The Baby Merchant

Kit Reed

TOR®

A Tom Doherty Associates Book
New York

THE BABY MERCHANT

Copyright © 2006 by Kit Reed

This book is printed on acid-free paper.

A Tor Book
Published by Tom Doherty Associates, LLC
175 Fifth Avenue
New York, NY 10010

www.tor.com

Tor® is a registered trademark of Tom Doherty Associates, LLC.

Library of Congress Cataloging-in-Publication Data

Reed, Kit.
    The baby merchant / Kit Reed.—1st ed.
        p. cm.
    "A Tom Doherty Associates book."
    ISBN-13: 978-0-765-31550-2
    ISBN-10: 0-765-31550-5
    1. Pregnant women—Fiction. 2. Unmarried mothers—Fiction. 3. Adoption—Corrupt practice—
Fiction. 4. Adoptive parents—Fiction. I. Title.

PS3568.E367 B33 2006
813'.54—dc22

                                                                2006040385

First Edition: June 2006

Printed in the United States of America

0 9 8 7 6 5 4 3 2 1

For Katy
for many reasons

The Baby Merchant

i.
First

Change always comes as a surprise. Stricken, you look up. *What just happened? You never saw it coming. It is that gradual, unless it hurtles down on you, screeching. You scream, what.* **What?** *One day you wake up with the dry swallows, thinking: I want* **that.** *You won't know whether this crashing need for a child is visceral or cosmic, whether it's embedded in human DNA or if there really is a star out there with your name on it. You only know that you are forever changed. You* **want.**

You can't know that wanting is just that. That's all it is. What should be natural isn't always easy. It may be impossible.

You don't really want to know what Tom Starbird does. You don't care what he does, as long as he can help you.

You never guessed it would come to this. The change in you was sudden, and suddenly deceptive. While you weren't looking the birth rate dropped: radiation, herbicides, preservatives, something you don't know about. You said, "That's interesting," because you were still so young that you both were scared of her getting pregnant.

Then Ebola, AIDS, avian flu leveled cities and you said, "Thank God that's half a world away."

You barely noticed when Homeland Security locked down Immigration— to keep out disease and terrorists, they said, when in fact it was to keep out everybody but us. Doors clanged shut before you grasped the implications. You felt sorry for couples stopped at the border with their third-world babies but their stories were just sad, the way something happening to somebody else is sad. Being childless was, after all, their problem, not yours. You said, "Why didn't they adopt American?" You never thought it could happen to you. **Not me.** *Was it your prayer or your incantation?* **Not me.**

Now it's all you think about.

By the time you go looking for Tom Starbird you have started down the same sad trail. You're used to getting what you want but this time, your bodies failed you. You've been through every known medical procedure. Adoption wait lists are endless, and if you thought you and he could buy a baby, forget it. In this time of limited supply, a baby is a treasure. Like high end pets, every newborn is chipped with a tracking device because like forests, babies are natural resources. You think it's so nobody will steal your treasure, but, look. It also tracks your baby's development for your government. If you're lucky enough to get a baby. You and your mate exchange looks drenched with blame; is it his fault? Hers?

Starbird is your last hope. You hear about him from a friend of a friend. Cautiously, you make contact. Hard as it is for you to admit failure, consider yourself lucky. The man is, after all, in an extremely sensitive business. Thank your stars that you come highly recommended. It's the only reason he agreed to meet. Be glad your salaries are in the high six figures. Cheap at the price, you think, because by this time need rips through you like a forest fire. What is it you really want here? Love, or perpetual life?

What are you afraid of? Loneliness? The empty table at Thanksgiving? That at the end there will be nobody left to cry?

Tom Starbird can help you. He's the kind of man it's a pleasure doing business with, although, God! you never guessed this **need** *would become a business matter.*

You like his sweet, irregular grin, the chipped front tooth. Beginning crows' feet. Black-Irish coloring, with blue eyes and brows like brushstrokes on rice paper. The coarse dark hair is cut close by a high end barber whose work you know. The Hugo Boss suit and pale shirt are just right— nothing too showy, nothing too matchy. Only a dot in the left earlobe where the stud came out hints at a life beyond the business of this meeting. He's half your age. Why are you afraid? Because this is by no means a done deal, and you know it. It won't matter how rich you are if you don't fit his parameters. It won't matter how much you have to offer. If you are a bad fit your man Starbird may like you, he may even be sorry for you, but nothing you can do or say will make him help you.

If you pass, he sets a second meeting. Your place this time, because you have survived the interview and aced the psychological tests. Remember, Tom Starbird is as thorough as he is selective. This is the crucial onsite visit. Not an inspection, exactly, but you've spent days preparing. You don't know what he expects of you but you think it had better be perfect. You spent a long time dressing for this encounter, practicing faces. He's brushed the dog and sprayed the plants to make them look glossy and well cared for. She put a pie in the oven because you want Starbird to walk into a bright, sweet place where dogs frolic and children will be happy.

These are all tricks realtors devised for homeowners who are selling, but in this case you are selling yourselves.

Everything hinges on this meeting. What comes next? Is he supposed to begin? Are you?

The smile is nice but my God, the eyes bore all the way in to the center of you. Still smiling, he begins. "Tell me one more time why you think you want a baby."

One
The Provider

1.

Waking up on the worst day of your life so far you won't know why you are uneasy, only that everything looks OK, but something is not right. Sun's up, coffee's good; Sasha Egan is in pretty good shape, considering. Nothing wrong, exactly, but she can't quite shake the feeling.

"Go away," she says to no one. "Just go away."

About the obvious: Sasha is nothing like the sweet little hicks murmuring in the solarium, but here she is, trapped with a gaggle of betrayed prom queens and unwitting cheerleaders, castoff girl-friends and beaming fundamentalist kids bobbing in the sunlight like so many giant chrysanthemums. The regulation pastel scrubs, the Lite Rock piped into every room, the resolutely cheery decor, even the potted trees in the hallways make her despair, but she made an informed decision. Now she is here. It's not that she's pro-life, exactly, although she is at some deep level still a Catholic. She's here because she's pro *this* life.

Luellen Squiers tugs on her arm, wheedling. Nice kid, has the room next to hers. "Party in the solarium, Sashie, are you coming? Cookies from Mom."

"Great," she says.

"So come on. Come on, Sashie, aren't you coming?"

"Soon, OK?" She'd rather die, but usually she manages. Why do these kids look up to her anyway? Maybe because she is older. She smiles until Luellen lets go.

"Why not now?" At the end of the hall, pregnant teenagers lounge on flowered sofas striped with sunlight, giggling over their morning milk and disintegrating brownies packed in wax paper by mothers who don't have a clue. Whatever their anxieties before they moved into the sunny dormitory at Newlife, whatever their second thoughts, the moment is past. They're happy to sink back into the arms of Newlife, which is the trendy new name the agency has given the Agatha Pilcher Home for Unwed Mothers, which is what they are.

It is— face it— what Sasha has become.

The timing couldn't be worse. In real life she is an M.F.A. student, a printmaker whose soul blisters the surface of her work. She spends all her work time chasing a vision she hasn't quite caught. The year she and Danny Gray lived together in Santa Barbara, she almost broke through. It wasn't breakthrough work but it did get her into the Massachusetts College of Art. When she's working sometimes she forgets to eat; she'll pass a window on her way out of the print shop and suddenly discover that she forgot to comb her hair. The work means more to her than Danny or any other man, and this baby . . . God, what was she thinking? This just can't happen. Not now, not now! Until the test strip turned pink, her mentor at MassArt was grooming her for a fellowship in graphic arts in, oh God, Venice. A year in Italy, apprenticed to a printmaker she respects. Instead she's in the third-trimester wing at Newlife, stalking the halls like an outsider, which is also what she is.

Too bummed to be nice right now, she tells Luellen, "I can't."

The pregnant child's voice trails after her. "Oh-kaaaaay."

She ought to go down there and mingle but right now she isn't feeling strong enough to look into their bright, hopeful faces or deal with their emotional demands.

Poor kids, they're all here for the usual reasons: he hit like lightning— first love or date rape, how do you draw the line— or they never want to see him again— a relative, sometimes, those are the worst cases, or it was some boy they thought they loved and learned to hate. Unless they're here because they're still in love but he wants her and her only, but not this, as in, as soon as she told him, he ran.

Some of these girls checked in because embarrassed moms made them, or because they love being pregnant but are just too young to keep it, and others because their beliefs preclude the alternative. Some were in denial for so long that by the time they got around to facing facts it was too late, and the rest? Their folks kicked them out or they came because they don't have anywhere else to go. It's odd, how even these times of great shortages and eager single mothers, the old social order still prevails in certain circles. As though time and change will never completely erase the stigma.

The others are here for the usual reasons, and Sasha?

It was the fumes.

The inks and solvents she and the other artists use in the university print shop just aren't safe. She knows printmakers whose fingertips are dissolving and a couple with patches on their lungs and one woman whose hair is coming out in patches, and she personally turned out to be allergic to the ground she mixes to prepare the copper plates for her prints; the compound gives her headaches in spite of the rubber gloves.

Is that anything you'd expose a fetus to?

Why she's hosting said fetus is another question, and the answers are so many and so complex that Sasha can't unpack them; she can still feel the surge that knifed up into her when she found out she was pregnant, that strong, sexual twist. At the time she put it down to fear. Now she knows it was wild joy. The rush. Without even trying, she had done this amazing thing. Shaking, she laid the pregnancy test strip on the windowsill in the women's bathroom in the Fine Arts building and went back to the print shop and packed up her stuff and left. She won't go back until this is over.

Just because you love a thing doesn't mean that you have to keep it, which is the real reason Sasha is here.

Her baby, she thinks, is like a firefly; you have to let it out of the jar so it can fly away and light up its scrap of sky. The issue is autonomy. Without it, how can he soar? She plans to have this baby, put her thumbprint on his forehead and say goodbye, but whoever the new parents— and in spite of institutional prodding Sasha is taking her damn sweet time culling the Newlife folders— whoever the new parents and wherever he goes afterward, this baby will still be hers. A unique print stamped with her mark.

After she has this baby, after she sifts through the sad stories of the parent-wannabes and picks out exactly the right ones from the welter of moving letters and heartfelt videos; after she's observed the finalists through the one-way mirror in the dayroom and questioned them at length; after she rips off these people's scalps and looks into their pulsing brains to make certain, she can put her baby into the right parents' arms with a clear conscience and walk free.

Eventually Sasha will meet the man she wants to love forever and wake up next to every morning for the rest of her life; by then she may even want children, but Gary Cargill was never that man. An OK guy, pleasant expression but not anybody you want to see a lot of. Face it, she hardly knows him! He was, she thinks, just a comfort fuck in the depths of a hard New England winter, like that pint of Rocky Road you accidentally scarf because you're lonesome and depressed. Sasha's hopes are not tied up in him. She has her work to think about, which is why she left Cambridge without telling Gary. If she does this right she may get back in time to take the Venice fellowship, and nobody has to know. She didn't tell her family; Grandmother is the last person Sasha would tell and believe her, she has reasons. She didn't phone Danny in Santa Barbara, even though they are best friends. It's her secret— safe in the heart of the former Agatha Pilcher home.

Like most artists, Sasha is a control freak. She chose Newlife because the agency promises complete confidentiality. Nobody has to know. Unless the birth mother opts for disclosure, even the adoptive parents will never know. See, if you're the only person who knows a thing, you can absorb it. You can adjust and move on. Do this pregnancy right and it can't hurt her; do it right and there will be no change in the fabric of her life, no interruption in the pattern, no unsightly holes. As far as the world knows, this baby never happened. In a funny way, Sasha was never pregnant and none of this ever came down. As long as nobody outside Pilcher finds out that she is here.

After she wrapped her half-finished copper plates and her engraving tools and took them out of the print shop, she went to the dean. She thanks her stars that the university is so big that the dean of the art school didn't have the foggiest who she was. She pleaded artistic difficulties and arranged for an academic leave. It took her a few weeks to plan her next step.

She started with phone calls. Then she let her fingers do the walking on the Web. The Newlife Web pages are thick with the confessions of happy adoptive parents and digital photos of other women's badly timed, OK, unwelcome babies beaming in adoptive mothers' arms. One phone call and Newlife sent the paperwork and a set of psychological tests. She aced the onsite interview. Sasha packed and gave away the cat and got out of town weeks before she started to show. Good timing, good management. Perfect control.

Then why is she on edge? Tense and brooding, as though in the middle distance, beyond her range of vision and just out of earshot, events are spinning out of control?

She doesn't know. Unlike Sasha, the girls in the solarium murmur along happily. They have surrendered to process. Relieved of responsibility, the accidental moms slap leaf-patterned cushions on the bamboo sofas and drowse in the sunlight without a care for what happens next. Let the institution do the heavy lifting while the world spins on however, without input from them. After all, their babies will have the very best. Newlife moms send their babies home with people who can afford the very best because this is, after all, a seller's market. They will grow up with advantages that their teenaged moms never had and live well-furnished lives that these girls can't hope to touch. These girls have the great good luck to be pregnant in a time of unprecedented shortages. How lucky they are that thousands of women who grew up scared of getting pregnant— can't. When did it change? How did it happen anyway, was it the march of technology that did it or two-career families or zeitgeist or hormones in our food? Is it the toxins we breathe or something in the water that caused the shortages, or just too many women waiting until Too Soon turned into Too Late? The heartbroken childless couples who come to Newlife are many. The ones who rise to the top of the placement list are the best. The world is running out of babies. There just aren't enough babies to go around.

So what the hell is wrong with Sasha today? Nothing, she tells herself uneasily, it's nothing, just pregnant nerves.

Her belly is out to here. The Pilcher obstetrician tells her the baby's dropped. The ideal parents are out there somewhere; they're waiting, all she has to do is pick them out. She has to do it soon! The responsibility is tremendous. What if she makes a mistake? Her ankles are swelling and she can't wear contacts because her eyes have changed; she's breaking out and she looks awful all the time. The local water smells like sulfur and comes out of the tap brown, so her dark hair stands out from her face like a frizzy cartoon of a bad hair day. Today's scrubs are bright yellow, splattered with orchids in a car crash of colors; it's a good thing nobody she cares about has to see her this way. She doesn't even want the girls in the solarium to see her this way. Even though Sasha keeps her distance the poor kids seek her out, like, she's older, so she must know what to do. Usually she listens and gives advice like a no-fault big sister or a kindly surrogate mom, but she can't be that person today, even though little Suzy begged her to come.

On any other day she would tell herself to get over it and go in, but she is not fit company for anybody right now. She turns away from the door.

Too late. Suzy DeLoach shrieks, "Sasha, you came! Over here."

"No no, Sasha, it's my turn."

Elsie-somebody mutters, "So Sasha, I've got this, problem?"

"Sasha. Sasha!" Tubby Betty Jane Gudger waves Discman earphones, desperate to catch her eye. "Over here."

"Look, picnic pictures!" Redheaded Luellen is fanning snapshots like a card shark, sweet little pest with thick, pale eyelashes and that Smurfette squint. Kid adores Sasha, not sure why, maybe because Sasha got up and went to her when she woke up crying the other night; she drew a cartoon for Luellen and made her laugh and ever since she's followed Sasha around with that gooshy smile. Crush, she supposes. Poor little kid.

Sallie Bedloe begs, "Brownies, Sasha, then let's do our eyes."

I would give a fortune to have a grown-up conversation. Faking a grin, she falls back on the old in-joke. "No thanks, I'm watching my weight."

Janice Ann-something squeals, to get her attention. "Sasha, Betty's hurting me!"

"Nobody's hurting you," she says, nailing Betty with a look. "They wouldn't dare." Never should have come in here. Got to get away before they find out that even grownups get depressed. She doesn't know why, she just knows it's her responsibility. As senior inmate, right, *inmate,* she owes it to these girls because against all indications, these pregnant children seem to look up to her. She knows exactly which tone to use to make them giggle and agree. "Right, guys? You wouldn't dare."

"Sasha, look at my . . ."

"Gotta go." Swamped, she has to improvise. She lurches for the doorframe with a little gasp. "Braxton Hicks, guys. I think. Better go get it checked out. No no, keep on doing what you're doing. Nurse hates it when a whole gang of people come."

Luellen jumps up as if to start CPR and two others flock to follow but Sasha is spun on her heels by plump, grim Viola Nagle, the supervisor on the third-trimester floor. "Egan, I need you."

Grateful for the rescue, she turns. "What?"

"In the office. Phone."

"No way."

"They asked for you."

"No they didn't."

"By name."

Sasha, why are you shaking? "Nobody knows I'm here." *Nobody knows my real name.*

"That's what you think," Viola's fingers bite into her upper arm. "Egan. Egan isn't your real name. It's Sarah Donovan, according to the book."

"Not any more." Never mind why she is estranged from her family. She is estranged from her family.

"Is Egan your married name or what?"

It was her father's name. Sasha glares until Viola lets go. "What were you doing in my files?"

"Is that the Philadelphia Donovans?"

"Never heard of them."

"Construction, right?" They are in the glass breezeway leading to the main building with Viola in the lead. She spits, "They asked for you by name."

Who did? She snaps, "You're supposed to play dumb. It's in the contract!" Even though she had to present her driver's license and her passport as proof of identity when she signed on here, Sasha's real name is supposed to be safe in the vault. Right, Viola, Egan is not her real name. "What the fuck happened to confidentiality?"

"They made certain threats."

When you're hiding something, you can't let down. "Like what?"

Viola smirks. "They said get you to the phone or Mrs. Donovan's lawyers would come down on us. With the FBI."

Grandmother! "You've got the wrong person."

"Sure I do." Viola never liked Sasha; her grimace can't disguise the triumphant smirk as she opens the office door and shoves her inside. "Lawyers, get it? I had to call the shot."

Sasha makes clear that she isn't picking up the phone until Viola leaves. When the door clicks shut she shouts into the receiver. "Grand?"

The other person listens just long enough to make sure it's Sasha speaking and hangs up.

"Who," she shouts at the dead phone. "Who!"

Telemarketer, Sasha tells herself crazily. Wrong number. Stupid mistake. Biting her knuckles, she bursts out into the hall with possibilities following like a swarm of hornets. She wants to grab Viola and grill her, but Viola is gone. Sasha paces on a loop, juggling contingencies until thought blurs like white sound and the compression sends her hurtling outside. She explodes into stunning noon light: harsh Florida sunlight strikes white buildings and white walks and ricochets off white sand. A shadow knifes across the blinding white cement.

She throws her arm up, as if to shield herself. "No!"

"No, hell. Yes. Don't you know me? Sasha, it's me!"

For a minute she doesn't recognize him, their night together was that short, but then she does. It's Gary. Cargill, he told her, but that was afterward. She hardly knew him before that night. Hell, she doesn't know him now. He's supposed to be in Boston, where he belongs. He was supposed to forget her but Gary that she slept with exactly *once* back in Brookline, Massachusetts, is here on the grounds of the Newlife Institute in central Florida, baring freshly whitened teeth in a grim smile and running his fingers through that retro spike. It defies logic but here he is, the laughing dancer from the studio party, the cute guy she took home after her friend Myra's opening at MassArt: regular features, pleasant expression, bland and, OK, out of shape— five more years and he'll be running to fat. Nice and uncomplicated, she thought, and at the time she was grateful. Not too smart. But her thoughts fly ahead of the memory: *We hardly know each other and here he is. What does he want?*

Clearly Gary's smarter than she thought. After all, he's here. He's tracked her down and come a thousand miles. Nobody gets into the building without a visitor's permit so Gary used his cell phone to yank her chain.

"You."

Grinning, he pats the Nokia on his belt. "What kept you?"

Stupid. I'm the stupid one. She assumed he was safely in her past, when he's been out here waiting the whole time. *Here is Gary*

Cargill standing in our courtyard, and he knows more about me than I thought. "That was you on the phone." She does not ask: How did you get my real name?

"And that's you standing there, bigger than a house."

"You son of a bitch."

The grin just misses being engaging. "That's not very nice."

"What do you want?"

"Aren't you glad I'm here?" The gesture he makes— that curve outlining her belly— is condescending. "Look at you!"

"What's it to you?"

"Why didn't you tell me?"

Trapped here in strong sunlight, Sasha considers, but only for a second. A lock inside her clicks. "Nothing to tell."

"You're going to have a baby . . ."

"So?"

"It's mine."

No, my baby, she thinks, surprised. "You don't know that!"

"You know damn well it is."

Careful, Sasha. Keep it light. "What makes you think it's your baby?"

Gary has a pleasant face really, nice blue eyes, nice way he shakes his head at her, a little bit sad, a little bit sweet. Why does she hate him, then? Maybe it's the smug way he says, "You're not the kind of girl you think you are."

"You have no idea what I'm like."

"When you dropped out I did a little research."

"Research!"

He laughs. "Call it my bio project for the term." He thinks they are still kidding; when she doesn't laugh he says, "So, everybody knows you're a serial monogamist, Sash. You're famous for it. Even when it's a one night stand."

"OK Gary, what are you really doing here?"

"I heard you were in trouble."

"This isn't trouble, it's something I chose."

"I came to help."

"You want to help? Then go away."

"Sasha, don't be mad at me. I came as soon as I heard. Don't be ashamed, you should have told me. Every baby needs a father." Then he gives her a wise look that makes her want to kill him. "You should know."

She flinches. Direct hit, but Gary can't know that. He can't possibly know. Damn him, he won't stop smiling even when her voice turns cold. "If I wanted a father, don't you think I would have been in touch?"

"I thought you were being brave."

"I was being realistic. Nice talking, Gary. Gotta go."

"Wait, OK?" His thought processes are grinding like heavy machinery. His face clots with the lie he is about to tell. "I love you, Sasha. I want to take care of you."

"No you don't."

"And I want to take care of our baby." Gary grabs her wrist; he is sweating with good will. Smiling, he repeats the lie. "I don't know you very well but I do love you, OK?" Smiling.

Like I'm supposed to be thrilled. Oh yes this is creepy. What does he want with her, really, or is it the baby he wants? God, what does he want with it? "You came all the way down here because . . ."

"Dammit, it's my baby too." The gel in Gary's hair has dissolved in sweat; in another minute his head will melt. He digs his front teeth into his lower lip and Sasha is surprised to see blood. "I want my baby and I want to do right by you, and besides . . ."

"Gary, you hardly know me. Just don't."

His eyes keep shifting from left to right and back again so that he is perpetually looking not at Sasha but over her shoulder, scoping the facade of the Newlife building with that terrible, unremitting smile. "Newlife. They do placement, right? So, what. Are you, giving my baby away?"

"What I do is my business."

"Wait a minute, it's my business too." Raking her with that blind smile, Gary Cargill, who came all this distance, plods toward the conclusion he had in mind before he started on this trip. "Hey, if you don't want the baby no problem, I'll take it."

"The hell you will."

"It's mine, OK?"

Her anger is so sharp that they are both surprised. "No. It's mine!"

"Listen. No kid of mine gets handed off to some high roller just because they write the biggest check. Not when he has family out there and they want . . ." When she stiffens, he breaks off to refine his pitch.

What family? His or mine? Sasha jerks away. Gary moves with her. Her wrist is slick under his fingers but she can't get free. There's the outside possibility that Gary means well, but her mind is running ahead to the Donovans— Grandmother— and if he hasn't sold her out to Grandmother, what must his parents be like? Just like Gary: genial, passive-aggressive chunks of flesh with stupid minds and stupid, agreeable smiles. Which is it? Which is it anyway? She shucked her name and came all this distance to save her baby from Grandmother, but which is worse? Either way her beautiful firefly is trapped in a Mason jar, battering himself to death against the glass.

Gary gives her wrist a little shake. "Are you listening to me?"

"What do you want with a baby, Gary?"

His face films over with earnestness. "I want to take care of him, and besides."

Grimly, she tries to loosen his fingers. She'd like to break them and pry them off, one by one. "Besides, what?"

"Goddammit, he's my blood."

What does he really want with this baby, quick sale to the highest bidder, or does he actually want a living shrine to his genetic set? *Damn you, Gary. Go.* "What if I tell you it isn't a he?"

"Work with me, Sasha. We were in love."

"We don't even know each other!" She is revolted by the reddish fringe that passes for eyelashes. She wants to smash away that shiteating grin but he still has her wrist and nothing she's tried here is working. "OK, Gary, what do you want?"

"OK," he says, and Sasha is treated to the sight of Gary Cargill thinking. "OK." She can't tell whether the machine in his head is turning up cherries or lemons but she can hear the tumblers click. In spite of the tremor of insincerity that won't let his voice settle on one note, he's trying to sound cool. "Tell you what. If you don't want to come with me right now you don't have to, I'm cool with that. If you don't want to keep the baby, fine. Promise I get to pick him up when he's ready; sign off on him and we're done."

It's a struggle but she lightens her tone. "How did you find out where I was?"

"I told you," he says, "I know a lot about you."

She studies him. *What, Gary, did you hire detectives?* Anger isn't helping, Sasha. Play it cool. Try hard not to ask. It's time to stop fighting. Instead she says mildly, "That's interesting."

Encouraged, Gary presses, backing her into the cement flowerbox outside the main entrance. She dodges this way. That. Like a guard in pro basketball, he thwarts her every move. He is so close now that her belly bumps him and the contact makes her shudder. "Come on Sasha. You know you want to get rid of it."

He is so close to the truth that it makes her flinch.

"What difference does it make to you who takes him home?" Then, because he thinks he has her, he blows it. "You can't be doing this for the money. Everybody knows your grandmother has pots."

Sasha's jaw tightens. Yes he hired detectives. Or Grandmother did. Gary's scheme unfolds like a slick travel brochure. He'll go up to the big house holding her baby in front of him and Grandmother will get all sentimental and pay and pay and pay. Worse. Grand will want to bring him up. She will bring him up the way she did Sasha, wreaking her will on him. "OK," Sasha says, scooping up sand from the cement planter. "OK."

Gary's grin sprawls out of control as, surprised, he lets go. "OK really?"

"What do you think?" She tosses it in his face. Then she swipes her card and is inside the building before he can rub the grit out of his eyes.

She can hear him shouting, "Sasha, is it a girl or a boy?"

On the worst day of her life so far, Sasha does what women do after a rape. She goes upstairs and gets into a shower turned on so hard that hot water pelts down on her head in a little hailstorm. No way, Gary, she thinks, shivering and scrubbing her hair with a bar of soap. No way.

The knowledge rushes in on her like a runaway freight. *I can't stay here!*

In ordinary circumstances she'd be more resourceful, faster, strong enough to fight, But Sasha Egan is eight months pregnant. She's huge and unwieldy and tired all the time now, and so short of breath that she can't act fast and she certainly can't run. She'd never even make it to the main gate. She doesn't know how to get away but she has to go.

Her issue, then, is how to disappear.

2.

Rumpled and engaging, Jake Zorn is a willful dynamo. With that smile he can get anything he wants, and he usually does. Maury's gruff, grinning husband never gives up, which is why he, and not Maury, is in Atlanta today, making the pitch. He's in the offices of the Fayerweather Agency, pleading for something he didn't necessarily want when this whole thing started. Jake always wanted a baby, but when he looked into its face he expected to see his own face, looking back. The perfect child to complete the perfect picture, but they are going to have to settle for less than perfect. Now that they're at the end of the trail, he's willing to adopt. In fact, he's in Atlanta, trying to make it happen.

Poised on the curb in front of Departures, he broke Maury's heart with that brave, uneven grin. "I love you, babe. I'm going to get us a baby."

Ten years of trying and this is the last stop. Jake will do anything to make her happy. All their colleagues, everybody they care about has at least one, what's the matter with them? They started out with such confidence, and now look. They are reduced to begging.

Nobody really wants to adopt, Maury thinks, not if they can have their own, but for too many women now, that's getting harder and harder. Jake doesn't, in spite of his gallant attempt to convince her that he's fine with it. "Whoever he is," he said, grinning, "We're going to love him."

At this stage in their efforts, it's their last chance. Jake is in Atlanta, pleading their case. He's turning on the charm at the Fayerweather Agency, one of the best private adoption agencies and,
face it, the last on their list. The others turned them down because
they're older than the usual. Maury and Jake are in their forties
and— OK. The other thing. The deal breaker, she thinks, sagging.

Maury ought to be down there arguing this, after all she's the
lawyer, but frankly, she's too wrecked to argue anything. She's
holed up in an empty courtroom in the federal courthouse in
downtown Boston. She doesn't want people watching when Jake
phones with the news. Good or bad. She has to be alone when she
gets it.

To look at Maury Bayless, you'd never guess that she is desperate. She looks young and confident: great profile, good hair and
good jewelry, beautifully cut suit. Prada bag. Cell phone in a silver
case. Cool boots. Bestseller in paperback, so she can pretend she is
reading. Fresh sprouts in the sandwich, she could be any busy
lawyer grabbing lunch between court dates. Nobody has to know
that she can chew but not swallow and stare at a page and stare at it
with no idea what she is seeing.

For the last ten years Maury has zig-zagged between hope and
despair, hostage to her own body, and now the next thirty—
sixty?— years of her life are hanging on Jake's phone call. The Fayerweather meeting began at eleven, which means that deep as they
are in this last ditch effort, she can't talk to the only person in her
life she can really talk to. Her failure stands between them like a
wall of ice.

"You go," Maury said at curbside check-in. "I'm too messed up
to do this interview."

Jake raked his fingers down her arms as she pulled away. "But I
was counting on you."

"I'm the wrong person." Bright woman, senior partner, but she
has a history. "They won't see me sitting down with them, all they'll
see is my files."

"Oh," Jake said, and she thought she heard his heart crack.

She murmured, "I'm so sorry."

He dropped his bags and kissed the pale insides of her wrists. "Oh, my sweet one."

She waited until she was back at the Park and Fly to lock herself in the car and cry. So Jake is alone in Atlanta, pursuing their last hope. Sweet Jake with his great gravelly voice and that disarming grin and the things he's willing to tell you about himself to get you to unbutton. When they were twenty, Jake got Maury on board, no problem. The coolest guy at the party. Spilled his beer and picked her up so her feet wouldn't get wet, so nice! He convinced her to marry him right out of college. The man can sell anything, charm strangers out of their deepest secrets, expose liars and have them thank him for it, could sell snake oil and make people believe it really cured them.

Maury thinks bitterly, *And I can't even have a baby.*

Interesting and terrible, what failure does to you. Whatever you thought you were when you started out, you are only this now. The sum of what you have tried and failed to do. Of course you have to go out and show yourself to the people, dress like a winner and smile like a champ, but it won't change what you are feeling. The worse you feel, the better you have to look. Believe it. Put on that grin— lady, accessorize!— and hope to God that nobody knows that inside you are hung with gauze and shadows, a shrine devoted to everything you've lost.

She isn't depressed, exactly. She's just in mourning for something she knows she should have had.

If only they'd gotten pregnant when Jake first brought it up. First-year law student, what did she know, she was only a kid! Her Jake was breaking into TV news— weekend anchor; it was small town TV, but, hey. Not bad for a go-fer just out of college. Charismatic Jake shmoozed his way into a terrific story. His pals at town hall suspected that the town clerk was shooting kiddy porn with a city camcorder. Jake brought him down. He dug up the tapes, which he duped and turned over to the police. The angry parents even let him interview the kids involved for the first-ever Jake Zorn

Exposé. Now he's famous for them; the Television Conscience of Boston. These days the Jake Zorn Exposé airs nationwide.

After that first show Jake ran the tape obsessively, looking for— what? What turned him on? It wasn't vanity, she doesn't think. She thinks it was a passion to— what, transmit his image, sending part of himself hurtling into the future, to live on and on. She came in and found him on his knees in front of a freeze frame, fixed on his close-up. Still kneeling, he looked up at her with a bright, amazing smile. "Oh, Maury. What if we had a baby?"

It rolled in from out of nowhere. Stricken, she blurted, "We're too young!"

"But look at us. Wouldn't he be beautiful?"

Her mind ran ahead to the real question: could she have a baby and still make the Law Review? Men get to the top however, but for any woman who cares about what she does, professional life is like climbing a wall. You cut hand holds and notches for your feet, hacking them out of solid rock. It's hard work, the climb is slow and you can't let down for a minute or you'll start to slide. Keep at it long enough and in the end all you want is to reach the top so you can rest. If she told Jake, he'd think she was weak.

She punted. "What makes you think it would be a boy?"

With a foolish, loving, confident grin, he said, "Trust me."

"You want me to quit law school?" *Oh, Jake.*

Standing, he hooked his arms around her, drawing her in. "Just for a little while. How long could it take?"

When a couple has a baby, it's the woman who pays. Maury set her jaw. "Try eighteen years."

Professionally, they were both hanging on by their fingernails. She argued the parallels, which Jake refused to recognize; they had a fight.

"'s OK," Jake said in the end, with a new smile that she didn't understand at the time but has come to know by heart, like a Top-Ten song that you keep hearing long after the guy you thought you were in love with has dropped you. TV has taught Jake exactly how to modulate the voice so viewers buy everything he says without wondering whether it's true or not. Her skull vibrated as he put his mouth to her temple, rumbling, "We have plenty of time."

They honestly thought they did. It was a sweet lie, but it was still a lie. Taut with waiting, Maury says to the empty courtroom, "You only thought you had time." She is her own prosecutor now.

Maybe she should have given in after she passed the bar. That summer Jake caught the suburban cops taking bribes; he got it on tape and the exposé won him an award. THE CONSCIENCE OF BOSTON SCORES AGAIN. The headline ran the same day Judge Aylward offered Maury the clerkship; she could hardly wait to get home. Laughing, she and Jake hugged and squealed like high school cheerleaders after the big touchdown. He took her out to celebrate.

Then her lover, her husband, wonderful guy, wrecked the celebration. What did he see in her eyes? Maury, or only himself reflected? "The plaque plus twenty K," he said— so proud! "Now you can afford to quit."

"Is that all you think about?"

"We're great together. With a kid, we're our own corporation. You and I and Jakey."

"I can't yet." *Why do you want a child so badly, Jake? Am I not enough for you?* "I just can't." Maury doesn't know why, she can't explain it. You just aren't ready until you are. Having a baby is such a big thing, especially when it's your body. "Give me time," she begged, unless she was praying.

Wistful, he took her hands. Her Jake. Terrible in hope, he was pleading. "OK, honey, but let's do it soon."

Privately, she set her timer for thirty-five. It's perfectly possible for a woman to stay on the pill without the man in the house knowing. Thirty-five seemed like a safe number, partly because it was so far away. Forty looked even better to her. Hell, women in their fifties have been known to conceive— with a little help. The biological limits expand all the time. At the back of Maury's mind there was the knowledge that when she did get pregnant, her professional life would roll onto a siding while Jake's roared ahead full steam: *It isn't fair.* In spite of his pointedly not badgering— in spite of his wistful, insistent charm, they let it rest. When you're young and running hard you think you have plenty of time. *Idiot bitch,* Maury thinks, despising her stupidity, *you thought life was like business.* Wasn't having a baby supposed to be like an arraignment or a court date that you could schedule and bring off by the numbers? One. Two. Three.

Hard-driving, high-jumping Maury. So organized. She landed a job with a top firm. She made partner. She cleared her calendar. A thirty-fifth birthday present for Jake. A surprise.

Nothing happened. Now, that was a surprise. Fine, all those years on the pill, don't expect results right away.

It took her more than a year to conceive.

Once you get committed to a thing, it's all you think about. Every disappointment is like a little death.

The first disappointment was exactly that. A little death. She had a miscarriage so sudden and dramatic that it was over before the airport paramedics reached her. Her fault, she thinks, for running hard when she should have laid back as advised, but she was in the middle of a copyright matter that couldn't wait. Her plaintiff was a Boston novelist who had been ripped off: his novel to their major motion picture, opening next month in a theater near you. He could prove it, line for line; they needed a settlement meeting before the opening, while they had the power to keep it out of the theaters. The studio said we meet in Los Angeles or forget it. Maury never knew whether it was the stress that did it, or the rough flight in bad weather or some tragic biological flaw, but she flew from Boston to Los Angeles in her first trimester and she lost the baby. She won her client a six-figure settlement but she lost the baby. Her baby. Jake's. It happened— this was so awful— in Chicago on the way home. The cramping started at LAX, but what did she know, she'd never been pregnant before. She hemorrhaged as she was running to make her connection in O'Hare.

Jake flew to Chicago to take her home. He brought white flowers and a white plush Teddy. "Oh, honey!"

They were both crying. You always do. "I'm sorry."

"It's OK, this isn't the last baby in the world." Careful, Jake. That which you don't know enough to fear is closer than you thought.

They had no way of knowing what was coming. All Maury knew was what you did to get past it. Pick yourself up, girl. Attend to your look! She felt something new on her face. A few more miscarriages and it solidified, like a layer of makeup that won't wash off. The chronic failure's carefully constructed smile. "It's OK, Jake, I'm OK."

But Jake's a born overachiever. He took it as a challenge. *Nobody beats us.* "As soon as you're all better we can try again."

They've been trying for ten years.

When things go wrong the woman always pays.

Maury and Jake have tried everything: obsessive temperature taking, hers; hormone-sensitive paper strips, hers, because in these matters it is she who bears the burden; breathless midafternoon meetings in downtown hotels because all signs indicated that her cycle was high, followed by the hours Maury spent on her back willing the sperm to ignite. There would be days of hope followed by ambiguous home pregnancy test results followed by the blind, rising excitement no woman can stifle followed by her period, which was only late, followed by the next attempt. The next.

Too late, they turned to technology: the flurry of sperm counts and comprehensive ultrasounds and exploratory procedures and, when it was indicated, courses of clomiphene, with Jake stifling her worries with that ruthless, hopeful smile. "So what if we end up with triplets? Cheap at the price."

When things go wrong the woman always pays.

Now they are at the end of the trail.

Alone in the echoing courtroom, Maury Bayless checks her silent cell phone and flips it shut. Then she bows her head over her knuckles, gnawing until the blood comes. She won't cry. She won't! She can't call Jake and she can't change or prevent whatever is happening from happening.

Now that she and Jake are at the bottom line they will do anything to get a baby. Anything.

ii.

Your source tells you Tom Starbird's mission is placing unwanted babies with people who are sick with want. You gulp because this so perfectly describes your situation.

The **want** part of the equation is key to him. It explains the psychiatric evaluation before the first meeting. If you want to be his client, you have to prove you're more than a high ticket consumer bent on the next acquisition. If you're shopping for a baby the same way you score cars and beach condos, he will know it. Babies aren't furniture. They aren't Beemers or trinkets from Bulgari. A baby is by no means the porcelain your decorator brings in to complete a perfect picture. If you think you're securing your own little hostage to posterity, he will know that, too. One false note and he'll walk away. You have to want the baby for itself.

And the **unwanted** part?

You won't know precisely what "unwanted" means. Ask and a raw, sad look streaks across his face like a storm over the surface of the moon. "Just somebody who'll be better off with you."

Unwanted. You think of babies dropped in high school toilets or left in dumpsters or on church doorsteps, but that's the sentimental view. They are no more. The government's taken care of that, thanks to the march of science— elements added to the water in low-income projects, gum they hand out in the public schools; it's in the pills kids pick up like candy at the bar in every club. Babies are *hard to come by, but the government doesn't want just anybody to have a baby. Ironic that you, who would make a perfect contribution to the national gene pool, can't get pregnant, while there are still a few in the. Um. Undesirable demographic.*

*In your ignorance, you thought of "unwanted" in terms of babies by the thousands stuck in Dickensian orphanages, holding out their arms to you, begging, **take me, take me**. As if you could walk in and pick and choose.*

By the time you meet Tom Starbird, you know better. If there were still orphanages, you would not be sitting here pleading for his services. You have no idea what he means when he says, "unwanted." You want to ask. You're afraid to ask.

After all it is you, not Starbird, who is under scrutiny here.

Smile as he looks up from his keyboard, studying you. Smile and look him straight in the eye, even though his scrutiny frightens you. Remember, he can help you. If he approves your application.

3.
Tom Starbird

Now, my mother thought she was a poet, and I paid for it. She was so deep into art that she lost track of life. It made me hate illusion. I never talk in figures. I deal in truth and truth only.

What I see is what you get.

The truth? I steal children. I am very good at what I do. I'm willing to tell you more, but when you engage my services you don't want to know, not really.

No, don't back off and don't for a minute think that this is in any respect creepy. My motives are pure. I fill a need and in the process, I'm saving disenfranchised kids. The ones turned loose in the world unchipped, which makes them ciphers in this country. I pull them out of bad situations and drop them into good ones, for which, believe me, I am highly paid.

Understand, I don't in any way get off on this; except for my few *pro bono* jobs, it's strictly transactional.

My clients' motives must be equally pure. If you expect to do business with me this is a given. Our transaction depends on a complete absence of sexual baggage. I won't tolerate anything overt or, trickier: anything latent. The screening you undergo before we meet is calibrated to pick up the slightest hint of corruption. If you are lucky enough to survive it and we arrange a meeting, look deep into the baggage that you bring to the table. If your desires are anything less than parental, I will know it.

If you're hiding anything, be warned. If I pick up the slightest hint that there's anything funny about you I will not only drop you as a client, I will hunt you down and expose you for what you are. Then I will destroy you. Anything to keep this operation clean.

My reputation depends on it.

Now, as for you. Don't for a minute imagine we are friends. This is a business arrangement and you are the client. Like the product, the client must be top of the line. If we are talking, it's because you have survived the background check, scored high on the psychological screening and passed the physical. I want my parents-in-waiting young enough and strong enough for the long haul, which means no psychic breaks in the history and no physical ailments, congenital or otherwise. My clients have to be in shape to see it through. And what do you get in return?

Early upheaval makes a man resourceful, resilient and meticulous. You are getting the best.

The few clients I take are top drawer. You know the type.

You *are* the type.

You come to me in a time of great shortages. When you come you are all at some level grieving. I know this and I'm sorry, even though I don't show it. I can't get emotionally involved. You don't want me to, not really. In fact, you think when this is over you can thank me and walk away. Of course you're wrong, but we'll get to that. You are, furthermore, embarrassed to be here; aren't you supposed to have it all? You worked hard to get where you are, fast track careerists with high-profile jobs, so congratulations, you've made it to the top. I see it in the way you walk in here in your hand-tailored suits and your discreetly high end shoes. You have the big house, the weekend place, the cars; by the time you come to me, you have everything you want except the one thing you really want, and at this point I have to ask you, what went wrong?

Is it something in the water or the air that dried you up or did you hear your biological alarm clock going off and hit the snooze button one time too many?

You have everything you want except the one thing you can't

have: the child who loves you more than anybody, beaming up at you like a worshiper looking into the face of God. You want to know that when you go, you'll leave at least one person behind to cry for you.

Now, who puts you in touch with me?

Like any high end provider, I don't advertise. This is for my security and yours. You come through someone I trust and you must come highly recommended, although if you are resourceful enough to find me on your own and consent to the forty per cent surcharge I may consider you, and you? You have it on excellent authority that I can be trusted to deliver top value.

You come to me because you know I'm the best.

I never meant to get into this line of work. The first time was an accident, as in, I had no idea there would be money. It was a *pro bono* decision, you know? I did it for my best friends from college. Killing two birds, I guess— rescuing a baby for Jim and Marie. They had a baby long enough to fall in love with it and then it died. They were devastated. I would do anything to help them stop hurting, so . . . Where to start?

With the screaming, I suppose. Every night I sat with Jim and Marie until I couldn't bear their grief and every night when I came home I heard a baby crying nonstop. It came from the apartment across from mine; it was the hottest summer in years. We were in an old building and I kept the windows open because I could. Every night this pitiful wail went spiraling up the airshaft and every night I heard a man's big, hard voice shouting, shut up, shut up. The more he shouted the harder the baby cried. Shut it up, he yelled at the mother— his girlfriend, wife, shut the fucking thing up. It cried, he yelled, the woman screamed: shut up you little bastard, shut up, shut up, I heard furniture crashing and I may have heard his fists thudding into her flesh; I know I heard the smack of a hand on bare skin and over everything I heard the phlegmy, rattling wail that comes out of a baby when somebody's shaking it to make it stop crying and that just makes it howl louder because it can't and they will do anything to make it stop.

I didn't know what to do. Should I go over? Call the cops? Ironic, my best friends were grieving over the baby they lost and here was a couple with a baby they didn't want. Do you know what that's like? Terrible. When nobody wants you they think you don't know it, but no matter how little you are, you know. Night after night after night it cried, while Jim and Marie . . .

I had to do something.

In college we did everything together, Jim and Marie Jansen and me, I've changed their names for their protection. They got married while I was in business school and instead of breaking up the threesome it bonded us, I was Godfather to the baby they lost. Where I was floating between temp work and crap job offers, Jim designed a genius piece of software and made half a million overnight. The Jansens had everything they wanted and then the baby died. She went in one morning and it was lying there stiff and cold in the crib. Raw agony is painful to see. I would have done anything for them. Nights I hung in and talked and let them cry and talked some more until I couldn't bear another minute of the pain, and when I went home no matter how late it was, the baby across the way was screaming. I don't know how the conversation started or what Marie and Jim said to me, I only know what I said.

For everybody's protection, I will withhold the details. Let's just say I performed a rescue. I solved two problems at once and when I walked away the Jansens had their baby and I was holding enough money to float me until I could swim on my own. Of course I refused, I refused it twice, in spite of which Jim made a wire transfer into my account. The amount staggered me.

Sure it gives you a rush, making people happy. They loved the baby and the money was amazing, but I thought it was a one shot deal. I didn't expect to do it ever again. Funny, I think that every single time. If you want to know the truth, the first job nearly destroyed me. Their raw grief and the sobs, the sound that came out of them when I put that baby into their arms. Then there was the responsibility. A benevolent God is expected to look after His creations. How could I? I was only twenty-four.

When you play God the pressure is tremendous.

Jim and Marie said, "How can we thank you?"

I hugged them both. I touched the soft spot in the baby's skull. A scar, but no implant. I asked the Jansens for a single favor. "Get him microchipped. Forget about me and, please." The big favor. "Please don't look for me."

I left town. I still wonder if the couple in my building ever thought to look for the baby I took. I think not. They'd had the chip removed, so it's pretty clear that I was doing them a favor too. I never saw anything about it in the news.

I moved to Chicago, great place to stay lost. Open all night, perfect for a young guy. The money floated me for almost six months, which I spent reading. I was considering my options. What did I really want to do? Not certain.

As for the business, I never thought of it as a business. I thought I was done.

The Jansens sent another couple. My best friends, and after I made them promise. First lesson: *don't do business with friends.*

Nice people. I had to get rid of them.

"I'm sorry. You've made a mistake."

The new people were terrible in their pain, with tears standing in their eyes and those moist, urgent grins. That wasn't the only thing troubling me. I couldn't figure out which of us the Jansens thought they were doing the favor.

The wife said, "They said you could help us. They promised." She wasn't much older than me.

It was awful. I backed away.

Her mouth was so dry that her lips stuck together; he kept licking his, they were that hungry. "You know, like you helped Marie and Jim?"

I knew him from the picture: one of the Fortune Five Hundred. He grabbed my hand: steady grip. "Don't say no."

"I just did."

He named a figure.

"I'll see what I can do for you."

The money was even better than the first time. I spent the last of the Jansens' money on a midrange scanner because I had to be sure. I found a deserving baby for my new clients. I put the cash in a Viennese bank. I left town because the connection was too intimate. I couldn't get sucked into their gratitude.

As I said, the pressure was tremendous. Then there's the pain. I took the lesson: *depersonalize.*

To keep from breaking your heart every time, you have to detach.

I developed tactics.

I maintain a professional distance, like a doctor. In the operating room a surgeon can't afford to think, *my poor friend;* he has to think: *this liver, this kidney* or *this heart.* This distance is essential to precision. Get emotionally involved and you start making mistakes. Terminology keeps it cool.

Objectify and you can protect yourself. There is a logic to rhetoric. Use the right words for things. From here on out, think of me as the provider. I am an expert technician in a volatile medium, which means close attention to every detail. No I don't want to hear your life story. All I need to know is whether I want to take your case. You are here because I am the best.

In professional terms, the baby I will put into your arms is the subject, until the pickup is made and I know I can guarantee the product. There is, of course, a supplier, but we don't need to get into that.

When we finally come face to face you seem surprised; you paid so much for this appointment and waited so long. Now you are nonplussed. I look like a kid to you. What did you expect, the ancient and powerful Oz? You're all alike— put off by the disparity in our ages but impressed by my bearing and the firm's reputation and, I think, the Saville Row threads. Do not be deceived. I have the power. "Starbird? *The* Tom Starbird?"

"Yes."

"We have a problem." The shuffling and throat-clearing begin. You're getting ready to sob out your story, which I already know. I've met too many of you in your big, silent houses where no children come; I've seen too many perfect, empty nurseries— why must you always buy the crib and the Teddy bear before you're sure? I don't need to know what stops you had to make before you played out your string and came here. It's all too sad. "We . . ."

I cut you off. "I understand."

"Can you help us?"

"Probably." By this time I've researched suppliers as thoroughly as I've researched you. I may even have a subject ready for pickup, but before we sit down to the paperwork, I have to observe you. I need to see how you play your hand. If I see anything I don't like, we're done.

You're here because you know I can put a baby into your arms. Your lips are turning white the way they do when you've been in the waiting room too long and finally get in to see the latest renowned doctor. You've spent so much time with doctors that I feel sorry for you. You have put your faith in science, and look how far it's gotten you. One of you says, "So, you have a new technology."

"Not exactly." I know what you are thinking. I see visions of cloned babies dancing in your eyes. You want to hand on your genetic material any way you can. You want to do this in spite of the bungled experiments that put the first commercial labs out of business. We still see them on the nightly news, with their botched bodies and vacant, smeared faces, all of them tumbling like kittens waiting to be drowned. God knows you've been warned, but in spite of everything, you want to see your own DNA rolling into the future. "It's hard to explain." In fact, I won't. The less you know, the better I can do my job.

But you have put your faith in science for too long. "We don't mind being guinea pigs."

I hack off the rest of your sentence with the blade of my hand. "No need."

"Any protocol's fine with us." You've read about uterine transplants in South Africa, in Switzerland; none of them take, but every fresh try makes the news. You give a nervous little laugh. "As long as it works."

"I'm not a doctor."

"Experimental medicine's fine with us."

It is my job to break this to you gently. I begin. "Science can only go so far."

I don't have to finish. In your hearts, you know. After all, you have gone the rounds. I see this in your drawn faces and your sad eyes, the slight acquisitive curl of fingers that tighten in spite of you. Between you, you've spent too many hours crying, the sorrow has sent you pacing through your quiet house on too many nights, stalking as though the thing you most want will be in the next room if you can only get there fast enough.

You know I work on the wrong side of the law and you come even though you have reservations. As soon as I lay it out for you, your reservations evaporate. You like my looks, and when push comes to shove you are more than grateful for my service. I see the hunger in your eyes. I see the pain and believe me, I'm sorry. You think I couldn't possibly know what it's like: the cold hearth, the gathering silence, but I do. I saw into the void well before you felt it opening, but we don't need to get into that. If I like you I'll help you, so you can rest your heart.

But we are still feeling each other out.

The men in these encounters arrive with varying agendas but you, you mothers in want, you are all the same with your lovely, drawn faces. You are trying not to cry and my heart goes out to you. "Can you help us?"

Nice as you seem, I remain cautious. "I think so."

You brighten, even though I don't exactly smile. "That's wonderful."

"If you can meet my price."

One of you— he, with his bruised ego, you, with your breaking heart— one of you says, "Whatever it takes." You, the mother-in-waiting, will do anything to keep from feeling this way. His motives are more complex and harder to pigeonhole. Maybe he just wants an end to your nights of silent weeping.

"You understand this is a high risk profession, which means my service is not cheap." There are expenses, even though I keep my establishment small: an office for these meetings, because I refuse to eat where I shit; the database, which is essential to my searches and encrypted so nobody can hack in. Now, as for staff: aside from the doctor, who works on retainer, there's only Martha, the receptionist, who is also a licensed practical nurse. Sitting down with you, I have to consider the cost of the operation, beginning with the search for a close match, equipment for the pickup and a contingency fund, in the event of unforeseen trouble with the law. The real expense is the post-transfer coverup. It's not cheap, locating a subject and removing that subject to a safe venue without leaving a trace.

Even though they treated these unwanted babies badly when they had them, didn't like them, neglected them, were no good, some of my suppliers will go to great lengths to get their property back. To protect us both, I spare you the details. I simply name the raw figure. "And that's just the expenses."

You say, "Satisfaction guaranteed?"

"If we agree on the terms." My eyes drill deep into you. "And you have to make me a guarantee."

"Wait a minute, this wasn't in the . . ."

For emphasis, I wait. Then I say, "You guarantee the product a good home."

"Oh, that. No problem. We can afford the best of the best."

"Fine, but there's more to it than that." While you hold your breath I pretend to calculate. You know how these things work, you secure your order with a cash advance. I produce the child you want and I do it to order. If anything goes wrong I am bonded, so you are indemnified. I hold it another beat and give you the figure.

You don't even wait to hear. You are reckless in your anxiety to seal the transaction. "Fine!"

"That is, pending the home visit." I give you a long look in which I satisfy myself that you are on the level. I can see you holding your breath but I have to make sure I want to find a child for you. At last I say, "Assuming the home is right, then . . . OK."

I see you exhale: *whew*. I know where this is coming from. No more back alley deals with unscrupulous lawyers for you, no more cold speculums, no more routine humiliations in examining rooms, no more desperately functional sex complete with charts and thermometers and no more paper cups and *in vitro* sessions; no more trying to fix the blame and better yet, no heartbreak at the adoption agencies, and this is the best: no risk of the birth mother going to court to take back her baby, never mind how much you paid. For the first time since this started you can relax. "Thank God."

"Don't thank God, thank me."

I love that inadvertent, joyful murmur of relief.

Money changes hands. Cash, never checks or money orders and certainly not plastic— wire transfers from the usual banks are too easily traced, which is definitely not good for either of us. I take the envelope.

Your gratitude is embarrassing. "We can't tell you how much we . . . Oh Mr. Starbird, we . . ."

To shut you up I stick out my hand and let you shake. "You can call me Tom."

You, the mother-in-waiting are weeping with happiness but like me, your man is all business. He pulls out his PDA to enter the details. "When do we start?"

"The meter's already running." What you see is what you get and you get what you pay for with Tom Starbird. Top value.

We get down to the specifics. You are snobs, all of you. It is a given that your new child will come from the approved demographic. If you want to tie a bow on your particular genetic package, I guarantee a thorough search and a close match. And if you want to try for an upgrade, a baby you can count on to grow up smarter or better looking than you? Specify and I can deliver, but it will cost you.

Next you must decide how old. Of course I can provide heirs of any age but you should know that for both provider and client, the older the subject, the more complicated the job. Remember, I am an altruist. I find great parents for great babies, in the end everybody's better off. Still, even when they're begging to be rescued the older ones do come fitted with memories, so be advised. You're going to see trauma and crying plus residual from the first imprinting. To say nothing of the danger of its being recognized. I prefer a subject too young to know where it used to live or who its birth mother was but, by the time I make the pickup, old enough to sleep through the night.

Naturally these meetings run long. By this time he is growing impatient, perhaps because this was her idea and he wants to get it over with. He is a businessman after all. "Where do we sign?"

I pull him up short. "Not so fast."

I see her soft lips tremble. "Is there a problem?"

Oh, ma'am, not you! I don't mean you! I smile to reassure her and then I skewer him with a glare. "Not if you agree to the conditions."

"I told you, whatever it costs!"

"You understand, this is going to take time." If we've reached this point you have agreed to the downpayment, expenses and of course the per diem, as well as a large cash reserve put by for unforeseen exigencies. Now all you have to do is prepare the baby's room and wait. In locating the product, I study potential subjects just as carefully as I do the clients, and I am looking for more than a close genetic match. I know which ones are loved and which are neglected or despised, but you don't need to know. My database is filled with prospects whose parents didn't care enough about them to have them chipped. All you need to know is that when I'm done everybody is better off.

You're angry. You want a baby today. "How much time?"

"As long as it takes." If you want instant gratification, take your business elsewhere. There are no overnight deliveries here. You can't rush a quality operation, and given time, I will come up with exactly what you ordered. Only when the transfer is made and all parties are satisfied— when the circumstances are exactly right— then and, OK, only then, will we sign the final agreement, and be advised, I reserve the right to assess the situation and if it's indicated, return your money and cancel the deal. "Unless you want to find somebody else."

"No!" We both know there is nobody else.

You have to be willing to wait for as long as it takes, and do not pester me.

Delivery day is by no means the end point. You aren't buying a child. You are taking on a lifetime responsibility to a singular, irreplaceable human being. Before we're done you will agree to devote yourself to this child until it's grown, which is why I set a cutoff age for clients. More. You will agree to onsite spot checks. You will guarantee funding for private schools, four years at a top college and if indicated, full support for graduate school. No waiting tables for my products, no crap night work. I couldn't do these jobs if I didn't know that my rescues are better off with you than they would be in their old lives.

Now, the agreement. Before I deliver you will swear to this in writing, and this is the make-or-break clause:

To love the product without qualification, put this baby's wellbeing before your own, and in every moment of every day, to honor its integrity and its individuality.

This is the bottom line.

And if I am telling you all this now?

That's another story.

4.

The light is changing, casting long bars on the polished floor of the empty courtroom, and Maury still hasn't heard from Jake. It's their last hope. What will she do if he comes up empty? She doesn't know.

By this time she's been through so many medical procedures that her confidence hangs in tatters around her ankles like exploded pantyhose. She used to be a competent professional, a control freak who refused to be ordered around. Now she'll do anything. Worse. She used to blanch at the sight of a speculum. Now she'll spread her knees for anyone. Anybody who claims that with help, she can conceive.

The long, degrading effort has spilled her out deeply exhausted, not from the drugs or the shots or the invasive protocols, but from the pressure of Jake's expectations and his unwavering sweetness when they fail, compounded by his fatal inability to quit.

He can't stop hoping.

Neither can she. God knows why she is still hopeful, but she starts out hopeful every single time.

"It's OK," they told each other the first time. "We can always adopt."

It's what you say to each other in the early stages, especially when you've done so well at everything else that success seems inevitable; it's coming, it is! It's just a little late. You exchange blurred, hopeful smiles and one of you says— kidding!— "Well, we can always adopt."

Frankly, Maury was ready after the second miscarriage. Two boys. She would have had two boys. She thinks she was the first to turn that smeared, desperate smile. She thinks she was the one who swallowed a sob and said, "Well, we can always adopt."

Then one of you— Jake in this case— said, "One more try."

It made her want to weep. "It's not your body, Jake."

"Oh honey, let's just try this one last thing, OK?" He's an investigative reporter after all. Alert to every new development. "The odds are good."

At Jake's urging, Maury's tried them all. When she still couldn't conceive they moved on to *in vitro.* Difficult. Expensive, but they were both well into the six-figure bracket by then so, hey. Some took, some didn't. Even when Maury went to bed for weeks after implantation, even though she was prepared to stay down for as long as she had to just to make it work, none of them, not one of those flimsy, might-have-been babies stayed with her for long.

Later, when she was still shaky from the last loss, she said, "Jake, let's adopt." Not the knee-jerk usual, this was a considered decision. "We have to. Please?"

Fixed on the future— his genetic material!— Jake, *her Jake,* turned his handsome head that the camera loves so much and wouldn't look at her. "Sweetie, let's don't go there."

She said in a low voice, "Not even now, after everything?"

He made a sound she didn't recognize. "I can't."

"Jake!"

Glaring out the window at something she could not see, the man she thought loved her was so fixed on what he wanted that he didn't respond. After too long he turned back with a look so bleak that she could see into his skull. "What would be the point?"

"Oh honey, I just want a baby!" She didn't when she started, not really. Now it's all she thinks about.

Oh Jake, oh, that Top Ten smile. Does he know that when he turns up the voltage like that it isn't personal, it's only that invented smile that won a million viewers? "I don't want just any baby."

Oh God, don't let me cry. "Jake!"

Then Jake said with terrifying gravity, "We're not just anybody, Maury. This is us. Your body. Mine. We're too good to waste."

Amazing, what comes out under pressure: the truth. "Mine isn't working, Jake."

"I know."

Like it was something she did. "Then let's adopt."

"We're not just anybody, OK?" Why was he so angry? "I don't want just anybody's baby, Maur. We have to keep trying."

"We used to be funny together." Her voice tore like a rag. "Now this is all we ever talk about."

"Work with me here."

"You want me to get pregnant." *Oh my God this is so terrible.* "I can't."

"But *we* can," Jake said, and then he said the unthinkable. What is it, Jake, why the burning need to lay down your own DNA like an animal scent-marking, or a scout blazing a trail in the woods? Good reporter, does his research. "There is one more thing we can try. I have some names."

She loved him. She still does. Grieving, she agreed.

The first surrogate couldn't conceive. Common phenomenon these days, but Maury thought with a savage righteous pang that, in spite of all the testing, maybe their problems had less to do with her than they did with Jake. During the screening process he was relentless, grilling and discarding candidates because they tested badly, because they said the wrong thing, because they didn't look enough like him. He settled on a Brown senior trying to bank grad school tuition. Maury came away from the meeting in tears; the girl was lovely, she was intelligent, she was still young. She'd have Jake's baby and it would look like him and Jake would fall in love with her. He'd leave Maury and start over with his nice new family, his very own baby safe in the world at last, with the potential for dozens more.

Instead of turning up at the clinic for insemination, the Brown senior took their down payment and vanished.

In the end, even Jake was defeated. He lowered his head like a dying bear determined to stay standing. "OK. We'll adopt."

"I'll call the state agency." God, it was a relief.

Jake flashed his palm like a figure in a No Smoking poster. "No way. We can afford a private agency, Maur. If we're going to do this . . ." His breath shook. "No Korean babies for me."

She grimaced. "We don't have much choice." No more Korean babies for anyone, none from China or Romania, the Center for Disease Control and the immigrations authorities saw to that. No more babies from outside these heavily protected United States. Even before Immigration shut them out she knew Jake would never go along. He's not that kind of guy. *I don't want just anybody's baby.* Agreeing to adopt, Jake set down parameters: he expects a child from their demographic, a close genetic match.

He wants to look into the face of his new baby and see somebody who looks like him looking back.

On the surface of it, any adoption agency would be happy to see the Bayless-Zorns coming: handsome, high-powered professionals— yuppies once, but young is receding into the past. So is the "upwardly mobile" part of the acronym. These two are at the top. Maury's a valued senior partner in a first-rate firm. The Jake Zorn Exposés, the ragged hair and that distinctive voice that sounds like it's been kicked downstairs, the professional charm put Jake next in line for a job as anchor on the national network news. They make enough money to keep bushels of babies, and in style. They just took a little too long deciding to adopt.

Although they're, ahem, older, the Bayless-Zorns have a nice way about them. It's clear that they'd be good with kids, although they wouldn't be where they are in life if they weren't ambitious. He has an immediate grin and a firm grip, but even when he's smiling, that intent look lets you know that when he's on the job, Jake turns into somebody else, and the wife? In these interviews, Maury glows as if somebody's lighted a cosy fire inside her head. She plans to quit the firm as soon as they put a baby into her arms, after all it takes everything you've got to see a child through the crucial first six years. If she does go back to work, she tells them, it will be part time.

Alone today, waiting, Maury's surprised by the sound of her own voice. "Plenty of lawyers work from home."

Sitting in the back of the empty courtroom pretending to read, she is in fact making her case. If she gets this baby, she will be home for this baby and when he goes to school she'll leave work early to be home when he gets there. A good mother never, ever lets her child come home to an empty house. Maury's child will come home to a warm, bright kitchen where every day is like a little party, milk and cookies, a big hug; they'll make brownies on snow days; she'll read to him! She wants her kids— how did they get to be kids instead of just one?— she wants her kids to associate home with the smell of dinner cooking. Home, where it's warm and safe and they know they are loved.

Then why do agencies keep turning them down? At first glance the paperwork's impeccable, but that's only at first glance. Sooner or later the case worker researching the Bayless-Zorns discovers Maury's hospitalization and drops them. Hospitalizations are OK, especially when a couple has spent so long trying to have a baby. It's this particular hospitalization that stops them cold. The reason behind it.

This is what failure does to you.

Nobody wants to give a child to a woman who's been hospitalized for depression. Not without close scrutiny. Not after they find out that she tried to off herself.

"What would you do," Maury says to the empty courtroom. Public defender now, pleading her own case. "Ten years," she says aloud. "Ten years of trying and failing. What would it do to you?"

Lame, Maury, she thinks. *Lame.* "But I got past it. I'm all better!"

It's late. What happened in Atlanta? Jake should have been in touch hours ago. She trusted him to win over the board at

Fayerweather, the last agency on their list. God, she thinks, did I make a mistake? No, with her benched, it's bound to go better. The recognition factor alone will do the job. Sweet, gruff Jake is a brilliant pitchman. His reputation walks in the door ahead of him: *The Conscience of Boston*. People defer. With that calculatedly rumpled, diamond-in-the-rough manner, Jake Zorn looks like a man you can trust.

Maybe his meeting ran long because everything is going right; they love Jake so much that they've brought out folders so he can take his pick. Unless everything is going wrong. They brought up the hospitalization. That must be it. Fine. Jake can explain it away. If it can be done Jake will do it and if he can't he'll con them into giving him and Maury a child. The man could charm concessions out of a cobra and when charm doesn't work he knows how to threaten with the best because— face it. Much as she loves him, Jake isn't always very nice. Look. Without Maury hanging in his shadow smiling her ashen, desperate smile, the man can do anything. Anything, she tells herself, sliding into the sweet, familiar loop between despair and the merciless hope that won't let go and never lets you quit.

No wonder she can't let anybody see her right now.

Crazy, what Maury does when her cell phone finally does vibrate. She switches it off and waits. She'll know soon enough, but right now she isn't strong enough to get the news first-hand. She'll wait until Jake is done talking. Then she'll give it another couple of minutes to be sure. When he's good and finished, she'll pick it up from her voicemail.

Jake Zorn didn't get to the top in television with sloppy sound bites. The message he leaves is one of those thirty-second teasers: you'll pay anything just to hear more. It does less than Maury wanted but more than she'd hoped.

"Honey, it's no go, but are we surprised?" Nice Jake, he keeps it light the way he always does when things are at their worst. "No sweat. I'm getting us a baby. Details when we talk. Too sensitive to do by phone." Then, not like him! He lets a silence fall. Only the electric crackle of his breathing tells her not to click the phone shut. Deep breath. He takes a deep breath. What comes out next comes in a throaty bark wrenched out of some place she doesn't recognize. Jake, forceful and jubilant. "I've found a guy."

iii.

*U*nderstand, Starbird presents as an individual without back-story. *Don't ask him what he means by* **unwanted.** *Not if you expect to do business with him.*

Whatever you do, don't ask about his life. There is too much at stake. Haven't you ever thought you wanted something and then gotten it and discovered it wasn't what you wanted after all? This explains why he works so hard at what he does.

His mother the failed poet thought a baby was just what she needed to make things right, but she was wrong. The man she chose was out the door before the baby came. Starbird counts himself lucky that the dude sometimes sent presents— out of guilt, proba-bly. The occasional post card from Darjeeling or Damascus or Hong Kong; they still come. Summer or winter the card says, **Happy Birthday, Tom.** *If Daria Starbird thought having a baby would make her a successful poet, she was wrong. All it did was make her tired and distracted and profoundly sad.*

Tom was her mistake. She said it out loud before he was old enough to parse it. She didn't blame him, exactly, but Tommy knew. She told him with crap meals and bleak evenings, long silences at the supper table, which served as her desk until six P.M., when she swept aside all her books and unfinished poems with an ostenta-tious sigh. Most nights they lived on canned soup and Hot Pockets because for a poet, life is too short to waste it cooking dinners.

Daria never reproached him, she didn't have to. He sensed her bitterness every time her rivals published books or won prizes; they got the world and all she had was him.

Gracious, handsome woman. Elegant— you'd never guess. Only Tommy knew she was miserable. He tried his hardest to make it better, but he didn't have the touch. Try and she'd turn on him. "Get out, how can I concentrate?" "Why are you always in the way?" "If it wasn't for you . . ." Once, before he knew better, he ran at his mother and locked his arms around her rigid body, sobbing. He gave her everything he had. "Oh, Mommy, don't feel bad!" The look she gave back when she pried him off and backed away was so forbidding that even though she apologized with tears running, he never touched her again.

Who exactly knows what "unwanted" means? Who has the right to decide who is welcome in any house? Better leave that to the experts, if you expect this man to help you. If there were snapshots in Starbird's paneled office instead of eighteenth-century water colors and that single extraordinary oil, you'd see that little Tom certainly didn't look unwanted; his mother dressed him in good clothes, kept the house tidy; she gave up her career ("now clean your room, I gave up my career for you!") and went to work. She took a crap office job to pay for pediatricians and dentists Tommy needed, tuition at good schools, wouldn't any mother do the same?

And what else are mothers supposed to do? What's the first thing they're supposed to do?

Starbird knows the answer well enough. If you have to ask, you can't afford it. He is looking for it in you.

*Before he got old enough to know better Tom convinced himself his mother loved him, she just wasn't good at remembering to tell him. He had to believe. She is, after all, his **mother**. How else could he make it through? Then he found the papers. Don't ask about the papers if you expect to stand anywhere smiling ever again. He found her papers and he knew. Oh, they went through the formalities all right, good-mornings and school lunches and night-nights, sleep-tights and cool hugs on the expected occasions, but it was* *empty, all of it. She said "I love you" but only when she had to, to make a point. It didn't help. He knew. No matter what Tommy did for Daria Starbird, no matter what nice thing he tried to say or do, he was nothing more to her than the unfortunate outward and physical sign of a bad career move.*

5.

Tom Starbird

When you get blown out the door of your life it's never just one thing that does it. In the realm of proximate and remote causes, known way stations on my road out of the rescue business, Morgan Sterling was the spark that lit a very long fuse. And the charge? Until I ran into the Carsons, I didn't even know there was a charge set inside me, just waiting for detonation. By the time I finished with Rita and Geoffrey Carson I knew damn well that it was there and sooner or later it would go off.

And why? We'll get to that later.

This all came down when I still talked in figures. I honestly thought if I could just find the right words for things, I could do what I had to and know it was right.

The hell of it is that the Carsons looked right. Nice couple, ran a private school, lived like churchmice, scrimping to buy my services. Or I thought they were. I checked them out on the Web before I opened their application. Kindly headmaster, A-1 school, laughable salary, the guy had to be an altruist. He'd turned his back on his rich dad's empire to work with bright, unconventional kids who from all reports loved both Geoffrey and his wife Rita like parents. On paper, they looked terrific.

They looked terrific in person, too. Attractive, energetic. They'd passed all my tests, no problem; they looked good, coming into my office. They interviewed well— a little too eager, but that's to be expected.

It was time to study them in their native habitat. All brick and ivy, I supposed, great place for a kid, first-class ticket to a first-class college guaranteed. Young, energetic, hands-on parents, I thought, no handing this one off to some old lady for the day-to-day, no daycare, no nanny. This is what I want for my kids, and I have reasons.

Their nice brick house was everything you'd hope for: on a hill overlooking the brick quadrangle. That came with the territory, I assumed, one of the perks of the job, no headmaster could afford a place like that. They offered tea and cookies in a lovely room with Persian rugs and museum quality furniture, which should have been the tipoff. If you're a headmaster you get the house free, but the Utrillo and the Chagall?

I don't know what I expected.

Afternoon tea segued into the cocktail hour, Perrier for me, thanks, I don't drink when I'm working ("Oh, but surely a little wine for dinner . . ."). She'd roasted duck and made a pie ("Don't leave, I did it for you!"). As a provider I keep a professional distance but this time I stayed. I had to be sure. OK, I was psyched at the idea of somebody cooking for me. They were wine snobs and the labels on the wines Geoffrey brought up from the wine cellar (the headmaster has a wine cellar?) had that you-can't-afford-this sheen. Although I am especially careful when someone else is pouring, they'd both had too much of Geoffrey's Chateauneuf du Pape and even I was a little boiled.

When people want children they always want them for a reason, but most people's reasons are, maybe, less obviously venal? The penny dropped after brandies in front of Ye Olde Englishe Fireplace under the ancestral portrait in their oak-paneled library.

"It's so painful," Rita was saying, "giving our lives to the children, watching them grow up and loving them, knowing all the time that no matter how close we are, we'll have to send them home at the end of the year."

"So this is wonderful," Geoff said, because by that time I was Geoffing him. "And you can get us a baby by . . ."

I had a great prospect scoped for them, ready for the pickup. It was easy to finish his sentence; I all but promised: "Christmas."

"A month before your big Four-Oh," Rita sang.

"The *big* birthday." Geoffrey laughed. Then he went: "Ka-*ching*."

She purred, "Our hero," with a grin that made me wonder if she was getting cranked up to hit on me. Then she moved in and I knew she was; in her careless need to touch me she slid one warm, soft hand down my jaw, turning my head and leaning in close. Her lips made contact with my ear and she whispered, "It's this fucking will. Not one fucking penny unless we have kid!"

It cost me to get out of that one. We'd all signed. I'd made promises. Cheap at the price. Bastards.

The Pottingers, talented, nice sculptors from Chicago, were an easier shot to call. It just took a little bit longer. They tested fine, right up to the transfer of property. They made the mistake of bringing the live-in nanny they'd just engaged to fly back with the kid while they stayed in New York and took in a couple of shows. I pointed them to the escape clause I'd had written in especially for such cases, but by that time I was . . . What. I'm not sure, exactly. Just uneasy.

Then I got a call from Sterling Enterprises and I thought: fine. This is a meeting worth going to. Funding for my secret project, if it works out. Everybody knows Morgan Sterling, high-voltage Manhattan corporate exec, she's on everybody's A list and trustee on a dozen boards. Odd, the way in some circles, looks and power make you a celebrity. In all the print journals and videos I studied after her assistant phoned, Sterling comes off as smart, beautiful, powerful— a noted philanthropist. She's that chic, salty, fabulous-looking woman who shows up on magazine covers and red carpets and sits front and center on the sofa on all the best talk shows. The woman is an opinion-maker, and I needed her help.

The bait: an offer from the Morgan Sterling Foundation to support my secret dream. Remember, I didn't call her. They called me.

The switch? So what if I didn't see it coming? Isn't life a transaction?

She sent a car, which meant she valued my time. Bozos in black met me at the curb and took me up to an oval office at the top of a Manhattan building you probably know on sight. The bozos who saw me into the building and up to the penthouse office were replaced by bozos in soft gray suits that weren't quite uniforms, who settled me in the boardroom with coffee and the *Financial Times*. There was a lot of money here: gray velvet walls, gray ceiling, deep gray carpeting, oval glass table with what looked like brushed steel Brancusi knockoff as a base. Indirect lighting rimmed the oval ceiling, deflected by a mirrored band: two-way glass. If they wanted to observe this meeting, fine. I wasn't here on business.

I was here to get her to do something I can't do. I'm looking for ways to help all the babies nobody bothers to chip. Franchising the disenfranchised, I suppose. In this paranoid society a baby without a chip is an uncitizen, shut out of everything a kid has a right to expect in this and every other country.

In a country in high bunker mode— right, Homeland Security!— it was easy to sell the public on tiny tracking devices so no child gets lost. Embedded in the fontanelle. Once the skull closes, they can't be removed. If anybody snatches your treasure the signal leads cops straight to the perp before she can put the baby down.

Of course they were playing on other fears, as in, No Child Left Behind. That was the second prong of the campaign for the legislation: tracking intelligence so your child gets into the right preschool and grade school, the right high school, a college that will make you proud and shoehorn your young graduate into a paying job and success in life. All those couples who stayed up nights getting pregnant and all the climbers and overachievers crazy to see their kids score big bought in and started lobbying. Microchipping is written into the law.

Now I have to wonder if it's so no child can hide.

You, who were so afraid of losing your children, you voted for chipping without looking ahead, but I work with the babies nobody cared enough to chip.

Understand, the chips can't be counterfeited and each device is numbered. Usually they pop them into the soft spot before your baby leaves the hospital, but the window of opportunity is open for several months. And you pay a handsome price for it, after which your child's name is officially entered into the system. Once the fontanelle closes, the baby's future is pretty much carved in stone.

Sure they sold you on a chip that would keep your treasure safe. They soft-pedaled the fact that every one of these chips stores data as well as transmits and you have no control over what goes in. The thing will keep storing and transmitting for the rest of your child's life. Never mind how much data or what kind of privileged information gets input before the implant goes into your baby's head or which details are entered every time that baby goes to the pediatrician for its shots, goes into daycare, starts school. Never mind the routine scanning every time your growing child walks into a bank or a computer store or goes through airport security or registers for its SATs . . .

Security. Sure, no outsiders in our fine country, but:

The bottom line?

The screening technology is in the early stages so results are not yet obvious to you, the public, but the implications are clear.

Without that numbered chip, a kid is a cipher. Bottom-tier schooling at best, and you can forget college. When security technology catches up with the chip, doors all over the country will slam shut. The unchipped child will never be able to walk into a bank or through an airport without setting off alarms. May not be able to get a driver's license, go into or out of a supermarket, get on or off a subway or a metropolitan bus. Will have a hard time getting a job. The kid may end up at one of the juvenile centers. In jail.

The implantation tax is already in place, and it's stiff. Not everybody wants to pay. Some people can't pay.

There are so many unchipped babies that I could work all day every day for the rest of my life and never place them all, never get them chipped, never make them entitled U.S. citizens. There are too many for me to help.

I can't help them but I can't just walk away.

Saving these kids won't just take a village. It'll take a foundation. I need millions to do the job and an organizing genius to set it up and get the word out. A charismatic figure to win nationwide support. Me, I fly under the radar. I couldn't do the job even if it was safe for me to show my face. Morgan Sterling is C.E.O. of a major conglomerate and the kind of celebrity audiences love on sight.

I came to this meeting because I thought she wanted to help. Why else did she track me down and set it up?

God only knows what I was expecting.

I never expected to see her flounce in like a Rockette with her arms spread and a phony, incandescent smile crossing her face like the display on a Times Square LCD, and I never expected her to say what she said to me instead of Thank you for coming, or Hello.

"Mr. Starbird, I want a baby."

I never expected her to be so old. "Ma'am?"

"You heard me, I want a baby. And don't call me Ma'am." Even the voice was old.

It made me wonder who did her up for TV and photo shoots. How many face lifts there had been, and what acting coach taught her to project eternal youth. But you don't say that to a billionaire with her own private foundation. You get out as best you can. I should have been pissed at the deceit but I was just depressed. "I thought you wanted to talk about my project."

"Afterward. When can you deliver?"

"I can't."

"It's your business, right?"

"That's not why I'm here."

Her face shrank into an ugly squint. "But you *do* steal babies."

A match flared inside me. *What?*

"I need one . . ." She looked at her watch. "Nine months from yesterday. My boyfriend thinks I'm pregnant."

"I can't do that." We both knew I meant I wouldn't.

She didn't care. She just went on. "This is a picture of Trey. Get me a baby who looks like him."

"I'm sorry."

"Don't worry, I'm good for it. All Trey's friends have children now. I could do it, but I'm too busy. After all," she said with the ease of an expert at self-delusion, "I'm still ovulating. I can certainly get pregnant, I just don't have the time." She went on carefully, making clear that this was transactional. "And you need something from me. Something about a foundation. Now, where's the paperwork?" She tightened her grip and I winced as her nails dug in. "Let's do this!"

I couldn't just walk away from her billions. I fell back on boilerplate. Starbird's first question. "Tell me why you think you want a baby."

That big head lifted and she threw back her hair in an odd, showy gesture lifted from some vintage movie I was too young to recognize. "Doesn't every girl want a child?"

So that was it. Up front and stark naked. Richest woman in New York, needs more than anything to think she is still young. She thinks a baby will prove it. I got up to go. "I'm sorry."

The girl in Morgan Sterling vanished. The executive turned to steel. "Get me this baby."

A spark kindled inside me. "No."

OK, forgive me, all you unwanted, unchipped, disenfranchised babies that I will never help. I walked out on her. Behind me she thundered, if a woman sobbing with rage can thunder, "You'll never do business in this town again!"

The fuse ignited. *Right.*

I don't want to do business in this town again. Not really. Not ever. I knew that even before Morgan Sterling knew that she and I were done.

Instead of going back to the office to sign off on all the cases on my wait list and return the stack of petitions laid out for my consideration, I went to one of my garages and took out the rusting Hyundai I keep for low profile followups. I needed to remind myself why I'd gotten into this business in the first place so I left the city by the Lincoln Tunnel and drove for days.

I needed to make sure my people were OK.

I went to every New England town where I had placed children and I went to their houses, every one I could find. Some were shuttered against night. Others had new tenants or For Sale signs on the lawn, and that gave me the creeps. Where had they gone? Why did they go? Had something happened to the baby I had found for them? Was it something they'd done that they didn't want me to know about? I didn't know. I made wider circles, jittering with anxiety until I located a few of my first clients, still settled in the houses they'd been so anxious for me to inspect. I spied on some of them at the playground and at the supermarket. I don't know what I was expecting but they looked ordinary to me. When people are going about their daily business they aren't necessarily focused on their children and there's only so much you can tell, so I followed them home and drove around until nightfall, when I doubled back. When I reached their houses I cut the motor and watched for a while. Then I got out and went on foot. I wanted to see all the families I'd made, laughing together. I wanted there to be hugging, signs of joy. I didn't want them to thank me, I just wanted to know. In a dozen places I circled their houses, craning to see into their living rooms, and when they drew the curtains I prowled around the back, staring into lighted kitchen windows and for all the babies I saw waving in their high chairs, babies tucked in bouncy chairs and toddlers paddling around on screen porches I saw only the ordinary.

What was I looking for, what did I expect really? I just wanted to know I'd done some good. I needed to see them laughing and content, but for all the time I spent watching the children I'd worked so hard to help, I couldn't tell if they were happy.

I couldn't tell!

Interesting, how you can start out thinking you are doing one thing and end up doing another, how you break your heart trying to help and end up shooting yourself in the foot. Interesting and terrible.

All that and I still didn't know whether I'd done even one good thing. It might be time to quit.

6.

The glories of pregnancy are a myth dreamed up by women who forgot. In the final stages, it's hard to sleep. When your body's been carjacked, it's impossible. You're no longer a person, you are a vehicle, with an unwanted passenger driving you God knows where. Pregnancy jerks you into a new trajectory and sends you speeding along toward a destination you don't want and can't escape. At the end there will be pain and blood, and in Sasha Egan's case, grief and responsibility to a baby she never asked for and can't keep.

How would she take care of it? Worry alone keeps her tossing and turning, but with this new belly, turning won't work. Can't sleep on her front, can't sleep on her back either, can't roll over without groaning; in the night her feral passenger's elbows jab into her soft places, stirring up bad dreams. Anxieties roll in like waves, eroding sleep.

Tonight, it's worse. With Gary Cargill stalking the Pilcher grounds, she'll be awake until the night goes away— or Gary does. Dry-mouthed and taut with worry, she heaves herself out of bed and pads out to the hall window to check. There's always the possibility that she'll look out and catch him leaving, or that the still air, the bleached sand outside will tell her he's gone.

Instead she sees a smear of darkness rushing past. Hurrying down the long hallway she sees it from the next window and the next: Gary Cargill's moving shadow, leaving its track like a snail.

He's been out there for hours. When she ran inside yesterday he phoned and phoned. He hit *redial* on his cell before the door slammed behind her. He called the office and kept calling until Lights Out, but in spite of Viola's sudden concern (what is it, Viola, did he offer you money?) Sasha refused his calls.

Now he is out there in broad moonlight, shaking his fist at the building while she watches from the darkened solarium. Let him yell, his threats won't make it through the Thermopane. Pilcher's sealed tight. Still it makes her uneasy, having him so close.

Shaking, she goes back to her room. *He can't get me here,* she tells herself, but no place is safe. Gary looked like such a nice guy the night she fucked him, sweet-faced and easygoing with a goofy, slightly hammered smile and flakes of glitter caught in his fair, curly hair. Now he is someone else. It won't matter what she does or what she tells him, he isn't giving up and he won't go away. He didn't track her down and come all this way just to let it go. Every time she gets up to look she sees that same shadow like a running smudge: her one-night stand Gary Cargill on a loop. One slip, and now they are eternally linked.

What does Gary really want from this?

He doesn't want a baby of his own to take care of, not Gary, not at his age. That was a lie. So, what? Did Grandmother make him an offer he can't refuse or is he planning to sell this baby to somebody else?

She has to plan but plans elude her. Everywhere her mind runs, Gary is.

Her first instinct is to leave, but the risks are too great. If she stays put he'll make a scene in the office and get her kicked out of here or else he'll go to court to take her baby away. If she calls the police he'll turn them on her, charging God knows what. It will get into the newspapers and Grandmother will find out.

If she walks out any door, he'll pounce. He could blindside her and throw her into his car before she got the breath to scream. He could tie her down and drive without stopping until they were a thousand miles from here, keep her locked up in a shack or trapped in a motel until she goes into labor, and then what would Gary do? Follow her into the delivery room and stay until the baby comes out— happy father, Nurse, let me hold him for a minute. There. He could tuck the baby under his arm and make a run for it as soon as their backs were turned. If she lets him get his hands on it, he can do whatever he wants.

If Gary's that crazy, would he bother with the hospital at all? Or would he keep her locked up after the contractions start? My God, imagine having this baby without help, stranded somewhere, squirming on a dirty mattress while Gary hangs over her with that blind, possessive smile. Imagine being trapped miles from the hospital, fighting contractions until she is torn wide open and the baby slips out into Gary's hands.

Shaking, she backs into the bed and sits down hard. Get over yourself, Sasha. Get a grip.

She's— God, does Gary already know where she is in the building, or is he on a surveillance run, checking all the windows, waiting for her to flip on a light and show herself? If she does show herself will he lie to fat Viola in the morning, or will he bribe his way in? For all she knows, he's down there prying open one of the sealed windows right now. Or he's found an unlocked door or an open window and has slipped inside. Is he on the ground floor yet, is he upstairs, creeping this way? What if he corners her in her room? She doesn't know.

Gary is a complete stranger. She has no idea what he will do.

For all she knows he's waiting for her to come out and apologize— after all, it's his baby too. Or he thinks she's secretly in love with him. *You know you're asking for it. No!* Unless he expects her to rush into his arms and beg him to marry her so this baby will have a father. Or he thinks she's so stupid that by morning, she'll forget and wander out. As if she'd sit up and stretch, yawning, and blunder outside in her bathrobe to enjoy the pink morning light. Surprised: *Oh, Gary.* What are you doing here? Unless he's trying to flush her out so he can spring like a panther and bring her down. She isn't safe anywhere.

She can't go out. Not now and not tomorrow, either. Not without a plan. She can't go on the way she is, frantic and vulnerable. She has to do something, but what?

Just when she ought to be deciding, Sasha is torn. She has everything she needs here at Pilcher: bright, sunny room for the duration, comprehensive prenatal care. Case workers eager to place this baby when it comes. To her surprise she has friends, a handful of sweet, uncomplicated pregnant girls who never heard of Donovan Development and could care less who her grandfather is. She has responsibilities— grinning, needy little Luellen Squiers. She has excellent doctors and experienced labor coaches, three squares and no responsibilities, and right now she has autonomy: no craggy grandmother reminding her that she's just like her mother, bad fruit always lands under the tree. She can't do that to a kid.

There is, furthermore, the lure of the nice new parents the Newlife agency has contracted to find, the perfect, loving family she's promised this unborn child. When you make a unique print you hope for wealthy, wonderful patrons who will take it home to the ideal setting, somebody who will appreciate what you've done and frame it right. You want a sweet couple who will love this creation of yours and keep it safe in a beautiful place. It's more than Sasha can do for him, and the guilt is eating her up. So far the parent candidates have all been duds, but satisfaction is written into the Newlife contract, she's begged them to try harder and they still have time to search.

Now, if the agency would contract to protect me from Gary, she thinks, if they would pledge to help me fight for my rights . . .

A click on the Thermopane brings her to her feet. She's afraid to look. Is Gary down there throwing stones? Fear sends her back to the bed, where she clings like a shipwrecked sailor rocking on a raft. It isn't safe!

She can't go home. She won't. If she wanted to see the Donovans she'd be there by now, but where her grandparents are concerned, Sasha is a hard sell. It's her baby and she plans to give it up, which means they must never know. Catholic girls go ahead and have their babies, which is what brought her here. Good Catholic mothers keep their children, Grandmother drummed it into her before she was big enough to hold a spoon. Didn't she force Sasha's mother to get married while she was still in high school and see to it that the irresponsible girl brought her baby home for Grand to feed and fuss at and supervise? Sasha knew the litany before she was old enough to understand.

"Get down on your knees and thank God that I kept her from paying some clinic to scoop you out."

Didn't Grand keep Sasha even after handsome Jimmy Egan took off in the middle of the night and Lucy ran away? Oh, yes Sasha heard about it. She heard about it every day. "And thank your God for giving you a grandmother to take care of you!"

Maeve Donovan, that grudging model of Irish rectitude. Sasha knows what that rectitude demands. She's never going back. If she went home her grandparents would buy Gary just the way they did her father, forcing a marriage down her throat.

Unless, Sasha thinks bitterly, they already have bought him. Gary's sudden possessiveness, violence not threatened, but implied. Have he and Grand already struck a deal?

While the younger women sigh and groan in their sleep, Sasha lies spreadeagled, taut and dry-eyed with concentration, working on a plan. It isn't much but she thinks it will fly. Anything is better than waiting for Gary to hit the end of his tether and turn on her like a junkie's Rottweiler. Gary. She hardly knows him, which is the worst part. She has no idea what he will do. Even though they're strangers, she does know that Gary isn't particularly swift. She's sorting through ways to slip before he has time to figure out that she's gone.

Friday, she thinks. She will go Friday. If she can last that long.

On Fridays there are day trips, outings, supervised comings and goings in the Newlife vans. She will sign up to go shopping Friday with Betty Jane Gudger and Luellen Squiers and a half dozen other giggling high school kids. With the black panes in the air conditioned Ford Expedition sealed tight Gary will have no way of knowing Sasha is slumped in the back behind the others, or that her shoulder bag contains the last civilian dress she owns that almost fits. Gaudy and embarrassed in their pastel flowered scrubs, the Newlife residents always stick together on these outings, moving in a phalanx down the wide main street of the one horse town, which means that later anybody asking questions will have a hard time finding out how many unwed mothers went to town and how many came back. The girls will all be jabbering, happy and distracted, but Sasha will remain vigilant. When the time's right and she is certain nobody— especially not Gary— is watching, she will duck into the bathroom at the local clam bar, do the quick change and wedge herself through the back window and slip away on the afternoon bus. Tomorrow she'll go down to the computer room and research Greyhound routes on the Web. She needs to pick a location, some wide place in the road on the far side of the state line. She needs somewhere big enough to support a decent hospital, some large town or small city where a pregnant stranger won't stand out on the main drag like a wild duck in a plastic wading pond. Once she gets oriented she'll check into a good motel to wait this thing out. Her credit limit is high, let Mastercard pay for this; she'll find a way to place the baby and figure out how to disappear long before the Donovans or the Cargills or anybody else thinks of calling in the law or hiring a detective to track her down through the receipts.

7.

Tom Starbird

Martha, I don't care who's on the line, the Everetts and I are closing here." When we're done, I'm looking for an island where I can sit down and go inside myself to think.

"I'm sorry, Tom, it's an emergency."

"It had better be."

"When you hear who it is . . ." Martha's embarrassed because in a no-calls situation, she let some outsider bully her into putting him through. She evaporates before she can finish her apology.

At the other end of my private line a man whose voice I think I recognize says, "Do you know who I am?"

It's the last voice I want to hear. We all saw him tear into the Nebraska baby ranches and the clone labs on national TV. If this is Jake Zorn, the Conscience of Boston, I am probably fucked. The name is famous and he expects me to say it. Instead I say, "No."

"Jake Zorn." He throws it like a rock.

"What do you want?"

"And you're Tom Starbird."

I should deny it, I should ask how he got this number and what threats he leveled to make Martha put him through but I have clients waiting and I can't play that scene. I should hang up now. Instead I nod, even though this isn't TV. "I am."

"Then you know why I'm calling."

"Um." Oh, yes I am stalling. This is, after all, Boston's celebrated exposé guy, his hottest stuff airs nationwide. How much does he know? "No comment."

"It's not about that!"

"OK goodbye."

"I know where you are and I know what you do."

Bad. This is bad. "I'm hanging up now."

"I'll just call back on your cell."

"Nobody has that number!" *Oh, shit. He really does know where I am.* What he doesn't know is that I have a backup plan for this eventuality. My passport's in order, the house is in somebody else's name. The bulk of the money is in Vienna. A few wire transfers and I'm gone. My cell vibrates: busted. I check caller ID, just in case. It's definitely him. My voice shoots up as I snap it shut. "Nobody."

"Relax," he says with a broadcast-quality chuckle. All of a sudden he's Mr. Congeniality. "It's not what you think."

"Then what the hell is it?"

"Are you alone?"

"I can't have this conversation now."

"But you will."

Cover the mouthpiece, smile at the couple perched on the sofa like refugees stranded on the dock at Da Nang; the tide's going out and your captain must set sail. OK, I do talk in figures; I lied. "I'm sorry, I have to take this."

Jane Everett's eyebrows shoot up. *Not now, when we're so close!*

I cover the mouthpiece. "Can you come back tonight?"

The husband is angry. He thought we were equals in a simple business arrangement. Tai Everett isn't used to dealing with people he needs more than they need him. "What are you trying to pull?"

"I have to take this call."

The wife touches his lips to keep him from saying any more. Her anxiety is so sweet that I give her my best reassuring smile. Relieved, she tugs him to his feet. "We'll just . . ."

For her sake I am trying to be gracious. "If you don't mind."

I feel sorry for them. Stopped just short of the finish line. Where they came on strong when they walked into the meeting, now they both look unaccountably shabby, standing there. He bristles. "We were about to close on this!"

"Tai, please!"

They eddy in the doorway while Zorn's breathing crackles in the receiver and I re-think. The Everetts are here because they tested better than any of the others on my wait list. I bumped them up and rushed the meeting because it's my last for a while. I am a short-timer here. The last subject is ripe for rescue and plans for the pickup are in place. I prefer a longer lead time but I am wrapping this one up tomorrow. Supplier I've been watching is juggling an oversized family, there's neglect, maybe something worse going on. Clearly there's a reason she never had this last baby chipped. If the kid gets lost, he's doing her a favor, that's how much she cares. You might call it an emergency rescue. The doctor I keep on call will come in tonight, check out the baby and see to the chipping; he brings registered government chips ready for programming and implanting, so tomorrow at the airport and every day after that, the Everetts' new baby is cool. The sooner we complete the transfer of property, the sooner I can move on.

"OK," I say to them, "we'll finalize. But you'll have to wait. Now, if you'll excuse me . . ."

He scowls. She puts her hand on his arm. "Tai, don't!"

"Martha will make coffee for you."

I'm usually pretty cool but I die and get buried a few times too many before they finally leave the room. Meanwhile the power player at the other end of the line is buzzing like a hinky generator; Jake Zorn isn't used to waiting. Guys like this have assistants to do the waiting for them; they place his calls and when they get his party, he makes them wait. It's a power thing. That makes this call automatically different.

He placed it himself because he doesn't want anybody to know.

Holy fuck, he needs me more than I need him. "Sorry, Zorn. I can't help you."

"I don't have much time."

"How did you get my . . ."

"Does it matter? I need your services."

I am done taking clients, at least for now. I can't get sucked into anything with Jake Zorn. I need empty time, so I can think. "I'm sorry, I'm on hiatus."

"I *said,* I need your services. How soon can we meet?"

"I can't help you." Translation: I won't.

"Beg to differ." The voice rattles like stones in a rock tumbler. "If I decide to expose you, you're fucked. Just think of it as long-term insurance. If we bring this off you know I'll never go public with what I know because I'm personally involved."

"What do you think you know?"

"That you steal kids."

I am quick to say, "It's a placement service!" but the fuse burns a little faster.

"Fine. Place a baby with me."

"Can't. Even my wait list has to wait."

He barks in that *do you know who I am* tone: "I don't wait."

"I'm sorry, shop's closed."

Zorn rolls on like a piece of heavy equipment fixing to mash me flat. "Not before you do this. Understand?"

I don't budge. There is nothing between us but the sound of Zorn waiting.

Finally he says, "You have to help us." That familiar break in the voice turns spiky Jake Zorn into just another needy human. "You have to help her. Please."

"See, that's the problem." Oh, yes I have been thinking. Not for nothing was Daria Starbird a poet. My intuition kicks in. "Your wife had an episode."

It's like a punch in the belly. I can almost hear him go *ooof.* "You're not supposed to know that."

"I know a lot of things."

"It's over, it was nothing," he says. Then he says, "Look, Starbird, my wife. That was a passing thing. She's fine now, I have hospital paperwork on that. I was getting it in order for . . ."

"One of the agencies . . ."

"A lot of agencies . . ."

"That turned you down."

Rage roars out of him. "We need a baby!" Having exploded, Zorn stops. The silence lasts a long time. I am shaking the receiver to see what else is going to fall out of it when he adds:

"Just steal a fucking baby for us, OK?"

The more I talk to him the more I know I don't want to place a kid with this guy. He's a yeller. Probably a hitter too. "Look, Mr. Zorn, there's more than one problem with this."

"What?"

He isn't listening to reason, which means I end up piling on too many reasons. He isn't a vanity client, like Morgan Sterling, so I tell him, "There's your age."

"If this is about the money, we pay up front, and in cash."

"Everybody does." What are they, late forties, fifty? The gravely voice and the relief map face are Jake Zorn's TV stock in trade. This guy hits hard. He could have a heart attack and leave the kid fatherless. He could stroke out. "Even if your wife is strong enough to do it, you're too old to bring up a kid."

"We can handle it."

"You want to go to his graduation on a walker? If you live to see him graduate?"

"Fuck that shit," he growls. Not even Zorn wants to admit that he's old. "We'll be great parents!"

"You look more like grandparents."

"And what the fuck do you look like, Starbird? Scum."

Filthy. He makes what I do sound filthy. I make wrapping-up noises. "So that's it. You'll have to find another guy."

"Not so fast, Starbird. We're not done."

I don't answer. I am waiting for him to hang up.

"Starbird?"

"I'm here."

"You know what happens to people who cross me. You might as well know . . ." Pause for effect. "My people have accessed your files."

Right. *Oh, careful, Starbird. Be careful what you say.* "Nobody accesses my files."

"What makes you so sure?" He waits. When I don't speak he says, "Do you know what I can do to you?"

"You don't have anything on me."

"Do you want to put money on that? If I decide to do the show, and believe me, I *will* do the show . . ."

Nobody knows exactly what I do or where or how I do it, but if Zorn is on the level, he has an idea. This isn't like you knowing. It's like having the Supreme Court or the Attorney General know. Exposing me to the light. I wait.

He rumbles to himself for a minute, like a boiler fixing to blow. "Here's the deal. I'll give it to you in writing. Your baby for my silence."

It seems safer to pretend that I'm out of words.

"Starbird, I don't hear you answering. If we're talking, you know I already have enough on you to put you away for life."

Doubtful, but it's clear where he's going with this. If I refuse him, he intends to go public with whatever little shit he has on me. This is bad, but it is by no means the worst. I'll tell you what's worse. The thing about the law is, the law is blind to motives. If they do come after me they won't just try me and put me away. I'll be charged with kidnapping, death penalty implied. "I don't think so."

"Do you really want to take the risk?"

Push has come to shove and I make a tremendous discovery. "I really don't care." *Did I really say that?* Wow. It's true! This is nothing I chose.

BANG. It's over. I can't do this any more.

"So get me a baby."

"Or you'll, what. Expose me?"

"Yes."

Where I should be cowering, maybe, or re-thinking, for the first time since I took on my very first clients, I feel liberated. A thousand tons lighter. He just made it easy for me to turn my back and walk away. "That's cool. If you think you can put me out of business, go for it! I'm through, as of today."

"You can't quit." Something inside Jake Zorn is grinding. I can hear it in his voice. "You can't afford to quit."

"But I am. And if you think you're taping this conversation, you can forget it. My filters shred all signals, going out or coming in. Whatever you're using to record this, your equipment's already fried."

"You're lying."

"So if you don't mind . . ."

"Like you think I don't mind, Starbird." The rest comes in stages, like the first blobs of slurry slipping out of a cement mixer. "Do you really believe I'd start this without a backup plan?"

I kick it out of the way. "If you can find me, let me know when your big show is running. Can't wait to see it when it airs."

Then the slurry rolls down on me for real. Zorn says in a cold, still voice, "Oh, I'm not going after you."

Starbird, asshole, listen to yourself, blundering on while the stuff piles up around your ankles. "OK then, goodbye and thanks."

"Don't thank me yet."

"You can't hurt me now."

Listen to the man! Jake Zorn continues in that cold, still voice, graver than his usual. "Why would I waste time on you?"

It's been a long conversation and I'm sick of it. To tell the truth, I'm too busy writing my farewell speech to notice. "Spare me the threats and don't bother me again." I'm about to flip him into oblivion when he comes up with the one thing that will suck me in.

"The big story is Daria Starbird. Feminist poet, comes on all sacred and holy, but her backstory is a bitch. You and she are related, right?"

This fixes me in place. Zorn is waiting but no words come.

"Right?" I can hear him looking at his watch. He may need me more than I need him, but in this one respect, I need his silence. The bastard has me and he knows it. This time he doesn't bother to wait for an answer. "You've wasted enough of my time, Starbird. You know where I am. Tomorrow at three."

8.

Like certain men, the escape plan looked good in the dark but now the sun is up.

Clinging to her raft, bobbing aimlessly a thousand miles from shore, Sasha stares at the ceiling. She hasn't slept. Gary's out there doing God knows what. Unless he's downstairs right now, sweet-talking his way inside— Gary Cargill, whom she barely knows. He's on the move and she's lying here with a half-assed plan that fell apart at first light. Can she stay? Should she go? This isn't only her future. There's the baby. How can she plan when she can't even sleep? She should have left last night, when she was sure.

She should have called a cab, called the cops, called it quits last night here but it was weird out. The footing was uncertain. No matter which door she chose he could be standing there.

She heard his footsteps circling for hours, but some time before sunrise she heard a door slam and the throaty snarl of a cheap car scratching off. She didn't need to hear Gary shouting, *I'll be back.* She knows he will. Crazy, she thinks, he's crazy to assume that biology constitutes possession. He came in grinning like a carnival prizewinner primed to pick up the plush elephant, the Nokia or iPod, the Twin Towers paperweight that he won with a lucky shot. As if one shot makes him a dad.

The incursion leaves her jittery and possessive. *This isn't your inalienable right, you jerk, it has nothing to do with you.*

Sasha knows better than anyone that it doesn't. She's carrying this baby, and she has no right. As if a dumb college fuck like Gary could actually take care of a child. As if she can. Biology doesn't make you a mother. Or give you a father's rights. When it comes to a freshly hatched baby, she doesn't know what to do. She wouldn't know where to start. Which, for God's sake, is why she came here in the first place. To find somebody who does. She wants a real mother and father to throw their hearts into taking care of this baby she is having.

If she leaves, what will happen to her baby then?

Gary's mad sense of entitlement frightens her. *Mine,* he said. They are like kids fighting over a rubber doll. *No. It's mine.*

God, she can't stay! Worse. She is afraid to go.

It's pathetic but her time here has made her lazy and dependent. It was the relief, she supposes, after all that uncertainty. Somebody to take care. Before Newlife, Sasha was taut with worry. What on earth would she do with this tiny, breakable thing, how could she manage a child without hurting it— specifically, without messing up the way her mother had? How could she keep from replicating the pattern, yet another Donovan woman crawling home? The solutions the agency offered were beautifully simple. Ideal.

We will find a perfect home for your baby. Sign here and let us do the rest.

Decided, she drifted along like a holiday rafter with no fixed destination and no deadlines, floating down a stream she had no desire to divert, or to escape. With everything taken care of she simply let go, humming along without worrying about what day it was or what to wear or when to go down to the sunny dining room, or what would happen next. She slept a lot, who wouldn't? When all your decisions are made for you, you have time to dream.

In dreams she's only a container for the beautiful firefly she can release at the end. She loves it, she supposes, but in an abstract way. The way every artist loves her work. She can't wait to let it out of the jar. No. She can't wait to stop being the jar. She can watch it fly out to light up the sky. Think what beautiful patterns he'll make! Dreaming, she let the pregnancy take her; at the end of nine months she and her baby would part with a kiss and a wave, Sasha and her firefly free to light up their separate parts of the world. Next time they meet, she thought before Gary intruded, it will be as equals, two joyful, free spirits— *Oh, so this is what you're like. What a nice surprise.*

Then Gary.

For the first time since she hit Newlife, the decisions are back in her lap. Last night she thought it was clear. This morning, she doesn't know. Is she better off running? Safer here? The chasm between now and her due date stretches and Sasha teeters like a ropewalker. Can she make it across without Gary jerking the rope out from under her? What if she can't?

The rest of the pregnant world is up and dressed and downstairs for the day, happy to waddle through the morning, laughing in front of daytime TV without a care while, alone in her room, Sasha broods. She should be showering. Putting on today's flowered scrubs. Shuffling out to face the day. Instead she lies here, parched and anxious, while her imagination darts like a trapped ferret trying to gnaw its way to an exit without knowing which way.

"Sally?"

When you don't sleep and sunrise finally tells you it's OK to quit trying, sometimes you drop off out of sheer relief. Sasha blinks and sits up, flailing. *Did I sleep?* "What!"

Maureen Storch, the placement officer, is standing over her with that nice-nasty Pepto-Bismol breath: "Sally, get up!"

"It's Sasha."

"Whatever, Sarah."

"Sasha."

The woman blinks bulging thyroid eyes. "Why aren't you ready?"

Sasha's head jerks. "What?"

"Don't you remember? Today's the day!"

She wonders what Maureen knows that makes her so officious.

Has Gary been down there shooting his mouth off? She's afraid to ask. "What time is it?"

"Quit stalling. You know damn well it's time."

She's running out of time and she doesn't even know what time it is. "What's happening?"

"Didn't you hear the bell? It's almost ten. You're late."

"Late for . . ."

"The prospects." The placement officer says with exaggerated patience, "You knew they were coming at nine. Why aren't you up?"

"Then this isn't about . . ." Better not finish this sentence, she realizes. If they haven't heard from Gary, fine.

"They're the last on your list, Egan, so get moving. They've been in the special room for an hour."

Strung out on no sleep, Sasha rummages: what were those people's names? "Who have?"

"The Hansons! They're your last couple in this round." Maureen slaps her clipboard on the bedstead. Schedule for the day, check-off sheet, green folder. "Remember, you only get thirteen tries."

"I'm sorry." She is. If they don't suit her, her name sinks to the bottom of the list. Reject the Hansons and she loses her place in line; it'll be weeks before she gets another chance.

"You'd better be nice to them!" She taps the folder as though she has them clipped to the poop sheet inside. "Be extra nice to them because they're your last for a long, long time."

Sasha shudders. The Hansons are downstairs in the observation room, waiting for her approval. When she has her baby they'll take it away. Why isn't she relieved? She just isn't, that's all.

"Aren't you excited? What's wrong with you?"

There are so many answers to that question that she'd better not start. She scowls into the mirror. "Minute."

"You don't want to keep them waiting."

"I said, just a minute." It's going to take more than a minute. She's trying to figure out how to handle this. If she runs, Gary will hunt her down. If she stays and promises this couple her baby, Gary may swoop down and steal it out of its crib before they can collect. What if she and the Hansons love each other? Can they make the match and leave together, the three of them?

"No. Now." Maureen jabs a ballpoint at her shoulder, leaving a blue mark on yesterday's scrubs; last night she was too upset to change. "They've been waiting in the special room for an hour."

"Wait, OK?" Comb. Lipstick. Nothing helps. "I look like shit."

"Girl, what's the matter with you?"

"Bad day."

The idiot woman is happy to misread her. "Like you think they care how you look? They came all the way from Indianapolis, so get with the program." Maureen will say anything to hurry her along. Sasha's been a difficult client and she and Maureen are a bad match. It's taken the placement officer weeks to come up with these prospects and now she's twitching like Dolly Levi on the eve of an arranged marriage.

"I'm not talking about bad hair. I said I needed a minute, OK?" The Hansons. If they're as nice in person as they came off in the video conferences, they may be The Right Ones. Then she can give her baby two nice new parents and a good home. She can hand him over and walk away, knowing that he has the perfect place, nice house with a big yard, his own room— cute bunk beds and kid wallpaper, sailboats on the sheets— in some safe, comfortable neighborhood with people who know how to take care of a kid.

Better. She'll have allies. They're both lawyers. Let them help her solve the Gary problem, and she'll be free.

"One minute exactly," Maureen says. "No more."

"At least turn your back while I dress." You'd think once you decide not to keep a baby that you wouldn't care who took him home with them, but you do. This is, after all, your flesh and blood you are parting with. You need to do the right thing by this living being you've put into the world. This means you take your time deciding which parents, you owe it to him to make damn sure they're right. Smart enough and kind enough. Enough like you so they can understand him. Better than you so they can give him what he needs. By this time Sasha has made so many snap judgments that there have been staff meetings about her. Each refusal is a black mark on Maureen's fitness report.

"Sixty seconds."

"All right, Maureen!"

"I'm counting."

The Hansons think the agency has called them in as a special favor, to help them decide what kind of baby they want. They think they are playing with Newlife nurses' children to help out. They flew into Orlando from Indiana and rented a car and drove out to Newlife because parent-wannabes will do anything to ingratiate themselves with the staff. Actually, they are auditioning. In fact, they are here on approval. Approval only, Sasha reminds herself. Does she want this placement, or does she not want it?

"I make it sixty seconds," Maureen says.

If Sasha doesn't like their looks, by contract she gets to say thumbs down. She can return them, no obligation, no charge, like mail order clothes that don't fit. They'll never know they were in the running here and she and Maureen will be back at square one. When they began this, Maureen handed her a long list. Now all the other names are ticked off and they are down to one. Sasha is supposed to spend today watching the Hansons through the one-way mirror in the Observation Room. Maureen says she has a week to decide, but with Gary lurking, she doesn't have that kind of time.

"Ninety." Maureen flashes her watch.

In fact, she has no time. No time at all. She has today. Until Gary shows up. If she likes the Hansons' looks she'll just call the shot. She'll tell Maureen they're fine, let's do this. Then she'll check her lipstick and run her fingers through her hair one more time and when Maureen brings the Hansons into the observation booth to meet her, she supposes they'll all be so happy and relieved and glad to see each other that they'll hug. She'll promise the Hansons her baby and in return, she will enlist their help. Maybe they can get her out of here! Maybe she can wait out the last weeks of her pregnancy at their big house in Indiana and have her baby in Indianapolis, in the hospital of their choice.

Together they can keep her baby safe. She hopes. God, she hopes!

"Two minutes. Now move!" Maureen shoves her into the elevator and they go down. "You're gonna love them," she says grimly, propelling her to the observation room. "Unless you want to cut to the chase and sign the papers now."

"I have to see them," Sasha says through clenched teeth. With Gary hovering, she has to do this fast. The Hansons are lawyers, which is a plus. She needs allies to help her shed Gary. Sasha's a smart woman, she's just too pregnant to fight him without help. With Gary and Grand out there in a holding pattern, casting shadows whenever they pass overhead, she needs all the support she can get. Together, she and these nice people who can't conceive will decide how to cope with the guy who has zero rights in this matter but will do anything to prevent this adoption.

If Gary wants to crank up Grandmother and roll her in like a cannon and fire, well, the Hansons will fight back. If they really want this baby they'll fight it up to the Supreme Court. *But what if I don't like them?* she thinks, gulping. Her hands fly to her face. *What if they don't like me?* The doors open.

"Now, get in there and get started." Maureen Storch is one of those plain, freckled puddings who hates women who are better looking than they are. She doesn't like Sasha much. "In my ten years here I've never had more trouble with a placement."

"Don't push."

"Come take a look at your baby's new parents." Maureen thinks she is projecting professional cheer but her voice is tight with hostility. "Today's the day."

"I said, don't!"

"Now, smile." Maureen pushes her into a chair. "And when you buzz me to bring them in, make sure you're smiling. It's now or never, right?" God she is trying hard not to sound grim.

The darkened observation booth is small, lighted only by the glowing one-way mirror that opens on the nursery. Right. It's now or never. Now or never, but how can she think straight when she hasn't slept? No time for a shower and nothing to eat since the supper she was too distressed to swallow. She should have eaten. She should have begged for coffee. Oh, this is bad.

Maureen sticks her head in again with that atrocious, cheery grin. "Buzz me the minute you're sure."

Sasha does not say, *how do I know if I'm sure?* On paper, the Hansons look ideal. They've passed all the psychological tests with high marks; their sheet bears Maureen's Highly Recommended star. For days Sasha looked deep into the eyes of Jim and Carla Hanson via WebCam; she learned to love them on the tape she ran to shreds but it's daunting, having them here, bumping around on the other side of the glass. She is trembling as she looks into the bright nursery. Inside, the Hansons laugh and murmur engagingly as they help one-year-old Lonnie Dietrich stack plastic cups— ADD Lonnie, whose last two placements didn't take. Generic yuppie couple, she thinks, good-looking in their Levi's and Patagonia shirts; smiling and, OK, older, which is not so good, do these people have the energy to keep up with any child of mine? She knows without needing to be told that her firefly will be a little torpedo. Still she's OK with older, if they're good at what they do. At least they know how to make this hard-to-place kid Lonnie giggle, and Lonnie is borderline autistic. The man who wants so badly to be a dad is scratching his ribs and galumphing like a monkey: oook oook oook. With a look over her shoulder at the mirror, the mother-in-waiting tickles Lonnie and rolls him over and makes him laugh. Sasha's beginning to think this just may work out.

In the next second Mrs. Hanson does something that overturns her.

Rolling the child over on the floor, the woman who looks nice enough on WebCam looks up, as if a sixth sense has told her something has changed. Abruptly she stands, abandoning the laughing child like a toy she has lost interest in. Mystified, Lonnie begins to cry. Without glancing his way, Carla Hanson comes up to the one-way mirror. She leans into her reflection, pressing her face so close that her nose makes a grease spot and her lipstick smears the glass.

"I know you're watching, Mother," she says with the same hostility Sasha senses in Maureen. "Don't pretend that you aren't."

Maybe it's the proximity and maybe it's a flaw in the glass but with those moist eyes Mrs. Hanson looks a lot like Gary Cargill, leaning in with a single-minded greed that is every bit as naked as Gary's and, in spite of the barrier, overflowing into Sasha's personal space. Her naked hunger, that slack mouth make clear that this woman Sasha wanted so much to be right for her baby is all wrong. Peel off the smile and the granola clothes and she is every bit as mediocre and stupid as Gary. Carla Hanson won't see Sasha recoil but she's the kind of woman who would go on talking even if she did.

Hungry and anxious and— now that they are so close— ravenous!— she goes on, pleading in that creepy, condescending kindergarten teacher tone: "I know you're in there, Sarah, and Sarah, I want you to know that Jim and I will take wonderful care of this sweet little baby boy of yours. I can't wait to have a baby, Sarah, and I'm just so . . ." the word squeezes out, "so *happy* that we're going to have yours! I mean, I'm sorry you're too busy being a big artist to take care of him but look at it this way, with us he's bound to be much-much better off . . ."

Hanson may be embarrassed by his wife's gushing, but he can't shut her up. "Always wanted a boy," he says gruffly. "And since you can't handle it . . ."

Maureen, you bitch. What happened to confidentiality!

On the other side of the mirror Carla Hanson warbles on. "Oh, I can't wait to hold my brand new baby, I wish he'd just pop out right now so I could pick him up and take him home!"

Smiling into her own reflected face, the woman does not see Sasha bristling behind the mirror: *Not my firefly, you don't.* She mutters, "Did you have to come on so fucking strong?"

The woman is so close that orange lipstick smears the glass. "Come on, sweetie, give him here."

Carla Hanson can't hear Sasha's involuntary, feral growl and she won't see Sasha's belly jump as the band of muscle protecting her baby clenches and she backs away from the glass murmuring, "Oh no you don't, you stupid bitch. No way," shaking her head as she comes crashing out of the booth and smack into Maureen.

"Too soon, Sarah." Maureen fans the door, trying to push her back inside. "For Pete's sake, take your time."

"Get out of my way."

"You're too close to term to go making snap judgments. Now get back in there and let's wrap this thing up."

"It's not a package!"

"Bundle, then. As in bundle of joy." The professional sweetness is undercut by spite. "Hurry up, please. It's time."

"I'd rather die."

"You weren't in there long enough to know."

"Have you *seen* them?"

"Yes I've seen them, for crap's sake I picked them out for you! Now get back in there and give them a little time."

"They've *had* time." She feints but everyplace she turns, Maureen is, wig-wagging like a basketball guard. "Move, Maureen."

Professional smile. Unprofessional rage flickering too close to the surface. "Oh, it's much too late in the game for that. Now get back in there and give those nice people a chance."

"They aren't nice, they're all wrong!" They are at an ugly little standoff here in the hall. They aren't exactly grappling, but it's close. Inching toward the elevator, Sasha hears herself pleading, "I can't."

Maureen snarls but the charge nurse is watching from her station, so she can't hit or grab this recalcitrant patient, inmate, whatever Sasha is. She warbles, "You mean you can't do this today."

"Ever!"

The charge nurse pads up on white, rubber-soled shoes. "Is everything all right?"

Sasha whips her head around so fast that the tears spray. "Not really."

"Don't worry Margaret, I'm on it." Maureen glares at the nurse until she goes away. Then she raises her voice so Margaret will hear her asking, as per Newlife policy, "Sarah, are you all right?"

"No." Pulling free, Sasha darts for the elevator panel and stabs the UP button. "Get out of my way!"

As per Newlife policy, Maureen nods with that phony by-the-numbers smile, but when she speaks it is coldly, firing icicles like darts. "Sarah, this is the seventh set of probables that you've turned down. We're running out of possibilities. You might even say this is your last chance and you are just about to blow it."

"I don't care."

"Yes you do, you're just upset." Do these people get bonuses for every successful placement or is Maureen just a controlling pea-brained bitch? "Get back in there."

Thank God the elevator comes. "No."

"I mean it. You're out of time."

Sasha stumbles inside. "I know!"

Maureen thumps the closing doors with a plump shoulder. They roll back with a jerk. She pokes her head in and what she says next is quick and vindictive and nothing like the Newlife party line. "You'd better pick somebody soon if you don't want to have that baby in a ditch."

"Shut up, Maureen." She stabs the button again. Again.

"This is my case!" The bitch has her foot in the door.

"Not any more." Sasha grinds her heel into the bitch's open toed Birkenstock, which Maureen withdraws with a yip. Stumbling backward into the hallway, she won't hear what her patient says next. The doors close on Sasha's last words, which come as a surprise even to her. "I can't stay here."

Two
The Subject

9.
Starbird

With this meeting with Zorn hanging fire, there are things I have to do. Before I meet with him, I make certain preparations. Another rule of life: when you quit a job, move out and move on.

Before I meet Zorn tomorrow, I have to tie up all the loose ends. I've already made the apposite phone calls. Certain clients. My realtor. The banks. My financial officer is coming in after the Everetts leave with their new baby. Assuming all goes well they'll be gone by nine and he and I will begin. It won't matter what time we finish or when he completes the list of tasks I have for him, finance never sleeps. The lights are going on in some financial institution somewhere on this parallel as we speak; international markets open for business on the hour and bank vaults swing wide sequentially, time zone by time zone, girdling the earth.

Even before I liquidate, I have plenty. I can afford to walk away.

As soon as I close the books on the Everetts. The pickup on this one was penciled in for tomorrow until Zorn's call came in. Apologies to the Everetts for rushing you out of the office like that, and apologies to everybody on my wait list, I won't be getting back to you.

Meanwhile I have this transaction to complete. It's risky, making a pickup without prep time, but I have do this today. If things go smoothly, my clients will have the product sooner than they thought and I can vaporize, but this is assuming every small detail falls into place. Conditions are volatile. So are suppliers. Winds and weather affect schedules, along with health conditions and outside events. If things go right I'll complete the pickup by six tonight and prepare the product for delivery; we'll meet at eight and I can get shut of the pair of you, but high rollers that you are, you Everetts, you might as well know that in this instance, there's no guarantee. If I can't secure the subject today, I'll have to sign off on you. I'm sorry, but I need to close the books on this matter now. Tomorrow's anybody's ballgame.

If for some reason I do abort, naturally you get your money back, along with enough cash to cover the insult plus travel and hotels. If I return your deposit it means I can't proceed, and I wish I had better news for you.

Although I usually keep subjects on reserve for a week between acquisition and delivery, I expect to bring this one off quickly, barring the unforeseen. Lucky for you, the subject and the supplier are close by. Because of the risk factor I usually avoid working locally, but even before Jake Zorn rattled my chain, this one was ordained.

See, the Everetts' request was broad in most respects and specific in only one. They want the child of a Juilliard graduate, with potential musical talent assumed— funny what some people care about. Gender: either will do, and coloring? Not an issue, but they expressed a preference for fair. I hacked into the Juilliard database and worked from there. The search yielded five in-state matches and over time I settled on the right one. I've been watching the family for weeks. Overworked mother, too many kids and as a result, plans for a career as a concert pianist gone to hell, Juilliard, remember.

There is obvious resentment; there's been neglect, potential for abuse. I think by overlooking the chipping, this woman who never made it as a concert pianist was getting her revenge. No college for this baby, not unless I make the rescue and have him chipped. This one needs to be saved. In case you wonder whether my babies really end up in better homes, the Everetts say it all: top talent manager in Los Angeles, wife works at ICM— nice people, been trying for years. They want this so badly that they've flown in for three meetings and aced all the tests. Plus we've shaken hands and curt as he is right now because I put them off, I like the guy. Nice mother for this baby, good dad. Company Learjet, which means they can afford to give the product better than everything it needs. And will love it more than the supplier.

I think.

In this instance my supplier and the subject live in one of the boroughs— don't ask, confidentiality prevents— which means I can wrap this one up fast. The Everetts think they're coming in to finalize the paperwork, and I can guarantee you that there will be a bonus for me when they find their order's been filled and transfer of property is scheduled for tonight. With high-level professionals like them, quick service is an issue. In a way, I love this job. Forget the money. I get off on the power, that smile when they take the baby, the gasp of delight.

It's time to prepare.

For pickups, I dress on an occasional basis: what's right for the venue and the specific time of day. Although I have been known to wear off-the-rack Armani and drive a high end car for pickups in certain circumstances, I usually go in uniform. There are times when a provider in my line has to dress to impress but in most cases the anonymous service person is a better base identity, that face you look at and don't see because you never look past the emblem on the cap. For a local pickup, it's the only way. There are service trucks in every neighborhood and nobody looks twice. Now, as for transportation. I use the service truck with removable panels and changeable top devices: mall security emblems and roof lights for one job, exterminator logo and roof insect for another and because of bad associations— pederasty, kidnapping!— never, ever the ice cream truck. I am, in every other respect, adaptable. The stable I keep garaged in the crosstown Park and Lock includes a mail truck and a U-Haul moving van, useful for interstate transfers because there's room in the back for a cubicle complete with crib and all the necessaries for a long haul.

Today I will use the UPS truck, which means the brown uniform, with brown shorts even though it's raining buckets. Something about those naked knees inspires trust.

Now, on to the rescue. Do not feel sorry for the suppliers of my subjects, I am doing them a favor. I don't snatch cherished infants out of their cradles. I'm not that kind of guy. The last thing I need is a baby somebody wants. I specialize in the category nobody talks about but everybody understands, and this is a very special service that doesn't cost them a cent.

Removal sounds too abrupt. Let's say I bring relief to women overwhelmed by too many kids, like the one I will intercept today. My average supplier is a mother who already has too many kids. Here she is, pregnant. Again. She tries to put a good face on it but she hates what she has become and she blames the infant intruder. She's overworked and frantic. Spread so thin that for one reason or another, she doesn't bother to have the baby chipped. My scanner can read tracking signals in a house full of kids— and like the government issue model, it detects the absence of same.

I won't touch onlies— unless the parameters are unmatchable anywhere else and the price is right because love them or not, these woman are too sharply focused. My typical supplier is the one with a new baby that, I swear to you, she does not want. Don't listen to what she says when you run into her in the supermarket and say what a cute baby, look into her eyes. Just scan and see if you pick up a signal. Not on your life. Now, don't judge her and for God's sake don't judge me. Just try to understand. This interloper in her life is ripe for rescue. In the end she will thank me for it although she can never, ever admit it, at least not out loud and never right away.

The absence of a signal makes it clear. The rest is a matter of timing and susceptibility. Now, a woman with too many children spends her life juggling particles— one too many and she hits the wall. Look for yelling. Silent tears. That's when I move in.

The best time of day for these actions, incidentally, is twilight. Night makes people edgy and puts them on guard, but at the end of the long, exhausting day there is a fleeting window of opportunity, that murky moment in late afternoon when the eyes can't trust what the mind tells them that they see. Everything changes at twilight. People let down because they're close to the end of another hard day. Women who are ordinarily edgy and vigilant relax. In the shadows, motives slide. Outlines blur.

Now, as for location. Locations vary. I prefer public places because the multitude of witnesses means that even though bystanders may be looking, they don't see. Nobody sees anything.

For my money, pickups on private property are unnecessary and intrusive. Now, if I find my supplier's child carrier set down on a back porch or in a garden and the target strapped inside it, temporarily alone, that is another matter. Leave the baby outside for long enough, snoozing in its car seat because it will cry as soon as you wake it up or sleeping in its stroller on your sunny terrace and I may seize the opportunity, but be assured I never, ever enter the house. I do not invade your privacy because I am a professional. Only the vindictive ex-husband or a deranged pervert would break into a house that's occupied. Only a thief would sneak in through an unlocked door, creep upstairs past the rooms where the others sleep and take an infant out of its bed in a private home.

There are dozens of better arenas for the action, anywhere a woman with small children goes: pharmacy. Supermarket. Mall. I choose times and places where stress gets to her and she's most likely to let down her guard: busy playgrounds and bus stops, mass transit stations; any clearance sale anywhere, because mothers rolling strollers into department stores will shuck their coats on the spot and run to the nearest mirror to find out whether the bargain they are stalking fits; movie matinees, because that kind of woman won't care what happens as long as the baby is quiet so she and the half-dozen others present can gum chocolate and watch the show; the post office at Christmas, when my unwitting suppliers stagger in under piles of unmailed packages, fed up with their duties and exhausted from standing in line; busy supermarkets near suppertime, when the shopper in question forgets for a second and turns her back on the baby in the cart.

Absolutely the best place to complete a pickup is your supermarket parking lot. The most confusing time for any mother, worthy or unworthy, is when she should be home by this time and ready to start supper and she's running late and instead she's yoked to the shopping cart, with one child crying and another yammering and the others whining and she's half out of her mind with getting the week's groceries into the car.

The easiest way to remove the subject is from a shopping cart and the second easiest, from a stroller, although the surest is after the supplier thinks she has her children strapped safely into the car. Only in extreme cases will I try to detach a new baby propped on the seat in one of those harnesses that mothers strap to their chests. It's been done, but I detest the necessary jostling, the specially honed cutters it takes to separate those bulky straps. My favored method is much subtler. I wait until my supplier is swamped by demands— children tugging here, squalling there. I like to see her hampered by groceries and overburdened— one in a stroller, one in a Baby Björn or a Snugli and one in a backpack with the fourth hanging with its full weight on the one free arm— a woman like the one I will relieve of her unwanted burden today.

Today's mark buys her food for the week at the Stop and Shop on Thursdays, perfect for me. Of course she has packages, and whether she is loading children into car seats or transferring her purchases to the trunk, eventually she has to undo the harness and put the new baby down. Of course I've been surveilling her; I am meticulous in my work. Usually she detaches the harness from her front first, undoing the baby and buckling it in the infant car seat with an audible *whew*. When I hear that, I think, *Oh, lady. I have come to help you,* although she won't see it right away. The older child gets snapped into its bucket in front; by that time he's hungry and whining and she pushes him down a little bit too hard into the seat. When he yowls she does the snaps with a little crack: "There!" Then she takes the one in the stroller and buckles her into the car seat in the back, next to the baby. I see her thinking: There's all *that.* Now for the packages.

Now.

I've done this so often that I can tell you exactly how it will go. I wait until she has the children stashed and she's loading the collapsed stroller and that fetishist's dream of a baby harness and all her purchases into the trunk. This is when I strike.

Generally I start with Tootsie Rolls for the toddlers, effectively cementing their teeth shut and while they are mumbling through that combination of drool and melting chocolate I plied them with I extract the subject with a slash of my prepared Exacto knife, and slip the infant into the specially outfitted parcel and snap it shut before the product can squeak. Truth? The older siblings are awed; they are drunk on the chocolate I gave them and ravished by my grin. They won't admit it but since I am removing a source of irritation that's kept their mother too busy to do anything but yell at them, they are also glad.

"Mom," the older one cries dutifully and at least three beats too late.

"In a minute," she says, as I wink and back away with my prize.

"Mo-om!"

"I *said,* just a minute!" Unless she says, "Shut up."

"Mom," the child repeats as I seal the container and duck into the shadows and out of earshot, "Mo-om!"

By the time the supplier turns around with an impatient, "What!" I'm gone. By the time she figures out what's happened, I'm well gone.

In these actions, I count on the initial moment of confusion to cover my retreat: *Oh my God, where's the baby?* She ruffles the blanket, which I have left in the car seat in a confusing heap; she looks on the floor and peers into the trunk. What happened to the baby, did I leave him/her in the store? Did I forget to bring him, did I miscount? Did you children do something to your baby sister? Does his father have him? Did I forget and leave him in the shopping cart? Desperate, she runs back into the store.

The manager will have everybody looking soon.

By the time the supplier figures out what's happened, my charge and I are locked into the speeding truck light-years away, heading for a better life.

She will tell the police later that she loves her children, she loves them *so much!* but in disappearances and kidnappings the over-wrought mother is uniformly the first person police suspect. The detectives will turn full attention on her, so prejudice works in my favor. By the time they are done badgering her I'll be so far out of the picture that they'll never guess I was there. If they do, they'll never find me. They won't have the foggiest idea where to look. In these cases the product and I are off the scene before she can call 911.

Meanwhile investigators are pressing her: "Ma'am, are you sure you didn't . . ." Naturally she protests but they remember other disappearances, you read about them in the papers every day. These cops remember dozens of sad stories other weeping mothers told— elaborate lies that police swallowed in the heat of things and then had to disgorge en route to the ugly truth. Experience makes the police hard on her and she begins to cry. She loves her babies. She does. She's a good mother, she does her job!

Officer, don't be too hard on her. Even the most scrupulous mother has to turn her back on her children some time.

By the time the police understand that she isn't the only suspect, the product is under observation in my safe house in Chelsea, being examined fore and aft by my pediatrician and cleaned up and outfitted for delivery to wealthy new parents far better than you.

Oh, yes I am good at my job.

Usually my people do the vetting and prepare the product for transfer, but this is a rush job. When I get back to the city I leave the truck at the Park and Lock and pick up my own car at a better garage three blocks down. I take my pickup out of the parcel only when we are inside my building, and getting out of the elevator at the top. I don't usually handle the product between pickup and the transaction meeting, when I hand it over, but in anticipation of the meeting with my accountant, I dismissed Grace tonight. This means I have to feed and bathe and dress this one myself, which is how I get to see him up close. Cute little boy. Fair, just what they specified. The subject is at the optimum age for this: three months old, old enough to goo and sleep through the night and young enough to forget there was ever anybody else. I'm taken by the big, soft head with airy red down instead of hair and that strong jawline obscured by multiple chins, the clients wanted a winner and this one will knock them off their feet. Ordinarily I'm not interested in babies, but today's catch is really cute, maybe because he's the last. Instead of being larval, like most of them, he's interactive. He snuggles down and takes to the Enfamil like we are old friends. After I do the bath and the diaper and get the onesie snapped I tickle him a little bit. Every time I put my face close enough for him to make it out, he smiles.

I'm not taking this child out to the doctor tonight, not with him just settling in, but he'll be flying out with the Everetts in the morning, so he needs a chip. I make the doctor come to me. Sweet kid; he doesn't even cry when it goes in.

Hard to explain why this particular transfer of property pleases me so much, or why *tristesse* creeps in just when I should be feeling good because the job is done. Maybe it's the business with Zorn and maybe it's something about seeing this one up close and knowing he'll be better off because of what I'm about to do. He has a nice, goofy smile. I should be happy and satisfied at putting him into a good family, but I worry. Will the Everetts love him enough? Will he be happy with them? When I do one of these jobs I can feel the psychic energy draining out of me. There's not much of me left. When the Everetts ring at seven and I buzz them in, I have to force a smile.

Oh, look at them. Nice, but assertively chic in custom rumpled Armani one-offs bespoke especially to impress me, beaming because I just told them we aren't only signing, tonight's the night.

"Oh," she says with her eyelash extensions wet with tears of anticipation, "You're wonderful."

I can't help smiling. "Thank you."

He gives me his hand with that flash of teeth he keeps for top of the line clients. "Can't tell you how grateful."

"I'm glad." I am. I saw the hunger in their eyes, afterimages of pain burned into the irises. I know what you are feeling no matter how cleverly you dissemble. In spite of the fact that they can and do buy anything and anybody they want, this couple has been through it, trying to score the one thing they want most and couldn't have, an item careless teens used to abandon in Dumpsters or high school toilets in the days before the crop failed.

Childless men Everett's age have all done time with the nurse and skin magazines and the humiliating paper cup and they have done it whether they are ordinary guys or piranhas circling the tank in Beverly Hills, which is what Everett is. This kind of grief spares no one, not even the powerful Tai Everett of ICM. And his wife Jane? It's always harder on the women, because these are their bodies on the line. Screenwriter, beautiful but scarred, tried everything, endured every medical indignity and still feels guilty, like it is her fault.

Her mouth won't hold still. "Can we see him now?"

"Soon," I tell her. "First, the papers."

He says, "Look, if you want me to sweeten the deal . . ."

"That's not the issue here." I make clear there is no need for him to open the alligator case for me, no need to rifffle the stacks of bills or make a show of counting them. Money isn't all I want. "You need to agree to the terms."

He's an agent. He knows. "Show me where to sign."

I stop his arm. "No. First read it. You have to agree to the terms." They have to guarantee to give the product everything it needs. More: to love and take care of him for as long as it takes.

This is a man who spends his life vetting contracts. I see him combing the prose for loopholes, unexpected fine print, subtle traps. While they read I hover like a hawk. One sign of hesitation, one attempt to hedge and I'll cancel the arrangement. In the other room, the product's begun to cry: hungry? Wet diaper? Did the doctor hurt him when he put in the chip? What are you trying to do, Starbird? Keep this baby for yourself?

They execute the agreement quickly, initialing every clause. He signs.

She signs.

I sign. "Done. Do you have a name for him?"

"Tai. Tai Junior."

"Don't call him Junior, OK?"

"When can we see him?"

"As soon as you want."

"And when can we take him home?"

"He's just getting settled. Tomorrow's fine." What am I doing here, playing for time? Looking for an excuse to dodge the meeting with Zorn? Dangerous to keep the product onsite, and I know it. Still I am watching the Everetts for signs of hunger or fatigue, anything that will send them to a hotel now, so I can keep the baby overnight. "If you want to stay over, the hotel's on me."

"No thanks." Everett scowls. "You just promised we'd have him tonight."

Sad truth about me? I am a hardened professional, but every time I turn over one of these kids there is the doubt. "Right."

He's all business but she could die of happiness right here. "I can't tell you . . ."

"Here."

I put the baby into her arms and her face blazes. "Oh!"

"I know." For an intense half-second I get to feel like God.

I hand them the starter set: car seat and clothes, premixed formula and bottle warmer, disposable diapers for the trip. One of those bunting things for him to wear in the car. Does he have enough food, should I change him again, do I need to tell them to keep him warm? The baby grins at me one last time. The newly cemented Everett family thanks me and they go.

In the end I want to leave my mark on life, everybody does; I want to do something big and I want to fall in love and have my own babies before I get too old to love them right; I want to use my money and whatever talents I have to surprise the world, but first I have a problem to solve. Tonight I have made these people happy. On a good day, that should do it, but not this time. Tomorrow I meet Zorn.

10.

When you've been in *want* for as long as Maury has, you run in every direction, looking for straws in the wind, unless it's straws to grasp. A new procedure, a new agency. A new hope!

This is how bad it is. When she comes home at night she goes here, there in the darkened house convinced that she hears children's voices. She imagines them sitting down at night with her and Jake; she sees them running through her empty rooms. Every time she sees a baby now Maury's mouth dries up and her heart turns over. It takes all her self control to keep from leaning too close, running her hands over the fuzzy heads or cupping those soft little skulls; it takes everything she has to smile and keep on walking instead of stopping to beg. "Oh please, can I hold her just for a little while?"

She's excited but she knows better than to be happy. They've been so close too many times. A guy, Jake tells her he's found a guy, but he won't give her any details.

"I don't want to get your hopes up," he said when he was leaving the house this morning, but you do not blow off a woman like Maury Bayless with platitudes. She's too smart. She's been through too much.

A specialist who works under cover and only in privileged circles, Jake said finally, don't ask. He wouldn't tell her much even though she pressed, and like any lawyer, Maury is expert at asking questions, looking for holes. If this doesn't work out he's going to get a hell of a story out of it, he told her, hesitating just long enough to make her uneasy. Then he laid it out for her in that slick broadcaster's rumble. When did he start using studio inflections on her? She said, "Oh, be yourself Jake."

His eyes were bright: "I am!" The job is more important to Jake than the baby; this she knows. For years he's been hearing rumors, Jake said, but around the time the first surrogate mother backed out on them, he turned up his first solid lead. An opera singer who'd been dropped from this guy's list because she'd failed some kind of test, naturally she was bitter because she'd been turned away because she's a star and felt entitled but it isn't about that. Listen, Maury, this guy does a high ticket business for high end clients. Celebrities use him, why shouldn't we?

"What are you trying to tell me, Jake?"

"I got a meeting with a guy it's impossible to meet," he said with that sweet grin. Like any good reporter, he thanked his source for the information and promised to get back. Then he started backgrounding. Laying stepping stones to this hard-to-get specialist's front door. Now Jake has him. "I have the goods on him, honey. We're in," he said, but Maury never knows when he is bluffing. Fool luck that he followed a lead that took him to the exact and only person who can get them a child.

"What does that mean, get us a child?"

"I didn't want to say much until I had him in the bag. We talked. We're meeting. He's flying in today."

"Who is he?"

"I can't tell you."

"Jake!"

"Not if you want this to go through. All you need to know is that he can give us what we want."

OK, Jake's enthusiasm made her nervous. "No, Jake, that isn't all I need to know. We're talking about a baby, not a new car."

"Can't stop now." He was halfway out the door. "Going in early to prepare."

It was barely seven A.M. Maybe it was Jake's tone and maybe it was the brown envelope he was carrying that snagged her attention; it looked like a private detective's report. She took his arm. "What do you mean, prepare?"

"This is a high end service, Maur. Heavy demand. The guy isn't just playing hard to get. He is hard to get."

In their exhaustive search for a baby, service is a new word. She said, "What do you mean, service?"

"It's a special placement service, OK? Practiced technician."

"That sounds so vague."

"It's all I can tell you right now. He puts the best babies into the right hands."

"How, Jake?"

He wouldn't answer. Instead he disengaged her fingers and pulled away. "He'll find us a baby so right for us that you'll think you had him yourself."

"I see."

"Our demographic. Discretion guaranteed."

Why couldn't she let it go? Jake was leaving. She reached out to stop him. "It doesn't have to be our demographic, Jake."

When her man turned, the lines around his mouth were drawn for battle. As if he could crush her with blunt teeth. No argument. Just this. "Yes. It does."

"Who is he, Jake? What's his name?"

"I can't tell you until I've got him signed and sealed."

"I'm not going into an agreement without meeting the other party, Jake." Yes she was using his name like a weapon. Repeating. Wham. Wham. Wham.

"This is not the time."

When did this turn into a fight? "The hell it isn't. The meeting's in your office, right? What time?"

"I said, no."

Need made her savage. "Jake, fuck it! We're in this together."

"Not this time. Maur." *Take that.* "It's one of the conditions." *And that.*

"Conditions!"

"I told you he was hard to get." Jake was drumming on the open door with those blunt, ridged fingernails. No apologies, no explanations, just, "We're meeting one on one. Call you at five."

Fine. Smart woman like you, you ought to be able to figure out how to make it through the day. Maury spends the morning in the firm's library, researching precedents. She is preparing an opening statement. When you can't have a baby, you retreat into work because it's the last safe place. Here she has control over her circumstances. She makes facts march in line. Concentration keeps her steady until late morning, when she closes her folder and takes her PDA into the park. She won't work, even though she thinks she can. She can't even find a bench she likes. She can't stay still. Dressed for the office and carefully combed and made up, Maury wanders the paths like a starving woman at a street fair, watching mothers pushing strollers and mothers sitting on benches with their babies, hungry and reduced to feeding on what she sees because none of this bounty belongs to her; she can look but she can't touch.

A young mother in jeans passes, pushing a tandem stroller, toddler perched up front kicking and blowing birdies, infant nestled in back.

Maury presents herself shyly. "He's beautiful." This always brings a smile. Make them smile, but don't let them know you're hovering, looking deep into their babies' faces. "Great eyes!"

This mother can't help smiling. "Thanks."

"How old's the baby?"

"Six weeks."

"Is it all right if I peek in?"

Some mothers mind, some don't. "I'm afraid she's asleep."

"I don't mind." Even though she knows it's too soon to be happy Maury offers, "I'm having one myself."

This makes some mothers back up and hurry off. Not that Maury looks old. It's just not something you say until you begin to show.

"That's wonderful." In this case the girl is too distracted by her toddler to see the telltale laugh lines; Maury has never looked her age, so the young mother may look right at her and not know.

"It's scary."

"Tell me about it. How far along are you?"

Oh, God! Maury swallows hard. "Too soon to tell."

Now she does look up. Her expression goes flat. "Oh."

Everything wells up in Maury's face. The losses of the last ten years, wild hopes. Everything. "But I can't wait."

What's the matter? Did her tone give her away? The girl makes an abrupt about-face with the stroller and turns to go. "Have a nice day."

Even the smartest women are all about the body: orifices and seepings and biological accidents. Never mind Maury's long, sad gynecological history. This is Maury today. Strong, resourceful, brilliant in court and reduced to the sum of her eructations, effluvia, physical events that she never asked for and can't help. Resorb the tears, lady, brush your hand across your mouth and buy a sandwich. Eat until you have to run for the public toilet because your miles of intestine are threatening to let go. When the cramping stops and you think you can smile, clean up and go to the basin. Dash water on your face, refresh your makeup and find that your lips are trembling and nothing you do will keep them still. Use your comb and the Clinique spray to turn yourself back into yourself. Straighten your shoulders and go back to the bench where, if you concentrate, you just may be able to stop your hands from shaking so you can look for security in your PDA.

"Can I sit here?" Who is she, where did she come from, tired-looking middleaged woman with a baby straddling her hip.

A baby. When does the desire move out of your head and into your secret places? "Of course."

"Sometimes you're just too old to have a baby." Dowsing with one hand, the woman parts her coat and comes up with a cigarette.

"I hope not!"

Shifting the baby, she sits with a little plop. This mother looks older than Maury, but she isn't. In spite of the sagging, pouchy body and the exploding hair, the face remains smooth; the cheeks are still padded because the flesh hasn't begun its inevitable slide. "They never tell you what you're in for, you know."

"But he's adorable."

"Yeah, right. And I'm dead beat. Gregory, stop that!"

"He isn't doing anything."

"He's a pest."

"How old is he?"

"Six months. Six months of shit and no end in sight." She gropes for a match as the baby starts slipping down her thigh.

"Watch out!"

Absently, she pulls him back into position. Sort of. "Can't sleep, can't put him down, now I can't even find a fucking match."

"I'm sorry, I don't smoke."

"It figures. Everything sucks when you're sleep deprived."

Now she knows better than to say, *I'm expecting one myself.* "But he's wonderful."

"I guess. It's the day-to-day that's the killer. He's high mainte-nance." She's found the matches but she can't seem to juggle her matchbook, the baby and the cigarette. "Want to hold him? Just for a minute, while I light this." Before Maury can answer, she drops the baby in her lap. "Here."

Only years from now will she be able to process what happens next. There is the thud of flesh on her flesh: a squirming, compact little tub of guts and aspiration and unformed intelligence and whatever else informs a beginning person when it first gets started in the world. On contact, Maury comprehends the union of earth and spirit that makes the baby what it is— this individual, like no other. Who will grow and become a person in time. This is the weight of humanity landing in her lap. The connection is imme-diate. Electrical. Running on without her, Maury's body fills up. Confused and astonished, engorged, she rocks in a pre-orgasmic tremor. For the moment all Jake's promises come true. She gasps. This is going to be HUGE.

Relieved of her baby, the woman lights up. She turns to thank Maury. Then she sees her face. "Hey, what's the matter?"

Words won't do it. They never can. Breathless and rocking with the tears streaming, Maury says stupidly, "He's so cute!"

11.
Starbird

Nothing's worse than doing business with someone you don't like. Unless it's pretending to like somebody you don't want to do business with, but that is what I have to do today. Think of this trip into deepest Boston as an exploratory operation. It wasn't Jake Zorn's threat that put me on the shuttle today and sent me nosing through the bowels of the Big Dig, it was the open question. To find out what I need to know, I have to make him think I'm here to negotiate.

I'm here to find out whether he is bluffing. Two counts. First, the obvious. I need to do this fast and get out without letting him get near the other thing.

The obvious: if I don't do this job, Boston's TV gadfly claims he can bring down the Feds on me. Kidnapping charges, several counts, with capital punishment not implied, but inevitable. If they can find me.

Question: can Zorn? What does he have on me?

It isn't really the threat that stings, it's the implication that tears into me like a fishhook and snags in a place that hurts. Fuck Morgan Sterling, I'm no thief and I'm not a kidnapper. I hate Zorn for proceeding on the assumption. It's like I'm some cold-blooded mercenary out to grab a kid to make a buck, or one of those filthy, deranged freakazoid pervs who drag little girls out of their beds at night and carry them away screaming. I despise Zorn for his ignorance, so this encounter is already doomed.

I never place babies with people I don't like and I'm not about to start.

That's what I'm here to tell him.

But first I have to find out what he has on me. And on the other thing, which I won't touch unless I have to. Find out what he has. Fob him off. OK, before I leave the country I need to know he can't hurt her.

Which is why I am cooling my heels in Jake Zorn's office in downtown Boston. On TV you always see Zorn lounging behind the gleaming mahogany desk plunked down in the middle of plush carpet, flanked by sleek sofas where the parade of witnesses sob out their stories for an audience, but it's just a set. Zorn's real office is cluttered and borderline shabby. This is where he researches the stories that earned him his stripes as the unofficial Conscience of Boston. Felons run at the sound of his name; petty politicians cower when they see him coming. A wooden wedge sits on the dented table with a legend where his name should be. Somebody has punched it out on a label maker: *Knowledge is power.*

Making people wait is power too, and Zorn knows it. The coffee urn and china mugs, the candy dish and his stack of distressed magazines make clear that I am not the first fool to sit here waiting. How long do the doctors and cops and federal prosecutors this guy interviews spend waiting for him anyway? How long do U.S. senators wait on the average? Road company stars promoting their shows? Longer than I intend to be here. Listen, I have plans: limo downstairs with the motor running, a plane to catch, but Boston's exposé king is famous for making you wait. He wants to make sure you think he's busy with somebody far more important than you.

Well, I've got news. Where Zorn is concerned right now there is nobody more important than me.

But he won't know that at least not right away. When he finally does come in I'll lay back, right up to the either/or moment when he orders me to get him a baby or he'll rat me out. I can't wait to see his face when I blow him off.

As far as he knows, the celebrated exposé artist with the sandpaper voice and that fuck-me grin has me in his power.

I'll never get a kid for him. So let him air whatever tape he has on me. That is, if he has tape, which is an open question.

Frankly, I hope it comes to that. It would solve a lot of problems. I'm leaving for a while anyway, and believe me, I've made preparations. The question is whether or not to come back.

See, every psychiatrist knows that deciding to do a thing and doing it are two different things. Morgan Sterling lit the fuse but I need one last kick. If you're on the edge and you haven't jumped because you can't quite jump, you need to make somebody mad enough to push you. See, if I let things go along the way they are, then they'll just keep going along the way they are and I'll end up doing this job forever. Trying to make people happy. When push comes to the ultimate shove, I don't want to be that person. I'm not a generous God, I'm just a guy!

I need to clear some space in my head. I need time to figure out who I really am, or what I could be, given the freedom.

The trouble is, it takes guts to walk out on those legions of miserable, unwanted babies on the road to un-citizenship and, OK, it's hard to turn my back on the endless ranks of hopeful, aching childless couples lined up for my services, but I'm only one guy and there are thousands times thousands of them. If I can't help them all, who am I hurting if I don't help any?

I am half-hoping Zorn will call the shot.

If the bastard has something on me and he goes public, let him. Let him get an Emmy for the story of the year. Cool. Then let the FedGov or Interpol try and find me. By the time it airs, I'll be so gone that there's no coming back. Department of burned bridges.

I have put myself on the table here in Jake Zorn's office, your living Gordian knot.

So come and get me, Mr. Television Conscience of Boston. You stupid son of a bitch.

Not that he's come. His dish of M&Ms is gathering dust.

Too much time passes.

To make him come running, I pretend to leave. I start by wigwagging for the security guy watching the half-dozen screens in his cubicle. Let him get the great man's attention. I shrug and flash my watch. I make a big show of putting on my coat. Then I make faces at the surveillance camera winking above the door. It crosses my mind to give it the finger on my way out.

Take that, asshole.

Zorn smashes into me. "The fuck are you going?"

"Leaving."

"In hell, Starbird. We have a meeting."

I look at my watch and disarm him with the kid question that only pretends to be asking. "Like, an hour ago?"

"Whenever." The clock is crunching toward four. I need to get out to Logan soon. I try to shoulder him out of my way. Zorn leans into me like a brace of fullbacks lunging at a tackle dummy. That lanky body in the cashmere jacket is denser than I thought. "Sit."

Interesting, letting somebody else make your decisions. I sit. Zorn sits on the other side of the dented metal table that passes for a desk. I'm surprised by what I see in his face now that we are sitting close. The scowl is intentionally forbidding, but his hands are shaking. Does finding a baby mean that much to him? It's odd. Underneath the investigative reporter mask, this is probably a decent guy. Nice, if you catch him right. Funny, even. Or prepared to be. In any other circumstance on any other day I might even like him. I can't let him know. In negotiations like this one, it's important. "So OK, Zorn. I'm here. What do you want?"

"You know what I want."

"And you're used to getting everything you want, right?"

Zorn looks easy in his body, strong but studiously rumpled. Older, he looks almost old enough to be my . . . Starbird, stop. Don't go there. Don't go getting sorry for him.

Focus on the framed certificates, the award statuettes spreading their wings on his cluttered shelves, the lovely woman looking back at me from a silver frame— that must be the wife. Usually I research these things, but I'm not doing this job, so why bother? Zorn may be in charge most days but right now he's squinting the way you do when you don't want the dentist to know that the root he's scraping out of your tooth hurts in spite of all the stuff he gave you. It's a silly, brave look that makes me think: *Oh, shit.* The Conscience of Boston is as vulnerable as the rest of us. He clears his throat and the sound that comes out is so sad that it makes me sad. "Except for the one thing. My wife Maury and I . . ."

I cut him off before he can begin his pitch. It's time to lead him where we have to go. "Why do you want a baby at your age?"

"What do you mean, at my age?"

"How old are you, really? You're forty-what." I start on the low side. "Six?"

"Wrong answer." The flattered grin tells me I estimated way low. Next time this guy jumps his head will hit fifty. He lies. "Forty-four."

"And your wife?" I do not say, your wife who tried to off herself and ended up in the hatch.

"What does that have to do with it?"

"I tried to tell you on the phone. There's a cutoff age for placements. So. What. Did you start too late or did you keep trying and coming up empty until she got too old?"

"That's fucking rude."

"I'm sorry, these are standard questions. Age is a factor. You're forty— . Um. Four. And your wife is . . ."

He knows it is. "None of your business!"

"I'm afraid it is my business." I pretend to be sorting through the M&Ms in his candy dish, looking for the purple ones. I set a row of them on the table and then I try to lay it out for him as I pick them off. "Or it was."

"What are you trying to tell me?"

"That I won't do it." I give him a grave, regretful look. "There are the rages."

I hate what happens to him next. What happens to all of you. That flinch. You see the future rolling in on you: the point when your body stops doing what your mind tells it. The long slide into death and the hope that if throwing a child onto the skids in front of you doesn't stop it, at least taking care of one will slow you down. Zorn needs this so bad that his eyes get wet and he tries the word he is least used to saying. "Please."

He looks so miserable that for a second, I waver. I think, would it be such a bad thing if I did one last job before I go? Would it hurt if I scored a baby for him? But it's only for a second. Short answer? Yes. It isn't only that I feel sorry for him even though I don't like him. If I help one more couple there will be another and another. And another. I'll never get out of town.

I am at now or never. Fake passport in my jacket pocket, along with tickets in that name. Nonstop flight to Paris already booked, open return. First Class check-in begins in an hour. I'm either going to end this now or miss my flight and spend the rest of my life mired in your pain, fixed in this time in this place in this part of my life while whatever is meant to come next flows on without me. "No deal."

"Triple what you usually get."

"It's still no deal." Shit, here comes the familiar half-grin with all his teeth showing, that rictus of naked grief I've seen in so many faces. Maybe he would be a good parent. Anybody who wants it that bad . . . Don't, Starbird. You came here to piss him off so you can walk away. To do this, I have to get mad at him. Bring push to shove so I can cut loose and leave.

He pushes: do this job.

I shove: no. Go ahead, Zorn. Threaten me.

One last push here and I'm over the ledge whether or not my chute's in place so, excellent. I start building my bill of particulars. He thinks I'm a fucking kidnapper. *That's one.*

"You'll rethink when I name the figure."

Money. He thinks I'm in this for the money. *That's two.* "You can't change my mind."

"Please." Hot as he is right now, Boston's TV news king is getting old and he knows it. The eyes have begun that descent into the skull, fresh markers on the inevitable road into the chasm. He wants me to feel sorry for him. That's the hell of it. I always do. There's a tremor in the voice. "Maury and I are so . . ."

Poor bastard. "I can't keep you from dying."

His look surprises me. So this is what piercing means. "Hope can."

Don't do that, Zorn. Don't make me sorry for you. I do what I have to, fall silent and wait him out. I'm waiting for *Three*.

Zorn does what people do when you stop answering. He can't handle the silence. He has to fill it somehow. Words roll out one after another in spite of him. "We just want somebody around to miss us when we die."

"Not everybody gets what they want."

His head comes up. "Do you have any idea what it's like?"

I don't want to hurt him, I just want to get this part over with. "I'm sorry. Even if . . ." No way to explain. "You're really too old to start with a baby now." Listen, I should know. Daria Starbird was too old to have me and we both paid for it.

"Fuck that. We're both in perfect health."

I want to add vanity to the bill of particulars, but it won't wash. Instead I say, "Then there's your wife's hospitalization."

"There wasn't any . . ." He still thinks it's their secret.

I read about it in the *Daily News.* It was that day's "Daily Dish," gossip before breakfast, regular as Page Six. "If she cracked again, what would happen to the kid?"

"Stop." The sandpaper voice crumbles. "You don't know what it's like."

"Wait!" I'm at the edge, but when I look down all I see at the bottom is his need. Don't look, Starbird. It's too sad. I lift one hand like a crossing guard stopping traffic or a priest giving absolution, take your pick. We are in an extremely odd place.

There is a little pause in which Zorn's face changes. He leans back. "I thought you'd come around."

Splat!

I hit the wall. Maxed out on the pressure of your expectations. The tension and anxiety. The grief! You're all just too sad for me.

The Everetts were sad and the clients before them were sad and Zorn is sad in spite of his success and the beautiful wife who wrote on the photo: *We are everything together.* There's a sad Mrs. Zorn at home smoothing the sheets on a sad, sad, empty crib, that I know. Otherwise he wouldn't be ready to slay for a deal with me. The rescues are sad, even when they make you happy. Maybe old age— twenty-nine and counting— is making me sentimental but it's getting harder to say goodbye to the babies. How can I be sure you'll take good care of them? How can I know whether they will be happy with you?

"Name your price."

I'm ready to go but anger rolls right over me and comes out before I can stop it: "Kids aren't commodities, you stupid bastard."

His head comes up. "The fuck!"

"Like they're the last item on your laundry list and if it doesn't work out like you thought, just add money and stir." What's driving me here? Zorn or something I don't know about? Wherever it came from, I am shaking with rage. "You think you can order up a baby just like a Beemer or a Lexus and the firm will deliver, well, I'm over it! I'm over your kind."

He swivels, trying hard to follow.

That noise you hear is the sound of my fist slamming down on the table. "I'm sick of you all!"

"What are you, crazy?"

The words won't stop coming. "You buy the house and you get the cars and whatever the hell else you want and then you try for the kid to complete the picture, and when it doesn't work you figure hell, medical miracles, and when that fizzles and you've been to all the agencies and you still can't score that *one last thing* so you come to me."

So push really has come to shove. God he is grim. "Sit down, Starbird."

"Or you have the baby and when it doesn't solve your problems you blame the child. Well, forget it. I'm done."

Before I left the city I took certain precautions. I go from this meeting straight to the airport, papers ready, along with a second passport with another set of tickets booked in a backup name, limo waiting outside to take me to International Departures at Logan.

All that remains are the phone calls I make from the boarding lounge once I've cleared Security. The house belongs to the Star Foundation as soon as I say the word, and my accountant will follow through; as for future placements, the nuns at San Remo will be in charge and all you needy people with aching hearts can apply to them. My broker will liquidate the portfolio as soon as I call and the money will get to Europe before I do. One wire transfer and it joins my other money in Vienna, where it's sitting in a numbered account. Listen, it's time. I suppose I should thank Zorn for putting me on this road, him and his fucking assumptions.

I turn to go. "It's done."

Zorn's fist slams into my shoulder so hard that it spins me around. His fingers clamp down. "You only think it's done."

"Let go."

"Don't make me take off the gloves."

"I mean it, let go!" But he doesn't. We are locked in the dance. So we are down to the moment where Zorn threatens to expose me and I find out whether he can make good.

"Fairly warned, right?" Grinning, he lets go. The barracuda in him breaks the surface with its blunt snout. "You know what I can do to you."

"You want to drop a dime on me? Do it." *That's three. What else do you have?*

"I can drop the dime in a very public way and I can promise, you won't like it." The man has just threatened to ruin me. Now he looks almost sorry he is going to have to do it.

"That which doesn't kill me only bores me. It's just TV." Time is getting away from me and so is this conversation. I want to go but I can't seem to get out of the room. There's something else between us, the thing I've been suppressing.

"It isn't only TV," he says. "I know where you've been and I know where you're going. I can lead the Feds to your doorstep in any country, so don't think you can go flying off to Paris and disappear."

"How did you . . ." know about Paris? I ought to walk but the question nags. *What else do you know?*

"There isn't a mountain high enough to hide you, Starbird, or a cave deep enough, and when they find you, you will come to trial and I *will* testify . . ."

"Go ahead." I hang in place, waiting for *Four*.

". . . and you will fry."

Oh, that. "If that's all you've got, I'll just . . ."

"You have no idea what I've got." Like me, he prepared for this meeting. More carefully than I thought. "I have files on this other business," Zorn says disconcertingly. "Your backstory. I have witnesses. I have stills and I have vid." Without taking his eyes off me, he eases a rectangle out of his pocket and slaps it on the table. It is an old fashioned VHS cassette.

"I don't care what you've got on me. I can't help you."

Thud: that big hand on my arm. Final. Restrictive. "Won't."

"OK," I say. "Won't."

His hands change venue. Those gorilla fingers grip my wrists. It's odd: Zorn looks even older now, bigger. His glare is terrible.

We are done talking. Hissing, I try to wrench free.

In both versions of the movie *Psycho,* the mother speaks in a man's voice. Out of nowhere I hear Jake Zorn aping my mother's tones, "Sit down, son. Shut up and sit down." It's like hearing Daria Starbird on a bad day and I am knocked off center. So we have come to the thing I know in my gut, that brought me out when I should have blown him off and walked away. Zorn pushes me into the chair, giving orders like my eighth-grade teacher: "Sit down and look at the fucking tape."

It is not my best hour. Authority plows into me and pushes me back into my seat. "Tape of what?"

"I know your secret, Starbird." Zorn is like an open heart surgeon with the chest spreaders, getting ready to drive the first wedge. "I know what your mother did to you."

Sick. I am unaccountably sick. "She didn't do anything!"

But first, the incision. "Don't shit me, Starbird. I've researched it and I know what she did."

"No you don't." Nobody does. It was never in the papers. "There isn't any tape."

"That's what you think." Zorn raises the scalpel and makes the first cut. "My people found witnesses."

Quick, Tommy. Stop him! I try but no sound comes out of me.

He extends the incision. Like the best surgeons, he makes a line so fine that it will be several seconds before his patient feels it and even longer before he sees the blood. "This poet in Cambridge. Doesn't want kids, but she gets pregnant to, what, expand her poetry. See, there's that little vain kernel inside her that will try anything because the work isn't going well and she'd sell her soul to be famous. But you know the story."

"It's only a story." I am sick deep down, the way you get when you've broken a bone, surprised but still safe in the instant before the pain starts.

"Sure, Tom. Sure it is. Shall I go on?" He stops. He is waiting for me to knuckle.

"Don't bother. That kind of thing happens all the time. Or used to, before the shortages." Joke, Zorn, get it? Ha ha.

"She tells the couple this baby is her mistake. You don't have to listen if you don't want to, Tom."

"Don't call me Tom."

"Why not? After all, I own you."

"Get to the part about the witnesses."

"Oh, that." The calculating bastard makes me wait. "It took some digging, but I found the couple in question."

The Levengers? "That's bullshit."

He is playing nice, like any surgeon fixing to insert the chest spreader: *This is for your own good, son.* "So, if you don't want me to go public . . ."

"About what, me stealing babies? Go ahead . . ." I am flailing and we both know it.

"No." He slips the cassette into the VCR.

". . . I've got nothing to lose. Hey, I'll even give you an exclusive." When you have nothing to lose, it makes you generous. Before he can hit PLAY I tell him, "As soon as I get where I'm going I'll tape you an interview. Sixty minute special. Whatever you want. You can call it *Secrets of the Bad.*"

Now it's Zorn's turn to create the uncomfortable silence.

I count thirty.

Fifty.

He is beyond the scalpel. He lifts the hammer. "Do you really want the world to know what she did to you?"

Too late, the operation is underway. "She didn't do anything."

"What she did to you then? And afterward?"

"She didn't! She didn't do anything."

"You know better. You know it made you what you are."

"Nobody knows anything, Zorn." My guts are twisting. This is awful. "Even I don't know."

He says, "Your mother knows what she did to you, Starbird."

He pushes PLAY.

"Stop!"

"And so do you."

"It's our word against yours." Whatever he's got, we'll just deny it. She is my mother, after all. That's what they said to me at the agency right before they made us take each other back. *She is your mother, after all.*

"And my witnesses know."

There they are. The Levengers. "Oh, shit."

Look at them, blinking into the camera, two old parties propped up on their living room sofa, patting their hair and fixing smiles. There they are, itching to tell their story, two people I don't necessarily recognize but know, beginning a story I know too well and don't want to hear. On the tape Jake Zorn trumpets, "These are the

Levengers." The self-appointed Conscience of Boston rolls it out for the millions: "They have an interesting story to tell."

"Fine, go ahead. Air it!" I shout loud enough to turn heads outside the glass door. "So what if she tried to give me away?"

"Wait!" Zorn's bark spins me around. I thought witnesses on tape was *Four,* but it isn't. It's only the beginning of *Four.* "One more thing."

As it turns out, the exposé artist knows something I don't. He knows exactly where he is going with this, whereas I am sitting there staring at the Levengers, thinking if he wants to humiliate me, fine. I can handle it. I may think we're finished, but we're nowhere near. So this is how the righteous Jake Zorn cracks me wide open and reaches in with both hands and stops my heart. "I'm not going after you, Starbird. I'm going after your mother. Walk out on this deal and I bring Daria Starbird to justice on my show."

BLAM.

When I leave his office I make the calls anyway. First this. Then I'm done.

12.

Sasha is too pregnant to walk far. She may not be all that big compared to the others, but she's unwieldy and short of breath and much too big to run. Never mind. No matter what happens, she's going. Tonight.

She is all process now.

She knows better than to pack. In spite of the Newlife gloss, most of the old Agatha Pilcher staff is still in place, with all the old institutional attitudes— stern nurses, a bunch of grinning, nice-nasty house mothers ready to tell you that whatever happens, it's for your own good. Departures are discouraged, so she has to act fast. No time for the conversation. Not a minute for one of those intense conferences in which the attending psychiatrist asks eight different ways if she's sure.

Dressed in that day's atrocious scrubs, chartreuse with red hibiscus blooming across the belly, Sasha presents herself in the office with a gracious, shiteating smile. "Just a minute with my lockbox, please. It's my nephew's birthday and I need to write him a check," which she does with a flourish, slipping it into the greeting card she filched from the gift shop. Worst luck, the administrator's out and Viola's in charge. *Semper vigilans,* you cow. She takes a good long time constructing a gushy note to this imaginary nephew with Viola looking over her shoulder, supervising every word. She keeps writing until even Viola gets tired of standing guard and turns to something else. Quickly, she scrawls a phony address and gives Viola her five— the only cash residents are allowed to carry, to discourage petty theft. "Here, I need a stamp." As Viola paws through the stamp drawer, Sasha darts into her wallet. By the time Viola comes up with a first class stamp and fumbles in the cash box to make change, the wallet is back in place. Smiling like a good girl, she gives Viola the card to mail; if the nurse wants to sneak away and steam it open and read it, fine. By the time it comes back stamped ADDRESS UNKNOWN, RETURN TO SENDER, Sasha will be light years away. She pats the checkbook into place next to the wallet. When Viola checks the contents before locking the box, she'll find the fifties Sasha brought when she signed in here still in the envelope. The woman is too stupid to look further, but Sasha has a few bad moments before Viola finishes fingering the wallet, the passport and what little jewelry Sasha has and snaps the key in the lock. She doesn't guess that the driver's license, Sasha's plastic and her ATM card have been removed.

Now all she has to do is make it through the day. This is hard enough on any day, but now she is in a footrace with Gary Cargill. How do you outrun an opponent you can't see? Where is he anyway, and what is he doing now? She hopes to God he isn't talking to a lawyer. What custody rights does he have? Time congeals like Jell-O. She keeps throwing herself at the day but she can't seem to get through it and she can't move it out of the way. She can't leave until the building, the staff and all the pregnant women in the place have gone to sleep.

Meanwhile Gary is out there somewhere, describing decreasing concentric circles that will inevitably close on her room at Newlife like a noose at her throat. She hopes to God he isn't smart enough to bring the law. She hopes to God he hasn't called Grandmother, and more than anything she hopes that he won't cut to the chase and storm the building, or sneak in or charm his way in. She has no idea what Gary will do.

"Some man called the office today," Eileen says at midmorning. "Said he was your husband. You don't have a husband, do you?"

Take a deep breath, Sasha. Smile and dissemble. "Would I be here if I did?"

"He wanted an interview, but of course our policies . . ." Unlike Viola and the placement officer, the charge nurse is a friend. Eileen says, "You might as well know, Viola's thinking about it. Is that a problem for you?"

"Who, me? No. No problem. Just give me a heads up."

Imagine Starbird's root canal and now imagine a root canal without anesthetic. Imagine the dentist pulling out the nerve, strand by strand. Think about Sasha Egan, shuffling past the day's landmarks— lunch, Lamaze class, art, without screaming, taut and rigidly controlled. God, they are finger painting today. In a miracle of compression, she goes through all the right motions: answer nicely when somebody speaks, manage a smile for the sweet, pregnant girls in the solarium because these huge children need her to be happy, they count on it. Sit at the supper table with them and talk brightly so they won't notice that she can't eat.

Go have a long shower and wash your hair, lady. You don't know when you'll get another chance.

Gary is a little time bomb. Tick.

It's all she can do to wait until Lights Out.

Once the building finally goes dark she has to wait another few minutes, until Eileen has finished tapping on every door on the hall in her unofficial bed check. The nurse calls good night and one by one the— OK, inmates— the inmates call good night. It's more civil than a roll call. *Egan?* Mandatory answer: *Here.* Better, but not by much. The drill goes: *Tap.* Then: "Good night Mary/Janey/ Luellen." Then, "Good night, Eileen." And if anybody fails to answer there's the flashlight check and if the person by that name is not in her bed, the lights go on for the full building search that won't end until everyone has been counted and the lights go out again. Sasha holds her breath as one by one the girls respond as expected, signifying that instead of gossiping in other girls' rooms or in the little pantry stealing food they are in their appointed places, safe in bed. Good nights ping-pong down the hall, approaching

Sasha's room. She is in bed in her underwear and tightly laced sneakers, with the covers pulled up to her chin. *Tap.* "Good night, Mary." *Tap.* "Good night Luellen." *Tap.* Eileen is at Sasha's door now. "Good night, Sasha."

"Good . . ." *Oh God please help me do this.* "Night." *Remember your manners.* "Eileen."

Two. Three. Four. Wait. Click. The hallway is finally dark except for the running lights.

Then she waits another hour. When the rustling and sighing subside as the others drop into sleep like flies off a wall, when she's certain even Eileen is in bed for the night, she puts on the only civilian dress that still fits her and slips out into the hall, going quietly because as they do in hospitals, the doors on this corridor stand open all night.

Luellen's sleepy voice curls out of the room next to hers. "Sasha? Is that you?"

Sasha ought to ignore it and skate on by but the child sounds so pitiful. OK face it, she's only a child. She hesitates.

"I can see your shadow, Sasha. Come on, I know it's you."

"Shh, Luellen. Gotta go."

"But I need you."

"Please, Lu. Just shhh."

She doesn't shh. They never do. They just get louder. "I can't!"

"What's the matter?"

"Would you please just please come here?"

The tone of urgency brings Sasha into the room. "Oh, sweetie, are you having contractions?"

Luellen sounded urgent but she looks all right. Like a child, she knows she has to come up with a reason. "I had a bad dream."

"Should I get Eileen?"

"Just stay with me, OK?"

"I can't, sweetie."

"Where are you going?"

"Nowhere."

"Then why are you all dressed up?"

"I have to make a phone call, Lu." She whispers to make Luellen whisper too. "Are you all right?"

"You're not doing anything weird, are you?"

"Of course not, Lu. So you're not in labor or anything?"

"I wish!"

"Take care then. I have to go." She pats the girl's covers and before Luellen can whisper *wait* she backs out, holding her breath. She doesn't exhale until she's cleared the exit at the end of the hall and is heading downstairs.

It is a little like running away from home. The women who run the establishment at Newlife are either too trusting or too Southern to imagine theft from inside so the office lock is easy work; Sasha opens it with her ATM card. Inside, she cleans out the petty cash drawer and feeds the contents of her folder to the shredder. It takes her longer to frame the note. She leaves it on the superintendent's desk, stapled to an envelope with jewelry still warm from her body, the only personal items she was allowed to keep when she checked in here— her diamond studs and an ancestral ring that will more than cover any debt to the institution. Then without a clue as to what she'll do once she has walked off the Newlife grounds, she hits the roll bar on the door outside and leaves the safety of the Pilcher home for good.

Three
The Pickup

13.

Tom Starbird presents as all surface. Nobody is, but he's working on it. He wants to live without subtext. As though there's nothing going on inside. What you see is what you get, he insists. Item by item, he is discarding even that.

In the studio apartment where he's holed up for the duration, he owns: his computer. The oversized coffee mug he brought from home. His clothes. The book of the day. The management supplies a microwave and a Mr. Coffee, two plates, two knives, two forks, two spoons, two glasses and two cups. The place comes furnished with a bed, a desk and a chair. Cable TV.

It's like living nowhere. Perfect for him. For Tom Starbird right now, this is enough. He loves the featureless fabrics and bare surfaces. Nothing to look at but a generic print on the curtains and quilt and expanses of white formica. No strong colors to distract. After the number of people and things he's spent his life taking care of, he loves the absence of objects, the silence. The minimalism would impress a monk.

On short notice, he turned everything he owns into cash. Essentially, money is an abstraction, so when he's done here, to all intents and purposes he will have nothing. Invisible and undemanding, it sits in a European bank. After he signs off on Zorn and his wife, he will be free. If he wants, he can fly to Vienna and collect it. Then he'll have enough to do or buy anything he wants.

If there's anything he wants.

This is one of the things he's here to figure out: what he wants.

It's not a question he is ready to address. He has to strip down to the bare walls before he can even think about it.

What does he really want to do, beyond divesting? He doesn't know. Just something different from this. Something he knows is *right*.

Ask Tom Starbird exactly what he's doing here and he won't be able to tell you, although he could tell you what he is trying to make of this room: a cell, or the next best thing. Ask him whether he means cell as in monastery or prison and he won't be able to say. He doesn't exactly know. Understanding is a function of process, he supposes. As a first step, he is decluttering his life.

Once you start divesting, you get hung up on it. In its own way it's a little bit like being drunk— get hooked on anything and snap decisions run up the heels of the considered ones. Sell it, throw it out, give it away without worrying about whether you'll ever need it again. When he shut up shop and moved out overnight, Starbird turned his clients over to the Star Foundation, along with the responsibility for followups, which he has covered with money transferred from a bank that can't be traced. He released Martha and the consulting pediatrician with handsome severance packages. The house in Chelsea, he deeded to the nuns, along with the books he bought and never had time to read. He transferred titles to his rolling stock— all but the Miata— to his accountant, who is welcome to keep any profits the sale brings in, although he's pledged to turn over whatever the paintings and drawings and his beautiful maquette collection fetch at Sotheby's.

Starbird is empty handed now, and by design.

Closing out the operation, he swept the hard drives on the office machines and turned over the keys and closed the door without looking back. He has brought nothing with him but a small bag: black suit, black python boots and a half-dozen shirts. He lives in sweats and washes his underwear in the sink. For a man who two weeks ago ran a risky, complex and highly profitable business and maintained a town house and an office, who loved to collect eighteenth-century drawings and twentieth-century art, this is an astounding moment of liberation.

The freedom is seductive. The absence of responsibility to objects, sublime. As for people, that takes work. He would like to be in a desert where no people are. This is the state he is creating here. Nothing to take care of. Nobody around to speak, to need, to hope. No things he should have done or not done and nobody here to reproach him. No conversation. Nothing to distract him from the business at hand. If he can truly clear the space, who knows what great thoughts will come in like strangers into an empty room? What will he begin to know? Starbird is sneaking up on the existential.

What it is like just to *be*.

Isn't there something you're forgetting, Tom?

Right. He has one more job to do. If he could dodge this last assignment, which leaves him feeling disrupted and, OK, dirty, he could get on with it. But bullish Jake Zorn reached deep into his past and grabbed him by the entrails, and he is twisting hard. He won't let go until he has what he wants. Run and the self appointed Conscience of Boston will destroy Tom Starbird's mother on TV.

Interesting, how you need to take care of and protect a person you don't particularly like.

All Starbird wants is to sit quietly and consider, but first he has *this* to do. If he could, he'd skip the country and get lost with the monks on Mount Athos, straining upward, toward he's not sure what. He could climb the high Andes and stand alone at Machu Picchu or escape to Kathmandu and not have to do this, but he can't. All he can do is procrastinate.

No wonder he's so busy building his own little world. He'd like to spend the rest of his life like this. In flux.

Unless he is in stasis.

He can't be sure. Bright and ambitious, organized and driven all his conscious life, Starbird tells himself he is preparing. But for what? When Zorn tracks him down, and he will track him down, he'll tell his sort-of employer that it's this last job that he's preparing for, but he knows better.

He is resting his heart. For now, he's escaped the pressure of other people's expectations. He is out from under their hopes.

"Hello," he says experimentally, precisely because nobody is around to answer. "So. Hey," he says into the empty room.

Laughing, he throws his cell phone in the toilet. He doesn't wait to see whether it drowns.

Tom Starbird is getting off on being alone.

Why was I so busy, he wonders. *Why was it so important to keep busy? What have I been doing, really? What was I doing all that time?*

Instead of popping up seconds before the alarm blurts he wakes up whenever and lets the day take him. His days are gloriously simple now. Routine obviates the need for decisions, and Starbird relaxes into the simple schedule like a convalescent at a desert spa. When he wakes up he showers and looks out the window for a long time, watching nothing until even that disappears. Then he folds up like a camp stool and sits crosslegged, facing the spot where the walls meet to make the empty corner he has selected for this. His open hands rest lightly on his thighs, palms up, inviting whatever comes. It will come in time, he knows, if only he can clear out twenty-eight years of trash— isolated facts and unwanted memories, desires and worries and old needs and the half-digested lyrics to a thousand songs he ingested as a kid who went through school plugged into a Discman so he wouldn't have to talk. Item by item, Tom Starbird is reducing the number of particles in his head.

Folding into lotus position, he hits a low, subverbal hum, a little bit more than breathing, less than speech. He doesn't have a mantra because there's no way to put words to what he is doing here. Franny, he thinks, in the old story, this girl Franny worked out her angst and misery with the Jesus prayer, but Starbird is not anxious and he is far from miserable. He is, right now, what passes for happy. For the first time in a long time, serene. This girl Franny's prayer wasn't really about the deity, it was a nervous breakdown spelled out in a language she didn't understand, whereas he is trying to damp down to alpha waves. The kind of pure concentration that empties the mind so something bigger can come in. What exactly this will be, he does not know, he only knows that there is more out there than the parts of his life that he can see.

Unbroken concentration? He isn't even close. He needs to lose it all— words, thought and volition. He needs to empty himself.

Tom Starbird is crunching toward something he can not yet identify. He can't see it yet, whatever he's looking for— he certainly can't give it a name but today . . .

He lapses and comes back with a start. Tom Starbird in lotus position, facing the meeting of two featureless walls. It happens so fast that his neck snaps. "What!" He can't find words for the thing he is inviting but suddenly he can, in a stupendous feat of understanding, imagine it. He imagines its existence and in that moment it is out there for him. Whatever it is. *Wow!* Excited and shaking, he jumps up. *What was that?*

Starbird hears himself calling, "Who? Who!"

No telling. Nothing he can name. What a rush! Something's out there, he's sure of it. He knows it as surely as he knows that his ankles are sore and his legs raw from the industrial carpeting where he has been sitting— how long? So long that the light has changed and it is late morning. In the next second the red numbers on the digital clock flip and the thing or the intimation or the awareness— whatever that was! is gone.

He's running late. Time to go out. Every day Starbird buys three papers. *New York Times, Wall Street Journal* and *Financial Times,* which he consumes over coffee and at the corner coffee shop. Morning walk uptown. Back by two with a paperback from the Barnes & Noble on Union Square, a novel the size of the Manhattan phone book; for the first time in his life he has time to read things like *House of Leaves* and *Infinite Jest.* The books he chooses are huge but no problem, with nothing left in his life but this order to fill for Zorn, he can sit up nights reading; with nobody around to interrupt he can read a book straight through to The End and get rid of it. Divest. He dumps the book in the return box at the branch library. This little act of generosity is key; his daily gift to literacy entitles him to buy a new book. It's OK to own books now, as long as he never owns more than one at a time.

Content in the tight emotional space he has created, Starbird expands in the silence, and if Jake Zorn's long shadow keeps pace with him like a raptor trailing a funeral cortege, he chooses not to know.

Every day or so he fires off an email to prove that he is on Zorn's case, and the replies? No idea. He's written a filter that dumps them straight in the trash. If the threats are escalating, he doesn't want to know. The rest of his mail, he deletes. It gives him a kind of vindictive pleasure, like Gulliver severing the ropes that tie him down. Take that, whoever you are. Take that. And that.

He gives the job a couple of hours a day. Last week he finished the XYZs in the database on his laptop, sorting extant potential subjects— unchipped possibilities he's been following with rescue in mind. Probably because he really is procrastinating, he confected reasons to discard even the likely prospects for the Zorn family, even though his inventory is first rate. He nixed a half-dozen babies according to gender and availability, coloring, body type and demographics, with special attention to physical and intellectual potential as determined by each genetic package, soberly noting why each was disqualified in long, thoughtful mails to Zorn. No to this one, too phlegmatic for you, no to that one, IQ potential low, you would be ashamed of him. No to that one and that one and that one, Zorn, no. No. No. Maybe he'll get the message and give up.

Starbird knows better. When Zorn does catch up with him he'll come down hard. When the Inspector General comes, look busy.

Which Starbird does. It isn't what you do but what you look like you're doing that makes the difference, so he's hacking into the servers of state agencies. Time isn't of the essence but it's an issue here. If he can find what he needs, he'll double back on the doctor he's kept on retainer and let him solve the problem of the chip. He has less of a conscience about skimming a subject out of the public sector because public is what it is, wards of the state often end up worse off than they would going home with Zorn. Sure Zorn will be the hard driving kind of dad who'll ride his son hard, but there's plenty of money for good schools, great dentists, that first car. Hey, he could be doing some orphan a favor. The problem, of course, is that these babies don't fit the demographic Zorn expects. Correction: demands.

So far he's kept hands off the private agencies because when they enter a secure server, even the most gifted hackers leave tracks. Given time, Starbird can hack into anything. He can breach any firewall and decrypt all your classified data, no matter how brilliantly it is coded or how obscure the key; he can penetrate your secure server and open your files no matter how deep they are stored and if he has to he will, but piracy is a dirty business and Tom Starbird stays clean.

Two hours on Zorn. No more. Then he is free to sit down in this quiet, featureless room and read his brains out. Amazing how your mind wanders out and what it comes back with when you are reading. Meditation is hard and in a way, he thinks, reading brings the same kind of concentration. The moment when you forget who or what you are.

He breaks at seven every night and goes out to eat. He won't have food on the premises. He doesn't take home leftovers. He is hooked on the stark white interior of his empty refrigerator shelves. No Styrofoam containers or plastic forks in this pristine room. Six-packs of Evian water and that's it. No products, no vodka in the freezer, no wine, not even a piece of fruit. After dinner he buys a grapefruit and a magazine and sits down under a strong light in Washington Square. He peels his fruit and leaves the detritus in the refuse bin. He skims *Harper's* or *The New Yorker* or a news magazine, depending. As soon as he's turned the last page he goes back to the apartment. He recycles the magazine on his way in. No need to keep things around once you are done with them. They are, after all, only things.

The simplicity is ravishing.

Even better: the not speaking. Except for the necessaries when he prepaid— cash— and moved in here, Starbird hasn't spoken to a single living person in two weeks. At the bookstore and the newsstand and the market, he puts his purchases on the counter and pays. Smiles. In restaurants, he never speaks. Grimacing like a foreigner, he picks up the menu and points. Perfect.

Nobody knows where he is.

Living this way, it is possible to lose track of time. Suspended between what he thought he was and whatever he is becoming, Tom Starbird moves dreamily from thing to thing. Possessions don't matter to him now. They never really did. For him, no object has any more value than the others. What he did in life before and what people thought of him won't matter either. All Tom Starbird is right now is, and this is the delight and the terror: in flux.

In the featureless world he has created here, significant events do surface, although he suppresses them. If they make a difference in his perception of the simple life he is designing, Starbird is in denial.

For instance, today.

It's his fault, unless he can blame Rick Moody. He picked up this novel about a young guy taking care of his debilitated mother; in the end he threw it into a corner. It wasn't the taking care of the mother part. He just has zero patience with alcoholics. Starbird hates addicts of any kind, those pathetic, weak sons of bitches. Who cares about a guy who can't get a grip?

Big mistake, man, tossing away the book you bought to get you through the day. Stay here. Read on until evening, when it's safe to go outside because the working world is homeward bound and nobody expects you to interface.

Instead he goes out. It's late spring. He drifts into Washington Square when the sun is still high and women are out with children in all sizes, from infants and toddlers in padded overalls to swift, feral older kids who play rough. Remember, Tom Starbird has made it up until this moment without human contact. He is wide open and receptive, vulnerable precisely because he is off guard.

Then a child waddling along in a bunny suit trips and smashes on the sidewalk in front of him, splitting his lip.

Don't cry. Blood and snot are running down as the baby howls as if the world left him behind at liftoff. *Oh please don't cry,* Starbird, who is not used to children, thinks, *This is awful.*

"Davey." A mother's frantic fluting rises behind him. "Davey?" She is crosshatching the park behind him, calling, "Has anybody seen Davey? Oh, please!"

What Starbird does then is as foolish as it is instinctive. He picks up the kid, rocking and hushing it. Where he's usually like steel he is all *there there,* ransacking for some bright trinket to take the baby's mind off its grief, calling, "Ma'am. Ma'am!"

The mother sees them. "Davey, oh my God!"

"It's OK, it's really OK," Starbird says in that creaky Tin Woodman voice that no amount of oil will make functional. Napkin from Dunkin' Donuts to stop the bleeding, bright plastic keyring for the baby to put in its mouth, coating it with blood and snot and, as it snuffles and starts to feel better, a film of drool.

"Davey," the mother cries. "What are you doing to him?"

"It's OK, lady. He's OK," Starbird says to her, holding Davy under the armpits like a puppy, handing him off. "He just fell."

She susses him out and concludes that he has done a Good Thing here instead of a Bad Thing, which is what young mothers in Manhattan usually expect of strangers. Her expression makes clear she believes she has nothing to fear— nice, clean-cut yuppie-looking guy like him. "Thanks so much," she says. "I was so scared!"

And this is Starbird's mistake. He looks directly at her. "Welcome," he says, but he is overturned by the feelings written on her face: love and anxiety and relief and the infinitely complicated spasm that grips a mother with a hurt child, even though the baby in the bunny suit— late Easter or what?— has forgotten all about it and smiled. Now she is smiling too. It blazes so bright that he has to turn away. "Bye."

"Take care," she calls after him in a sweet voice.

Contact is terrifying. Leave!

Starbird has done well so far but nobody can keep the world at bay for long. Bad omens drop into his life like the light rain before a storm. One day he finds a Manhattan phone directory in its plastic sleeve propped against his door like a little rock. Leaflets and misaddressed mail that the super has slipped under the door slither like roaches and every time he goes out somebody tries to force a flier or a free sample on him. The world keeps handing him small objects that he didn't ask for and doesn't want; if they keep piling up at this rate there won't be any room left for Tom Starbird in this tight space. At the end of the week he comes home to find mail heaped on his mat and sitting on top of that a carton— a large end table or small appliance correctly addressed to him. Odd, he hasn't ordered anything. Some fool neighbor signed for the damn thing and he has to lug it inside. If UPS can find him, it's only a matter of time before Zorn comes barging in.

He gets up the next day and slips on the routine like armor, but it's a bad fit.

On his daily bookstore run a sales rep for some big novel thrusts a gaudy Advance Reader's Copy on him as he's leaving the store with his book for the day. "Here, it's signed." Disturbed, anxious and burdened, he cuts through Union Square and hands it off to a pretty girl. Their hands brush and she smiles and tries to hand it back to him. Again he flees; he's lost the unwanted book, but he can't shake that incandescent smile.

It's hours before he feels safe again. There is no fulltime job as demanding as willful isolation.

Starbird manages, at least until ten, reading along as though none of this has happened, but he is not himself. Unsettled by so much human contact, he marks his place and drops the book. So what if he doesn't finish tonight, so what if he has to keep it an extra day? He can't sit still. After days of freedom, people have come back into his life. In another minute some fool will knock on his door or the goddamn phone will ring. He has to get out!

Alone in the night, Starbird walks across town and back on Houston, but where he should be lulled by the night air and the happy knowledge that not one of the dozens of carefree Saturday people he passes will look into his face, he is edgy. A drink, he thinks. After all, alcohol's a known depressant. It's not that he wants to be depressed, he just needs to come down a little.

Dumb, walking into a bar. Although he lives without subtext and tries to pretend that he is freshly minted, Tom Starbird is more firmly rooted in the world than he admits. Like everybody else out there, he has a past. Grammar school class pictures, one a year. High school yearbooks, college transcript, medical and dental records, rap sheet (small one, one speeding ticket and a busted store window when he was sixteen) plus an indelible mark in several people's memories; all right, he was stupid for going into this business without growing a beard or paying for a face job. And stupider for leaving it without trying to make some changes in his looks. Like everybody else out there, Starbird is trapped in his body. He is not only what he's trying to be, a faceless New Yorker with plenty of money and few possessions; he's a man who has lived in this world for almost thirty years, which means he is an ordinary person equipped with a history, just like everybody else.

Therefore he knows exactly who that average looking under-thirty guy is, squinting at him across the horseshoe bar: *I know you,* He's been made, as surely as a perp in a police lineup. Stupid, Starbird. Do you actually believe you can duck out the back before the guy rounds the bar and grabs your arm? Like a fugitive in a cheap movie he slaps a twenty on the counter and leaves, only to discover that the back door he thought opened on an alley ends in a tight hallway with two doors marked Stars and Garters. Very Village. Very much a trap.

Fine, he thinks. Wait it out in the men's. It's shitty light to read by, but at least I brought the book. Before he can barricade himself in a stall the outside door opens.

"Tom, Tom Starbird. I knew it was you!" This guy who knows him advances with a big, bland smile. Name is, what is it: Barton. Willie Barton, same floor, senior year. They were never friends but they used to run into each other going out and coming in.

"Yeah, I guess it is." Starbird sighs. "Hello, Willie."

"Yo, Tom! Excellent! What are you doing in New York?"

"Oh, you know." Smoothly, he maneuvers Willie into the hall.

"Man, you so look like a New Yorker."

"So, Willie. Are you here for a convention?"

"Bingo. But nobody ever had to tell you anything, you always knew. I could tell you were going to be some big deal!" What the fuck, he is *beaming*. "Man, it's great seeing you."

There is a moment in some human transactions when you become aware that you are more important to the person you're talking to than they ever were to you. They remember you. They set great store by you back then. You see it in their faces even as you think guiltily that you never gave them a thought. "You too."

"So, cool, what are you up to?"

Why are we stuck in this hall? "You know, this and that."

"You didn't come to our fifth."

"Yeah, I guess I just got busy." Duck and cover, man. Split!

But Willie persists. "We thought we'd see you at our fifth."

"Sorry. I don't do reunions." But, why? He knows what reunions are like. He can see them all— people he barely knew and the few he was close to, all studying him like the board of some big company: A Group to Report To. Nice looking guys just about his age with nice new families, good jobs and kind faces. What would he say that they would want to hear? What could he possibly say? "This is great, Will, but I've gotta go."

"You should have come, dude."

"Busy. You know."

"It's been a long time."

Starbird tries to leave but his new best friend hooks him with aggressive speed. Grimacing, he tries to get free. "Guess it has."

"Damn straight, dude. We missed you."

When you are committed to disappearing, this is the last thing you want to hear. "No you didn't."

"OK, then, we wondered where you were."

"I've been around."

"You know what I mean." Willie here means: What have you been up to? In case Starbird doesn't get it he says, "Like how's it going, and how's your life?"

"Busy."

"We're all busy, man. What about we catch up over a drink?"

"Love to but I can't."

"Can't or don't want to?"

"I'm kind of tied up right now," Starbird says, making a feint at the door. "Nice seeing you, guy."

Slow-moving, nice enough schlub, but a schlub, Barton covers him like a basketball guard. "Come on, let me buy you a drink."

"I can't right now, I have to see a person about a thing."

"One drink. After all, you haven't exactly been in touch."

"Sorry, I've been busy."

"Nobody gets too busy to . . ." There is that flash of hostility because you are more important to him than you knew. "One drink."

"OK. One drink."

It is a mistake. They are standing at the bar when Willie starts. "Married much?"

"Not so's you'd notice." This is getting more and more uncomfortable. "You?"

"About to." But Willie won't stop and let him ask the questions that would derail this investigation, now that he has Starbird in his power he just keeps boring in. "Still seeing Marie, I hope."

Arg. Is this iron man Tom Starbird gnawing his lip and trying not to turn red? "Not so's you'd notice."

"Somebody better? You always did have a . . ."

"I told you, I've been busy. Look." He shoves his hand in his pocket. "Phone's vibrating, and I've gotta take this call. Sorry. Be right back."

Willie has no right to look so hurt. "No you won't."

"OK. Take care." Starbird pats him in place and goes.

This does not stop Willie from scrambling after him. "Got a card?"

"Not on me."

"E addy?"

"It's a lot of numbers and stuff. Look, I've really gotta go."

Reluctantly, Willie lets go. "OK my e is funicular@aol.com. Easy, right?"

"Very easy."

But his voice follows. "So mail me."

"Sure, Willie. Right now I've."

"Later, OK?"

"Later, sure. Gotta . . ."

"Fershure, then."

"get . . ."

The voice trails after him; the asshole can't let it go. "That's funicular@aol.com."

Out of this town!

14.

Waiting for the bus in the Florida moonlight, Sasha is tense; at any minute Gary could lunge out of the palmettos or swoop down in his Neon and drag her off screaming. She's too huge and clumsy to put up much of a fight. The bus looms up in the Florida night like a wish fulfilled; anxiety drains out of her as soon as the doors hiss open and she makes it up the steps. Embraced by the dimness, she blunders along between rows of drowsing passengers and falls into the last available seat. She drops into sleep like a stone and sleeps until dawn, when passengers begin staggering back and forth to the toilet, cleaning up for the next big stop. In a way, Sasha wishes the bus would roll on past the terminal and keep on rolling. She feels protected here in the back of the Greyhound, warm and snug in her plush reclining seat with her feet propped on the collapsible footrest; never mind that her ankles have begun to swell. On another day she'd have stayed on the bus and ridden forever, due north to the border and up to Canada; she could get off the Greyhound in some small town and disappear in the great north woods, but not today. With her belly clenching in phantom contractions, it's time to call the shot.

When they roll in to the Greyhound terminal at Jacksonville, Florida, she gets off. Big, stupendously indifferent, it's a good place to start. Built along the St. John's River, the city of Jacksonville is an overgrown, confusing industrial hick town where it's easy to get lost: quadruple lanes of clashing traffic, sulfurous haze, your vision obscured by toxins layering in the morning light. Yes there are glossy highrises, expanding areas of gentrification and megamalls in abundance, but it's still an industrial city and it still smells bad. Sasha picks up a *Jacksonville Journal* at the terminal newsstand and hides out at the nearest fast food place, studying the Classifieds until the used car lots open for the day. It doesn't take long to find the kind of dealer she needs: a guy committed to moving used cars in a hurry, no questions asked. She picks up a rusting black Toyota for a few hundred dollars, title? More money changes hands. Honey, nobody needs a title on this kind of car. Grinning, she gets in and heads for the coast.

Finding a place is easier than she thought. She finds the DelMar around the time her appetite alarm starts jangling; she sees the DelMar Diner sign from the road, motel attached. Now she is holed up in this seedy, genteel motel marked for death, situated in the shadow of an expanding megamall so far outside Savannah, Georgia, that even if he could guess what city, Gary Cargill wouldn't have the wits to figure out which place.

Nice clean room she's found to bring the baby back to, Fifties knotty pine paneling with a duck print over the bed, floral repros over the matching dresser; once forest green chenille bedspread with the peacock spin-dried to death, shag carpeting scrubbed so often that she can't guess what color it used to be, but clean. Clean. The tile in the tiny bathroom is baby pink. The DelMar looks less like the Bates Motel than a fugitive from a Coen Brothers' movie, it's only a matter of time before the eighteen-wheelers and land yachts come nosing into the lot outside like animals at a watering hole, because the motel is situated on a frontage road and there's a liquor license posted in the diner attached. But the mall is encroaching and the place could go on the market any minute.

"It's yours for as long as you want it," the queen-sized manager tells her, sweeping furry Delta Burke eyelashes in the direction of Sasha's bulge, "but be warned. The place could go on the market any minute."

Seems like a nice person. The room is clean. It's half the price of a Holiday Inn. "I'll take my chances," Sasha says.

"You won't be sorry," the manager says because they always do.

She puts down cash. She has to save her plastic for the hospital, no idea what that will cost, but her credit limit is 20K, should be enough. Plastic when the time comes, not before. Even though Visa knows her as Sasha Egan, she could be traced before she's fit to travel again. Cash machine, small withdrawals, she'll be fine. The DelMar's manager thanks her. She writes out a receipt, but she doesn't leave. Lonely, Sasha thinks, she's probably alone here. The woman is big as a house trailer but she dresses like a star: big prints in gaudy colors, to suggest she is proud of her size, or that she is beyond being ashamed. Costume jewelry and heavy makeup. She hovers with her lips pooched in an expectant, frosted coral O. Hoping to release her, Sasha says, "Thanks." Her gesture takes in the green bedspread, the curtains, the tacky furnishings. "This is really very nice."

"Any minute we might have to sell." Poor lady, her eyes fill up. This motel is more to her than just a job. What did she, marry into the DelMar? Who was Del, and what happened to him anyway? Did he love her, or did he make her manager so he could run away and be free? Did she eat to console herself, or did he die, so eating's all she has? Sniffling, the fat woman went on in a beautiful contralto, "The state could come along and condemn us any time and take the land."

"You can always fight it," Sasha says.

"Sweet girl. I'm giving you the monthly rate." She shows Sasha where the blankets are stored. "You are so lucky," she says. "Girl or boy?"

Oh, the baby. She'd almost forgotten. Something makes her say, "I don't know," even though she does.

"So lucky! Isn't pregnancy the most wonderful time of life?"

Are you fucking crazy?

"Look at you, getting so big, and soon you'll have a nice, sweet baby to love. I miss mine so much!"

Sasha grunts. There are no words for what she feels.

"I think the ninth month of pregnancy is just beautiful, don't you? And when that sweet baby comes, the *feeling . . .*" She maunders on, running her hand under one of those huge breasts, burrowing in the fold as though trying to reach her heart. "When mine were tiny it was the happiest time of my life."

"I see." Maybe it was. How's Sasha supposed to know?

"If only they stayed that way, all helpless and sweet and satisfied with a little toy." She opens the metal casement window, you turn the crank like this. "Will Daddy be joining you?"

"No." Sasha is waiting for her to go.

But the manager moves closer, squinting. "Honey, is everything all right?"

Sasha shrinks. Huge as she is right now, she's not a patch on this woman, who could be hiding triplets in there. "Yes Ma'am."

"Please, it's Marilyn." When she folds those pendulous, marbled arms, every Lurex stripe shimmies. "Marilyn Steptoe."

Just go. "Is there anything else you need me to sign?"

"I'll give you my old crib for an extra twenty-five."

"A crib?" Odd, this comes as a shock. She has become a person who needs a crib. Until now Sasha had managed to think of this pregnancy as happening to someone else.

"Every baby needs a crib."

"A crib." Sasha made it this far on hope: that she'd have this baby and kiss it goodbye. Nice new parents would whisk him off to a nice new home, and they'd be better parents than she could ever be. What does she know about bringing up a kid? She'd get herself back, no questions asked. Could have, too, if she'd stayed at Newlife, but she ran. Now that she is off the premises, she understands that in spite of the flowered scrubs and cosmetic rhetoric, Newlife was never anything more than the Agatha Pilcher Home for Unwed Mothers. Which is what she is. With a baby she'll have to take care of day and night until she finds somebody better to do the job. The information rolls in and hits her so hard that she groans. "Oh God." Correction: smile at the lady, keep it bright. "I mean, sure. Absolutely. A crib."

"Whoever the bastard is, he doesn't deserve you."

Sasha doesn't hear. She is stunned by the exigencies. A baby, here. Given time she can probably manage an adoption, but until then. Here. Oh good grief, I'm going to have this thing. No preapproved parents waiting, there's only me. I'm having this baby and I have to bring it back to the DelMar. A lurking checklist hatches so fast that she blinks, necessity spreading its wings and pecking away inside her head. Obstetrician, she needs. Hospital, prepaid cab on call in case she is too bent to drive, Huggies or whatever, infant size; alcohol, Q-tips, what else, oh my God we don't have clothes. Blindsided by the *we,* she says, "Hot plate and refrigerator, unless that minibar thing is cold enough?" Hot plate to warm bottles, she thinks, start the baby on formula so when they do part company it won't be a problem. She'll be able to do it fast. She is planning out loud. "I can always bathe the baby in the sink."

Marilyn is assessing her, as if subtracting the belly. "You know, I wasn't always this big."

Sasha says politely, "You have a very pretty face."

"After the babies I never got my figure back. I'll send Dancy to fix the little fridge for you."

"By the way, cool shoes."

"I'll have him bring down the microwave."

"That would be wonderful." How did she get so tired? Oh, lady, please go. "Now if you don't mind . . ."

"Honey, are you going to be all right in here?"

"Fine."

But Marilyn has gone all mother on her, prodding in that musical voice, "What was he like, honey, did he love you? What was so terrible that you had to run away?"

"What makes you think I ran . . ."

"Nobody wants to have their baby all alone. Truth, honey. Did he beat up on you?"

"No, nothing like that."

"Then why don't you call the boy and make up with him? Every baby needs a father, honey." Marilyn misreads the snort of disgust.

"One phone call is all it takes. Why not kiss and make up with him, so you can go home?"

The truth pops out. "I don't want to go home!"

The manager's face shakes like Jell-O in an earthquake. "Sugar, did he hit you?"

"Can we not talk about this now?"

"I know, I know," Marilyn says nicely, "You're one of those girls who can't cry if there's people watching, so I'll just go. You go ahead and let it all out, honey. Why don't you lay down?"

Sasha stands like a movie lobby cutout, blinking at Marilyn until she leaves. Her body says, let me sit down.

The minute she lets down, the door clicks open. "Remember, you have friends here."

"Thanks." Sasha covers her face so Marilyn won't see her losing it— not laughing exactly, but close.

"OK then." Long silence. "Goodbye now, and you take care."

For the first time since she hit Newlife, she is alone.

For the first time she commands the space she occupies, expanding into the silence, the absence of routine. For the first time since she left Cambridge, Sasha is in control.

At Pilcher she had been like a lab rat on a treadmill, chasing the bait with a sense of purpose but no place to go. Now she is her own person. She has *things* to do. Short nap. Next, food. Clothes. Pick a doctor and make an appointment. Emergency, she'd tell the office, because by her watch she has maybe three weeks. Maybe a how-to book so she'll know what to do. Pick up art supplies at the mall. Until the baby comes, she'll work. She won't be making prints in this pastel rabbit hutch, but she can sketch.

That night she comes back with a skeleton wardrobe and a few baby things; she walks in to find a crib jammed up against her bed and a china lamp with a rose silk shade installed. It is in the shape of a lamb. Groaning, she lets her plastic shopping bags slither into the crib and throws her new black scarf over the monstrosity. She pushes the crib into the far corner and opens her new pad— Arches paper, quality stock. She picks up the best of the soft lead pencils, thinking to get back to who she used to be. A few months ago she was an artist. Now she has become an instrument. No. She will *not* let biology preempt her free will. You're an artist, remember? Work fast. Rigid with self-consciousness, she tries. Nothing comes. Her brain's been co-opted but at least she looks the part. After months in pastels she is wearing black.

The few clothes she'd chosen for, OK, The Final Days are generic— leggings and oversized T-shirts in black or athletic gray. Perfect for now and afterward, no matter what shape this baby leaves her vacated body in. Tomorrow she will add a sweet-looking pastel top selected to delude doctors' receptionists, but sweet is not how Sasha sees herself. She is a commando dressing for her next raid on the outside world.

15.

Once you have been made in a town you moved into minus backstory, that town is over for you. Willie Barton is the first clod of earth on the coffin. Starbird has to get out before it starts raining dirt and he is buried alive.

Ugly feeling Starbird gets, coming into his building. Detritus that won't fit in his lobby mailbox is heaped on the mat at his apartment door; mail accretes even when you're known only as OCCU-PANT, which is all he is. He kicks it aside and slams the door fast, but not fast enough. The world is out there shifting like a great beast. Sooner or later everything he tried to leave behind will filter in.

Shaken and queasy, he sits crosslegged in his corner, humming on one long breath; he will do anything to get into the zone. He wants to get to a place where no thoughts can follow.

Tomorrow, Starbird. This is the last day of your vacation. To-morrow you're back in the job, like it or not.

That's one bad thought. It turns out to be the least of them.

The clutter drives him to his feet. Stretching, he looks around the featureless room. At least he has kept this pure. The solitude is particularly sweet because he knows it's coming to an end. In an odd way his hiatus here has been like a convalescence. The limbo where he floated, a free agent, until tonight. Now everything out there is crowding in. If he's been convalescing, is he over it? He doesn't know. It doesn't matter any more than it matters what the *it* was. It's time to move.

Over it? Checking his hands, the pink rims where the blood runs underneath healthy nails— no tremor that he can see— Starbird wonders for the first time, *Have I been sick?*

He goes to the mirror, sticks out his tongue. *What was that?*

When there's something wrong with you, it's supposed to show in your face: veins bulging, transparent skin with the blood running green underneath. Starbird looks obscenely healthy. Fine.

What was it anyway? He isn't sure. So, what. If there was a sickness, if he's getting over it and it isn't his body, is it something with the business? He doesn't think so. That's just something he did. Underscore the past tense. *Did.* He took pride in the work. He did a lot of good. It made him rich. No matter how well you do at something, sooner or later you hit the wall and it's time to move on.

If it was just himself he had to think about, Starbird could walk out on Zorn, the needy Conscience of Boston, and disappear. He could leave tonight. He could exit without a trace. But at their face-off in the Boston studio, Zorn dropped a central piece of Starbird's life into the room. It plunged to the bottom of his heart like a little anchor, tearing a hole. Forget the first class seat and the limo waiting. Starbird's thought balloon had the Air France 777 with feathered wings on it, flying away.

You think your life has flowed past all the old shit and then Zorn tells you, "My interviewers did preliminaries on all the other people Daria tried to hand you off to when you were a baby, so be warned."

And you understand that like it or not, stuff you thought you'd outrun is part of your life. *Others?* "Explain warned."

Zorn popped a Pez out of a plastic Goofy's mouth. "If we have to, we can go live with this story next week. Want one?"

"No thanks."

"So are we going to do this or what?"

The anchor dug into Starbird's soft tissue but he didn't scream. He went back to the table. He sat down and pulled out his PDA. Like any vendor, he said flatly, "Tell me what you want."

"A boy." Zorn had a checklist. "Naturally, our demographic. Coloring like mine, so he looks like mine."

"You understand this is going to take time."

Zorn rolled over him like a tank. "Within the month. Oh. One more thing I need. The birth parents should be arties. Actors, sculptors, some kind of talent that will show up in the kid."

"That's cutting it kind of fine."

"I don't have to pay you at all, you know."

"I don't care about the fucking money."

Zorn whipped his head around so fast that his face blurred. He hit the remote. The tape rolled.

"Turn it off!" The more he saw of this macho performance artist the more he knew he was wired to ride a son hard: something about the pearly fingernails with the cuticles gnawed down to raw flesh. He temporized. "How would you be with a little girl?"

"This isn't a negotiation, Starbird. A son. Within the month."

"These things generally start with the home visit. Your wife."

"That won't do."

"It's important. I need to know if . . ." *if you're fit to be parents.* Zorn cut him off.

"No way. I won't put her through that." Then the Conscience of Boston faltered. The voice rattled downhill over bad memories and cracked on the truth. "She's been through too much."

His mutter of sympathy popped out in spite of him. "I'm sorry."

"I want it to be a surprise."

"I don't do placements sight unseen."

"Your mother thinks she's coming into the studio to talk about Save the Children," Zorn said. Push making things clear to Shove.

Now he is here. If he walks out on Zorn, if he turns his back on this job, Starbird will look up at the screen in his empty room one day and see his mother being eviscerated for the studio audience and millions at home, with tie-ins: unauthorized biography rushed

into paperback, with outtakes bannered on the covers of every supermarket rag followed by the Lifetime MOW, aired endlessly on
cable and burned into a DVD in case he wants to replay his
mother's humiliation without commercial breaks. Shit, he thinks,
tote bags and T-shirts. The woman who dropped him into the
world and tried so hard to walk away will be made to suffer which,
when you come right down to it, would serve her right.

It would serve her right, but here he is. He is here on behalf of
Daria Starbird who for better or worse he loves, but does not like.

Funny, he thinks, getting hung up on this, especially when he
knows Daria doesn't much like him, either.

Once you have been made for who you used to be, the pressure
is intense. He despises Zorn for sending all this old kludge rolling
into his pristine, newly emptied life. Bad memory is like a tape-
worm. You don't know you have it until you yack it up. He doesn't
like Daria, he understands now, because she doesn't like him, a fact
he doesn't often think about. He supposes she never did. The
woman is all surface, closely contained: *don't touch.* He spent his
childhood trying to make a dent in that facade. He didn't exactly
love her when he was little, although at the time he thought he did.
He can admit it now that he's outgrown the child's sense of the way
things are supposed to be. What he felt was more like awe, the stillness that takes you when you see your first Grecian marble up
close: *look on my works ye mighty and despair.* His mother carries
herself with that stern, beautiful lift of the head: *leave me alone,*
but he knows better now. She is vulnerable too.

The poems make clear that there's all this *stuff* going on underneath, want compounded by the knowledge that as poets go, Daria
is good, but she'll never be brilliant. Which she takes to be Starbird's fault, viz. her poem called, "If It Wasn't for You." She was so
proud that it was in *Ploughshares* that she signed a copy for him.
What was she thinking? Did she forget? There was worse news en-
coded in the unpublished poems he found in the attic of that narrow house in Jamaica Plain. The carton was marked: TO BE
PUBLISHED AFTER MY DEATH. By now Zorn's investigators have

probably scanned the things and put them back exactly where Starbird dropped them when he was twelve.

She thought of herself as an artist first, so what do you expect? The baby was her "mistake," she said to friends, not caring that he understood. Is he something she did wrong or something she did accidentally? He doesn't know. She was decent to him but grudging; she still is. He supposes when Daria looks at him she sees lost chances, books she never wrote, the job she took when she should have been living single at Yaddo or some damn place with box lunches and rustic studios and arty dinners where she could read her stuff aloud and have people go, ooooh. She talked about poetry the way other people talk about sex. In that narrow house with him she was only going through the motions ("If It Wasn't for You").

She's grudging every time they meet, so they just don't.

And he's hanging in here for this woman's sake because? It's odd. Why does he always have to prove himself to her? Maybe he just wants to put this in her lap and say, *I told you I was worth it. See? Look what I just did for you.* He can't be free until he makes this huge sacrifice and Daria recognizes it for what it is. Whatever losses she blames him for, he'll redeem himself by making this save. OK, she wasn't the warmest. She wasn't even particularly nice. Listen, she fed him and kept his clothes clean and took him to the pediatrician and got his teeth straightened, isn't that enough? In grade school Daria touched all the bases. She shoehorned him into Boston Latin and fronted for a good college and if she didn't call or write or come to his commencement, so what? They don't need to talk or see each other to know the other is still there.

In its own way it's been a motivational experience; when nobody wants you, you have to prove yourself. You run faster and jump higher. Isn't he always the best at what he does?

With the brute logic of an artist's self-destructing machine, the phone shatters his solitude. His time alone here is done. The carefully constructed life is gone for good. Heedless Starbird. When he moved into this place where people he know can't find him, he never thought to unplug the phone. Unless he was asking for it. "Shut up," he yells, close to losing it. "Just shut up."

He tells himself *you don't have to answer,* but he does. "Hello, Zorn."

"Where the fuck is your cell phone?"

"Whatever happened to hello?"

"We left hello behind the day you took that meeting."

"How did you get this number?"

"If you picked up your messages, you'd know."

"I don't get messages."

"You'd better get this one." At his end of the line, Zorn is eating. Starbird hears the tiny crackle of fractured M&Ms. "I've lined up some amazing witnesses for this show we're doing. Your father in particular."

"I don't have a father, Zorn."

"Tell that to the kid who taped his statement. Now what have you got for me?"

"I told you, these things take time."

"You've had time."

The old anger flickers. Rich, heedless clients. Fucking consumers. "You can't always have what you want the minute you want it, Zorn."

"By the way, I've got your mother's psychiatric records, for when I talk to your dad."

A father. Has Zorn really unearthed the guy who sends the post cards? Surprise, he doesn't want to know. End this conversation, just do it. He lies. "Hold your water. I've found a subject."

"Who?"

"I can't divulge."

"I think you'd better put your mouth where my money is. Details, Starbird."

"Sorry. Security."

"If not who, at least tell me when."

"Can't."

"Ballpark."

"Trust me, you'll be the first to know."

"OK, last warning. In two weeks this puppy's set to air."

Starbird does what you do. Crackles paper. "You're breaking up!"

"Don't pull that shit on me."

"Can't hear you. Gotta go."

Only one way out of this that he can see. Do the job.

As the sun comes up, he sits down to the search he's been avoiding so conscientiously. He has to score a kid for a guy who hasn't been tested and a woman he's never met and isn't sure he can trust to take good care of it. He's going to find a baby for Zorn.

This is all wrong. Everything about it is wrong.

First he will do something he's never done in his life in the business. He's going to poach. Definitely not done, and never by Starbird, but he has to work fast. He opens his laptop and begins an advanced search. It's time to raid private agency files. The search engine dishes up a list. He sorts them and settles on the best three.

This particular pool of subjects comes pre-vetted. The information he needs is in the agency database: demographics, health records. Due dates and birth dates. The mothers have signed releases handing their babies off, which means he has a fresh pool of subjects waiting for nice new parents. *Nice new parents*— what, hair-trigger Zorn and the wife he hasn't met? Don't go there, Starbird. This is bad enough. He doesn't have weeks to spend negotiating with a mother-to-be. Zorn won't let him wait.

He needs a baby that's already on the ground.

Starbird had to put thoughts of hell behind him when he agreed to this deal with Zorn. Then he decided to poach. Now he has to do something obviously wrong. Once you do something that's just not done, you will do anything.

Good as he is at this, he's taking a risk. State agencies are big and understaffed. Personnel get careless and if they do catch you prowling, nobody cares enough to follow up. This is different. It's almost like pinging the personal computer of some nice girl you thought you loved. Broaching any private server is risky, he knows, because even the most subtle and accomplished hackers leave tracks. Fine, he thinks. By the time they subpoena the agency's hard drives, I'll be gone.

An advanced search of the first two agencies yields nothing. The third server is harder to break into but when he does, he finds something likely, and if it isn't? So what if he can't bring Zorn the match he wants? Then he finds exactly the right one. Male. Name of the father not recorded, in Starbird's book A Good Thing, no collision over parental rights. No birth date registered but if he reads the file correctly, it should be on the ground any minute now. According to the file, the mother's some kind of artist. Coloring . . . who gives a shit about the coloring? Looks good, he thinks. Looks good to me.

What he can't know is that this particular file is still in the agency database only because the records clerk is out sick and hasn't updated the files. Crazy hoping-against-hope man that he is, Starbird pays cash for a cell phone and makes exactly one call. The street's noisy so he goes into a booth in the Soho Grand. Pretends to be the supplier's anxious brother, congenital illness in the family, treatment urgently needed, family's worried about her and worse yet, her newborn will need immediate special care. A blood exchange, or it will die.

"I wish we could help you," the administrator says, "but the patient isn't with us any more."

"And this is because . . ."

"She's gone."

"Oh, so the adoption's been finalized."

"No, she's. Um . . ."

He feints. "Tell me where she went and the family won't sue."

"She left on her own recognizance."

His mind closes on this like a bear trap. "So she ran away."

"No she didn't, she . . ." Did she hear the steel in his voice? She freezes. "Perhaps you'd better take this up with our lawyers."

"Did she leave an address?"

"The bitch ran off. Who is this anyway?"

Starbird clicks the woman into oblivion and grinds the phone to rubble under his heel. He heads back to his place, running scenarios. It isn't that hard to trace a hugely pregnant woman when you know what you're doing. When a woman is close to term airlines refuse to take her, which means she can't go far. It's even easier to find one who's just given birth. First he'll go down, win them over with some story, and then? He doesn't know what comes after *then*. Once he gets to the place in Florida he'll have to wing it. Study the situation, play it by ear. There will be plenty of time to write his lines and lay out alternative scenarios once he's on the plane. Then he can study downloads of the tri-state area map. He can hack into the likeliest hospital databases as soon as the NO SMOKING light goes off.

Starbird is in it now. Whatever was the matter here, stasis or sickness, if that's what it was— when he fills this last order, he is over it. He will be goddamn cured. He is well and truly done.

First, he has certain arrangements to make. Plane tickets. The car. Do this, Starbird, save your mother's bacon before it shrivels on the plate and she is wrecked and you are permanently wrecked. Do whatever you have to, to bring this off, and do it fast. Job to be done here, not much time left to do it, get in and get it done and get it over with. Get it over with so you can get out.

Pack quickly, you don't have much, leave nothing of yourself behind. Sweep the place clean of fingerprints, try not to agonize over DNA samples trapped in the sheets and in the shag rug, you're so good at what you do that it won't come to that. And if it does, by the time they come looking you'll be in Hong Kong or Marrakesh and another dozen tenants will have moved in on top of any traces you left. Wipe the doorknob after you step out into the hall. When you shut the door behind you, try to pretend that you feel five hundred pounds lighter. Psych yourself as you get in the cab.

You can do this, no problem. You can.

Once he's headed for the airport, Starbird gets busy with his PDA, running ahead of the sick feeling that has grabbed him by the balls and begun to spread, crawling up his loins and into the great gut. Humming along at high speeds, preparing for a job he does not want, Tom Starbird knows in the part of him that he thought he had slammed shut and turned the lock on years ago that this last job is going to ruin him. He isn't sure how or why, but it will ruin him; he knows it and he has to do it anyway.

16.

On her second day at the DelMar Sasha goes to the public library to research local obstetricians on the Web. She narrows her choices on the basis of genteel Southern names, adding some plucked out of local history, Doctors Weed, Ribault, Oglethorpe, Calhoun. Then she starts phoning offices, shmoozing receptionists: how long had the doctor been here, oh, he's from here? Wonderful. Smart woman, Sasha found out enough about old Savannah society to know which names to drop, and thanks to the private school, she knows exactly what to say to get the receptionist to put her through. In an alternative universe, Sasha might have been a writer; once she has the doctor on the line she knows exactly what story to tell— college friend of Miranda Upchurch, in Savannah for the big wedding, Doctor. Friend of Sally Yerkes, from Jacksonville? Beattie Pinckney from Beaufort gave me your name, baby isn't due for weeks and weeks, but just in case I get caught short . . .

He sees her the next day. Charming Southerner. "Of course I'll take care of you if the baby comes early." The doctor has Muzak in his examining room and a repro of Monet's *Water Lilies* posted on the ceiling, so the patients immobilized on his table can lie there thinking serene thoughts while he looks into their deep places and judges. What he has to say is somewhat more disturbing. "But you might as well know, your due date is sooner than you thought."

"I'll get my doctor to send my records," Sasha tells him with a saccharine, good-girl smile. "Just in case."

When she comes home to the DelMar there are pregnant-woman offerings from Marilyn laid out on the bed: two vast, hideous print blouses. Flowered. So much like Marilyn that she doesn't want to touch them; she drops them in the Dumpster but the bed still smells of Trailing Arbutus perfume. There is a note:

SO YOU'LL LOOK PRETTY FOR HIM.

Don't even think about it, Marilyn. Got to put her off but do it nicely, remember, she's only trying to be nice. Unless this is a hostile act. Sasha picks up the house phone and then rethinks. Go on up to the office. Do this in person. Make it stick.

It's like blundering into a catfight.

A tangle of growling, squalling noises overflows the DelMar office. The words don't factor. Somebody yowls and then Marilyn's beautiful contralto splatters like an egg hitting a fan. Inside, she and a kid saw back and forth, and the words? Ugly words. There are threats and reproaches, there is whining, "You this," "I didn't," "You that," "Did *not*," cut short by a smack and an outraged howl. The office door falls open and an angry toad of a child runs out, spraying her with a hateful glare. He isn't as fat as his mother. Yet. He's almost as tall as Sasha, but he's sobbing like a toddler. He stumbles along on Marilyn's high heels with his face rouged and his body hobbled by a rucked up evening gown.

Marilyn explodes into the doorway. She's been sweet— no, syrupy— with Sasha. Now she's somebody else. "God *damn* you, Delroy Steptoe, you wrecked my formal!"

"Did not!"

"Look here, you . . ."

"Leave me alone."

"You ripped the shit out of it."

"Who cares? You're too fucking fat to fucking fit in it."

"You'd better the fuck care."

"Fat, Fat!" The bawling child vomits up his worst. "O-beast."

"Shut up you little fuck, I'm your fucking mother." *You're so lucky, babies are the sweetest things.* Marilyn rages on, the way you do when you have no idea that anyone sees. Would she have said what she said to him with Sasha standing there? "I wish you were fucking dead."

Delroy pulls his mother's ruffled skirts up over his big pink butt and moons her, howling, "Well I wish you wasn't o-beast."

A white hunter Sasha dated once said in all seriousness, "Don't let a rhinoceros get you between it and the water." This is Marilyn now.

"Well, I wish I never had you." The fat woman brings her fists down on her fat child's temples so hard that something in his nose ruptures and blood flies. "So there!"

Fleeing, little Delroy sees what Marilyn doesn't. He sees Sasha riveted at the edge of the parking lot. He pulls loose and heads her way wailing, running hard. Poor kid. Is she supposed to save him from his mother, hug him, what? But— weird— even from here she feels it: the furious, squealing child is one of those rare people who trigger instant dislike. Where Sasha should have tried to help she backed away. She didn't stick out a foot and trip him, but it was close. Shaking, she stood aside and let the parade of grief go by. "Um," she says helplessly now. She reaches for Marilyn's arm as if to slow down her charge but her mind is rushing ahead: *I must be abnormal, a real mother would help. God, what if it was my kid?*

At her touch, Marilyn whirls. ". . . the fuck?"

Sasha is too upset to speak. "Um."

Halted, angry Marilyn can't recover her sweet tone any more than she can cobble a feasible smile. "Fuck do you want?"

Think fast, get it over with. "I can't go back because he threatened to kill me," Sasha says.

Like *that*, Marilyn morphs back into whatever she was pretending to be before the image slipped— sweet, decent woman, only a little plump. Her voice plumps up to match. "Oh, you poor girl."

"So don't go finding the father for me."

"Girlfriend, you're covered."

"I need your word."

"I've got you covered, girl."

"Promise."

"Really." She smooths Sasha's hair in a clumsy, motherly feint. "If the bastard shows up I'll call the cops on him."

Raging Marilyn was scary; sympathetic Marilyn is worse. In another minute the woman will be plastered to Sasha like a new best friend. She's assailed by nightmare visions of Marilyn bonding, confiding, Marilyn dragging out dressy clothes and laying them out on the asphalt for her to admire; she'd expect Sasha to come into the office for coffee and sit on the red leatherette sofa, sliding in to bump haunches while they looked at wedding pictures, or she'd act all the roles in The Marilyn Story while they did each other's hair. "I hope you don't think Delroy and I were really fighting."

"Who, me? Oh, no."

"We just love to take on. Now how about a cup of . . ."

"Can't. I've gotta go."

"You aren't having contractions, or anything, are you?"

"No!" Shaking, Sasha flees Marilyn's voracious smile.

At least Marilyn has stopped barging into the room. When you're glad to get rid of somebody it makes you feel guilty and paranoid. Maybe it's hurt feelings over the refusing to come in for coffee. Maybe she's ashamed because Sasha caught her real voice coming out of her true face that day.

Unless Marilyn's afraid she'll find Sasha in labor and have to help until the ambulance comes. Or cut the cord and clean up because the ambulance is too late. Unless there is, as Sasha believes, something so obscenely *different* about this pregnancy that even Marilyn, who's had two children ("We never talk about Earl"), doesn't want to be exposed. As if desperation is something you can catch. When Sasha looks in the mirror now, she is embarrassed and surprised. Nothing like this has ever happened to her body before. It's like the final stages of an arcane, contagious disease.

At least Marilyn's stopped coming around. OK, so be it, fine. It is a relief not to have to deal. When Marilyn does get in touch, it is in writing. Sasha comes in from another supply run on the mall to find a note on the shag rug. Instead of letting herself in with her passkey, Marilyn had shoved the paper under the door. It must have taken several tries because the note is mashed into zigzags and partially ripped.

DO YOU WANT TO KNOW IF ANYBODY COMES SNIFFING AROUND?

Even a week ago she would have roared into the office and asked. She would have collared Marilyn, a neat trick given her amplitude, and shaken an answer out of her: "What do you mean, sniffing around? Was somebody looking for me?"

But she is beyond it now. Inertia caught up while Sasha wasn't looking. It's getting harder to move. She can't sleep, can't concentrate, can barely make it through the days. It's hard to get up in the morning. Half the time she can't bother to dress and the other half, she dithers, moving small objects in a desperate attempt to prepare.

There's nothing Sasha can do to keep what's happening to her from happening. There is no way to reverse the process, so she does what extremely pregnant women do. She brings her unit in the DelMar to an obsessive, twice-scoured level of readiness, imposing an order that would astound and delight the headmistress at her old boarding school. Truth? It's the one thing about her life that she imagines she can control. She lines up supplies the way you do when you think that no matter where the next trip takes you, you may not make it back alive.

Unlike the pristine space Tom Starbird created for himself, or emptied, so he could bear to be in it, Sasha's room is carefully decorated and piled with useful objects and, if you thought you were going to have a baby, a hundred per cent ready. Whenever she thinks of a necessary item she struggles out to the mall, ticks it off her list and scores a chocolate bar; on her last foray she had a box of pralines sent to the girls, no card but Luellen will know and stop worrying about her. Meanwhile she is socked in here for the duration, fully armed for whatever is to come. In fact, she overprepares. Receiving blankets, baby washcloths and towels, wipes and formula and bottled water, what else. Maxi Pads, for after, because she's read the book. She is beyond ready. She perceives herself as safely hidden here in the dingy outskirts of Savannah, Georgia, and Gary? She doesn't know.

She takes out Marilyn's note. DO YOU WANT TO KNOW IF ANY-BODY COMES SNIFFING AROUND? Not really, no. I'm too pregnant to cope.

Later in the week: knocking. Shit. Marilyn.

Groaning, Sasha grapples with the covers: *was I asleep? Again?* No way to pretend she isn't home: curtains drawn, car out front. When she hears Marilyn's key in the lock she struggles to the door, calling, "Coming!" when she means: don't come in.

"It's me, honey. I had to warn you."

"What?" At any other stage in her life Sasha would have pushed past the manager, run for the car and scratched off like a NASCAR ace. She should have! At the sound of the word "warn," she should have left her stuff behind and disappeared, but she's too scattered to think fast and too big to move. She droops like a blown dandelion in the warm, damp air, waiting for a breeze to lift her and carry her to higher ground. Before she can choke it back she gasps. "My God, is he here?"

Marilyn fixes her with that squint. "Is who here?"

"I don't know, I thought you were coming about . . ."

"No listen! They stole a baby out of the hospital. You hear?"

"My God."

"Turn on the TV."

On the screen, another of television's hypnotic, disorderly and riveting, unscripted real-life dramas is unfolding. Live. Day-old girl stolen from the neonatal ward. Before she could be chipped! They see tearful parents, grim Savannah police, experts on kidnapping, trauma counselors, stunned relatives, the works. Watching with her knuckles crammed in her mouth, she forgets about Marilyn until Marilyn speaks.

"Isn't it awful?"

Absorbed, Sasha murmurs, "Terrible," but her emotions are disturbingly mixed.

"Those poor parents, that poor little thing." The bed shakes as the manager sits.

There is Marilyn's perfume, there is that cloying, personal *ponk* in the air because Marilyn is carefully made up but not quite clean; the combination should have driven Sasha out of the DelMar forever but she's entirely too pregnant to go. While Marilyn shifts on those fat haunches, while she mutters and squirms, grunting with each televised blow, Sasha is unnaturally still. She watches from a strange posture of detachment. *Solve a lot of problems,* she thinks and then she thinks she deserves to be extinguished on the spot.

"I'm so glad I'm not pregnant," Marilyn says. "I'd be worried to death!"

"They'll find the baby."

"Can you imagine? Can you just imagine? It's probably lying murdered in some ditch."

Sasha shudders. "Don't say that! I bet it's some poor woman trying to replace one she lost."

"From your lips to God's ears."

"If she lost her own baby, you know she'll take good care of this one."

"What if they can't catch her? What if she doesn't give it back?" Marilyn's anxiety buzzes, filling the room like a flock of gnats. "It will kill the parents, think how awful, your brand new only baby gone, she could be dead, she could be anything, and you'd never *know.*"

"They'll find her," Sasha said.

"You be extra careful at the hospital, honey,"

"I will. Oh, look. She's found!" *They always do.* It was simple enough, the chief of detectives was saying, we went through the register of still births, we researched all those women and we followed up. Sasha punches the remote and the picture disappears. With that hateful, unaccustomed effort, Sasha gets to her feet. Valedictory. "So that's that. I'll see you later Marilyn, OK?"

Marilyn doesn't care, she chatters on. "Whatever you do, once you have that baby, you be good and careful with that baby."

"I will."

"Girlfriend, you gotta take care! Once you get that baby, don't let that baby out of your sight."

Oh, move! Sasha thinks. *Leave while you can,* but she's too far along for that. She's too far along for anything. Whatever is going to happen, will happen. Careful, she's too far along to be careful. Yawning, exhausted, she gets Marilyn out the door with a muddled promise. "Don't worry, I will."

17.

"Excuse me, did you lose this?"

Luellen Squiers knows she didn't but the extremely cool, black-haired guy in the black T-shirt and jeans worn all the way down to silver is so cute that she doesn't care. Also the silver plastic phone thingy he is holding is very nice— will definitely fit her cell, when she finally gets it back from where Eleanor put it when they checked her in. She smiles her nicest. "Who, me? Well, yeah."

"I found it back there."

"Well, thanks."

"Glad I caught up with you."

This makes her smile even wider. "Me too."

Nice smile on him too. Standing here, happy to be in this conversation. He says, "So you're um, having a baby?"

"Pretty much." It's Friday again, probably the last Friday Luellen will be making the special trip to town. She's so big now that she's like to pop and if she has to carry this baby ten more minutes, she'll die. She's gonna be pooping out this baby soon, no problem, everybody says the second one's always a lot easier than the first and her first slid out like a greased piglet, no big deal, she'll get done with it, she'll get her figure back and then she can go home. Looking at this guy, Luellen wishes it was over with and she was skinny and cute this very minute but if she was, she'd be home with Mama instead of talking to him here. "Probably next week."

"Congratulations."

I love the way you look when you smile. "I guess."

"No, really."

"That's not what Mama said. She said don't come back until you hand it off. She dudn't believe in birth control." She gestures at the mini-van with the Newlife seal.

"Heh. Institutions."

"Tell me about it."

He looks around. They are the only two people standing here. "Don't you guys usually travel in a group?"

"Oh," she says. "You know about us."

"I do." The smile spreads into a grin. "So where is everybody?"

"Them all? They're all in Ruby Tuesday eating onion blossoms. I don't do onion blossoms, they give me gas." They are standing under the awning that shades the strip mall restaurant where the driver likes to stop on their way back to the Newlife grounds. She used to like hanging out inside the pet store with her girlfriend Sasha instead of bloating up on the Friday Special, but Sasha's gone. She left in the middle of the night. She left Luellen cold. Girl, you were supposed to be my labor coach? Luellen is beginning to feel sorry for herself. "At this point everything gives me gas."

"That's too bad."

"Hey." Smile for him. "It'll be all over soon."

"Sweet. Well, nice talking."

Oh, no! He's turning to go. Say something to him, Luellen, say something interesting to keep him standing here talking to you. You haven't been this close to a hunk like this since you checked back in at the place. "So. Are you from around here?"

He turns back just the way she hoped he would. "Who, me? Just passing through."

The man is mighty sweet in the black T-shirt, beginning tan on the face but the arms and neck are white. "You're from up north, aren't you?

"Portland, Maine. I came to get my girlfriend but she's gone."

"Oh, you mean Margie, Margie had her baby and a lady took it, so they sent her home."

"No, my girlfriend hasn't had her baby yet, I came to get her and she's gone. I love her to death and now I can't find her."

"Oh, you mean Sasha."

Oh, he lights up when he hears the name. Beautiful smile he gives her. Black eyelashes. So cute. "Sasha, that's her. Totally gone and the people at the desk won't say why."

"Oh, them, they're all bitches. Right," she says, rummaging for something to please him. "Somebody said you'd been around."

His head lifts. "Who?"

"You know, her boyfriend?" She prompts. "That would be you."

"Right. They won't tell me where she went."

"Shuh, it's not like she told them. That's how bitchy they are. We hate them and we never tell them shit." To keep this going she adds, "They took away my phone!"

"If only she'd waited for me."

"Well, she didn't." Luellen hasn't quite forgiven her. When your best friend walks out on you— your labor coach!— you've gotta feel a little bit betrayed.

"I feel so bad," he says, "I didn't get to make up with her after we broke up."

"That's terrible."

"I know. I didn't do it, breaking up was her idea."

"Really?" Luellen considers. She is thinking, is it really ever the girl's idea?

"I didn't even know about the baby, and now . . ."

"She never even told you she was preg?"

He shakes his head.

Aw, she is thinking. This is the kind of guy you want to take home with you, and put to bed and take care of until he feels better. Awwww. "That's so sad!"

"I really want to get back with her before the . . ."

"Baby comes. That's soooo sweet!"

"But I don't know where she is."

"She didn't tell?"

"Not really."

"That's awful." Luellen hasn't had a cute guy this close since Richie, and that's so over that she doesn't care if she never sees him again. Right now she is getting off on the attention, on standing here with this beautiful guy— older, with his cool clothes, great look, he has these brush-stroke eyebrows that go with the thick black lashes. The blue-gray eyes are so clear that you think you can see straight into his head, and they're fixed exclusively on her. She sniffs. "I loved her but she never told me much."

"If I only knew where she went."

"If I knew . . ." What should she do? What is she supposed to do? When your best friend takes off without an if, an and or a by the way, what is she saying about what she really thinks of you?

"I just want to make up with her. You know how it is."

"I wish I could tell you but." It's kind of thrilling, being in this tight with a man, like, he's perfect and he needs you because he's so sad. She would do anything to please him. "OK, where's Sasha? Let me think."

"If she'd left a note, you'd know."

"Not even a post card from wherever she went to." Squinting thoughtfully, she rummages for something to make him smile. "Oh, wait. You know what? I think she sent us a present. At least I think it's from her. We got this great big box of pralines from, you know, Stuckey's? It said Souvenir of Savannah on the top."

"She always did love candy."

"Yeah." Luellen doesn't know whether Sasha loves candy or not but again, she loves to make him smile at her. "It had to be her."

"You know what?" He makes a heart of his hands and cups her face. "You're wonderful."

"It's nothing."

"No, you're a really lovely girl."

"Oooh maaan, thank you." At her back there is a disturbance behind the stained glass restaurant door: the rest of the Newlife party bunched in the vestibule, fixing to come out.

He sees it too. Quickly, he kisses her on the forehead and re-leases her. "And thank you. You go have a wonderful baby, OK?"

Luellen is beaming. "Don't worry, I will."

"It's been nice talking, and by the way." He folds a bill into her hand before he goes. When she unfolds it later, it's a fifty. "As soon as you're all thin again, go buy yourself something nice."

18.

"Hi," Maury murmurs, low, so not even God will hear her. She doesn't want to jump the gun but now that Jake has somebody working, she needs to practice. The voice you keep for your own baby has to be special, she thinks. Not like any other. She gathers up all the love in her and says gently, "Hey."

Where she ought not to hope too much, it's all she thinks about. Who can possibly understand the hunger, or why it's so intense? No matter how hard she tries to take her mind off it, the hope inside her blazes, burning away everything but want. It's all that's left of her now. Jake says there's a baby out there for her. He's coming soon! If only she knew how, or when.

"I found a guy." Jake's promises are bright but fuzzy. Hard to get a grip on.

Ask him who, or how, and he gets all red and says through his teeth, "Just let me do this."

When he first got back from Atlanta he fell into a paroxysm of planning. He was half fairy Godfather engineering a gift and half vulpine Conscience of Boston, tracking fresh quarry. On the day of the big meeting she begged to go with him. At the door he threw a look over his shoulder. It lodged in her like a tomahawk, stopping her dead. She wanted to go; she was afraid to go; what if she couldn't control herself and started sobbing? What if she begged and the arrangement blew up because she'd handled it wrong?

Her voice failed her. She barely managed, "Take care."

That night Jake came home grinning. "Hug me. Fall down and worship me. We're getting a baby."

Her heart said: *when?* Her head made her ask, "Just like that?"

"Not exactly. But hey, I brought it off!"

"How?"

He avoided her eyes like a bad little boy. "It's complicated."

Maury's seen this kind of bright evasiveness in clients. In plaintiffs in a case she is defending. She said carefully, "Is that all you're going to tell me?"

"We're getting a baby, Maur. That's all you need to know."

"No it isn't. Whose baby, Jake, which organization, how . . ."

"Don't worry, we're in good hands. Takeout, or shall I cook?"

"That isn't an answer, Jake."

"Don't go all lawyer on me, Maur."

"I don't even know his . . ."

"Don't." The look Jake gave her then was charged with past history: all Maury's miserable failures, from her first miscarriage to her . . . never mind. He slid a big, gentle hand down her jaw and said, "Let's don't jinx this one by picking it to death, OK?"

She wants to trust him and be patient, but the hunger is getting worse. Sometimes she has to bite her knuckles to keep from gasping, but she goes to the office every day; she does her job. She eats lunch at her desk because the park's not safe for her.

There are too many babies with beautiful, wet eyelashes and faces like blown flowers, too many infants buckled into Snuglis or strollers, tidy and smug: *just think, this time last year I didn't even exist.* She has to clamp her elbows to her sides and hurry past to keep from touching them. Those tiny collisions with other women's children fan the fire and only make it worse. Better to work. The hunger enhances concentration. Arguments snap into place with amazing clarity; in meetings, she speaks with force. At work, sometimes she can forget.

In what little spare time she permits, she struggles to keep from setting up the baby's room— again. She remembers all those sad dismantlings after all those sad pregnancies. She actually gets through the days without going to Baby Gap or Babies Я Us, but nights, she breaks down and buys equipment on the Internet.

Being childless and in want is bitter. Knowing the baby you need is coming but not knowing how or when is worse.

At night, she and Jake meet in the kitchen like a pair of expectant fathers in a hospital waiting room: bonded even though they don't know each other very well. Tonight he's trimming his nails under the Tiffany shade. Instead of saying, *Don't*, she takes his hand. The conversation begins the way it always does. "Any news?"

"Not yet."

"When?"

"Soon."

"How soon?"

"When I know, you'll know." Jake sweeps the cuttings off the table and into the trash. The sweet, craggy man she's been in love with since they were kids is aging; Maury is surprised by the white hairs glinting in his rusty hair, which looks thinner under the kitchen light, changed by intimations of the scalp.

"I hate soon. I'm sick of it." She shouldn't be hard on him, he's doing this for her, but she can't quit, she's starving. "Can't you do any better than *soon*? He ought to at least have a due date."

"It's not like he said a week from next Thursday, Maur. This kind of thing takes time."

"That's not good enough!" Yes they are having a fight. This conversation has gotten so old that their responses are reflexive. Words that mean more than face value, personal shorthand as a timesaver. Usually Maury can fight and figure out what they're having for supper at the same time.

"It'll have to do."

They've had this fight so often that Maury's mind goes scurrying around a new corner: "No. Let me talk to him."

The response that pops up is one of Jake's macros: the easy sound byte people drop into place so they won't have to think. No matter who uses it, this one is laced with hostility. "Why would you want to do that?"

"I'm sick of getting everything filtered through you. It's my baby too."

"What do you want from me, Maur? What do you want from him?"

"A straight answer, for one."

"You think I'm not capable of getting a straight answer?"

"I think you're too close to it, Jake. Like, personally involved." This is not what she means. She means: your ego is tied up in this. When he gets this invested in something, Jake loses track of results. All he cares about is winning the encounter.

He slaps the nail clippers down on the table. "Be careful, lady, or there won't be any answers at all."

There are several bad things about the conversation, not the least of which is that they are having it with her standing and him sitting. As if he's making her, not his guy, the enemy here. She slides a can of peanuts across the table. Yes it's an offering. "Honey, please. If I meet him, I can tell if he's on the level."

"That's out of the question." He pushes the can away.

"I can't do business with somebody I don't know!" Angry, she goes into the freezer. Steak for dinner, maybe. Thaw in the microwave. A salad. We can eat by eight.

"You're not doing business with him, I am."

She tries out a smile that doesn't quite make it. When did all their encounters turn into *Family Feud*? "Jake, I'm serious. This is us we're talking about, something we've worked for and, OK, prayed for." She gulps. "Or I have. There are things we need to know."

"If you have questions, print them out. I'll run them past him next time we talk."

Fuck him, she'll nuke something. "Don't condescend to me, Jake."

"Maury, he's on it! Now get off my back."

Forget dinner. Is she mad at Jake for being secretive and high-handed or mad at her faulty body for bringing them to this? "You're so fucking close mouthed. You haven't even told me his name."

"It's not important."

"It is to me. Where is he, anyway? Why hasn't he come for the home visit?" She thinks about the smile she would give him. "The interview?"

"We took the meeting." He's so pissed at her that he forgets he refused the peanuts. He gnashes angrily. "We had the interview."

"No. You did. These proceedings always start with the mother."

"This isn't a proceeding."

Alarmed, she asks, "Is there something different about this one?"

"Maura!" Jake slaps the table. "Do you want this baby or not?"

"Of course. Don't yell at me."

Like *that,* he softens. "Then back off and let him do his job."

Maury is not stupid. She's a lawyer, one of the best. She proceeds cautiously, putting a question she can't necessarily afford to have answered. Sushi, she'll call Keiji's for sushi. "Jake, is there something about this that you don't want me to know about?"

"Sweetie, I've told you everything I can." Now Jake turns. They are finally having this conversation face to face. He doesn't hug her; he's smart enough to know that won't work. Instead he stands with his hands spread, to show her that he has nothing to hide. "If you love me, you have to trust."

Careful, Maury. Keep it light. Her voice trembles. "Tell me we're not into some kind of black market baby thing."

Flashing that grin, Jake falls back on an old network macro: "What's that supposed to mean?"

"Like, this isn't some shyster who ranches Peruvian immigrants or gets high school girls pregnant for pay." She's kidding, but she isn't. She says, too fast, "Kidding!"

"No," Jake says. His look says, *Don't press.* "Nothing like that."

"I'm glad."

He scowls. "Is that what this is about? You think I'm?"

Careful, Maury. Notice he doesn't complete the sentence. Smile and let it go. "I'm sorry, I just had to know."

"Well now you do."

"OK," Maury says after careful thought. When you want a baby as badly as Maury Bayless does today, no matter who you are, no matter how intelligent and ethical and scrupulous, you are willing to overlook a lot of things. There are things Jake isn't telling her and she understands they're things she doesn't really want to know. All she wants to know— the only thing she wants to know— is that soon she'll be holding her very own warm, loving baby. Therefore details she would ordinarily track down like a prosecutor and examine under a microscope are not important to her right now. There are things you have to do to get what you most need and this isn't a matter of morality, it's a matter of survival. So what if Jake's mysterious source isn't completely on the level? In the darkest part of her heart she is too hungry to care. "OK."

"So will you back off?"

"I promise, I won't ask questions. I just want to see the guy!" She wants to look into this stranger's face and know that he is on the level in one respect and one only. She wants to know he will follow through. That these aren't empty promises. "Just once."

Jake warns: "He knows about the hospitalization, Maur."

It's like a punch to the belly. "Oh!"

"He knows you tried to kill yourself."

"Then I have to see him, Jake. He needs to see me. To prove I'm not . . ."

"Crazy?" Now the Conscience of Boston departs from his collection of selected sound bytes and turns on his wife. This time he puts his hands on Maury's shoulders to weigh her down and hold her in place. They are standing too close. "Look, he's on our case and it's going very well. And chill, it's all aboveboard, and if I don't want to pull you into a meeting? He . . . Agh. Look, he says the parents have to be stable." Blushing, Jake coughs it up. "OK. What if he takes one look and decides you're too crazy to have a kid? I love you, but you could sink the boat."

19.

Caught in the current and rushing toward the falls, you know one thing is certain. That roar coming from the deep gorge ahead is indeed crashing water. There will be no last minute rescues or helicopter lifts for you, lady. You are going over the falls.

Sasha cabs to the hospital in all confidence.

The driver says, "We made it. Hope everything's OK."

"I can't wait for it to be over," Sasha says.

"Don't worry, most babies are born in the middle of the night. Take care."

"Thanks a lot. I'll be fine." She can do this. She's read the books. Without Luellen for a Lamaze partner, she's practiced alone. Breathing, everything. She's got it down. She knows what to expect. A little pain, nothing she can't handle. A temporary inconvenience. Then she'll be herself. She can pick up her life where she left off. In a way, it's exciting, knowing she's so close. They balk at the no insurance card; then they run her plastic. Given the credit balance they admit her, stat.

She's like a parachutist right before the jump or a skier at the top of a peak, ready to push off. Excited. Ready. OK, then. Let's do this. Compared to the long climb this part looks simple. Fine. I'm going down.

The rest comes as a shock.

Sasha isn't old enough to know the hunger. In fact, she's here to tell you that if Maury Bayless thinks motherhood is glorious, she's wrong. About the glories of motherhood: giving birth is not a woman's crowning achievement, it's scary and bloody and harsh. It hurts. You're helpless in a painful, messy situation you can't escape, just part of a process that is beyond your control. The sooner it's over with the better, and anybody who claims otherwise is either lying or on crack. The joy of birthing is a myth that professional mothers float, she thinks, women who have nothing else in their lives to brag about inflating a hard, necessary but perfectly natural process into something they personally did. Childbirth as personal triumph. A magnificent feat only they could bring off. Coming on to you like Marilyn with wet sentimental mouths and misty sentimental eyes, what the fuck happened to them, did they forget?

When Sasha gets back to the DelMar she finds Marilyn hovering, but instead of asking to see the baby— *my baby!*— she hangs in the doorway, muttering. "Don't worry, I didn't tell him anything."

Tottering with exhaustion, Sasha says, "What?" Why is she so wrecked, all she did was ride in a cab.

". . . asking about you, but I just sent him away."

"Who?" It was a terrible ride, threading through dense downtown traffic in a taxi, bouncing on hard plastic seats. She was riding along on twenty-some fresh stitches, and Beattie Calhoun's obstetrician signed her out at the height of rush hour. "I understand your finances are limited so I'm releasing you early," he said nicely. Then her guts crawled as he added, "But you're expected back Thursday for the chipping." Now the infant is bleating— no tears, but he's miserable, and Sasha is wild because this is a problem she has no idea how to solve. This puny, brand new human being is alive. He's here and she's in charge. It's not the newborn's fault that she is the way she is, weak and tearful and in no respect glad it is here. No, mother love did not kick in the minute they wiped it off and put it into her arms; like the fabled joy of squeezing out a baby without drugs to enhance the glory, this is a myth. Biology doesn't make you a mother. She doesn't know what does. Her brand new human is crying, it's squirming weakly— is it OK? She's scared to look. This is not the egg they gave you to take care of in high school Human Life class, which if you broke, there were eleven others in the box. It's real. Until four this afternoon, she could hand this tiny living creature off to a nurse, but now . . . giving bottles and changing diapers with a nurse there to fix anything that seems broken is one thing, but this is different. She and this brand new baby are on their own. This is her problem. It's all hers, and she doesn't know what to do. And here is Marilyn Steptoe leaning on the doorknob nattering about something somebody— a phone call, she thinks, but she's too distracted to think. *A phone call?*

". . . don't you want to know what he said?"

She's terrified of dropping the baby. She's weaving slightly— anesthesia hangover? What? "Somebody called?"

"He came."

"Who?"

"Oooh, is that your baby?" Marilyn reaches out. Sasha turns her shoulder protectively to block that fat hand with those shiny coral nails. "Oooh, she's so sweet."

"It's not a . . ." Something isn't right here in her hideout at the DelMar, she doesn't know what.

"Let me hold her."

"It's too soon!"

"Oh look, she's crying, poor little thing. Don't worry, babies love me. Sweetheart, come to Marilyn, Marilyn knows what to do."

"No!" Instinctively, Sasha makes another half-turn with her shoulder raised to shield the newborn; the DelMar manager is so big, he's so small. Then she gets it. *Oh, fuck. Gary.* "Was he kind of bulky with no-color hair?"

Marilyn manages to touch the baby in spite of her. "Soft little . . . Who?"

"Whoever came!"

"Oh, him. Nice looking fella, nice ways."

"Marilyn, what did he want?"

"In case you hadn't noticed, it's busy out. I don't know what the fuck he wanted. Come here, sweet baby, you know who loves you."

"What?" Sasha whirls in another half-turn. It's squirming, oh my God, what if I drop it, "or who?"

"He didn't exactly say. Just so you know." Marilyn is serene in aquamarine today, with plastic Navajo turquoise strung around her neck. Instead of for God's sake lending a hand or giving useful *advice* here, she is looking at Sasha through sequined glasses that magnify her eyes like night flowers. "If you were in trouble with the police you'd tell me, right, honey?"

When she doesn't answer, Marilyn prods her. "Right?"

In the delivery room they had to use forceps. That's why the episiotomy is so long. Twenty-something stitches. Twenty-what? Don't worry, they said. You'll be fine. What did Marilyn just say?

She repeats. "Right, Sasha?"

Swaying, Sasha nods.

"Yes you'd tell me or yes there is?— Oh, don't drop her!"

"Him!" Sasha hadn't intended to name him because she was giving him away and that was for his real parents to do, but when they plopped him in her arms to her surprise she knew exactly who he was. He's Jimmy Egan, like her absent dad. "Now if you'll just."

"And nobody else is looking for you or anything. Is there?" Marilyn fixes on the baby, advancing with her iridescent coral mouth pursed in a kiss. "I keep a clean establishment here and . . ."

"No."

"Like there's something you did? Poor sweetheart, let me hold you, I'll just . . ."

"No!" Sasha turns, shielding Jim. Jim!

"Oooh, he's just so cute, I'm just saying, if you're in trouble with the police . . ."

Get this woman out before you collapse; one sign of weakness and she'll pounce and devour you, she'll use poor Jimmy's bones like toothpicks to clean her big square teeth. The weight of Marilyn's attention is oppressive. "No, no trouble with the police."

Thank God Delroy broke the office window just then and at the crash Marilyn inflated and went steaming out. Sasha shot the dead bolt when the screaming started. She drew the chain latch before fuming, red-faced engine of vengeance monster Marilyn morphed back into nice Marilyn and came back.

Thank God the hospital sent her off with a starter set of Huggies and a six-pack of Enfamil, sterilized and ready to serve. Thank God new babies are pretty much flattened by the ride out of nowhere into the world. As soon as he eats, Jimmy drops into milk-sodden sleep and as long as he is sleeping, Sasha can sleep.

My God. I have a baby.

Days later she's still in shock.

One day you're going along fine, spawning uphill, maybe, but basically OK in spite of the fatigue and the increasingly grotesque body, and the next, fate runs into you like a steamroller and mashes you flat. Maybe pioneer wives really did drop their babies and go right back to the bean rows, but this is not early America. Sasha Egan is fitter than any farmer's wife, but as an organism, she's a lot more complex. She's never sick. Until today she had no idea what it was like to be physically weak. She isn't sick now, but she sure as hell knows something has happened to her. Trauma, she supposes. Her body is pissed at what she just did to it. It's all she can do to get across the room. Where she felt OK when she went to the hospital, Sasha is changed. It is an astonishment. A strong woman in her early twenties leveled by biology. For the first time in her life she is fragile.

Weak.

So fucking weak.

Sure there are women who pick up Happy Meals and skinny-girl clothes at the mall enroute home from the hospital. They even come home triumphant and energized. They love to relive every gorgeous moment of the delivery and dads capture it on video so you can look upon them in admiration, and despair. Maybe they really do sauté the placenta in wine with onions for a secret supper with the father, but Sasha is not that person. Yeugh! If she could just keep her hand steady she'd start sketching impressions of the ordeal. The lights. Masked faces hovering. She needs to prove she's still who she was before they made the cut and inserted forceps to yank the baby out. She pulls out her oil stick and a pad, but she can't work. Her concentration is shot. All she really wants to do is lie down and forget.

She cries twice a day now, which is not like Sasha Egan. It isn't like Sasha at all.

Not the best time to be given this infinitesimal *thing* to take care of, seven pounds ten ounces of potential human, an open-ended, nonstop demand that nothing has prepared her to meet. If she doesn't feed this baby, he'll starve; if she can't take proper care of him he'll die. It's so precarious: a thousand things waiting to go wrong. It's terrifying. She needs to find a good family for Jimmy here because inexperienced as she is, even Sasha can tell at a glance that it will be years before he can take care of himself. When she and Beattie Calhoun's obstetrician met in the delivery room she told him she was giving her baby away, so he suppressed the scowl and gave her the shot that dries you up. Mistake, maybe. It did the job just fine but in the middle of the night when Jimmy's howling to be fed she wishes she could just haul one out and shove it in his face. It's all she can do to cope with the business of bottles and formula: how can she keep him awake long enough to eat, is he supposed to empty the bottle or is this enough or what?

Days later, she's still a mess. Poor Jim here looks a lot more beat up than she does. Her baby has a dent in his temple from the forceps and he's so tiny it's a marvel he's alive. It's scary to see him bawling with his little hands flashing, my God you can see the brain pulsing through the top of his skull, the thing that makes him distinctively Jim is protected by a membrane so thin you could puncture it with a ballpoint pen. And this is where they want to drive in the chip. It's so fragile! He's too young! Mesmerized, she watches it pulse, is that healthy or not? Look how the belly pumps with that rapid breathing, is it OK, is he put together right, is he supposed to have that bony pigeon breast? Is it normal, all this passion and effort to stay alive? The flailing worries her, but what if it stops? He is hers to take care of. What if she messes up?

Sasha wakes in the night and if she doesn't hear Jim crying she heaves herself out of bed and shuffles over to check. Passes her hand in front of his face. *Are you OK?* Sometimes she holds up a mirror, is he still breathing, my God, what if he's died? In time she learns that even asleep, an infant is noisy: grunting and snuffling, breathing in and out. He's eating, she thinks she's doing this part right but who's to know? Can she mix formula and sterilize bottles in the microwave without poisoning him? Can he really, really breathe without her help? Is he sick, is this normal, is he OK? She's never been in this deep; she's never been this obligated to anybody in her life.

Then she wakes in the night to profound silence. She jumps up. *My God!* When she turns on the light and looks into the crib her baby isn't dead, he's awake and lying quietly with his arms above his head and his legs curled like a puppy on its back. His fists clench inside the oversized nightie. For the first time, his eyes are open wide. As if fixed on the afterimage of a first thought.

Oh my God! She looks into the small, squashed face, rocked by the slate black eyes that look out but take in nothing— Jimmy Egan, all there and linked to her by a process beyond her control that beggars the work of any artist.

Oh my God, she thinks, poleaxed by discovery. *I made a person.*

In the daytime, logistics obscure thought. Days are about worrying and feeding, running through the infant-sized Huggies she laid in without dreaming they would go so fast. What if she runs out before she's steady enough to drive? This isn't the kind of neighborhood where stores deliver. She can't send Marilyn. She'll do anything to keep the fat manager off her case. What will she do if she runs out, tear up sheets for diapers and wash them in the basin? Probably. Jimmy's too little to be left alone and too little to take with. But what if she runs out? OK, sheets. She already scrubs the onesies and nightgowns because she didn't buy enough. A woman with girlfriends, she supposes, would have told her how many and what kind. Normal women learn these things from their moms but hers is in Boulder, she thinks, unless it's Tijuana, with another new man. Grandmother would know; Sasha would ask Grand if they were friends, but they were never friends. It's why she's here.

If she had friends they'd tell her that with infants, everything is a stage: soon over, to be replaced by the next. Any woman who's ever brought home a newborn knows that at the time, everything, especially the worst parts, seems endless. The news would cheer Sasha, but there's nobody here to tell her. She can't imagine the future. When he'll sleep through the night. How big he'll get. Whether they will like each other. She is all weakness and worry, rubbed raw by exhaustion. Giving birth isn't glorious, it's a pit that she has to get strong enough to climb out of.

Days blur.

Jimmy's crying. Again. Six times tonight so far, and she just changed him and fed him and burped him ten minutes ago, she did all the right things! Didn't she? She was almost asleep. Then that little voice knifed in. Jerked awake, she yips as stitches tear. She goes to the crib and cups her hands over the howling baby's heaving belly. "Don't, Jimmy. Please don't." She wants to help him and she can't. She doesn't know how! She's weak and confused; even her voice is faint, as though she can't quite fill her lungs. Stupid and powerless, she can't even take proper care of him! Hugging the sobbing baby, she rocks and he rocks with her. She says loud enough for Jimmy to hear, "It's just you and me, kid, OK?"

Oblivious, he wails.

"You and me." They are both crying now.

It's a good thing nobody knows where she is.

20.

In a hotel closer to the DelMar than Sasha would imagine in her bleakest moment, Gary Cargill gets out of the shower. Soaked, he squelches across the carpet and sits on a brocade chair. When he gets up he'll see a nice wet print of his butt. This is exactly the kind of thing that tickles Gary. He is all body image, with the addition of a couple of small things that escape him right now. He spent a long time in the shower this morning, thinking. He stood under the spray so long that his fingers shriveled and the hard winter skin on his feet turned white to match. By the time he got out, the rims of his toes and the edges of his heels were all gross. Now he is busy scraping them off. Later he will use up some time trying to get his big toe in his mouth— stupid, but what else has he got to do? You bet he has been here too long.

In fact, he hit Savannah shortly after Sasha did, but she doesn't know that. If she did she would probably freak. The last few days have been an exercise in laying back. So what if he maxes out on his plastic? The payback is huge. Whatever it costs him to bring home Sasha Donovan's baby, it's an investment in his future. If he can't make her marry him, he'll move into the old lady's garage apartment like she wants so she can play with her grandchild every day. The deal is, she'll be beholden to him. Isn't he bringing her grandbaby home? Of course the pact includes assurances on both sides: parochial schools, Villanova, all that. Sure, lady. He'll even turn

Catholic to cement the deal. Given what he gets back? Cheap at the price.

Fixed, he thinks. Big house, company V.P. Fixed for life. Sweet. Above the hotel bills, which she's reimbursing, all he's spent so far is time. OK, given Gary's record in college, where he's been too long, his time isn't worth much right now.

With more empty hours than things to do, Gary is paying meticulous attention to his person. Who's more important, after all? He lingers at the bathroom mirror, clipping his nose hairs and checking for zits; he double shaves. He is thinking of getting some depilatory cream for his back, where brown hairs sprout on the beginning love handles, if he loses the fuzz maybe they won't stick out so much. Tweeze the eyebrows, back-comb your hair. Make nice for the girl you score tonight, who knows what will come his way? Although he came into Savannah not knowing a soul who could hook him up, Gary has had plenty of girls in this room, and not one of them a woman of questionable repute, Gary is too good looking to pay for that. Like, he's doing them a favor, right? His days are empty but with women flocking the bar at cocktail hour like gnats around a bug zapper, his nights are somewhat fuller. In the right light, Gary is something of a babe magnet, so what's with this Sasha bitch, blowing him off like the ugly kid at the prom?

Was there something stuck in his teeth that he didn't know about? The way she acted when he showed up in Florida you'd think he was there to hurt her, not help. Why did she fly apart before he could go, like, *I come in peace,* and why the fuck did she run away before he could get close enough to make her get in love with him?

Son of a bitch, he thought she would be pleased.

Gary Cargill is no stalker. He's not your mortal enemy. God knows he came down south to do this woman a favor, like, if she wanted to get married, cool. Tum dum de dum, tum *da* da dum. Or he could take the baby and split, it was a good deal for her either way. What's her problem? He may not be Mr. Right but no way is he Mr. Wrong. Plays Well With Others, it said on his report cards, although his grades sucked; frankly, he got into college because he can throw the ball around. That plus a great deal of personal charm, which he is pretty much the master of. In classes at UMass, Boston, he smiles his way through discussions on obscure points and his grades float up to passing. People like him. He gets extra help on his papers by boffing the smartest girl in whichever class, and you know what? These girls know it's transactional, but they like it. Gary Cargill is no villain, he's just a dumb college fuck. In spite of what Sasha thinks, he is in no way dangerous. It isn't even her that he wants, he barely remembers the girl he had B+ sex with during Spring Fling.

He just wants to make this work.

His reasons are partly practical but it's ego too. Gary is like a flower and Sasha stomped on him. He is not used to rejection. He started with his Amazing Free Offer— marriage, the whole nine yards— and she scraped him off like pond scum. You'd think he was some crater-face asshole with a humongous hard drive and not the cool, popular person that he is. Great at parties, invited to all the bashes at MassArt. In high school he was football captain and homecoming king both, which is a measure. Girls thought he was a hunk and OK, he does have some hunklike qualities, even Gary would admit it, and Gary is also modest. Even though he's going soft from weeks in a town where it's swampy and too hot out to run, the cute flight attendants and girl brokers who flow in and out of the hotel bar take to him on sight. The only nights Gary sleeps alone are when he decides he needs the rest.

So where does this Sasha get off? Hell, why waste time getting on her good side when all the grandmother wants is the kid? Better, he thinks, to walk into this arrangement unencumbered. Frankly, he's guessing old Mrs. Donovan would never sit still for a divorce so best he stays single until he meets Mrs. Right.

Yes. Score the kid, and fuck Sasha. He has his rights. After all, he is the father here.

He just found out it's a boy.

He knows it's a boy and he knows which day it went home from the hospital, but he doesn't know if she's named it yet. Never mind, he has a good name scheduled: Donovan Cargill, Donnie for short. Satisfying both constituencies, about which more later. Names, yet. He really has been in Savannah too long, bored much?

He even bought shoes for it, shitkickers, size zero. Cute. He tied the tiny shoelaces together and hung them on the mirror over his dresser, which also contains the antique Burger King *Lord of the Rings* action figure set, minus one, which he obtained on eBay and had FedExed to the hotel. Last week he had everything but the Gimli and the Strider. A lucky coup and now the Gimli is on its way. He swipes his card and checks the Web twice a day because he's still missing the Strider. Too much time on his hands here? Looks like it. Not that he had a choice.

When the Donovan detective's phone call brought him here, his first instinct was to rush in and grab this Sarah Donovan a.k.a. Egan and drag her back to Philadelphia, but Gary is too smart for that. Only a tard would pounce on a pregnant broad before the baby came. Look at their history. Try and she'd have taken off, baby on board.

He is a pageant of waiting.

Listen, he has reasons.

One. Divide and conquer. Although it seemed like forever he had to wait until the girl and the baby were not one unit but two. Why kill yourself trying to jam a big old Jiffy Bag into your pocket when the diamond ring inside it is what you really want?

Besides, once the present gets separated from the package, eventually you will find the contents alone in a room. Like, the container has wandered off or turned its back or some goddamn thing and you can sneak in and score. But he can't count on that happening yet. As Gary understands it, new babies latch on to the mom and suck twenty-four/seven, so she won't be putting it down just yet. Never mind. He has friends at the DelMar. Over time he's scoped the motel and built character with the fat manager, so what if he had to degrade himself and flirt with her a little bit?

Plus he had to establish his cover, in case. So it won't look weird the next time he goes around. This is how smart Gary is. The fat lady thinks he's scouting her motel as a vacation spot for his big old company retreat. Fuck, do I *look* like an actuarial? Plus he's in tight with that pissy brat of hers, smarmy kid eats his supper alone in the diner every night, buy him dessert and let him bitch about his mom a little and he's all yours.

When Sasha a.k.a Sarah puts this baby down, Gary will be the first to know. It's worth the fifty he promised the kid.

Reason number three for holding off? Timing. He has an instinct about this. If he goes in too soon, she'll go all 911 on him. Wait long enough and she'll be over the mom thing and let go without a fight. Wait long enough and, she'll go please, Mister, please, take it, anything to get it off her back. Every time Gary cruises the DelMar the kid is crying. He can hear it scream. Even filtered through the Thermopane it's enough to drive you nuts. Two weeks around one of those and any normal person would freak. So Gary's cool. Let his one night stand do the heavy lifting. When their baby's ripe, he'll step in and grab it, nine'll get you ten she won't call the cops. Shit, she'll probably thank him for it. Wasn't that why she came down here, to lose the damn thing?

He's deep into waiting. He has been holed up for so long that he's started nicking the bed like a prisoner marking off the days. Never mind, over time he's turned this room into a second home. He's fixed it up— Kmart chair pillow thing, Georgia Bulldogs Styrofoam cup holders and Bulldogs tray so he can eat in bed. Scarves to cover the lampshades when a new girl comes up with him from the bar, peach-shaped ashtray in case she's a smoker, books he doesn't read; she'll be impressed. He is content to hang in here and eat Domino's and watch TV until it's time.

The brat at the DelMar promised to phone when his baby's mother finally goes out to the movies or the hairdresser or some damn thing. Then Gary will drop in at the DelMar cool as anything and pick it up, and for the price of the XMen action figures Gary scored on eBay plus a fifty, the fat manager's fat kid will slip him the passkey so he won't have to break in. Another fifty and the brat will tell an excellent lie for him. Once he scores he is totally out of here and Sasha can go fuck herself. He doesn't much care if he ever sees her again, although he supposes old lady Donovan's detective will want to keep tabs on her. For God's sake didn't the same detective track him down and bring him in?

"I assume she wouldn't be having a baby," the old lady said, "if you two weren't in love."

"Who, me and Sasha?" He barely remembered her.

"Sarah."

"Pregnant." He was still absorbing it. "What makes you think it's me?"

"She's not the first tramp in our family," the old lady said. Steel glasses. Narrow nose. Judgmental look. "We keep close track."

"You been tracking her?" He was processing the news. Never mind why she was having it instead of running to a clinic to get it taken out; how did this tough old lady know so much? Girl was pretty, he remembered, but that was about all he remembered. "You've been tracking Sasha. Sasha Egan," he said. "Nice girl."

"Donovan! It's Sarah." Why was she so pissed off?

He flashed the smile he perfected in junior high. "Sarah. Right." Big house. A lot of money here. "What do you want me to do?"

They sat for a long time while Mrs. Donovan looked into her knobby hands and considered and Gary looked at the big, dirty diamonds on her rings. He could see her lips pleating under pink lipstick that she'd put on thicker than varnish. He could see the light changing through gauzy white curtains embroidered with flowers. He saw her skinny knees trembling under the navy blue dress and he was feeling explosive and uneasy because she was so old. What would he do if she just died while they were sitting there?

"Ma'am?"

Her head came up. "We have to plan."

A lot of money. "What do you want me to do?"

Simple enough. At least to her. At the time it seemed simple to him too. Her best case scenario was him and Sasha— no, Sarah— married before the baby came. She wanted them married and living here and she wanted the baby baptized Catholic when it was two weeks old because she knew, even if he didn't, that every soul is a treasure and you can't let a new soul slip into limbo because death pounced before it could be baptized into the church. All he had to do was go down there to Florida and propose.

"Married," Gary said, but he was thinking, *What's in it for me?* Then she sweetened it. V.P. at Donovan Development, she needed a man in place when Father got too old. That's what old Mr. and Mrs. Donovan called each other, Mother and Father instead of names, and from the glimpse Gary caught of Father heading out, he was already too old. He had that pale blue stare, like his brains had blown out of his ears. They'll die and it will all be his.

When Sasha scraped him off her that first day at Newlife he saw the money going up the tubes. He backed off and thought about it. What to do.

By the time he figured out a plan and went back out to the whelping box, the bitch was gone. He was scared the old lady would cut his left arm off for failing but he phoned her anyway, the way you call your mom when you can't get your shoelaces untied. If she couldn't help at least she could tell him what to do.

He didn't want to blow this deal! She already knew. Like *that!* she hit him with Plan B. "Wait there. My detective will find her."

"Detective!"

"How do you think we found you? He'll find her. Then you . . ."

Relief made him truthful. "She'll just scrape me off her shoe."

"I don't care what she does," Mrs. Donovan said angrily. "As long as you bring the baby here."

"Wuow." He went on in a hollow, careful tone. "You don't care what happens to her?"

"Not really," she said. "As long as the baby stays here. And you. We're prepared to take good care of you. The garage apartment, a nanny for our child. My great grandchild," she said in a tone that he could not begin to interpret. "Now bring him home."

"And you need me because . . ."

"We're not going to live forever," she said flatly. Like that.

Damn straight. "Yes," he said. All that money. "Yes Ma'am."

And what if she stiffs him? Then what? Gary is still a young dude with a life to live! What's he going to do with a kid? Let Mom take care of it. She won't ask questions, she'll be fucking thrilled to have a piece of Gary's very own genetic set to play with. When Gary went out the door to college he heard her begging Dad, "Oh honey, let's have another baby," fat chance now, couple years ago something inside her went wrong and she had her works cut out. It's crazy, old women like Mrs. Donovan and his mom getting weird about babies, but they do. What's so special about them anyway? Since the operation it's all Mom thinks about, what's gone. So if the Donovans don't want the baby, no prob. They're good for it, Mom will be psyched so one way or another, everybody's satisfied.

Long after the pipes have run with morning showers and the doors on either side of his have slammed on businessmen going out into the city, Gary sits musing in his rumpled, cluttered room. God the days are getting long.

Room Service jumpstarts this long day in Savannah. The guy brought a FedEx. It's his Gimli, you know, the *Lord of the Rings* dwarf guy? He was afraid he'd have to leave town before it came so he sprang for FedEx, he is that anxious to complete the set. When you point the ring in the middle at one of the *Lord of the Rings* action figures, it either says something or it lights up, it is a genuine antique. Now he has something to do. Unwrap the Gimli and slide him into the circle, only one empty slot left. Go down and check on the Strider, auction closes tonight, play it cool, Gary, don't get all bent about it and preempt. Long brunch in the coffee shop, cruise the DelMar, he can hear the baby— fuck, *his* baby— bawling from all the way out here on the access road; martial arts movie in the P.M., pizza supper in bed, go down to the bar for drinks badda bing, badda bingo, he scores again, goooo Happy Hour!

"Oh," the babe of the evening says, scoping the *Lord of the Rings* set, "my little boy would love those!"

This brings him up short. Like, this woman looks good but she's used or broken. "You have a kid?"

Another flight attendant, nice eyes, body to die for, which he is about to do. She freezes. "He's ten. Is that a problem for you?"

"Oh no," he says quickly. "I'm kind of a father myself."

"Kind of a father? You either are or you aren't."

"Are. I mean, am! His name is Donnie and he's two weeks old."

"You have a two-week-old baby and you're here?"

"The mom and I are divorced." Look at her, dark hair, really sweet face. They were about to get down to it but she has turned to the mirror and is tucking in her shirt. She's going to be out of here before he can get his hands on her unless he thinks fast. "She never loved me," he says in a tone designed to make her go, *oh, you poor thing*. "She pretty much kicked me out."

"That's terrible." Sympathetic but not. "What did you do?"

"I wouldn't let her give the baby away."

She softens. "She wanted to give him away? That's so rude!"

"I know." Opportunity beckons. "I'm here to get him back."

"You mean you're going to court?"

"Oh no," he says. "If I go to court she'll kill herself." He looks at her shrewdly. "Or him."

The girl is all his now. Everything about her flows his way. "Oh my God. You poor guy."

The rest of the night goes very well. In between, the stew tells him about her abusive ex-husband and how she loves her kid so much that she moved down here from Albany to keep him safe. She knows Gary's going to love his little baby the same way, once you get them in your arms you never want to let go, he's a saint to be doing this; there's champagne in the room by that time, there are breakfast rolls and Mimosas and fresh grapes and they are snuggling in front of the muted TV while world news flows by, patterned like a flying carpet heading somewhere else. At the end they exchange kisses and home addresses and phone numbers, all fake, and somehow Gary ends up telling her his plan and the whole time he is thinking, *why am I telling her all this?* But she is very sympathetic.

"Anything you have to do to get your baby, you just have to do it. You go, guy."

Sweet girl, she gives it to him one more time.

At the door Bonnie-whatever, says, "I wouldn't let it wait too long or you'll have a hell of a time getting custody." She wipes off his farewell kiss like so much excess lipstick, preparing to go out into the world. Gary looks so *Duh* that she stops to explain patiently, "Everybody knows that after the mother's been carrying it around for a while they bond."

Doh!

Turns out he can't hang around here much longer, waiting on the fat child's phone call and biding his time. Whatever time he had is boiling down to *now*.

Soon he has go out to the DelMar and collect the kid. He'll be going for it as soon as he buys a basket or something for it to sleep in and figures out the moves. Weird, now that he's up against it, he's kind of dragging his feet. Without his making a conscious choice, *now* morphs into *soon*.

He's excited to get going but in a way he's sorry. Living in a hotel sounds boring, but he's had fun here. He was flunking everything and it was time to get away. It's been a good time. Working carefully, he takes the *Lord of the Rings* figures off their bases in the magic circle and wraps each one in Kleenex so they won't get hurt bumping around in his pack, and the Strider? Should he hang in here until he knows he has the Strider or should he get on with this and get out of here? He can feel the empty spot, like the gap in a row of your front teeth.

Get over it, he tells himself. You need to get in there and do this. If it works out you get the garage apartment, the job in the company, salary in six figures. And if something goes wrong and you get stuck with the baby? When the old people die, your little heir apparent is going to inherit and you will get everything.

21.

It's interesting, the way you go along as though your life is a long dream that you actually control. Needy and ignorant, you think ahead. You hope. You plan. As you lay out a pattern of next things, what to do and how it will come down, you imagine that what comes next will in fact unfold according to the template you have made for it, never mind that blueprints for human endeavors are drawn in ash on something far less substantial than paper.

Before the day is out, Tom Starbird will make two mistakes.

He will show himself.

The second is bigger.

He will interface with the mark.

It's one thing for superheroes to put on shiny masks and zoom in on fluorescent lightning bolts to perform rescues, revealing flashy superpowers. Starbird is something else. His identity is secret, his best work covert. His rescues unfold in shadow and silence. To do his job, he must blend into his surroundings and disappear, the sixteenth degree of invisible.

All this is about to be compromised.

Pretty girl in trouble. Turns to him, what can he do? Anybody would do the same.

If life ran like an operating system, there would be a display on Tom Starbird's monitor, flashing:

Fatal error.

To do what Starbird does demands distance. Defend your position, which must be remote. Emotion makes you vulnerable. Get personally involved and you make mistakes. Never think of yourself as a person, you are a job function. Who you are when you are off duty is not important. For the duration of the job, you are this. All his working life Starbird has managed to objectify: the subject. The supplier— a mother who doesn't deserve a kid. He is the provider. The subject is just that until he makes the pickup. An object he needs. He picks the time and place, moves in and scores. He separates the product from the supplier and makes delivery. The method: go in fast, do the job cleanly and get out without leaving tracks. In this context he is not Tom Starbird, he is an instrument. His life depends on it.

But he will interface with the mark.

It will become personal.

Oh, this is wrong. From the beginning, the parameters were skewed. Zorn smacked him in the face with his own pathetic backstory and threatened his mother, which makes Starbird something less than a provider and Zorn something more than a client. This isn't just contract work. He is on a forced march.

God knows he's tried to take his time.

Temporizing, Starbird wasted a few days tracking the supplier from the Pilcher Home in central Florida to Savannah, Georgia, where the girl had gone to ground. After all, there was nothing he could do until the infant Zorn ordered landed alive and well. The days until then passed undisturbed. After he got what he needed out of that silly kid Luellen, he drifted through small towns in barren central Florida, stopping at roadside stands and gift shops, browsing through candied orange peel and dried alligators and religious objects made out of shells. He admired primitive alligators and palm trees painted on driftwood, but he didn't buy. He is done collecting now. Instead he wandered sandy main drags and went barefoot in the dirt, picking up sand spurs like a man with nothing on his mind and nothing pressing to do. He might as well take his time. No merchant as clever as Tom Starbird would spook a supplier by moving in too soon. There was no need to pursue this before the due date.

The trail of a woman in her ninth month does not evaporate. A woman on the run leaves wide tracks.

When it was time, he worked his way up the coast through sandy shore towns to Savannah, where he checked into a genteel, sleepy, period hotel he'd pulled off the web. Triangulating from the supplier's due date, he hacked his way through hospital databases, working methodically until he found the right one. Shmooze the night nurse in one of these places and you can find out pretty much anything you want. It never occurred to him that not every man has this power. There are still nights when Luellen Squiers pulls the phone case out of her pillowcase, replaying that wonderful smile. Even in big city hospitals like the one in Savannah, charm works. "Yes," the nurse said, smiling back, "she had such a hard time that we all remember her." *Oh,* he thought, *my poor girl.* "All alone, nobody to come for her. We had to send her home in a cab." Slip a fifty under your fake badge and the cab company dispatcher will open his files for you; it works every time. Given the date, the time and the pickup point, it didn't take long to locate the supplier at the DelMar— B minus motel on an access road, no security guy, no Policemen's Benevolent Association scarfing lunches in exchange for the protective shield.

He set a tentative pickup date. It had been a hard delivery, they told him. The charge nurse had confided that the poor girl was in for a long convalescence. Correction, lady. Supplier. Too much information for me. All he needed to know was that she wouldn't be leaving Savannah any time soon. Counting down, he set the date.

For Starbird, the four week waiting period was key. In ordinary circumstances he'd wait six. He didn't get where he is by moving too fast. He preferred to delay pickup until the product was big enough to transport safely. Further, the first month was crucial in developmental terms. It took that long for biology to determine whether the subject was going to make it in the world. No conscientious provider would deliver a product until he could guarantee its survival and assure the client that there were no organic defects and none pending, no glitches like colic or croup and no physical flaws. Starbird prided himself in delivering product in optimum condition. After all, the object of the operation was to put these babies into circumstances where they would thrive.

Any reasonable client would wait.

"Four weeks," Zorn yapped when he heard. "What the fuck!"

"It's just now on the ground. Too young to travel. I don't deliver until it's ready, understand?"

"You don't get it. My wife goes to bed crying every night."

"Not before."

"Why the fuck not?"

"Needs time to develop." Time for him to double back with the scanner, make sure the supplier hasn't re-thought and had the subject chipped, in which case the next square on the board is marked GO and he has to start over. "Even a month is cutting it close."

"If you think I've left off interviewing witnesses on this other thing you're wrong, Starbird. Bring me the damn kid."

"I told you, it's too soon."

"My wife cries every fucking single night."

"Sorry, man, but you can't rush biology. This isn't a box of Cheerios that you snatch off a dump in the supermarket, Zorn."

Zorn's voice froze over. "Watch your tone."

"Look. If you want somebody else to do this, I'm happy to walk away."

"Just try it. If you want your mother bare naked on TV."

"Don't."

He added, offhand, "As a matter of fact, I have her coming in for an interview."

Keep it cool, Starbird. Don't let him get to you. "OK." He surprised himself. "Three weeks. Not a minute sooner."

"Three weeks." Zorn's voice was bright with relief. "Hell, take an extra day."

Once he set the timing Starbird had to lay back, at least for a while— no problem. He needed to think. He spent some days meandering up the Inland Waterway, exploring the Sea Islands. He drove on up to Beaufort with no obligations and no needs, really, until it was time. This gave him the liberty to take his ambition out into the light and crack it open and look inside. For the first time it seemed important to him to find out how the engine that drove him ran, to disassemble it, see what the parts looked like.

Exiting the life that made him who he was, Starbird was compelled to learn what he might possibly become. Without the distractions of the job to diffuse his concentration, the desire to find out took fire. It burned like acid, eating its way out. What did he want, anyway? What did he really want to do now, or to become?

Something, he thought. *Something more than this.*

He was riveted, hung up on the mystery of aspiration. Where did it come from, this burning, elusive need to jump higher?

Wandering rural South Carolina, he tried to open himself; he wanted to spread the leaves the way he would an artichoke and look into the heart. He needed to look into himself the way a man in love sometimes spreads the petals so he can look into the woman he loves, and look deep. Insulated by years focused on the work, the crazed cycle of planning and completion, Tom Starbird had no time to confront himself.

Now he did. When he finished this last job, this part of his life would be done forever. He brooded, wondering, *What comes next?*

He crossed long causeways flanked by marsh grass and drove on into sandy territory tufted with weeds and overhung by live-oaks and Australian pines shrouded in Spanish moss. In a ramshackle enclave by a dirt road, a door fell open as his car approached. Yellow light spilled out like a trail leading in. Stricken, Starbird took his foot off the gas. He was drawn to the glowing interior, where simpler lives than his spun out on bare wood floors in front of an HDTV; it was like seeing into another life. He switched off his lights and backed up, yearning for something he could not name. He cut the motor and coasted in. Rocked by longing, he watched kids running around the spare, uncluttered living room. Then somebody called and they dropped on the spot, laughing and tumbling in front of the TV while a woman— the mother? bringing cookies she had baked?— wandered in from the kitchen with a plate. Here's a story he once heard: rich kid's grandmother drives him through a burned out neighborhood in some big city. "Martin," she says grandly, "this is where poor people come from." At this distance, it looked good to him: having not enough, because he knew now that too much was never enough. Simple, compared.

It made his mouth water. His heart went out. He wanted to go up and present himself. Hi, it's me. Get invited in. He wanted to move in, he wanted them to let him live in their lives. If he could, it would solve everything.

If he could only do this right, maybe they'd like him. If they liked him well enough they might ask him to stay the night. If he showed he was useful maybe they'd let him stay on. He could come to live with them forever, make repairs, pull his weight on the farm. Hell with the exigencies, he was ready to dig, plow, plant, mind kids when he was needed, and if there wasn't a bed for him in the house no problem, he'd happily sleep in the shed. Right now Starbird would give anything to sit down for supper in the family kitchen and sprawl on the floor in front of the TV with their kids when supper was done. By this time he had fallen in love with this family; he was ready to do anything for them, give them anything they asked. Want a wire transfer? Sure. Let them take the damn money and go to fucking Europe if they wanted to, live on the Riviera, buy a farmhouse in France, he'd do anything for a chance to hang out with them here under the live-oaks, with the sharp, hard outlines of his guilt blurred by shrouds of Spanish moss.

He thought it was a fair transaction, everything he had in exchange for their hard but uncomplicated lives. Sitting there in the dark in coastal South Carolina, Tom Starbird rocked with homesickness for something he'd never had.

God, he thought, these poor people! Didn't they know how vulnerable they were, laughing in there? Three kids with their nice mom, nice dad. Couldn't they guess that there was a world-class felon slouched in his rental car out here in the dark?

When did he start thinking of himself as a felon? Wrenched by grief he didn't understand, Starbird looked into his hands reflectively. He didn't know. He didn't know!

Anybody else would have put his head down on the steering wheel and sobbed.

The dog heard. It began to bark. A man came to the door. The father, protecting his family. Out here in the world there were loving fathers on guard. Groaning, Starbird stepped on the gas. He would be gone before the tenant farmer knew he was there.

It was pickup day minus eleven. Time to establish a staging area in Savannah, where he would retreat to begin surveillance and finalize the plan. The subject had been in the world for more than two weeks now. By this time the supplier would be strong enough to take it out in the car. Starbird had done the preliminaries before he hit the road— what were the parameters of the DelMar, where the supplier would go when she went out— how far were the doctor's offices and which were the nearest stores, whether she went to the Food King or to Walgreens and when. It was simple enough to divine patterns, the comings and goings, this supplier's habits regarding the subject. How vigilant she was. Who else was around, and when. Whether she let other people tend this baby and whether she ever left it alone. He was still studying methods for the pickup. A short-timer now, he was weighing the UPS truck and uniform— sure fire but demanding substantial groundwork, against settling for a slap-on Domino's lightup sign for the rental car. A break-in would be easy. The site was wide open and easy to crack. Rundown motel, plywood doors and spring locks any fool could open with a credit card, but that was for amateurs. Clumsy. Accident-prone. Starbird is a skilled professional. If you want to do something right you never do it the easy way, which is exactly what police expect. Big back windows sheltered by azaleas, sitting there like an invitation. But that would be kidnapping. Starbird will never be that person.

After this job, nobody will confuse him with that person. Ever again.

Even exiting the business, Starbird is a professional. As a provider, he is careful. Meticulous. His plans are always in place well before he moves on them.

It's time to prepare.

It is this cool precision that brings Tom Starbird to the Food King today. The supplier has popped the product into her rusting heap and driven to a big, impersonal supermarket a stone's throw from the DelMar. He needs to observe without being seen and this is the ideal place. Tom follows at a distance as the supplier circles the aisles with the subject in its car seat propped in her shopping cart. Cartoon Teddy bears dance on the fabric that covers the cushions and the ruffled collapsible hood. The little plastic bucket comes equipped with a white plastic handle— asking for it! The infant in the bucket is like a puppy in a carrying case or a shrink-wrapped Easter basket with the bunny inside, inviting the consumer to snatch it out of the display, but Starbird prides himself on subtlety. He didn't get where he is by grabbing an item in plain sight and running out of the store.

Expert at remote surveillance, he tracks the supplier at a distance; he knows how to see without being seen, following as she circles the store. The girl is bent over the cart, murmuring to the subject in its ruffled bucket; doesn't she ever turn her back? As she stops to study TV dinners he backs off, waiting in the next aisle. He is alerted by a disruption. Sounds of a confrontation.

When the yelling starts Starbird knows it's time to vaporize, but curiosity keeps him in place a beat too long.

He is in fact turning to leave when the girl rounds the corner, running fast. And she has left the baby— where? The second Starbird takes to consider this question is the one he should have spent exiting the picture. He's skilled at disappearing. After all these years he knows how. *How* isn't the issue here. It's *when*. He's seconds too late. The girl spots him and runs headlong with her hands out. "Please," she says urgently. "There's this guy."

"What?"

"Back there. He's following me!"

Behind her this overweight bozo in a Georgia Bulldogs sweatshirt hip-checks the corner display of salsa, smashing jars as he steams her way. Sauce splatters and he slips. Big guy; one of those athletes that runs to fat when the season ends, but the clenched fists and Popeye muscles make clear he's still tough. Distressed, the girl turns a face like a bruised violet toward Starbird and— God!— just as he turns to go, she grabs his arm.

A nerve spasms. It's as if she's run a fingernail down his naked spine.

"Please!"

Oh shit. I've worked too hard to blow it now. He turns. In his right mind, Starbird would not permit this encounter because his work is done without reference to the mark. On any other job, he'd be out of here like a shot. Concealment is S.O.P., but he momentarily loses concentration, perhaps because they are so close to pickup, it's the last, he is thinking like a short-timer here.

For the first time in his long life in the business, Tom Starbird is face to face with the mark. He has been surveilling her for days. Up close she is something else. Pale against the black T-shirt, skinny and insubstantial, a little shaky on her feet— right, the nurses said she had a tough time— all this and she's trying to smile. All this observed in the seconds it takes the numbnut marauder in the Bulldogs sweats to regain his feet and cover the distance between the puddle of salsa and his prey.

"Please."

One woman alone, she needs his help, does he have a choice?

Starbird puts her behind him. "Stay here. I'll deal."

By the time he muscles her assailant out of the supermarket and frog-marches him across the parking lot to the road, the girl is running after him, waving her arms.

The stalker, old boyfriend, whatever, shit, amateur kidnapper? Whatever he is, he's struggling to get free. He lunges, raising hammy fists. Starbird stops him with the blade of his hand, not hard enough to smash the larynx but hard enough to knock him out of his tracks. Black belt: yeah thanks, Daria. Karate lessons to get me out of your hair. Grinning, he throws the schlub into the dirt and heads for his car. Split now and the girl may not forget what happened, but she won't remember how it came down or who you are.

Behind him, she is calling: "Wait."

Oh, shit.

"Don't go."

Don't compound the felony, run. He pretends not to hear.

Behind him she calls, "Please wait."

Another second and he'd have made it. He'd be out of here. "Can't. Late."

"Please!"

"Late, really. Really late." Too late.

She cuts him off at the car. She's panting and unsteady from the effort. Her voice is shaky too. "I just wanted to say thanks."

Dammit, lady, don't smile. Don't smile at me.

She does.

He and the supplier are face to face.

Tom Starbird got where he is by setting protocols and adhering to his own strict rules. No personal contact. Once you've objectified, everything you do remains abstract. Elements fall into place like the cherries on a slot machine. The operation depends on it.

If this seems cold, Starbird has his reasons. You can get away with anything as long as the victim doesn't have a face. Mistake. The minute you start thinking of her as a victim, you're screwed.

Oh God, the girl's still talking. "I just wanted to explain. That guy is my. Was my." Her face is full of her story she wants to tell. She wants him to hear it but she can't find the words to go with. She tries to take his hands but he pulls away. It's like one of those games where you win if you can keep from getting slapped. She sees he's getting weird and stops. "Oh hell, just, thanks."

Don't get sucked in here. Don't talk to her. Get in the car now, asshole. Pretend you don't know what she's talking about. Like it wasn't me that rushed that fat stalker off the scene, lady. Must have been somebody else. Leave now, while you can. Like a goddamn fool, he says, "You're welcome." OK, you said it. Now go.

He can't go. She is bobbing between him and the car door. Nice face. Very nice face. Intelligent. Pale scar parting the left eyebrow, when she was little she fell, or some kid hit her with a toy. Embarrassed now. "I'm not usually so helpless."

Three weeks out of the hospital, it's perfectly normal. Don't say that! "No problem," he says in a neutral tone. If human lives ran with the beautiful, brute simplicity of an operating system, Tom Starbird's screen would be bannered with the red circle canceled by an X. Right now it should be warning:

This program has performed an illegal operation
and will be shut down.

"See, I just had a baby and . . ."

"It's OK."

She goes on anyway. "Something about the whole childbirth thing makes your brains melt and go running down your neck." If she'd only stop smiling.

Accidentally, he smiles. Fuck you for that, Starbird, get rid of her before you do anything worse. "Don't worry, you'll get them back."

"I just freaked."

"He's a pretty big guy."

"I don't usually freak. I'm usually pretty tough."

I bet you are. "Yeah, well, nice meeting you. Now I have to . . ." Computers, at least, when you do something stupid, computers beep warnings, but this is a person. Born into a gentler society than the one he inhabits now, Starbird can't get past her and he just won't push her aside.

"He's kind of an ex-boyfriend. Hell no, he was never my boyfriend, he's just a . . ."

Fatal error. "Don't worry, he won't be back."

"Oh yes he will. I just wanted to . . ."

Fatal error. With a sense of futility, he takes her shoulders and gently turns her so he can get into the car. The contact is like a little

shock: slight. Shaky. Warm. Lovely, really. Asshole, back off!
"Thank me? You're welcome. Now if you don't mind, I'm late."

"I thought he was going to take my . . ."

This program has performed an illegal operation. Think fast,
Starbird. "Baby? Lady, where's your baby?"

Her hands fly up. "Oh my God, the baby!" At least this gets rid
of her. Suppliers at this stage, they're so new to it that sometimes
they forget they have a baby and accidentally put it down.

And will be shut down. "Better hurry. You left him in the store."

Whatever comes down now, he will remember her.

And she'll remember him.

His systems aren't shut down but they are gravely compromised.

22.

Jake Zorn is in his office, beginning construction on Tom Starbird's worst nightmare. He doesn't have the blueprint in front of him but the cornerstone is sitting right here. They are about to go *mano a mano*. With Starbird out of reach and everything pending, he has to keep busy. Partly he is bad at waiting and partly, in the lexicon of threats made good on, it is essential. If the dude can't produce a kid, Jake will have this to show. It's going well. In fact, it's going so well that he thinks he'll do the show anyway. It's good. Very good. With this pretrial interview slotted in, the show will be gangbusters. Yes, he is thinking of this as a trial. An open trial before a jury of millions, never been done, not like this. First you expose the culprit. Then you destroy her.

Sitting opposite him is Daria Starbird.

"Thanks for coming in," Zorn says. "I need your perspective on something."

"I brought a list of agencies." Woman's activist, she thinks she is here to consult on health resources for women. Handsome woman past a certain age, smiling uncertainly.

"I'm more interested in you as a mature parent."

Daria says sharply, "I wasn't *that* mature."

"You were forty."

She blinks as if he's just slapped her. "I didn't come here to talk about . . ."

"How does it feel to get pregnant in midlife?"

"And I certainly don't intend to . . ." She trails off. She is looking for the thread but it eludes her. Daria Starbird is in her sixties now. Carved-looking head, expensive shoes. Man-tailored suit— new; good jewelry to make clear that she is definitely not a man, although she has the same pale eyes and strong chin as the son. Cut from the same cloth, different detailing.

Zorn is looking for the thread too, but not the one that draws a straight line through this conversation. When he's at the top of his game the thread he pulls tightens like a noose but he's a little bit intimidated by this woman. When he's working a subject like this one he has to circle like a woodpecker tapping here, testing there, looking for weaknesses. That hollow sound that signals rot underneath. Tap. "Pregnant with a baby you don't want?"

"Oh!" She shakes her head with a subverbal noise that will have viewers by the millions jamming the 900 number.

Tap. "And try to get rid of?"

"I didn't have an . . ."

"I never said you did. I said you tried to get rid of it."

Tears spring. "You have it all wrong!"

Bullseye. "By all means, correct me."

"I wanted that baby, and besides . . ." Her head lifts. "That was a long time ago. Now, as I said, for women in trouble there are dozens of . . ."

"What was?"

She rushes past the question. "My list. It's right here on my PDA. Don't you want your person to download and print my list?"

"But the memories are still fresh." Yes he is baiting her. Get her on tape and it won't matter what she says, they can fix it up in the edit.

"No," she says, cool as anything. She's too smart to ask *what memories?*

"Because?" Maury's psychotic break taught him how to work these women. He wants her to say, electroshock trashes your memory. Then he'll say, not ask, what electroshock. Or, which memory.

Instead she doesn't say anything.

"You can tell me. We're off the record."

"Nothing to tell." In a way it's sad, the studied absence of expression. "I'm here to talk about health services for women."

"Emphasis on fertility problems," he says.

"I don't know anything about . . ."

My God he's forgotten what lie he told to get her in here. Guesses. "And unwanted children."

"Don't."

"My audience is going to want to know how you, as a mother . . ."

"I'm not only what happened to me! I'm . . ." A poet. Proud.

"A poet." With the tip of his ballpoint, he flips to the verse Duane Xeroxed for him. His voice is gentle now, like chocolate on satin. When a guy with Jake Zorn's rugged face and tough affect damps it down to confidential, it's a powerful aid to seduction. The verse is performing its own little seduction. Rapt, Daria Starbird listens to her own words: "Surprised by life I fall," he reads, "and in falling deep I lose myself . . ." on and on to the hush at the last line. Smiling, he looks up. "That's very nice."

"Thank you."

"Do you want to talk about it?"

"No."

He keeps the voice where it is, warm and gentle. On a good day, Jake Zorn is a heartbreaker and he knows it. "Then perhaps you'll say how what happened with your baby affected your work."

"No."

"It's very nice work, Ms. Starbird."

"Thank you." He's definitely on target: that telltale blush.

"It says here you used to win prizes."

"Where did you get that?"

"You were doing so well." He keeps his voice low. Lulling her.

"I was."

"Before this thing happened."

"What thing?"

"You had the . . ."

"Baby. Yes."

"And then something happened."

"A thing. Yes. That happened."

"And after that . . ."

Tears drop. She is falling into his hands. "After that it was harder. But I'm here to talk about . . ."

"Anything you want."

"Resources." Just when he thinks he has her, the woman eludes him; one more miss and he'll lose her. "God knows women need."

Like a hypnotist, he repeats her, "God knows they need . . ."

"All the help they can get."

"All the help they can get," Jake repeats and then he adds in that same soft voice, "Like you." Do this right and she'll echo dreamily, "like me," and . . .

Shit. She snaps to. "Actually, that's none of your business."

"We aren't recording yet, you can be straight with me."

Daria glances over her shoulder.

"No cameras, I promise. Until we move into the studio, we're off the record. Better. If you're comfortable where we are, we'll get Anton in here and when you see the red light you'll know he is shooting." Take aim. "Did I tell you my wife and I are expecting?"

"No." Her face is a study. "That's wonderful."

"It's kind of why I'm doing this story, so we'll know what's there for us after the baby comes." Confidence, he tells himself. Confidence begets confidence. Middleaged but Jake knows exactly how to modulate so that he comes on all boyish: garish. Kind eyes. Reassuring grin. "You know, it's funny how you want a kid when you don't even know if you're going to like it." He watches her face for sign. "A baby, at our age. Do you think we're too old?"

"It depends on who you are."

"Like, midlife, mid-career, it's gotta be disruptive." Yes he is watching, he is watching her with great care. "Irish coffee?"

"It's early for me, thanks."

"Great way to start the morning." He signals. Duane darts in. Daria won't see the kid leer when he sees how close they are sitting. "Relax you, make you sing like an angel." Her smile slips off her face. He says quickly, "Duane, tell Anton we aren't shooting for another hour. So Daria, are you OK with us getting *entre nous*?"

"I don't make friends very fast."

"Maury and I want this baby so much."

"I see."

Duane brings the coffee: whipped cream on top. She flicks the top with her finger and then licks the finger; good. God, if he could only get her to slip off her shoes. Zorn says gently, "I gather your story's a little different."

"I had a baby I wasn't sure I wanted, if that's what you mean. Now, you got me here to list resources available to women who want to conceive and can't. They are . . ." She starts reading off names.

Terrible story, now that he thinks about it, this very woman outside the Quincy Market in a snowstorm, offering her baby to the first taker, and that's only the first time. His research kid tells him Daria never got over it. Never quite made it as a poet, either. To compensate she's deep into good works, the woman is on a dozen boards. "And while we're at it, let's talk about services for unwed mothers," he adds to stop the recital of agency names. "Like certain people here today."

"That's none of your fucking business."

"Placement agencies, then."

"Oh, placement agencies. Of course. I have another list."

It doesn't matter what Daria says this morning. In postproduction, Anton and Derek will edit the interview to serve Zorn's purposes. Oh, yes they are shooting. The four digital camcorders in his office are sited so cleverly that his visitors have no idea. "Isn't it interesting that you ended up in this line of work."

"I help where I can."

"And tell me, do you think having a baby hurt your career?"

"Wait a minute." Shadows of memory race across Daria's face. She scowls. "What are you after here?"

"No offense." Daria does not say, *none taken,* so he tries, "With this baby coming Maury and I are, OK, a little scared. We're both professionals. What happens to your life with a baby in it?"

Like that! she groans, "God only knows."

Gotcha. "So now you understand why I'm so interested in the late pregnancy thing. You're a poet and a mother too." He manages a thin smile. In post production, it's always digitally enhanced.

Flattery startles Daria into frankness. "I'm not exactly famous for that."

"What was it like?"

"You don't want to know."

Now it's Jake's turn to be silent. He does not even prompt with the usual, "Go on." The Conscience of Boston has learned over time that even smart people are intimidated by silence. They can handle hearing the most awful things— even the unspeakable. It's silence they can't bear. When it grows, it frightens them. If it gets big enough it just might fall like a tombstone and kill them dead. Given time here, silence will make Daria Starbird so nervous that she'll do anything to end it. In time she will say anything just to fill the space and once she starts talking she'll spill her guts no matter what she's trying to hide.

It happens this way every time. He is the man!

Like any good reporter, Jake Zorn knows how. It's like being a psychiatrist: *don't mind me, I'm not really here.* He knows how to become invisible. Keep your head down and your eyes on the clipboard in your lap and you stop being a person in the room. You are nothing more or better than an ear. Pretend you aren't listening, you're making notes about something else. Look out the window. Pretend your mind is wandering. Never meet their eyes. Over his years interviewing, Zorn has learned this lesson well. Wait long enough and his subject— his mark!— will spill everything. Be still and when she starts talking, Daria Starbird will forget he's here.

In the beginning silence, the baby merchant's mother stirs uneasily, studying her beautiful hands. As it expands she looks up nervously, but Jake doesn't move. She shifts in her chair and clears her throat to get attention but he doesn't stir. Somebody has to break the silence. They can't just keep sitting here.

The silence is huge.

Finally she cracks. "You don't know what it does to you to be going along like everybody else and then suddenly you're pregnant."

Bingo.

"You have no idea what it's like. You've lost control of your life."

Flipping his ballpoint, Jake starts drumming on his clipboard, soft and unintrusive at first but hypnotic, making a steady, metronomic beat. He thinks, but does not say, *Ready, set, lady, go!*

"I suppose this is all fun and games for you. Whatever happens, your wife does the job."

This is so close to the mark that Jake flinches. Fortunately his subject is studying her own scarred knuckles now, and does not see. Note to self: find out about the scars. He gnaws the inside of his mouth to stay quiet. Like orchids, silence is hard to grow.

Finally Daria says, "If you did any research at all you know I had a nervous breakdown after my baby was born. It was not my first." She shakes like a dog. "God, it wasn't my last. It may seem like small change to you but the pressures on a poet are tremendous. The prize that singles you out. The early promise."

Say nothing. Track her with your eyes. Bring her to ground.

"All the expectations! The financial sacrifices, your family's." It all comes in on her. "The lifetime wasted because you can't measure up. You may come close, but you never measure up."

Hold your breath, man. Bite your tongue.

Musing, she launches a speed-rap. "The career that founders no matter how fast you run. Poets aren't like rock stars, Mr. Zorn, but they are. Think Sylvia Plath, and think hard. She had two children, and look what she did to herself. It's the pressure, but what did I know? I thought I owed it to the future. I thought being a mother might unleash my best work!" Her voice breaks in two.

Gulping, she goes on. "I didn't rush into it, I looked for the right man, somebody solid to love us and take care of us. See, I landed in the Riggs Clinic after Smith. I wanted to make this gift to the future but I knew I needed stability, so I chose Peter. With my talent and his strength . . ." Daria is staring at something he can't see. Shhh. Wait.

"I should have used one of the Boston Glyphs, we gave readings and made love in a dozen coffee bars. Or David, at Riggs he was my nurse. He would have taken care of us!" She sighs. "Not the man I chose. When I had my baby I was unmarried which was no big deal except it was. I was alone. Alone and pregnant. I couldn't even manage my life! How was I supposed to manage a kid?"

The gaps between silences are getting shorter. This is the best interviewer's trick of all. Let your subject unburden until she topples. Then she can't stop.

"My sisters begged me not to keep him. They offered to adopt him. How could I let them when I *loved him so much!*"

Jake is thinking: that's not the way I heard it. He tries to scope this— where she's coming from— but her face is locked up.

"Of course I never told him how scared I was. I never let down. How can you lead an expedition when your baby knows the leader is afraid? I had another nervous breakdown about it. No. You can't make me go there. At least not now. We got past it, Tommy and I. That's all anybody needs to know. I loved him so *much!* See how much I love my Tom. I love him so much that he thinks I don't love him at all. I pretended, to make it easier. I had to, so I could set him free. I said I didn't want him. I did it for him, get it? When you're one woman alone you go crazy with the responsibility. You have to do it right. You alone. You will be judged! You go through the days stone cold terrified of doing it wrong."

She is either lying or she isn't. Even Daria doesn't know.

She says, as if Jake has asked, "No I don't know where he is right now but I should, right? Isn't that what mothers do? We are in touch, but not often and not all that much. As for what he's made of himself since college? Hard to say. He did very well in college.

Like me, he won prizes, but his were for logic and rhetoric, things that help you instead of hurting you. See, logic and rhetoric move you beyond feeling to knowing how to think."

She chokes. "All poets have is feeling, and now look at me!"

They are approaching the end of the arc. No need to lay on Irish coffee, Jake has what he wants. All he has to do is wait.

"Then Tommy got a job and he's done well. I don't know what he's doing but he's doing very well, he sent me checks until I started sending them back and then he quit. I can't say how Tom makes his money but he makes a lot. Every birthday he finds a new netsuke for my collection and some of them are extremely fine, maybe his job takes him to Japan. He's always been secretive about his work, just like a poet, but I think he knows exactly what he's doing whereas poets— poets never know. Sometimes I think he must be in some very secret service. Interpol or CIA or one of those extreme secret agencies that we don't know about. As I said, he did very well in college. After that I simply do not know."

There's more to the recital, but none of it matters. In the way of good interviewers Jake nods and murmurs the occasional mmm hmmm while he scrawls: *bla bla bla.* At the end he buzzes Duane. Anton comes in with an antique camcorder and pretends to videotape the Resources for Women interview: a half-dozen Barbie doll questions and answers about health care and reproductive rights and— Jake is grateful even though he's not sure exactly what he has here— at the end he lets poor Daria, rigid with purpose, repeat the names on her list.

"So those are some of the resources available to women in the Greater Boston area. Now if you'll just turn that thing off."

"You understand," Jake says, "this is only a preliminary interview. You'll need to come back to the studio when we do the show. The most important segments are done live." He is already drafting his indictment. Judgment by the audience. When he goes national he won't be just another talking head on a TV magazine.

Stiff with exhaustion, Daria stands. "If I can do some good."

"Oh, you can." He hits that warm professional note geared to reassure. "And you will." Then the devil takes him and he adds carelessly, "If we can work out the timing and make a satisfactory arrangement, maybe we can bring you on together with your son."

"Tom." Daria's face breaks open. "I have so much to tell him!"

"Mother-son reunion. Sweet."

"But will he be glad to see me? What will he say?"

"He'll understand. This is your chance to explain to him."

The woman is yearning like the Man Without a Country craning at the coastline from his prison ship. "That would be wonderful."

"I wouldn't count on it. But I'll do what I can."

23.

If life in this dimension was as clean and logical as a computer's operating system, Starbird would indeed shut down and reboot, but it isn't and he can't. He's got too much going on.

The encounter has left him disrupted and brooding. He retreats to the genteel confines of the sleepy, venerable Marshall House in old Savannah, which he chose for the sleepy and venerable part. Who does this kind of work in a magnolia drenched landmark where azaleas bloom in profusion and personal attention is S.O.P? Shady business is supposed to go down in bland, featureless motels operated by chains so big that nobody notices who comes and who goes.

God, when did he start thinking of what he does as shady?

Nothing looks the same to him. He keeps flashing on her face: torn mouth, smudges under the eyes like bruised petals. If he had to talk to her, he had to talk to her, but he never should have looked her in the face. The woman was frantic, he isn't sure why. Was it the stalker guy or this new baby? Will her life clear up if she gets shut of it, he's doing her a favor, right? He doesn't know. He doesn't know and that's the hell of it. To do what he has to, he has to believe that he is doing all parties a service. Otherwise he's totally fucked.

Starbird is so wired that he has to remind himself what you do when you come into your hotel: smile and if the girl behind the desk says hey, be sure and answer back, easy and Southern. Hey.

Remember to ask if there are any messages. Like it's expected that you have friends in this town. So what if you messed up today, it's cool. You're cool. Head for your room before she sees otherwise.

"Mr. Laird," she calls after him.

Is that my name today? "Ma'am?"

Smiling— nice girl, accent from somewhere south of Tara— she waves a plastic bag he doesn't recognize. "You forgot your things."

Today's paperback. Latest *Vanity Fair:* where did I get those? Her fingers brush his and linger; all he can find to say is, "Sorry. Thanks." He checks his watch and is surprised by the time. Distracted, he guesses, heading for his room. No. Absorbed. Bad when you start losing time and don't know where it went. Very bad. If he messed up on an ordinary operation, he'd abort.

This time he can't. He doesn't have the liberty to retool. It takes weeks. You don't just plunge your arm into any old cradle and grab the first thing you find. You research. Background your supplier and your subject. Triangulate. Scan for the chip because you need to be sure the subject is ripe for a rescue; if you accidentally lifted a wanted child, it would be a disaster. This is how disturbed and edgy Starbird is; he never used to think about it. Now he is staring moodily into his laptop without remembering when he opened it, scrolling through hundreds of downloads, making . . .

An advanced search for another match. He skims screen after screen. Makes a wireless connection and goes trolling for more. It's not that he expects to find alternatives, really; he isn't even sure what he's looking for. He just needs the comforting contact with the computer, where what you type is what you get. The cool beauty of the flowchart. The precision of the analog mind.

How long has he been sitting here? He doesn't know. When he looks up his stomach is sour and the light has changed. Sighing, he goes to the window and stares down into the shady street. All the outlines are softened by humidity as moisture rolls in off the salt marshes ahead of the Southern twilight. This part of Savannah is a miracle of restoration, contrived to lull you into believing you're back in the day. Cars crouch in soft shadows, waiting to fade into night. Only the skateboarder with one DayGlo green earphone lifted so he can hear music and still talk on his cell reminds Starbird that this is Savannah now, and not a hundred years ago.

A hundred years ago nobody did what he has to do.

It used to make him feel useful. Now he feels bad. Even if he axes Zorn's parameters and forages for an acceptable substitute— even if he manages to score an infant off the street and pass it off on Zorn and the wife, locating said substitute and prepping for the score is out of the question now. Jake Zorn is one mean motherfucker; he says he's going fucking live with Starbird's fucking mother, and soon. Unless.

Now, Tom Starbird doesn't believe in human sacrifice but if that's how it comes down, OK. He wants Daria Starbird startled and grateful, not reproaching him as Zorn raises his obsidian knife.

If he's discarded everything he knows and agreed to traduce himself, he is doing it to protect her: why? After everything, he has to be the hero to her. If he can't, he's really fucked.

Scary who turns up on your speed dial, like she's tracked you through a dozen cell phones, infiltrating your unwilling heart. Without thinking you hit *call* even though that person is long gone from your life. You don't have time to think: Lady, don't be there. If you have to be there, don't pick up.

"Hello?"

"It's me."

"Call me back, you're breaking up."

"This is a new phone so don't give me that crap."

"What? Who is this?"

She knows who it is, all right. He could hang up now but they haven't had the fight. "Isn't it time you got caller I.D.?"

"Oh." The breathy little lift that surprises him. Like she's almost glad to hear. "Hello Tom."

"Hi Daria." This is one of those women you don't call Mom. It's a category she rejects. In these conversations there's always a three-beat pause after which the woman who bore him usually finds something to say that makes his teeth crack; OK, lady. Let's fight.

"Why aren't you talking?"

"Nothing to say."

"What's the matter, Tom, do you need money?" That wary tone. His last year in high school, he made it necessary for her to ask, but they're a lifetime later. "Are you in jail?"

"Hardly." I am not in high school now. Make her wait.

After a while she says, "Is something the matter?"

"Why would anything be the matter?"

"I don't know. It's just such a surprise."

"What is?"

"You, calling. You haven't exactly been in touch."

And this is the woman who left him bawling in the Star Market parking lot. Four years old. Snot dripping into the snow. His voice is tight. "Just checking in."

"That's a first."

Use silence to smoke her out. He's not sure what's brewing here, but he's trolling. For what? Reasons to cut her off?

"Well, Tom." Polite. "How are you?"

"Look, if you're busy I'll . . ." But he won't. If she doesn't want to talk to him it's up to her to end this conversation. Let her try. Then they can fight.

"No, I'm glad you called."

"Really." There's the outside possibility that she is. It's always this way. Two strangers circling in a mud wrestling pit.

There is another of those awful pauses. "How've you been?"

"Fine, Daria. I'm fine."

"Oh."

Excellent, he is thinking; I know all I need to know. She is just as fucking cold as she ever was. He can end this conversation and go. "Nice talking to you."

"Wait!"

"Ma'am?"

"I have something to tell you." That lilt. Good God she really is glad to hear from him, a fact he can't let himself accept.

"Take care. Talk to you."

"No, wait, Tommy. Wait'll you hear! I'm going on TV!"

Right. Zorn has scheduled the show.

"I love you," she says as he hangs up, the bitch. Binding him tight.

He is definitely a short-timer now.

In ordinary times what happened at the Food King would be a disaster, but when he's delivered and Zorn hands over his Daria Starbird tapes and signs off on the transaction, Tom Starbird can walk free. After this project, he is done. Once he's bought his freedom with this woman's unwanted baby— remember, Newlife is an adoption agency, she's asking for it, baby isn't even chipped— once he's bought his freedom with this *unwanted* baby, he is off the planet. So what if the supplier in this particular operation saw him, he'll make goddamn certain she never sees him again. When he removes the subject she'll be too smoked to remember who helped her at the Food King that day or link that to this. And that overweight punk that he threw out of the parking lot? This could be a plus.

Turn the boyfriend— or stalker, whatever— turn the fat fuck into the big red herring that stinks up a dozen false trails. A woman whose baby disappears has to dial 911 even when she's secretly relieved, so, cool. Let the Savannah cops fan out and tramp through every hamlet between Vidalia and Yemassee. By the time they come up empty, he'll be out of the picture. There will be nothing where he once was. A Starbird shaped hole in the air. *Because*, he thinks— old poem he knows, by an old poet Daria recited instead of talking to him— *because I do not hope to turn again.*

Get in, he mutters. Yes he is psyching himself. Get in and get on with it, get it over with and get out. In spite of the catastrophic glitch.

Watch out, Starbird. You are blocking something, man. The thing that hung you up all day like a computer fixing to crash. *The inconvenience is temporary,* he tells himself, stripping for the shower. *Temporary.* Yeah, right. Like, *Just leave your number and we'll get back to you,* or, *The check is in the mail,* or *We'll keep you on file.* He starts the water and gets in without noticing whether it's pouring down cold or hot enough to peel his skin.

Then the memory he has been fleeing all day swings around and smacks him in the face.

God. He didn't only interface with the mark. They have spoken. Worse. They didn't just talk and that was it. He let her stop him again when he could have gotten away clean and he still isn't sure why. He and the girl have spoken twice. He stands under the spray, thinking. He stands there long after scalding water runs cold.

Fatal error.

Starbird is up against it. If the first encounter didn't damn him, the second one will. He should have taken off after they talked; he should have crunched up onto the divider and driven out over the ornamental plantings, digging ruts in the peat moss as he hit the road. He bought enough time when he sent her running back inside the store: my baby! as if it actually mattered; why didn't he split? He should have roared down the bank and disappeared into four lane traffic or ditched the car and taken off on foot, anything to quit the parking lot before the girl came running back outside, babbling thanks. Shit. What kept him there, was it circumstance or was it sense memory: the feel of her slight body under his hands, the bruised violet eyes? Did she make him so stupid that he wanted to see her again? If he'd mashed a few hedges he'd be OK right now, but like a car thief who makes a point of avoiding even minor infractions during the getaway, he stayed inside the lines.

Like a good camper, he followed the double yellow line around to the exit lane. Twin signs stopped him at the entrance to the Food King. The automatic doors whished open as he hit the brakes. The girl came running out with the baby bobbing in its little ruffled bucket. When he hesitated, she stepped onto the tacky asphalt and all but threw herself onto the hood. She tapped on his window. He pretended not to see.

She was laughing and calling, "Hey. Oh, hey."

Stonewall her, idiot. Drive away.

"Hey, listen."

He pretended not to hear.

"Please?"

He rolled down the window. "What!"

This program has performed an illegal operation.

She leaned in to tell him nothing of any importance. "I just wanted to say. Thanks for that."

"It was nothing." What could he do? He couldn't accelerate or he'd rip her head off. He couldn't roll up the window; she filled the frame.

"Believe me, it was major. I couldn't handle it myself. It's so. He's so . . ." She couldn't explain.

"My pleasure. Gotta go."

"I don't know what I would have done." The way she hung on the car you'd think she was starved for conversation. To make it worse, she looked right at him when she smiled. Pretty girl. It's been a while. A guy gets stupid when a lovely girl smiles at him and God help him she is, and she did. Sweet. "So, thanks and thanks again."

"No problem," he said, stupid and soft as a weenie bun. Fucking idiot, fucking unprofessional. He should have split, but it was the kind of smile you had to return. My God, what if they put him in a lineup and she identifies him by the smile?

Time is liquid now that he has seen her. No. Now that she has seen him. All Starbird's warning lights are flashing. He hears the terminal beep that signals an irrevocable crash.

And will be shut down.

24.

Careful, Tom Starbird. Haste begets folly. Move too fast and no matter how well you know the drill, you are doomed to mess up in at least one respect. This phase of the operation usually takes weeks; he has three days.

In a preliminary maneuver, Starbird is scoping the DelMar. He has been here before, but at his leisure. This time he has to set the game plan. Which approach to use. Which diversionary tactic, the device that will separate the supplier from the subject just long enough for him to slip in for the pickup. He weighs: the credit check that sends the manager down to drag the girl into the office. The power failure. Dummy phone call. False alarm. Unexpected fire. No. Fire trucks. Broken pipe. Too messy. Think.

Calculates: how long she'll feel safe leaving the product alone in the unit. He has to lift the subject out of the crib with the supplier still on the premises— in the restaurant, in the office, down at the ice machine. How long will he have to lie in wait? Add time needed to enter, score and get away. He'll do a dry run with his stop watch. Set the method: good old Domino's delivery trick, he decides. He can slip the subject into the red plastic pizza sleeve. The pickup itself will take seconds. The issue is getting away.

By the time he closes on the DelMar, it's after ten. He wants complete darkness when he walks the perimeter, but it never really gets dark here in the industrial South. The mercury vapor sheen from the freeway, the sodium vapor haze above multiple parking lots and light pollution from the surrounding city turn the night sky an odd pastel. Whatever he does will unfold in a poisonous artificial glow. Starbird is as clever as he is careful. He drives into the sprawling asphalt mall parking lot on the artificial plateau above the DelMar. Shot with green from the mall's fluorescent banner, the layer of smog glows with diffused light.

Even a cartoon superhero would know to beware; the stillness is ominous, the toxic glow is ominous, but omens are a luxury Starbird is too rushed to entertain. His options have narrowed. He cuts the motor and coasts to a stop in a remote corner of the mall. The thousand-car lot is almost empty. Except for the movie theaters, the mall is closed. He trots the quarter mile over asphalt to the stand of pines that separates the raised parking lot from the DelMar, which sits at the bottom of the manmade drop. Quietly, he enters the woods, sliding through dead pine needles and discarded candy wrappers, Styrofoam clamshells and ripped condoms. Where the trees end, the earth drops off. He is at the top of a little embankment overlooking the DelMar. The motel nestles below, two dozen neat units with air conditioners humming in all the windows— all but the one he has identified as hers. So, what? Did somebody tell the girl air conditioning was bad for a newborn? Good situation. Easy access to the window and thick cover, he sees. The back of the DelMar is sheltered by azaleas so dense that they fill the little runoff ditch, swarming the low-slung building like escaped house plants that have grown to tremendous size in the wild.

Lights on, he notes, in a number of the units. Not a full house tonight, but for a dump like the DelMar, as close as it gets. Music coming out of the diner: Johnny Cash. Reflected headlights of cars bounce off the trees overhanging the parking lot as regulars at the DelMar Diner come and go under the pink neon sign. Plenty of people around, which means this is either a bad time or the optimum time to scope the site. He needs to see the room where the girl and this baby have been living since she brought him home from the hospital. No. Quickly, he corrects himself. Never girl and baby,

Starbird. Supplier. Subject. Get a grip! These aren't people now. Not to you. They are no more to you than the means to an end. The product you will turn over to buy your freedom from Jake Zorn.

In spite of his size Starbird is light on his feet. He is swift; if he sees you he can go to earth so fast that you'll never know. Narrowing his body like a diver, he skids down the red clay embankment. Azaleas screen the back windows of the units, but Starbird knows which ones to part to see inside her room. He has, after all, been here before. Approaching, he moves silently. Inside, the supplier and the subject will be asleep. He knows from other surveillance runs that she crashes early most nights. Exhaustion, he supposes. It's the kid. I'm doing her a favor here. He will look in without waking her. He wants to observe the subject and the supplier closely: the configuration of the bodies as they sleep, whether she keeps this one in its crib or whether they are together in her bed, whether her arm is curved around him and a pillow propped to protect him in case she rolls over because she's scared of crushing him. Don't go there, man. Too personal. This is going to be hard.

In fact, Sasha Egan and her baby aren't sleeping inside. They aren't there at all. The unit is empty. Tonight the baby started crying and wouldn't stop. Not sick, exactly, just bitching because something's not right— she doesn't know— is he sick? Is he already getting spoiled? When she couldn't stand it a minute longer, when a disturbance in the bushes outside her window startled her, she wrapped him up and took him across the parking lot to the DelMar diner. She left with the baby before Starbird cleared the woods. By the time he reaches the stand of azaleas outside her window, she's long gone.

Sasha is inside the diner, ordering. She's retreated partly because the baby wouldn't stop crying but mostly because she's a little scared. She heard something outside tonight— crunching in the bushes that was even worse because it stopped. Animal? Intruder? Has Gary followed her here? Is he prowling out there? She can't be sure, but she thinks that this presence, or disruption— this *difference* in their surroundings is what set Jimmy off. He's been crying for an hour. What if a crying baby is like the dog that senses danger before its master, who punishes it for howling when, my God, there are wolves closing on the sledge? If Gary Cargill is really out there— no, if she tells Marilyn she thinks a man is hiding outside her unit, Marilyn will call 911 before she can say, wait. Maybe they can face Gary together, she and the cops, but if the cops call Grandmother . . .

No. Just don't be alone right now. Uneasy, fretful and disrupted, she decides to hang in at the diner until closing. Let Marilyn and the regulars distract Jimmy; by this time she understands her baby well enough to know that when he cries, lights and company sometimes do the trick— anything but her, so fine, let Marilyn handle him; she can even purse that big wet mouth and blow on his feet and cuddle him up, if it will help. Anything, if he'll only stop crying! With the baby depending on her for every little thing and twenty-something stitches beginning to draw and the terrible knowledge that Gary Cargill is in the area, it's the only way she can keep from crying too.

Starbird doesn't know the unit is empty. He proceeds without making a sound. As he approaches the bushes that hide the girl's window, the azaleas stir and flatten like grass in the first gust of an oncoming storm. Snorting and completely unaware that he's not alone here, a dense, misshapen figure blunders out.

Bristling, Starbird falls still. His breathing slows; he seems to exist without moving. An outsider on his turf, who is this? Pervert, marauder, competition, what? No. This is much, much worse. It's the girl's clumsy stalker at the Food King, and he's belching drunk. The kind of drunk who's looking for a fight. On a regular job Starbird would vaporize and come back later, he's good at that, but he has interfaced with the mark on this case, and she hates the guy. He can't forget her eyes when she begged him to help— that lovely, damaged face. He should vanish and come back later but he knows this one. No. The man knows him, and there will be no later.

"What the fuck!" Blinking, the drunk lunges, trailing spit.

"Quiet." Starbird crosses his arms like a ref calling a foul.

It's like trying to stop a wild boar. "Fuck are you, anyway?"

Starbird jams the heel of his hand into the fat drunk and spins him around in mid-charge. "What are you doing here?"

"Fuck you doing here?"

"Shut up. Keep it down!"

"Fuck I will." Gary is loud and clumsy and slimy with sweat and alcohol. He was drunk when he came here and he's drunker now. Grunting, he pushes. "Onna baby!"

"Not tonight."

"Fuck that," Gary says, too loud.

Grimly, Starbird hisses, "Keep it down."

"It's my fucking baby. Wuddiyou, wanna fight?"

"It's not your baby . . ." End this, Starbird. End it fast. Like a dancer with an expert partner, he spins Gary Cargill so suddenly that Gary ends with his fleshy arm twisted behind his fat back and the blade of Starbird's forearm pressed so tightly into his throat that all his breath comes out in a desperate wheeze. Grimly, Starbird finishes, ". . . It's hers. Now, go."

"Fuck right I'm going," Gary gasps, straining for breath. Taut with fury, he hocks up a threat. "'Ma fuck going for the cops!"

Starbird's response is as swift as it is reflexive. Outstripping thought, the arm clenched around Gary's throat shoots out and, fueled by rage, snaps back and, with the compressed power of bone and muscle, smashes into Gary's neck.

Anybody looking out one of the back windows a minute later will see nothing more than two drunks poised at the top of the red clay berm that rises behind the DelMar. They are heading into the strip of scrub pines that separates the motel from the mall parking lot. The heavyset drunk stumbles along with his arm around the tall one's shoulders and the tall man's hand planted firmly on the back of his unsteady partner's fat neck. Too bad about the limp, baggy one, he looks too drunk to walk, has to be dragged. No matter, the other guy will take care of him. The clumsy drunk's tall friend will get him into the car and put him where he belongs. Wherever that is.

There isn't time for Starbird to reflect on what just happened. He has come to a place there is no getting back from. What happens next has to happen fast.

25.

Odd: when Sasha comes back to the room at midnight the air has changed. It's as though some big creature has just moved out. She is at the door with her back stiff and her shoulders high. Squinting like a speed-reader, she skims all the surfaces, but the geometry of small objects has not changed. There's just more space in the room. Wary, she moves inside, alert to signs of intrusion. The stale layer of old smoke and takeout food that hangs in cheap motel rooms is gone. Did Marilyn fix the air conditioning or did Dancy come in and open the window? Maybe it's the silence. No neighbors' TV drumming in the walls, no rattling AC and for once, no baby wailing, the silence is amazing. At the diner Marilyn kept Jimmy in her soft lap until she'd conned him into thinking he had everything he cared about. Now the baby is draped over Sasha's shoulder like a plush puppy with its soft face mashed into her neck, sleeping.

With Jimmy quiet the room seems brighter, somehow. Unless it seems bigger. Once she's satisfied herself that there's nobody hiding here and nothing has changed, Sasha expands. She is getting herself back. *Maybe I'm finally over it,* she thinks. When you've never been sick, a difficult birth rolls into you like an eighteen-wheeler and leaves you weepy and gasping. What the fuck is this? I'm too weak to run, my lungs are so shallow that I can't even yell, am I always going to be like this? Every day Sasha marks signs of progress: last week she only cried once a day, and. Wow.

Today she didn't cry at all. Brilliant! Soon she'll be fit to pack up her stuff and leave. She can strap this baby in his car seat and drive him down to Florida and hand him over to people who know how to place babies: "There." Then she can walk away. Of course she'll snuggle him for a minute before she lets go, so he knows that she's doing this for both their sakes. She'll squeeze him tight so that at some level he'll always remember the feel and smell of her. She'll feed and change him one last time so she can hand him over to the Newlife placement staff in mint condition. Then she can say good-bye for good. Well, maybe until his college graduation, when he's big enough to handle the news: *look, I'm your mom.* He'll be grown and gorgeous and maybe they can be friends. She'll give him her best painting— if she's good enough by then, she may have work hanging in the Whitney or the Modern, so the gift will be worth a few dollars. Graduation present, son. Surprise.

Why is she crying?

I'm not crying, she tells herself. *It's the Air Wick or some damn thing. Thank God I'm strong again, even though the incision burns and I'm still dripping.*

Soon she'll be done here. Nothing can stop her now. And Gary Cargill? Just let him try. As it turns out, she's not alone. Women with babies have friends out there— that nice guy in the supermarket— dark hair, saturnine look broken by a sweet smile that she surprised out of him. If Gary shows his face again, I have an ally. He'll be there, she thinks, even though she knows he won't. Never mind, everybody wants to help a young mother. *Kidnapper,* she'll cry, unless it seems more expedient to cry *rape.* Tomorrow she'll call a lawyer and get a restraining order. Then if Gary follows her she can bring down the entire contents of the fucking Florida State Police barracks on him. *Nobody's going to get my baby. What am I saying? Nobody's going to get between this baby and the nice, grown up, perfect parents that he deserves.*

Why is she still holding him? Carefully, she puts Jimmy down on his back the way conscientious mothers do, no SIDS risk here; never mind that she is no mother and won't have to do this much longer. When her son throws his arms above his head like that they curve like little parentheses. He looks like a Botticelli cherub shouting *Mirabile.* Sasha looks into the tiny, mashed face of this larval human and thinks with a surge of excitement, *Look what I've done. Look at him!*

When you plan to give your unwanted child away, you can't look it in the face for long.

You should try not to look at it at all.

Jimmy wakes twice in the night instead of the usual three or four times; for once he eats readily and drowsy Sasha tends to him so the feeding and sleeping unfold like a gentle dream that lets you wake up fresh. When she opens her eyes it's almost eight A.M. and she feels wonderful, maybe because for the first time since they came home, she hasn't been yanked out of sleep by Jimmy's thin little rabbity squeal. The silence is sublime. For a minute she forgets that she even has a baby. *What does Sasha want to do today?* she wonders, marveling. *What would Sasha like to do?* She yawns and rolls over. Then she sees the crib and, even before the episiotomy sinks its fish hooks in the floor of her body, remembers. *The baby.* It's late, sunlight is coming in and Jimmy isn't crying, what's the matter, he's so still! *Oh my God, what if he's died?*

Panicked, she surges up in the bed, ready to dial 911, seize him and start CPR, whatever it takes— my God, what does it take— when her baby spasms and kicks with one of those atrocious piggy grunts that newborns make because they just remembered where they are and that breathing is a continuing responsibility. Then as her heart stops he settles again. Sleeping. He is just sleeping.

New as Sasha is to all this she knows that when your baby is sleeping hard and well, you don't bother him. Even though part of her wants to shake him awake: "are you all right?" "are you sure you're all right?" the rest of her yields to conventional wisdom. If it ain't broke, don't fix it. Let sleeping dogs lie.

It is like a gift of time. Thank you, my good baby. Sweet! Smiling, she stretches like a patient at the end of a long convalescence. A few more days like this and she'll be fine.

Better, she thinks. *We're getting better.* She feels a hundred pounds lighter this morning, like Edmond Dantes coming out of the Chateau D'If. Strong. Like any prisoner, she emerges feeling leaner, smarter because she has survived. She is definitely on a roll. She lost all autonomy when she got pregnant. Her body took over and sent her rocketing into something she didn't want but refused to stop because. Because what? Not clear. *It isn't just a Catholic thing,* she thinks. It's more profound. Altered by pain, she came out of the hospital diminished. Gradually she's getting back her strength. Soon she'll be strong enough to manage her life. One more night like this, she thinks. Please God, one more night.

Jimmy wakes up and she changes and feeds him and puts him down again with such ease that she hardly notices how much time it takes to maintain one of these demanding, unfamiliar little beings, and if she does notice? No matter. They will be going south soon. Before she puts Jimmy in the car she'll phone Newlife. She wants to confirm that arrangements are in place at the Pilcher home in spite of her defection. When she leaves Jimmy with his real parents and walks away she won't be an unwilling mother any more, she'll be an artist again. Instead of being a garage and filling station for somebody she didn't invite and doesn't know very well, she will be autonomous. All potential, with her best work still ahead.

During her ordeal, Sasha realizes, something fundamental changed. She is before everything an artist, but when she gets back to work it won't be etching or engraving or pulling tiny editions of lithographs. She isn't interested in multiples now. She has, after all, created this unique person. When she was pregnant she thought of him in the abstract as a monotype, a unique print, but even a monotype opens up the possibility of a second printing. In her case this translated to: can always have another baby. Not now, but somewhere down the road. Now she's not so sure. Whoever Jimmy is, he's distinctively himself. The discovery makes her breath catch. The next one will be nothing like him.

She is too pressed and confused to think it through, but she is coming to a decision. She can't spell it out. Instead, the decision she makes arrives couched in terms of her work. She is done with multiples. The bigger the print run, the less the value. It may take years to learn and longer to be any good at it but Sasha is committed now. Everything she does from here on out has to be one of a kind. She will paint.

Marilyn comes with a half-dozen doughnuts, a sweet ending to a morning that began well. Smiling, the plump proprietor opens the box: honey dips dripping with glaze, jelly doughnuts and iced crullers, which they are supposed to split although Sasha can only eat one and Marilyn will scarf up all the rest. She has brought flowered paper napkins and Frappuccinos so it looks like a party. Some women turn into fools when there's a baby around and now that Sasha has let her hold him, Marilyn is hers forever.

She says, all by-the-way, "Did you hear the noise?"

Sasha turns with her face flaked with sugar. "When?"

"Last night."

"What kind of noise?"

"Don't know." Straddling the desk chair like a Valkyrie in equestrian position, Marilyn disappears another cruller. "A couple of people complained."

"When was it?"

"Don't know. I sure didn't hear it."

"Maybe we were still at the diner."

"Maybe." Marilyn wipes confectioner's sugar off her upper lip. The smear of raspberry jam on her lycra top matches her lipstick.

"What do you think it was?"

"Maybe it was nothing."

Nervously, Sasha reaches for another doughnut. "Maybe so."

"These things," Marilyn says. "You never know."

Oh shit, just when I was beginning to like it here. "We didn't hear it," Sasha says, willing it to go away.

"Me neither."

"After we went to bed we didn't hear a thing," she repeats. "Jimmy only woke up twice, and look at him."

The carton has floated onto the end of the bed and Marilyn has to lurch to her feet to seize a frilled honey dip. "Sleeping like an angel."

Something creeps up Sasha's ribs like a set of disembodied fingers. "Or a stone."

"So cute."

"Is it OK when they sleep this hard?"

Marilyn glances into the crib. "Don't worry, he's just growing. Being a baby is hard work."

"He is, isn't he? Growing." This makes her smile.

"He's definitely filling out." Marilyn's cheeks are as pink and full, like Jimmy's. "Sweet thing. Nice and fat."

He is. When she got him, Jimmy's legs and arms were like sticks but in just three weeks he's begun to look a lot more like a baby than he did when they cleaned him up and handed him to her. Sasha was scared she'd squash him or accidentally fall on him before they cleared the hospital. She was afraid he'd shrivel up like a butterfly cracked out of the cocoon too early. Now he's getting fat and she's learning how to take care of him. Whatever he is right now is because of her. Sasha is too sensitive to her position to get wrapped up in this project, but she's pleased. It is a mistake to invest any ego in a person she's about to give away, but Marilyn's right. Her baby does look snug in the crib. Clean and snug and for the moment, satisfied. Well kept. "I guess he is."

"I love a fat baby."

"Do you think he's too fat?"

"Just right, I'd say. You're doing a good job."

"Do you think so?"

"Didn't I just say so?" Marilyn advances on the crib. "Didn't I tell you that you'd just love being a mom? When they're little and easy and need you, it's the happiest time of your life. Isn't it? The happiest time of your life?"

Sasha can't answer.

"Sweet thing. Isn't he adorable!"

"I guess he is." She manages to sound diffident but she is thinking: *At least I did something right.* It crosses her mind that the good-bad feeling she has right now needs some examination. *Hey,* she thinks, surprised. *Nobody says I have to give him away.* Marilyn doesn't give her time to think through to: *I could always keep him.* With her fleshy upper arms flapping, Marilyn bends over the crib.

"Hello, sweet thing. Is he always this pink?"

Sasha moves to intercept her. "Don't wake him up." She means: Don't you dare touch my baby.

Smirking, Marilyn thrusts her hand into the crib. "He feels a little hot to me."

"Oh my God."

Marilyn snatches Sasha's baby before she can stop her. He jerks awake. His arms fly out and he opens his throat in that poor little hurt-bunny squeal. "Wow, he's like a little furnace." Marilyn sniffs. "And the smell!"

"Don't!"

"Pheeewie!" She peels the diaper anyway. "Look at that. Just smell the sick."

"Give him here."

There is a wet, blarching sound. "Ewww! Poor little thing's got diarrhea, listen at him! He's running like a sieve."

"I said, give him here!"

She doesn't bother to phone the pediatrician. She takes him into the office. "Don't worry," the doctor tells her after the nurse takes pity and pulls her out of the dismal, packed waiting room, "if this doesn't work we'll get him into the hospital."

Never. Why can't she explain? There are just too many reasons. "Oh please, not the hospital."

"Don't worry, we won't admit him if we don't have to, I don't abuse newborns unnecessarily."

"What do I have to do?"

"Just be careful he doesn't dehydrate. Keep him hydrated and if he doesn't improve, there are a couple of other things we can try. If nothing else works, I'll meet you at the E.R. day or night and we'll get an I.V. into him."

The next few hours are hard. *To cure a baby of diarrhea you have to starve him:* Dr. Spock. Ice chips. Liquid, all she can give him is Pedialyte cut with water and even that won't stay down, until it does she can't start him on a soy-based formula. It is an odd night, so filled with desperate worry, terrible misgivings and Jimmy's misery that Sasha will register but not process the message that came in while she was on the far side of Savannah waiting for the pediatrician to assure her that Jimmy isn't going to die. Which he won't if he'll just stop vomiting the Pedialyte which, weeping, she coaxes into him quarter ounce by torturous quarter ounce.

Is this normal? The doctor will know. She picks up the phone to a series of buzzes. She can't call out until she clears this fucking voice message. How long has the phone message light been on, did the doctor call while she was on her way home from his office? God, what if he left important instructions and she's doing this wrong because she was too stupid to pick up? Trembling, she punches the code. Shit, it's Marilyn: *"Honey, a man phoned here. He said don't worry, your boyfriend's gone for good. Your baby's sick, honey, at least give his poor daddy a chance."*

"Shut up, Marilyn. Shut up!"

It takes the doctor's service forever to pick up. They put her on hold forever. There is another long interval before the doctor calls back. Sasha is desperate, rocking the baby and murmuring into his ear as she frames a pact. "Be OK, please, baby. I'll do anything you want if you'll just be OK." *My fault, oh God this is all my fault for trying to do this on my own oh God, I should have stayed at the goddamn home. Or taken him back to Grandmother. At least she'd know what to do. I have no right to keep this baby, I love him and I don't know what to do for him.* Wrenched by unexpected grief, she resolves: *I can't take care of him. Oh God if you'll just make him better I promise, I'll give him to somebody who can.* For now, Jimmy's stopped twisting in pain. He is sobbing in his sleep. Weeping, she puts him down.

By the time the doctor calls back with a prescription, Sasha is too upset to think about anything but picking it up. What is she going to do about Jimmy? He's too sick to go out and she has to get this new stuff for him. Miracle suppositories that will stop the vomiting, the doctor said, available at the all-night pharmacy now; if she can get one of these into him it will melt and quiet his insides before he can spasm again and push it out. Thank God he's asleep. Every time he wakes up he goes off at both ends so she's terrified of waking him up. There's been a fever. He's too little to leave and far too sick to take. Marilyn, she thinks. I'll take back everything I said about you. She phones and phones the manager's unit, sobbing, but she can't rouse her even when she goes up to the apartment and bangs on the door. Behind her in the dark motel, Jimmy is sick as hell but safe in his crib. Suppositories, she is supposed to save his life with suppositories. My God. Why didn't the doctor tell her this afternoon, was he afraid she'd freak and overdose her child? Hell yes she complained. "He's a very small baby," the doctor explained tonight before stumbling back to bed. "And you're a new mother. These things are very strong." Shave half a suppository down to a sliver as instructed, he told her, it just might do the trick. Yawning, he added, "And if it doesn't, take him to the E.R. I'll meet you at the E.R. in the morning, before I start my rounds."

God she hates to leave him. God she has no choice. She deleted Marilyn's voicemail but she has registered it. Somebody out there— the cute guy from the market?— somebody wants her to know that Gary Cargill is gone. Gary is gone and Jimmy is sleeping, the place is locked, she has to go! She'll be away for thirty minutes, tops. Away. It makes her sick to think about it. Sasha Egan doesn't pray, but right now she is praying. "Please God," she murmurs, locking the sliding windows and securing them with a stick. "Please God please God, please God." Going out, she tries the knob twice after she slams the door and in a fit of protective madness pushes the city's huge plastic recycling containers one by one in front of the unit door.

It's almost four A.M. The streets (thank God?) are empty at this hour. She loses five minutes when she takes the wrong turn but thank God it will take five minutes less to get home to Jimmy now that she knows what she did wrong. The drug store is right where the doctor said it would be. It looks deserted but an inside light is on and in spite of her fears, a bright-eyed teenager in crisp white comes to the door as soon as she rings the night bell.

The pharmacist turns out to be the holdup. Old. Stupid. Maddening. He looks at her over the high counter at the back of the store, paddling through a stack of prescription slips.

"If Dr. Drinan really phoned this in I sure don't have a record of it."

"Of course he did! I just spoke to him."

"I don't see it." As if she's trying to put something over on him.

"Don't you have it in the computer?"

He scowls. "Why would I do that?"

"He said he would call!"

"Well, nobody called. Toby, did you take any calls?"

"No sir."

"It's suppositories. For my baby!"

"And it's supposed to be . . ."

She names the product. "Please, I can't leave him alone."

He pushes up his glasses and rubs his eyes like an old person who can't process what you are saying. "How old is your baby?"

"Three weeks."

"What does he weigh?"

She guesses. "Nine pounds."

"And you want to use *these* on him?"

"I have to, it's urgent." Hurry, old man. "Nothing works!"

"Ma'am, I don't know."

"What?" She's ready to vault the counter and choke him. "What!"

The old man is still rubbing his goddamn eyes. "For a three-week-old it's a very strong drug."

"He's very sick."

"I don't think Dr. Drinan would . . ."

"He did."

"Well, I'll just have to see about that."

"Call the service! The number is . . ."

"One minute. Now, if you'll just wait here."

He goes into the back leaving Sasha in stasis, trembling and determined not to cry. When he comes back with the handset Sasha seizes it from him and punches in the number. The service picks up on the tenth ring. She shouts, "Don't put me on hold!" They listen. Desperate, she rages at the pharmacist, "They don't have a record, they have to call the doctor and wait for him to call us back."

The pharmacist is sucking his tooth.

Frantic, she trusts the phone at him. "You talk to them."

"No need." Crafty old bastard, did he think she was going to boil these things and find some way to get high? After all this he takes the handset, flicks it off and says, "Now simmer down. They know you. Consider it verified."

Once she has the damn things, the real terror sets in. How long has she been gone? What if Jimmy threw up while she was out and choked on it, or dehydrated and went into convulsions while she was driving across town, what if he woke up and needed her and got scared? What if something awful happened to him while she was trapped here in the washed-out fluorescent light waiting for the prescription that can save his life? Either or. Is this what life and death matters come down to? Either or?

Driving back to the DelMar takes less than five minutes but in five minutes a baby can wake up filthy and screaming, he can cry so hard that he vomits and chokes to death on it; in five minutes a baby can stop breathing simply because you aren't around, sometimes he can stop breathing when you're there and there is nothing you can do about it or, God, he can wake up all cured and then get so scared because you've left him all alone that he'll cry and cry and keep on crying so hard that he gets sick all over again.

She jumps out of the car almost before it stops rolling. Sobbing, she starts shoving the trash bins away from the door, did she really think plastic barricades would protect her child? Does she hear him crying? What if he's too weak to cry? Has something awful happened to him? Terrified, she vows never to leave him again.

Everything goes wrong the way it does when urgency runs up on the heels of reason: the bins are hard to move. Crippled by haste she drops her keys, drops the prescription, feels her purse squirt out from under her tightly clamped elbow as she bends to pick it up. The simplest operations confound her. Like an exercise in stop-motion photography she watches her hand thrusting the key at the lock first this way, then that until finally she wrenches the door open and hurries in and thank God the baby is right where she left him, in place and sleeping quietly with that little pigeon breast going up and down, up and down and when she doubles over the crib and sniffs. The sick smell is gone. The diarrhea has stopped.

It's a long time before her trembling stops.

It's an even longer time before she can rest. Jimmy wakes naturally and she changes and feeds him— Pedialyte and the soy milk formula the doctor sent her away with, after which she puts him down quickly so he won't feel the strength draining out of her, pats him in place and crashes, limp with relief.

26.

By the time Sasha wakes up it's late and they both feel better. Amazing how fast babies recover. By early evening Jimmy is himself again, but she needs to be sure he's OK to travel. Nice man, the doctor calls. Unusual in the twenty-first century, although Sasha's too new at this to know it; the pediatrician's a Southern gentleman in the deep South, where this kind of thing still happens.

"Yes," she says. "He seems to be fine."

"Then you want to start him back on Enfamil," he says. "And bring him in tomorrow so I can look him over."

"Oh, please!" Yes, she means. Yes and thank you. But, Enfamil. In her rush to get Pedialyte on her way back from his office yesterday she forgot to buy formula.

"Enfamil," he repeats. "The sooner he's back on his regular diet, the better. Give him a day and then let me look at him. As it is," he adds, alerting Sasha to a fresh problem, "there are a couple of things we've overlooked."

"Enfamil." She has to get off the phone! "I'll see to that!"

She can't go back to this doctor, she realizes. He knows this baby hasn't been chipped. Chill, lady. Just keep him well. Fine, but how? In the anxiety and confusion that roll in when a new baby gets sick for the very first time, she's run out of formula. In addition, her squirting baby went through so many Huggies and packages of wipes that she's almost out. Worried, she jumps up and in the next second, giddy and reeling— when did she last eat?— sits down hard. They need supplies. It's raining. She can't take a sick baby out in this, but she can't let him starve. In the way of new mothers she thinks dutifully that she has to give Jimmy exactly what the doctor orders. She can't take him out— he's had a fever!— and she's vowed never to leave him alone again. Rummaging, she finds a lone bottle of Enfamil in the bottom of the mini-bar. "It's going to be OK," she tells Jimmy, even though she knows this bottle is the last. "It really is."

Moving like a long-distance wader, she burps her baby and changes him and pats him down in bed.

"Start with the food," she says aloud, as though the words will bring order. Troubled, she steps out into the blond, slick light of a rainy Georgia afternoon. She is looking for Marilyn, whom she sees framed in the office window at the far end of the block of units. Thunderclouds merge. It starts to pour and the motel parking lights flash on.

For whatever reasons, the call angers Marilyn. "In spite of what you might think," she yells, "I can't just drop everything and come down there. I have a business to run."

"I'm sorry, I just." Sasha manages not to cry on the phone, but it's a good thing Marilyn can't see her face. "The baby's been sick and I'm out of formula."

Wrong tactic. "Honey, he was sick and you didn't tell me? I thought we were friends!"

"I'm sorry, I was upset." She elaborates: out of formula, out of Huggies and the DelMar hand towels are rubbing all the skin off his bony backside. "Oh, Marilyn, can you come down and watch him just for a minute while I pick up these things?"

"Can't it wait a while?"

"I have to get them before he wakes up. If I don't, he'll get . . ."

"Sick," Marilyn says sullenly. "You should have told me."

". . . sick again."

"Oh, that poor baby. You should of taken better care of him."

"Oh Marilyn, please!"

"OK. I should be done here soon."

"Thanks," Sasha says. She doesn't have a choice. Marilyn's the only person she knows here, except for Delroy. Behind Sasha, Jimmy stirs; she just put him down so he should be good for an hour, but at three weeks you never know. "What time do you think?"

"I already said! Two minutes."

At quarter to six Sasha opens the door and sticks her head out; why is she surprised that Marilyn's not anywhere? She phones, but the phone is on the machine. Probably so she can come down here for a few minutes as she promised, to keep an eye on Jimmy, right? *Just in the back getting her things,* she tells herself. *She'll be down in just another minute.*

At six she is on borrowed time, pacing to the door and back every two or three minutes until on her last pass she sees Marilyn's fat little boy kicking a soccer ball in the parking lot. Shameless, she opens the door wide and waves. "Hey, Delroy."

"Hey."

"You want an. Uh. A cruller?"

In seconds, he is hers, sitting on the desk chair with his cheeks filled and his stubby legs sticking out. "It's pretty old."

"It's all I've got. Listen, do you know where your mother is?"

"Momma? Yep, she's up there with some guy but . . ." Ripping through the stale cruller he clears his mouth and says, "Oh, right, she said run down here and tell you she'll be just a bitty minute."

"When was that?"

"Before."

Behind her Jimmy stirs. If he wakes up now, what the hell is she going to feed him? If he starts crying he'll spasm, she thinks, and go shooting off at both ends. "Delroy, I need a big favor."

That mean, narrow look: "I can't."

"Ten dollars?"

"You going at the mall?"

She nods. Because he's still weighing it she says, "Twenty."

"Plus Kentucky Fried Chicken," Delroy says. "The bucket."

"Fine. I need you to stay here with the baby until your mama comes."

"Plus corn muffins," he says. "And a quart of butter becan."

"Butter what? Oh, pecan." Wallet, she thinks. Wallet and coupons on the formula and the Huggies. "I'll be back in ten minutes. Don't let anybody in and if anything happens, get your mother down here." Car keys. Check the back window. *Oh, don't cry, Jimmy. Stay asleep and please don't cry.*

"OK. And get me one of them apple pies," he says. "And also too one of the cherry ones."

"Anything you want, but you take care of my baby, you hear?"

Sasha is moving so fast now that she won't see the little distortion of the face that's supposed to be a smile but always goes awry. "Oh yes Ma'am."

"Until your mother comes," she says, but she thinks to call Marilyn's unit to seal the deal. With her hand over the mouthpiece she says, "And if you don't do a good job I will murder you."

This time Marilyn picks up. She is flustered and breathing hard. Checking an imaginary watch. "Oooh sorry, it's later than I thought. Be right down, I swear. Two minutes, tops."

In the Food King Sasha darts to the baby section and scores the necessaries, wishing she'd run into that nice guy from the other day; she needed a hand with the errands right now. Delroy expects brand name ice cream and brand name fried chicken. Well, he can go to hell. That nice guy. Did she imagine she saw his car in the Food King parking lot? Department of wishful thinking, right? Not eating makes you stupid and you start seeing things you only wish you saw. Another time she'd go back outside and scope the lot in case. Strange town, God knows she could use a friend, but she has to get back. Jimmy will be fine with Marilyn, but she's worried all the same.

———

Broad daylight, practically. Well, the end of it. Busy street, lots of traffic at the motel, customers in the diner, plenty of people around, Marilyn in the office pinning up her back hair and fluffing up her breasts under the flowered top before she tucks the master key in the cuff of her One Size Fits All knee-highs and ambles down to the Egan unit with her neck still flushed from good sex with the spring water supplier, her regular, and uses her master key because Marilyn is the manager and the manager doesn't have to knock. Blowzy, sleek and confident she rolls in, letting the words spill into the room ahead of her, "Oh you sweet baby, you just come to Mama Marilyn, you sweet baby thing."

Marilyn won't find the baby in Sasha's room, nor will she find the neatly lettered card propped up on the bedside table; she isn't that concerned. "Huh," she says, backing out of the unit and closing the door, only slightly disappointed to find it empty. "She musta took him." Love to pick up that sweet baby and snuggle him, a treat for him after that twitchy mother with her undersized front, but hey, it's almost time for the Nightly News and she has other fish to fry. "All that fuss and she took him with her after all."

When Sasha gets back— it was only twenty minutes!— when Sasha gets back from the market with everything Jimmy needs and supermarket chicken and generic ice cream for Delroy, she won't find the baby in her room either. She won't find him up in the diner or propped up in the sand pit out back while Delroy digs for quarters, now that the rain has stopped. She won't find him in the diner and she won't find him in the manager's office and she won't find him kicking his pink mouse feet in the apartment upstairs with Marilyn tickling him on her quilted, ruffled bed. She won't find him at all. The only thing she does find is a note that strikes instant paralysis even as it seals her into its own little prison and shuts off all the exits. Although she picks it up, she doesn't see it, really. Rather, she sees but does not comprehend. Throwing it down, she runs outside shouting, "Delroy!"

Block lettering in black ink on an index card, symmetrical, firm and oddly beautiful— who? That child, she thinks. Please let it be that fucking child:

HE'S SAFE.
TELL NO ONE.

That fucking child, fobbing her off with a note. *Like you think I won't tell your mother on you.* More angry than worried, she screams, "Delroy!"

Four
The Transaction

iv.

*P*oor baby!
    When Daria chose a father for her baby, she did not ask a poet. With her long history of alarms and distresses, her psychiatrist warned her not to get pregnant at all. She was too volatile. After all, he said, playing to her ego, aren't you an artist? Validated, she beamed.
    An artist who **will** be remembered.
    The doctor frowned. "At what cost?"
    "I have to do this." Daria's eyes blazed. Why did she imagine a baby would free her work? "I need a child!" She was blocked; critics said her verse was pretty, but empty. What could possibly be missing? The answer came to her in a night vision. With a baby, she would soar. Nothing Dr. Furman said or did could stop her. She was herself again by that time, after the trouble at Yaddo— not such a bad breakdown, really, she was only a little tremulous, sobbing and gnawing her knuckles because the words wouldn't come. Doctor, fragility is written into the job description, look at Emily Dickinson.
    From infancy Daria had it beaten into her: **You are special.** It is her job to measure up so, fine. **Make me proud.** She can, she is a poet. She will, Doctor, don't you see? No more flameouts for Daria Starbird, let her out. Let poetry set souls on fire. Long after her body turns to ash her work will live, and, God, so will the baby you advised her not to have! In spite of her psychiatrists' warnings she

went ahead. She knew he'd have her wit and what was, back then, her beauty; a handsome face just like hers. Of course he'd be a boy. Her love and her solace, her muse and her best friend! She would be the shining center of his world, what more does any poet want? At the end he would be there to bring home her prizes, to collect her verse and edit her private papers, so the world would know how brilliant she was and how hard it had been. Life was untidy, her critics cruel, but never mind. With a baby to complete her, every-thing would come down the way it should.

I am doing this for my work.

To make sure she got pregnant, she went off her medication. **Yes, doctor, I know what you are thinking,** *she wrote to Dr. Furman: words written to be read in classrooms long after she was gone.* **Great work comes out of volatile minds. Don't worry. I will find a strong, capable father to take care of us.**

She began the search. The father would be older. Grounded in something practical, an organized, affluent, well made man who would love her above all. Let him look after her baby's physical needs while she took custody of his soul. In the end she got neither. When she told Peter Gavian she was pregnant she thought he would be happy and honored. They were, after all, complementary, she and Peter. Rock and song bird. She was offering the man every-thing she had— her talent and his strength blended in a grand ex-periment, no strings, who wouldn't be glad? Instead he wrote her a check and gave her hell for being so careless. Strange, within the week the oil company he worked for transferred him to the home office in Singapore.

She was forty years old.

Having a baby was harder than she thought. Keeping one was impossible. Daria thought that once she had her baby everything would change, she would stop gnawing at her vitals and suffering over every word; the verse would flow. Sure. Women friends brought presents, but nobody warned her. Why didn't they tell her what it would be like? Why didn't they stop this before it ever got started, tie her down until the feeling passed? The learning process broke her in two. She loved the baby. She did, but he was nothing she could reason with; when she held him he cried, when she fed him he refused. He never slept. When she put him to bed and sat down with her notebook, he shrieked, he shat, he needed! If she didn't help him he would die. This opened a circle of vulnerability like another circle of hell. What if something awful happened to him? The responsibility overturned her. Just having him in the house shattered her concentration. Didn't God know she was an artist? Did she have to do this too? Why didn't somebody help? She couldn't think. She couldn't think! She couldn't work; she couldn't sleep; after a while she couldn't manage to feed herself, all she did was tend to him. Again. Again. The job never stayed done. The endlessness sent her into a spiral. One desperate night she sat down with her notebook listing alternatives, scribbling and scratching out until she came up with a plan. She printed it at the top of a new page, in big block letters. It seemed like a good plan. Reasonable.

Later Dr. Furman told her that when she tried to hand the baby off to the attractive, astonished couple in the Quincy Market, she was suffering from postpartum depression.

At the time it seemed right! At the time in her condition it was inevitable. Get up. Dress the baby nicely, anyone can see he is extremely pretty even though to you he is like kudzu, blind growth stifling your creativity. Put him in the backpack you bought because you thought you would enjoy long walks with him, back before you knew. Explain, even though he listens without understanding. Go.

They rode all the way downtown on the T.

The rest is confusion. All she remembers is sitting on the curb sobbing until they came and took care of her, whoever they were. Winter. Both times it happened in the winter because for a poet, winters are the worst, remember poor Sylvia, only a little older than me. It was days before she asked who had the baby— name? She thinks she was holding him on her lap after she gave up trying to hand him off and plopped down. By that time she was at the Riggs Clinic. Located in Hong Kong, Peter paid. Imagine, the Riggs Clinic. She felt singular. Honored. Some of America's major poets did time there; she smiled through tears at Dr. Furman when the clinic called him in for a consultation and he came.

"Excuse me, Doctor, don't you think I'm in good company? Anne Sexton was here, I think, and I think Robert Lowell, and I don't think she ever came here, but Sylvia Plath, see, Sylvia Plath had a breakdown too. I'm in extremely good company, can you see what I'm saying here? Every great artist pays a great price."

He gave her a tight, gray smile and left her to the staff psychiatrists. "You have my best wishes," he said in a formal, almost rabbinical way. "Take advantage of this gift of time."

Thank you, doctor. Without the baby screaming she could write! At Riggs she started a verse cycle but she couldn't think. She blamed the baby but by that time he was in other hands. It had to be the meds. Hospitals, the good thing about hospitals is, they're safe. The bad? They rehabilitate you. They rehabilitate you and turn you back into the world. When she left Riggs she had a new set of coping skills. She also knew touch typing. On her next visit they would offer courses in computer skills, but at the time nobody predicted a next visit since everything Daria said and did led them to believe she was cured. Clever girl. Forty-two, but girl. No worry wrinkles or laugh lines on this soul.

At discharge they supplied meds that smoothed the sharp edges but unfortunately kept her from seeing clearly, which meant that as long as she took four pills a day she felt fine but her vocabulary was scattered and her perceptions blurred. They also referred her to a clinic-endorsed agency for a reassuringly undemanding job. If Daria managed well, they said, she would have her baby back within the year. They never asked whether she wanted him. You are expected to want the child you willed into existence, doesn't everyone? She never told them otherwise. It was like a death sentence, division of death of the soul: Do well and you'll have him back. She did, and she did. To all intents and purposes she was cured.

Not so bad when he was very small and spent most of his waking hours in daycare, but the weekends were hard. He was always there. She looked forward to Mondays but of course at the office she had no time for poetry. No space in her head for half-formed verses to take shape. Bitterly, she saw other poets half her age winning prizes while she coped, but at least she coped.

Winter, these psychic breaks always came in the winter, and only in the years before the child got old enough to understand the rules, after which they coexisted. When he was big enough to understand, she and the boy revolved in the tall house like Paolo and Francesca or orbiting satellites that pass repeatedly but never touch. That last bad winter he was home with the flu. It dragged on for weeks. She had to take off work to take care of him. They were together all the time. The child rattled around the house all day when she most wanted to hide in her work. She couldn't write. She couldn't think! She did what she had to, to get back her concentration, because art matters more than life. She went off her meds.

Daria changed but he was the same. He was there, he was always there! With the drugs cleared out of her system she was exhilarated and tense; every interruption sank claws into her belly, every sound magnified; all her perceptions were heightened, the suffering was acute and the verse still didn't come. She tried. She did! Since they were trapped together she sat the child down and read her work aloud to him, what little she had. She read to him thinking, **if I read to you, the least you can do is listen, I need audience.** *He tried to pay attention, but what could he say when she battered him with questions? This word, Tommy, or this one? This rhyme scheme? When he couldn't answer she fretted. Every night after soup and canned biscuits she tried again. He was four, she thinks. She had to read; how else could she prove that she was a poet? She'd read to him and then she'd ask questions; Tommy was desperate to please her but he always said the wrong thing; she should have stopped but she had to keep going and by the end they were both howling with grief.*

It was the vulnerability that destroyed her, she thinks. She doesn't know whether she means hers, or his.

Either way, it was impossible.

When the couple at Star Market wouldn't take him she blew

apart; she doesn't remember much, just the child blubbering in the cold wind and her hand flying out somehow, before she fled in a sleetstorm of tears. She left in a cab; she saw Tommy standing behind her in the snowy parking lot— she can't remember, was there blood? Four years old. With Peter writing checks from Jakarta, they kept her at the Riggs Clinic for a year. Electroshock therapy this time. This time in the exit interview they did more than question. They grilled her. Like any prisoner, Daria said what you do, to convince them she was well enough to go free. Last time she felt protected in the hospital; this time there was electroshock. Rude. Violent. Extreme. They strapped her to the table and put the rubber guard in her mouth and hit the switch; it hurt! She would have promised anything to get away. She dressed carefully for the exit interview. Made a smile. Sweetly, she agreed that she and her therapists had worked hard and that the electroshock had, if not cured her, thoroughly rearranged her. For the better, she assured them, exaggerating the smile. She agreed that she was a new person and together they planned her life after the release. This time they offered her a new kind of freedom: the child was happy enough in the home where they'd placed him, the foster parents wanted to adopt but. Chronic A student that she was, Daria knew what she was expected to say. She protested with tears in her eyes and they gave her what they thought she wanted. They gave him back. Home visits, of course, from the hospital social worker, who would find everything as it should be although for Daria it was a tremendous effort, pursuing her hopes with the clumsy intruder in her house.

Job as receptionist in a women's clinic, to keep her grounded.

For the first few weeks after her release she thought she could be herself even with the job. She wrote poetry at night. She was like a moth, blindly following the flame around the house— the idea for her greatest work— and this is the sad, truest thing about Daria Starbird: every time she sat down she imagined that this was her masterpiece. This, that she was doing now. She'd fret for hours. Then in a flash she'd see the finished poem shimmering, unformed but beautiful. Just then the boy would scuttle past on his way to the bathroom or kitchen— shit, did I forget to feed you?— with that agonized, apologetic grin and it would evaporate. There was no getting it back. Trying, she bore down so hard that her ballpoint ripped the first sheet and she'd tear it out and go on, with that star-shaped crack in her concentration, as if the child had smashed it with a rock. **Oh, it's you.** *Hurrying past with his elbows tight to his sides, like a polite stranger in her house.*

How could she think with him lurking with that needy little frown, willing her to look up and speak to him?

When he went away to school they were both relieved.

Well, everything is going to be different now. Her boy is a finished product out on his own. He's a success in the world. Handsome, she knows, from the snapshots. They don't see each other but he has kept in touch. Cards on her birthday. Presents at Christmas. The checks, which are sizeable. His way of letting her know that he is doing very well at his job. And didn't he call the other day?

He couldn't have phoned at a better time.

Just as Daria is getting some recognition, with the promise of more to come; didn't the producer tell her this TV show would make her name a household word? Interesting, she thinks, how the conversation with Jake Zorn opened up during their second meeting. He would do the show on resources for women in the Boston area, of course, but he was more interested in her! It was sheer luck that she was also a major poet. He was making her the subject of a Zorn Extra, in a sidebar dedicated to her work. She agreed to the interview after he promised to let her open the discussion with a reading of "Torn Hopes," an early poem that may be her best.

Fortuitous, she thinks, that Tom called when he did. She takes it as a sign. Of course they had a hard time talking, they always do, but that will change. Daria is coming into her own now that he is grown. They've never known each other very well but now that he is successful and no longer needs her, that will change!

Coming home from the studio, she was excited. She seldom thought about Thomas but she was thinking, how wonderful it would be for him to see this! Now he isn't the only success in the family; her work is getting the attention it deserves. How wonderful it would be if he'd join her on the show— foolish hope, she knows, because Tom is too important to travel on the spur of the moment, too many commitments, he must be working for the government, everything he does is so hush hush.

So she was thinking about him even before he called— handsome now, with her coloring and her features, and although they don't see each other very much she thinks they are a good match. She must not have done such a bad job after all. Now that her day is coming, it would be nice have him here with her in the light. She is planning a rapprochement because he does love her, she thinks. And in spite of the trouble he caused as a baby, she certainly loves him. The secret, greedy part of Daria sees herself going out on this handsome boy's arm; she looks so young that nobody has to know he's her son. Who wouldn't want to walk into a party on Tom Starbird's arm? He can come to all her poetry readings, after this TV show the invitations will come pouring in. She'll be a poet again. She'll be reading to hundreds but she'll be reading for Tom, watching his face shine as the words flow into him. Then he'll know what it was all about, the suffering they went through for the sake of her art. And when the applause has died and she's signed all the nice people's books she and Tom will sit down over drinks, and they can finally say all the things to each other that they should have said. They love each other but all their conversations go sour.

Naturally Daria was excited when he called. She should have led with the good news but when Tom calls she answers with a tinny edge to her voice. It frightens her because she can't control it and she doesn't comprehend the source. All her responses sound artificial, like computer generated speech. He must have caught it because he couldn't tell her why he'd called. Daria tried to open the conversation, but, God! Patterns: after a flurry of false starts she blurted, "What's the matter, do you need money?"

"Is that all you can think of to say?"

They have never known how to talk to each other, she and Thomas. Had to start somewhere, she thinks. She tried! She did, but he kept asking stupid questions. Making stupid silences. An extension of the long dialog that is their life. She had to turn the conversation somehow. Excitement made her clumsy and instead of leading in gracefully, with an invitation, she blurted: "Tommy, I'm going on TV." What's the matter, was he too distracted to read the subtext? **After all these years my time has come.**

She thought he would be more excited. She'll never understand. He should be proud.

They should be friends!

27.

Marilyn Steptoe meant to get down to Fourteen to check on the girl's baby, she did promise, but things happen when you manage an establishment like the DelMar, diner attached even though Elwood is managing it. You get busy with one of the suppliers. The sweet cracker who brings in spring water once a week, this Todd! Frankly she was pissed when Sasha phoned to ask her because she and Todd were practically You Know, couldn't the girl tell the difference between good times and bad times to interrupt? She picked the exact moment to phone when Todd was making up his mind whether he and Marilyn would start seeing each other regular; Marilyn could see him thinking about it while he pulled on his socks. It was the give-or-take moment when things can go one way or the other, very delicate, one nudge in the wrong direction and your whole arrangement will go screw-jee and you're fucked. Doesn't the stupid thing know how hard things are for a divorced girl over thirty, never mind that she's put on a little weight? So what? She dresses nicely. She knows how to please a man.

With Todd in her bedroom Marilyn does what she has to, to get out of this in one piece. She makes promises. To both of them.

"Half hour, honey, be there at five, five-thirty tops," she says, pulling Todd into her circumference, like one of those suns around Saturn or something; if you want to know how to generate heat, you just ask Marilyn. On a good day she can pull any man back into the soft and the warm; all right, they both got excited and she lost track of the time. Nothing lost today, in the sack she and Todd are getting down to where it might add up to something, and the girl? Frankly, Marilyn is a little pissed. She thought they were girlfriends and now it turns out all this Sasha sees when she looks at Marilyn is *babysitter,* well she can go to hell. Damn girl has been at the Del-Mar for weeks now and frankly, old tenants have a way of getting stale, whatever she wants, it'll keep.

After Todd leaves for real, but with a smile that just might be interpreted as loving, she dresses and goes down to Sasha's unit in a generous mood. She might as well take over for a little bit. Let the poor thing out for a few, Marilyn had Delroy in an hour, no problem no stitches, but this one had a hard time, that baby tore her all up inside and what with it getting sick and all, she hasn't had a minute to herself. Odd, the place is empty. Everything neat as a pin; Marilyn doesn't know what neat as a pin is supposed to mean, really, but it's what you say. Girl gone, baby gone, she must have gotten tired of waiting and left in a snit . . . In a way, it's a relief. OK, she and Todd took a little too long getting up to what they were up to, and the last thing she needs right now is sulking and reproaches because she's, OK, she is a little late. Hell, where does she get off? Marilyn is doing her a goddamn favor, so what if she is a few minutes late?

The unit's empty but she says, "Where's my sweet baby?" In case the girl has taken him into the john.

Nobody answers and nobody comes. Nobody is here. The strange, vacant smell of the place tells her it's been a while.

OK, OK, so the girl got pissed off and drove away with him to spite her. Fine. Unless the skinny twit locked him in the car and went bar crawling, looking to score. Easy for her to do. Size two at the largest, you'd never know she just had a kid. As for herself, forget it. She is just Marilyn, hulking and resentful, standing here. Thinking, without knowing what it applies to, *serves her right.*

She heads back to the office and pulls out last month's receipts. If Sasha comes in bitching because I didn't hop to and do like I promised, she'll see right off that I'm up to my neck.

Then fat Delroy comes in looking like he swallowed the cat along with the canary and Marilyn has to sit him down in a chair. She loves the child but she hates that he is getting fat. Thick, sweet breath on him, what's he been eating now? "Where've you been, Delroy, what's that on your face?"

"Nothing, Mama."

"Hold still."

"I can't, I have to . . ."

"I said, hold still!" Chocolate. The child's mouth is ringed all around with chocolate. She tries to rub it off but it's crusted dry. "Come on, what you been eatin'?"

"Nothing. Ow!"

She loves Delroy because mothers are supposed to but she does not like him. She never has. If only he didn't look so God. Damned. Much like his father. Every time Marilyn looks in the child's eyes she sees Del Steptoe, so no matter how nicely she starts, she can't beat it down; she sees Del peeking out from inside this boy and she gets mad all over again. Decent of Del to put the property in her name so she'll always be well provided for, but he didn't do it for her sake, even though she was thinner then. The bastard did it so he could pick up and go, which makes you think twice about shotgun marriages, even though she personally thinks they are a necessary thing. She doesn't know what's going on with the girl in Fourteen and the boyfriend, nice enough boy, he hasn't been around in a while but for a while there cute Gary kept dropping into the office just to shmooze. He played like he was from some insurance company but he's this sweet baby's father, that she knows. The girl may fight it but every woman is better off with a man, especially when there's a baby, her experience with Delroy has taught her that. If Sasha had let that Gary in when he came knocking she wouldn't be needing a babysitter at all. But it's still kind of romantic, she thinks, him wanting her back. Then somebody else called, and maybe the voice Marilyn didn't recognize is some rival; shit, this girl has two men when Marilyn only has one, and only part time? Maybe he ran Gary off because he wants her to himself. Still, Marilyn knows a baby needs his real daddy, why can't she just mash the two of them together and make them kiss and make up? Better do it fast, before this Sasha picks up and takes that sweet baby away. Cute thing that will not grow up fat and duplicitous like her Delroy, she can tell by the eyes.

"Mom. Mo-om!"

"Stop squirming or I'll smack you!"

"Mom, I have to go!"

"Not until you say what you've got on your mouth."

"Nothing." He uses the back of his fist to wipe it off, fingers clamped around something, what's he holding so tight?

"It looks like chocolate ice cream to me. Delroy Steptoe, what you got in your hand?"

"Nothing!"

"Come on, Delroy, what are you holding?" Damn him, he is giving her that old Del smile of complete scorn that she is most afraid of; she grabs him, prying at the fingers, "Give it here!"

"Let go. Ow!"

"Listen at me, Delroy, where'd you get this?" It is knot of bills. "Delroy Wilson Steptoe, did you steal this money?"

His face squinches up into a miserable knot. "No Ma'am."

"Don't play like you aren't lying."

"She gave it to me."

"Who did."

"Miz Egan."

Her heart falls from a great height onto nails. "What for?"

"Minding the baby, OK?"

"Delroy, she was paying you to tend that baby?"

"Yes Ma'am."

Deep down inside of course she is mad at herself. After she got off the phone her new man Todd made a move that if she followed up on it she sure as hell would see more of him and not just on delivery days. So her mind is pretty much on that when she asks Delroy, "But she's back now, right? She's back so she let you go."

"Who?"

"Miz Egan. She's back now, Right?"

He doesn't answer. She smacks him and he starts to cry.

"Delroy, hold still!" God, she was just down there, the girl isn't back, that is, unless she just came in; Delroy's lying and she's too upset to figure out which part is the lie. "Is she here?"

Chocolate like sin, staining that crumpled, deceitful face. "I don't know!"

"Be straight with me, Delroy. She paid you when she got back from wherever she went to, right? And then she took the baby and went back out in the car."

"No Ma'am." His face is going all funny. Lying for sure, but she can't tell which parts. "She paid me before."

"And you took off and got ice cream."

Sobbing, he nods.

She has him by the neck now, shaking hard. Her voice comes out like thunder. "TELL ME WHERE YOU GOT THAT ICE CREAM."

"I got it from the . . ." He's sobbing so hard that he can hardly breathe. "I guh-guh-got it from the Good Humor Man."

"In hell you did, he don't come here!" She smacks her cheek. "Shit! The mall."

"Yes Ma'am."

"What did I tell you about the mall?"

"I mean, no Ma'am."

"You know what you'll get if I catch you at that mall." God forgive her, she is so upset that she's slapping him now, smacking him upside that face like a cartoon mother, left-right, left-right. "Now, Delroy Wilson Steptoe, did you take that baby over to the mall?"

"No Ma'am!"

"You weren't looking after the baby at all, were you, Delroy?"
She smacks him one last time and then gets all guilty because tears
spray all over the place. "You stole that money."

"No Ma'am," he says, insofar as he can speak at all.

"You stole that money and lied to cover up."

"I didn't, I didn't!"

"Where did you get it, Delroy. What have you . . ."

"I didn't, I . . . Owwww." Grief comes out in a clotted howl.

This is not a question because no question she asks Delroy gets a
straight answer; she shouts, "What the fuck have you done!"

"Ow- oh-wooooo . . ." There is no making sense of what he's trying to tell her now.

Then she looks up and sees the orange Toyota pulling into the
lot. She drops him. Thud. Her heart implodes. "Oh my God."

She wants to go out; she's afraid to go out. In fact she is waiting
for Sasha to get out of her junk heap holding that baby because
Marilyn knows better than anybody that you can't believe anything
Delroy Steptoe tells you, and she is gold plated four alarm certain
that he's pulling her chain and that sweet baby's in the back of
Sasha's car after all, strapped into its little seat nice as pie right now,
he isn't lost or stolen, he's perfectly fine. In which case she will
snatch Delroy baldheaded for stealing money and lying about it.

But what if he's telling the truth?

Oh, she'll punish him for sneaking off the place to get ice cream,
but if the rest is true, awful as it is she'll have to make it up to him
some way. See, she hit him pretty hard; loving a kid you don't much
like bends you into peculiar shapes, she can make it up to him with
pizza maybe, there was a Domino's guy out there just now, which is
the source of her inspiration. Things are bad between them and it's
her fault. It won't hurt to let him off his diet just this once. She'll
sort this out and then call in a nice big order to Pizza Hut, she and
Delroy can make up while they're deciding which toppings, but not
until she sees that girl get out of the car and lean over in back and
unbuckle the baby and hold it up so she can be sure.

Instead she sees Sasha opening the back and pulling out . . .

Packages. Nothing but packages. Grocery bags. A freezer bag with ice cream. Baby, she keeps thinking. No, willing. Baby next. But wishful thinking doesn't make a baby and the girl lets herself into the unit and the door slams shut. So . . . What?

If Delroy Steptoe is lying, she is going to tan his hide for real.

Oh God, if he's telling the truth then they are in deep shit here, the depth of which she really, truly doesn't want to know.

28.

Once doubt slithers in it feeds on you, growing until it is tremendous. It becomes your creator and your lover, the alien stirring in your secret parts, the sick uncertainty you love and fear gnawing its way to the surface— the obsession you harbor precisely because it will destroy you.

He never should have interfaced with the mark.

In the course of what should have been a routine prep, he also killed a guy.

I am not that person.

Uncertainty rocks him.

God, am I that person?

He is not thinking clearly now.

It was an easy pickup, easy in, easy out, getting inside the girl's locked unit at the DelMar was like cracking into a milk carton with a butcher knife. Naturally he'd scoped the place, nobody of Starbird's caliber would do an on-the-premises pickup without making a dry run. He knew the lay of the land, the ingress and egress and the niceties of the access road. He was familiar with the DelMar in spades. He studied the terrain before the mark left the hospital. When she locked her door today and got into the car he was watching from the top of the berm. He knew the road between here and the Food King, he knew where she went to fill prescriptions and he knew the exact turnaround time for each. When the motel manager's kid popped out the door minutes after she left he slapped the Domino's sign on top of the car and went in.

The removal was a picnic. Motel patrons all checked out before he rolled in, supplier safely off the scene for fifteen minutes minimum. On his way in he did run into one late departure shambling along to the key drop, but he held the carrier high and dodged the DelMar patron with that adroit weave that pizza guys use to make themselves feel important. He passed without notice: Tom Starbird as generic pizza guy, think invisible. By the time he moved on the unit the last overnight customer was long gone. It took him no time to score and the subject slept through the pickup. It squirmed a little in the red plastic pizza carrier as he headed for the car, that's all. When he opened the trunk and slipped it out of its carrier the subject didn't cry. It didn't even whimper as he set it down in the dummy UPS box fitted out with bedding and a white noise machine— took it like a little trouper. The kid snuggled into the thermal blankets like a mouse into a nest. Correction. The product, packaged and ready to roll.

Easy out, too, or it should have been. He had it all timed out. Domino's sign off the roof— twenty seconds. Ten seconds more to clear the DelMar lot, sixty on the access road to the freeway, he'd timed it, blend in with the last of the rush hour and go with the flow. Forty minutes max to the spot where his second car waited; north to south, the state of Georgia's small; Tom Starbird should be out of state before anybody thought to call 911. Hell, by the time the local cops threw up their hands and called in the Feds, he could be halfway to Texas.

Instead he is here.

Stymied. Marking time in a motel in Myrtle Beach. While giggling tourists bob up and down in the Atlantic just outside his window and the product snuffles in its pet carrier, Starbird is considering.

He should be enroute to Galveston, his designated point for the transfer of property.

But he has botched the operation. Interfacing with the mark. That accidental killing. Of these two mistakes the first is the graver.

He keeps seeing her face. That he can't shake it has made him edgy and so badly disrupted that exiting, he left the note— *I left a note?* It's the kind of thing you do only when your systems are gravely compromised. Tom Starbird, up and running, would never have made assurances by voicemail. Which, God help him, he did the other day. Tom Starbird in his right mind would never compound the mistake by leaving a . . . *Fuck, I left a note.*

This is what kept him lingering in the DelMar parking lot a hair longer than is S.O.P. Considering. Should he go back and trash the note or leave it so she wouldn't worry? Cruel to trouble somebody you almost like, but still . . . He was hung up for only a matter of seconds, but in a clean pickup a provider has to keep moving, click click click. Instead of dumping the Domino's sign and scratching off, he sat behind the wheel in the yellow evening light, weighing it. A note. With that fat fuck of an ex-boyfriend planted in the sawgrass off the inland waterway, a bloating time bomb ripening up for the sniffer dogs, he compromised himself further by leaving that note. It was a stupid thing to do. Why did he think the girl needed to know the boyfriend was gone for good? Worse. Why did he need to let her know the baby's OK? In a precision maneuver, it was a slip. The kind of stupid mistake even an expert can make reflexively, out of some sick need to help.

Stupid, yes.

Unless it was suicidal.

When doubt creeps in, every decision you attempt looks hinky. You never know if you wanted to shoot yourself in the foot or you did it because somebody else wanted it, but it happens.

A note, he thinks, pacing. Granted, he fucked up. He could either leave it and color himself gone before forensics started pawing the evidence or he could slip back inside her room and retrieve it. The question spelled itself out in seconds. The answer took too long to come. Indecision was new to Starbird and it was making him weird— how long did he really sit there dithering? Straight answer? Too long. While Starbird idled in his car, circling the drain, the supplier's rusting Toyota rolled into the lot. The decision was no longer his. The note stays, Starbird. Now, leave! Weirdness made his hands shake and his mouth dry out. It stopped him cold. He should have been out on the Interstate by that time, heading for the state line on the route he had drawn due west to the Gulf coast. Galveston. Mexico and beyond.

Instead he slouched behind the wheel with his eyes on the rearview mirror and waited for her to get out of the car. He just needed to see her right then. He had to see her however, whenever, whyever. Why the fuck ever? Did he think she'd find the note and understand? Did he think she'd come running out to thank him? To beg him to take her with him? What? Why did the weakest part of him care what she did or what happened to her next? Granted, darkness is safer than daylight, but for what he does, it can never get dark enough. Sighing, he started the motor. Still he lingered. Fixed on the mirror, he watched the girl's progress: slender in her black T-shirt, you'd never guess she'd just had a baby, but walking as though some deep, soft part of her still hurt. Carried her head like somebody he knows and almost loved once, *where the fuck is this coming from?* It was stupid but he felt safe enough sitting there in the twilight, the Domino's sign and the dumb hat turned him into an object you don't see, a unit you may note but will not remember as a person with a face: pizza guy. It was still stupid.

Unless it was suicidal. He is not the person he was when he went to ground in New York and this colors all his decisions. He is in transition. There is no telling what he will become.

It took her a minute to get out of her car and collect her bags— the plastic kept slithering away from her— and another to cross the parking lot and another minute to unlock the door and schlep the supplies inside. He started the motor, idling long past the vanishing point. There should be nothing left of him but a vapor trail, dust settling. At this stage in the operation there should be nothing where Starbird was sitting but thin air. Instead he hung in place, watching her reflection. What did he want, her to turn around and recognize him and flash a smile like a gift, was he that crazy? What was he waiting for, really? Applause for what he was doing? Military trumpets and a large cash prize?

What shrinks call validation? Some sign that if not grateful, she was at least relieved?

She ran out screaming.

Doubt kept his foot off the gas even though she came tearing out into the parking lot, spinning to look here, there, in a frenzy. This girl was nothing like the other women he'd relieved of kids they didn't really want; they pretended to be upset, where this one was desperate. Her face was drained of light. The girl ran along with her mouth wide and her straight hair streaming. She was a little whirlwind. Shouting, she came on like a dust devil— in rage, woe or what? He had no way of knowing. As she bore down on him Starbird hit the gas and instead of flooring it he glided past her and God help him he didn't mean to, but he thinks he smiled at her. What did he think, she would ask to come along? Did she want him to take her along? Confusion slowed him down. She looked right at him. He thinks she saw the face under the hat. As he hit the access road she went running back inside— the 911 call or her car keys? It didn't matter which, by that time Starbird was in the clear and headed for the freeway with the product stashed in the trunk. He floored it, pretending none of this had happened.

And what if it had? What if she made him out and gave chase? Did she have any idea how hard it is to keep up with an expert driver in a car chase, especially in that Toyota? Piece of junk. What if she made him out back there, and called the cops? Did she know how long it takes to get a 911 response? He'd be long gone by the time they came.

But doubt boiled in his belly and when the girl ran at the car that way, doubt broke out of his chest like the monster in *Alien,* ripping him to bits and slithering off on evil errands of its own. Now it is lashing its tail in his path, filling every road he takes and, mysteriously, directing him not west, but north; wherever Starbird turns doubt waits like an anaconda with its great jaws wide, preparing to glide in and devour him.

Instead of driving nonstop to Galveston he is stalled in a non-smoking single at the EconoLodge in Myrtle Beach, South Carolina, considering next moves. Worry has him pacing the narrow room while on the bed, freshly fed and cleaned up again, the product slumbers in the pet carrier he chose for this phase of the job.

Odd, what brings you from *there* to *here*.

He took the glitch in the parking lot as a temporary aberration, but when he stopped to switch cars, he made another slip. He had the fresh car well hidden, gassed up and waiting on an overgrown peninsula. When he reached it, Starbird stripped the plates, took out the Domino's sign and stuck it in the trunk of the relay car, to be destroyed later. One more switch and they'd never catch up with him. For this leg of the trip he had picked an unremarkable navy blue sedan, a choice based in experience: the color nobody notices because it's so dull. Navy blue says, *reliable*, no matter who's driving or how fast; stay within the limits or don't, no cop will give you a second look. He took the product in its container and plopped it on the passenger's seat next to him. When he was done doing what he had to do for it, he would transfer it to the pet carrier and secure it with the seat belt.

"This will only take a minute," he said to the container; his heart jumped. Had it died in there? It stirred and began to whimper. He patted the case. "Hang in. I have to do a thing."

He ran the pickup car to the edge of the bank and pushed it into deep water off the point— quicksand in the channel; eventually they'll find it, but it will take time. The sign and the UPS carton, he would ditch on his way inland, in a place nobody will ever think to look.

Now he had to do certain things for the kid. This phase of the operation was never his favorite but he was used to it. Feeding. Requisite diaper change. When he flew in from an ordinary pickup, back in the days when he still had a staff, he only had to do this once. On this one, he's in for the long haul. First, the feeding, which took too long. On routine jobs, the kind he had the liberty of orchestrating, Starbird made sure the subject was old enough to eat efficiently before he picked it up. On remote pickups he and the product would fly into LaGuardia— in ordinary times. From La-Guardia, there were dozens of secure ways to get back to his place where he would have Martha waiting, and she was a trained nurse. He'd have Martha on hand to take over the feeding, changing, all the necessaries until the clients came in for the transfer of property; yet another good way to depersonalize. He had a pediatrician on tap to inspect the goods and solve any unexpected problems, all bases covered and everything under control. Then he made his third mistake.

He knows Zorn and the wife are on the mark, ready to travel as soon as he phones with the particulars. He'd planned to call Zorn tomorrow, from the halfway point. No air travel within the continental U.S. on this one, not with hyped security and airport spot searches, he is going by car. He knows the route. Although he usually flies, Starbird knows how to dance ahead of roadblocks. When you are as meticulous as he is, you are prepared for any exigency. Everything in place before you begin. He completed the requisite paperwork before he left New York: an arsenal of forged driver's licenses and passports, a handful of airline tickets in all those names, you can't be too careful. Once he signs off on this project he will head south— bound to have an easy time at the border with his bogus passport and credentials. He expected to use the London ticket booked for one Carlos Velasquez one week from today— fly out of Mexico City with his beautiful new Mexican passport, but even here, he has backup reservations in two other names. He always has a backup. His Spanish is perfect, piece of cake.

Now he's not so sure.

He should be bombing across Alabama by this time. He should have made his calls and lined up the next rental car he intended to pick up. Instead, he is here. The business is in shutdown, what little staff he had is gone for good, with bonuses to assure their silence. Nobody to call, nobody to consult, a long trip looming. This is Tom Starbird, proceeding on his own.

Not only has he interfaced with the mark, he has interfaced with the product, and this is what leaves him hung up in this drab room like a computer frozen in mid-crash. He has made the fatal error of personifying the product. Instead of dealing with calm detachment, he has looked it in the face.

29.

Sasha won't recognize the person she becomes when all her hopes explode and she truly understands that her baby's lost. She may not even realize that she is changing. She's moving too fast. At some deep level she may already know she has lost Jimmy, but she refuses to comprehend it. She can't. She has to believe the disappearance is a puzzle she can solve. One she can and will solve because not to do it is unthinkable. Loss does that to you: stuns the brains out of you.

The blunt instrument that makes a blind, deaf-mute of Sasha Egan is incredulity. She can't believe it. She *won't* believe he is gone. When it comes, the news will come in dribbles, like a beginning avalanche. Slowly. Until the end when truth thunders down in a rain of boulders and flattens her.

The first thing she understands without knowing how she knows it is that in spite of her promises, Marilyn never came. None of her little touches in the unit, no signs that Jimmy was changed or fed, which is the first thing she'd do if she came in and found him awake. If Marilyn had come in and found him sleeping, she'd still be here. The bitch left it to Delroy. Did she think a child could do the job! Her first response is anger. Marilyn's so fucking irresponsible, where is she? Wait. No mother is that irresponsible, something happened that you don't know about.

Find him. Then ask.

Frantic, she starts in the motel room, opening drawers and closets with her blood pounding, calling Marilyn, calling Delroy— calling Jimmy!— calling them long after she understands that there is no one hiding here. There's a card propped on the phone. A note. Delroy left a fucking note? Furious, she jams it in her pocket. A note. Fool boy, did he think he could take Jimmy out any time he felt like it? She runs out into the parking lot in rising anger, looking here, there, for the little sneak— what was she thinking, trusting him with the baby, he's not even twelve yet, and where the fuck was his mother? A car starts up— pizza man; she glances his way but her vision stops at the lit-up Domino's sign on top of the car. Nobody. Everything in her is focused on her baby. "Delroy," she shouts as the Domino's delivery car pulls out of the parking lot. She goes running along the ornamental border, shouting, "Delroy? Delroy, where are you? I brought your stuff!"

That ought to bring him out.

Sasha can't know yet that it won't.

Nothing does. Not the food, not the threats. OK, she thinks, Delroy and the baby aren't here but they're nearby, they're here but hiding. If Delroy thinks it's a game, well. I'll game him. Jimmy's OK— he's fine, she tells herself because loss destroys thought, sweeping logic before it; they're here somewhere, all I have to do is figure out where. Wherever they are, it's for a perfectly good reason; when I find them Delroy will explain what happened or Marilyn will and we'll all laugh. If I don't throttle him.

As she runs along calling, Sasha checks the ice machine, looks under parked cars and with her heart stopped cold, into the murky lozenge of a swimming pool and— oh, God— the Dumpster. Her voice is high and wild. "Delroy. Delroy Steptoe, answer me!"

It's OK, Delroy's a responsible kid. He didn't just take off, he left a note. TELL NO ONE. That means he hasn't taken Jimmy to the office, why would he, when the very sight of him makes Marilyn mad enough to rip his ears off? The last thing he'd do would be take a crying baby to her. Denial prompts a series of desperate scenarios. Jimmy wasn't crying when she left, but with babies you never know— it was only for two minutes!— just a stopgap until Marilyn stepped in, that's all, the bitch! *Delroy, I got held up, you keep care of that baby until I get there.* No wonder he's hiding. He's out here somewhere, walking Jimmy to sleep; he can't answer because he's scared of waking him. She'll round the next corner and bump into him with Jimmy in the Snugli, dutifully trudging around the building, good boy. Unless Delroy took him up in the woods so Marilyn wouldn't hear the crying and tear into him.

What do you expect from a kid? She should have stayed, she should never have trusted Delroy, she should have left more money, better instructions, she never should have left. But what if Jimmy woke up hungry tonight, bawling, what if he started squirting again— the rain, Jimmy's fever, she couldn't take him out, she had to buy his things!

Maybe Delroy carried her baby uphill to the mall to show him to his cracker friends. The thought of them peeling the diaper—*look at here*— is infuriating. If those prurient little weasels so much as touch her child . . . That's where they are, that must be it. Lazy, indifferent Marilyn doesn't know it, but Delroy and his mall rat friends ditch school most afternoons. They hang in packs, hocking loogies into the mall fountain and sock-skating on the terrazzo mezzanine; she's seen the cheap thrill kids circling food court tables like vultures around a dying man, waiting for him to stop moving. If Delroy Steptoe hurts *one* quarter inch of her baby she'll murder him. Sixth grader or no, she'll beat him with her fists until he is the one who stops moving.

Brooding, she doubles back on the unit. Where did they go, how long have they been gone, did he take off as soon as she got in the car? Or did he hang in faithfully until Jimmy started to cry? How long ago was that? There's no bottle cooling in the microwave to tell her; the spot in the crib where Jimmy slept is cold. When did Delroy Steptoe give up on this? God, if the child took off in the extra ten minutes it took her to get his rotten fried chicken she'll never forgive him.

No. She'll never forgive herself.

Two minutes. She sold her only baby down the river for two minutes. Like Marilyn was ever going to come when she said. She should have known! Marilyn was never coming down in two minutes and she wasn't coming in twenty, either, in spite of her promises. Sick with it, Sasha understands that Marilyn didn't even bother to check. If she had, she'd be out here in the parking lot right now, explaining, or beating Delroy to a pulp. Instead all the curtains in her place are drawn. She has a guy in there with her, they are having gross, unimaginable middle-aged sex, and even when she doesn't have a man around to distract her, Marilyn is not reliable. She's done a lot of things Sasha never asked for and didn't want, brought in gaudy shirts and crap lamps, sticky food, but she never did anything she promised. So this is Sasha's fault for trusting a woman nobody can trust. No, it's her fault for trying to buy an eleven-year-old, it's . . .

It's her fault for being such a shitty mother— oh yes oh God, like it or not this is what Sasha Egan is now and will be from now until she dies and maybe after. She is a mother. She will never give away this baby. He's part of her.

Missing.

Guilt collects, swarming her like a cloud of gnats as she tries this, then that, searching, plagued by an inner monologue that will run in her head nonstop for the rest of her life until or unless she finds him; it will play in her head forever even if she does. Should-haves roll into might-haves and could-haves. Hoping, Sasha spins futile best-case scenarios as she taps on the doors of deserted units and runs along the gully behind the motel, flailing at the overgrown azalea bushes that hide the air conditioned back windows, stumbling along in the dark looking for anything— a pink starfish hand waving or a scrap of blue blanket, whatever the uneducated heart expects when it goes looking for a baby.

The last thing that comes in before you run out of hope is the last hope.

Wait, she thinks. Maybe Delroy took him up to Marilyn after all. He needs her even though he is scared shit of her. That's it, she tells herself, pleased and relieved. That's where they are. The minute Jimmy started crying he ran to the office and handed him off to Marilyn, the woman is probably sitting in the back booth in the diner right now with my baby in her lap, giving him gooshy kisses with that smug Revlon lipstick smile of hers. *Don't you dare put that fat red mouth on my Jimmy.*

That's it. It has to be. Sasha can't know why she is so angry. When I go running in she'll be all superior and hostile: "What's the matter, Sashie, don't you know how to take care of a baby?"

She heads for the diner with every line in her body angled forward, plowing through the unnatural light that pollutes Savannah nights. She's on the herringbone brick walk that leads up to the door when a hand clamps down on her shoulder.

"There you are!"

Startled, she shrieks.

"Don't do that," Marilyn says. "You'll scare the people."

Sasha whirls. An expanding universe of fears clots in her throat. She cries in a little explosion of breath: "Where is he?"

The big woman stands under the ornamental lamppost with the squirming Delroy. She claps both hands on his shoulders and turns him around so he is facing Sasha too. The sodium vapor light turns Marilyn's magenta mouth black and her turquoise pants black and makes ominous black squiggles of the design in her nylon top, like words in a message Sasha is too distraught to read. She looks like a painting of a big dead person. Delroy's grown so huge in Sasha's imagination that she is startled by the disparity. In this light he is anxious and small. "Shh shh." Marilyn shoves Delroy forward. Her full voice is trembling when she says, "OK, Del honey. Now."

Squinting, Delroy opens his mouth but he's been crying so hard that he can no longer speak. All she hears is his breath bubbling.

Marilyn's musical voice hits a series of flat discords. "Honey, I feel really bad about this."

Sasha throws up a hand as if to fend off what is coming.

"Hold still, honey," Marilyn says. The monolithic face fissures in an unexpected collapse and tears run down in all the crevices. "Delroy has something to tell you."

Not all the shaking in the world will shake any more information out of the miserable Delroy. By the time Sasha is done trying they are both wrung dry. There is no truth the boy can give her, no real explanation, nothing on what happened to her baby after he walked out on him. He walked out on her baby! Jimmy was sleeping so nice, he only left him for a tee-ninetsy little minute, and the baby went where? He doesn't know, he wasn't there, he says, and she has to believe him because try as she does, running at the question from every possible direction, it's all she can get out of him. No matter how cleverly she re-phrases, Delroy recites the same sparse, dismal details over and over. Hungry, he was just hungry, that's all. Baby was fine, he wouldn't of left except it was totally asleep, all he did was run uphill to find the Good Humor truck but it was gone so he had to go inside the mall for a Klondike Bar, so what if the time got away from him? It won't matter how long Sasha works on the boy, questioning, probing, grilling him with carefully controlled anger, that's all he has, the poor, ignorant little shit. Let the police try to get more out of Delroy Steptoe, if they ever fucking come. He has told her everything he has to tell. She's wrung him dry.

Of course she has called the police. It's the first thing she did. Now she is done with Delroy and sick of Marilyn's guilty sniveling and the Savannah P.D. still haven't showed up. Jiggling with remorse, Marilyn begs her to wait for the cops up in the office with her so she can help— make coffee, maybe, cookies to get her blood running and perk her up, she says, when she means, *to make up for it*. Marilyn is desperate to make it all right but Sasha refuses. She can't bear to look at the woman's face.

Marilyn calls, "They'll be here in just a little minute."

It takes them forever to come.

When they do come the police are courteous, efficient, suspicious. Southern gentlemen in their neat summer uniforms— short sleeves because summer comes to Savannah before the north even sees spring. It occurs to Sasha as they begin their polite Southern inquiry that they think she and not Delroy lost track of the baby. She is so innocent in terms of what they are thinking at first that this is as far as she can take it: *lost track of the baby.*

Then the detectives come. Polite. Genteel, but probing. They are at the beginning of a long night of questions and Sasha is too stupid with worry to see what they are really driving at.

Questions, she has to answer their questions. She doesn't know anything but she has to tell them everything, in these things there's no telling which details count. She needs to keep her head clear, be precise. Say exactly when she left the DelMar. Where she went. Stunned, she rehearses the details like a chronic A student trying hard to come up with the answer that will ace the test. They are like a pair of harriers, following each answer with another question— why she left. Where she was in the interim. What she found when she came back. Anything suspicious, did she see anything suspicious, does she want them to contact her family?

Family? No!

The two who are tag-team questioning her exchange significant looks.

Why aren't they out searching instead of sitting in here harassing her? She rummages for the exact detail that will move the police out of her bland, dismal motel room and into the woods, onto side roads or up into the mall, wherever her baby is. Anything to jump-start the search. Nuances, she thinks, looking at the empty crib, the Teddy she bought for her boy even though he isn't big enough to see the expression on its brown plush face, the little blue quilt she bought neatly folded on the rail unused, because Savannah nights are warm. How can I get them on the case?

God, this is what it is now: a case. With her heart turning inside out she hears the detective in charge assign it a number.

Even though he is still polite the chief investigator is losing patience. "Ma'am, if you don't know what happened, is there anybody you can think of who would?"

Why does it take her so long to think of Gary? Was he that big a cipher in her life? Her hand goes to her mouth: "There's a boy."

"We know."

"Not a boyfriend, but the baby's father."

"We know."

Better not to ask them how they know. She scrambles for the little she knows about Gary. Pathetic: it isn't much. Gary, does she really think that dumb, genial Gary from UMass in suburban Brookline would break in and steal her child? She tells them about Gary anyway. She describes the day he showed up at Newlife, their ugly little encounter; the night, with him circling the building; it's why she had to run away. Just when she thought she was safe he confronted her in the baby aisle of the Food King. That was the last she saw of him. Cargill, his last name is, Lieutenant. Gary Cargill.

"When did you see him last?"

"It's been days. I never saw him after the supermarket."

"Yes Ma'am," they say, "that's what the lady in the office said."

This comes as a surprise. Of course there is another team questioning Marilyn and Delroy. What made her think this investigation only touched on her?

Gary Cargill. A techy at the precinct does a search and supplies the details. Moving violation in Boston, that's all. Family's from Iowa, we're waiting to hear from headquarters in Des Moines. Now, Ma'am, when this Gary Cargill came to see you, did he make any threats?

No, she tells them. But I heard something in the bushes the other night, you don't think he . . .

We don't conjecture, Ma'am. Would you call it stalking.

It could have been stalking. No, he didn't make any threats. The more she tells them the more she thinks Gary is a bungler but he means well enough; he would never do a thing like this because whatever else he is, Gary Cargill is an ordinary guy and the person who would steal a baby is not ordinary. He is nothing like. Corrupt, she thinks, sick with the implications. He would have to be corrupt. Or deranged. This makes her shudder. She can't stop. Don't think about what a thief may do to your baby, Sasha; don't go there or you'll never come back. You have to stay here because Jimmy needs you. She won't know it until much later, but she is in shock. She can't think about what's happening to her baby and go on sitting here talking to the police. She can barely keep from screaming. It's all she can do to go on breathing out and in, in and out.

I don't think Gary would do this, she says. It's true.

The detective leans forward. Then who do you think did it?

She doesn't catch the nuance. I don't know!

Do what you can, Sasha. Answer their questions. Answer questions they haven't thought to ask. Be calm. She tries. They are polite. They take notes dutifully as she supplies useless information simply because it is information and then, dutifully, they follow up, but it's clear that their suspicions stop right here and they are only going through the motions. By the end she and the Savannah police will realize they are on a loop, saying all the same things to each other over and over again.

As the night wears into early morning, Sasha sees without being told that they think she intentionally lost her baby, by which they do not mean *lost*.

The questions stop. For the moment, they are done with her. She is a foregone conclusion.

All Sasha can do, then, as the forensics people turn over the unit and scour the car and bring in other police with lights to walk the woods and comb the terrain around the azaleas, looking for some shred of evidence that will convict her— unless, oh, God, they are looking for Jimmy's body— all she can do is wait for this phase of the investigation to end.

They have to move on! Otherwise they'll never find the kidnapper. *He's been taken.* The realization she's been avoiding rolls in like a stone, sealing the mouth of the cave where she is trapped. *Somebody has taken him away.* Who did this? What kind of person would break into your life like a burglar and steal your child? The police won't look outside this room until they've run this ugly thread out to the dead end that it is, bastards, why can't they hurry?

Clear the decks and start an organized search for the man? Unless. Carla Hanson's face flickers on like a porch light, unbidden— that greedy mouth. Recognition makes her gasp. *Unless it's a woman.* Yes! Doesn't it happen all the time?

"Lieutenant," she says. "Officer? Somebody! Please."

They are all busy doing something else.

Desperate, she tries to get their attention, but as far as they are concerned, she is a foregone conclusion now. The mother. For all they know, the perp. Their polite indifference makes her shout. She begs them to check the records in neonatal units at all the hospitals, find out whether some poor woman who lost a baby is on the loose out there, mad with grief, she may have stolen Jimmy to replace her own stillborn. Check the fertility clinics. Check the records for stillbirths. Conscientiously, the junior detective takes notes— so fucking polite!— for all she knows he is scribbling, bla bla bla.

"Do you hear?" Sasha repeats. Anxiety makes her passionate. They look at her warily because she is taking the initiative, where in these cases they expect the mother to be inarticulate and helpless.

"Yes Ma'am," the detective says politely, because this is the first night and generally, in these cases you need look no further.

"Yes Ma'am," the state troopers say, because by this time there are state troopers too, but Sasha can tell by the way they look at her that to a man (and by this time there are several) they believe this disappearance originated with her.

As if she would ever . . .

Shuddering, Sasha understands that a month ago she actually thought she could give away this baby. What was she, crazy? Was she disconnected from reality and seriously deranged, thinking for even one minute that she could part with the flesh wrenched out of her body and glowing with life and walk away feeling better? She tried to think of it in the abstract, but this is no abstraction. Jimmy Egan isn't a unique print or a separable entity that she can send out to fly and be happy, he isn't a firefly or any other damn thing, he is a living person. He was never a spark waiting to be freed to fly upward or any other metaphor an ignorant girl could contrive, he is her child. He is Jimmy, Jimmy Egan, he came out of her flesh and he is HERS and she will do whatever it takes and go wherever she has to go and go on without stopping until she finds him. She loves him because he is part of her now, wherever he goes, and she is prepared to do whatever it takes to find him. As the television news truck rolls in, Sasha lifts her head. The night has changed her and she understands now that her baby is truly lost.

The television unit. This may be her last chance. Oh, God. It may be too late for last chances.

For the first time Sasha is face to face with it. All the desperate hopes she has thrown up like barricades between her and the truth have vaporized. Now that she's argued and protested, now that she's done everything she can, the police machine runs on without her. Huddled in a cracked plastic chair, she watches them work while the tears run down, reduced to what she really is. Sasha is no artist. She's a mother, nothing more and nothing less, sealed in the prison of her own helplessness, rocking with grief.

30.

Until now, Starbird has managed to maintain his cool detachment all his professional life. With plans in place and clients waiting, he is stalled here in Myrtle Beach and it's his own damn fault. Instead of faring forward back there, he lost it. He never should have spoken to the kid.

The thing is, by the time he'd ditched the pickup vehicle and walked back to the new car the product was crying.

"It's OK," he'd said to it, the way you would to an actual person, "Don't get your panties in a twist."

Blunders beget blunders. Tom Starbird, who was stupid enough to interface with the mark, was officially stupid enough to interface with the product. Conversation. He could swear the thing smiled at the end. Usually this kind of encounter wouldn't touch him but this was the last, and it's her baby. That lovely woman. What was he thinking? In his line of work you never spoke to the product; S.O.P. It was a matter of expedience. If you had to speak, you kept it brief. You did not relate because you ran the danger of getting invested; start making like a father and you're well and truly fucked. To do this job you could not under any circumstances get personally involved, but there he was. Alone on the job, changing diapers under the dome light on a godforsaken point in rural Georgia. This wasn't a problem that would be solved at the end of a short flight to LaGuardia, this problem was riding all the way to Texas with him—three days together in the car. Bad: this phase was taking too long. The product was crying, the problem was his to deal with, what choice did he have?

"It's really OK," he said to the carton, "It's OK really, there there," he tried, stupidly mimicking Sarah's falsetto croon. "Shhshh don't cry, baby. Tom will take care of you."

Rattled, he took the prewarmed bottle of Enfamil out of the hot pack and opened the box. He eased the little thing out of its tangled nest and tried to feed it but to make bad worse, it wouldn't eat. Its problem was, it was starving and it didn't know how to fix it; it couldn't get a grip. When these things are that small they want to eat every few minutes and they never know whether they're hungry or not. They have to eat every couple of hours or they'll die, that Starbird knew. This one was making hungry fish faces but it couldn't seem to get the hang of it. Tom Starbird was stuck trying to feed a starving baby that didn't know how to eat. Coaxing took time he should have spent behind the wheel, hellbent for Texas. When he was just about to give up on it the baby settled, at least for long enough for its tiny chest to stop heaving and the mouth to latch on. Cool, but it kept losing its place in the procedure and Starbird kept having to remind it. Talk to the baby, dude. Try to sound like a mom. Jiggle. Bump its gums with the rubber nipple to wake it up if it nods off. He heard advancing belly rumblings and wet squirting sounds. Burp it. Now I have to burp it. Next he would have to change it or it would get raw and scream all the way to Galveston. When that was done he took out the usual supplies: baby wipes in quantity because you never know how many you're going to run through cleaning up one of these things, the smallest size disposable diapers, bucket with bleach to destroy DNA traces before heaving the dirties into the marsh.

You can feed a product without ever looking into its face, Starbird has done it so often he can complete the operation in his sleep. He can do it without making eye contact with the item. It's harder to clean and change one, as you have to turn them on their backs face up, but he is practiced at that too. If you have to watch what you're doing, focus on the details—what's dirty or raw, which parts need wiping. Where you have to smear on gunk. For this you need the light; why was it so hard? He tried, but this living product squirming under his hands was her get and progeny, whether or not she wanted to discard it, and that's the source of his grief.

He didn't know. He still doesn't know.

He helped the mark in the Food King and she ran after him to smile and say thanks; the smile told him that she liked him.

Would she like him now?

Efficient as he was, still bent on making the transfer tomorrow in Galveston, Starbird finished with the diaper tabs. He pulled on a fresh onesie with that practiced hand. He was all set to stick it back in the carrier when, at a sound the baby made when he did up the snaps in the crotch, he inadvertently looked it in the face.

He thinks it smiled.

It had the girl's exact expression. The same eyes. He put it back in place, shaken. *Did I do the right thing?*

Doubt. The monster had Tom Starbird in its jaws before he cleared the DelMar parking lot. Hell, leaving the Food King. Its teeth met somewhere at the center of him when the product smiled and he groaned aloud. *Got to get rid of it.*

It has him now, no question. If he can't get his shit together it will swallow him whole. At this hour he should still be on the road, driving for his life. Instead he is slouching in this EconoLodge in Myrtle Beach, South Carolina with the living product asleep for the moment but snorting like a small animal, clean and fed but, OK, grunting and tossing in the fresh nest he made for it.

He is on the phone. *Got to offload it.*

In the realm of botched exercises, this is the cardinal mistake: rushing a transaction. He has to hand off this baby fast or doubt will paralyze him and he'll never hand it off. *Got to get rid of it fast.*

His party answers. With his operating system close to crashing, Starbird barks, "Zorn?"

"You've got my kid?"

"There's been a change of plans."

31.

It is near dawn.

The police are gentle with Sasha now that they have played out their string. They are winding up here. They turn to Sasha as the television crew enters the room. "OK, Ma'am, anything else?"

She is beyond speech. Demonstrating futility, she turns her pockets out. "Oh my God, I forgot this."

The note. Index card, yes. Firm printing. Broad strokes. She thinks as she hands it over that she was out of her mind last night when she stuck it in her pocket and forgot it, stupid, anxious mother hung up on best-case scenarios. Beautiful printing on the card, strong, broad strokes. Delroy Steptoe didn't print this. Neither did clumsy Gary Cargill. It's a message for her, of that she is certain, but it's a message from somebody completely other. This person took her baby, this bastard, this monster. He's out there and no matter what she has to do she will by God find him, she will do this no matter what it costs or how long it takes, she will . . .

HE'S SAFE.

TELL NO ONE.

Someone— news anchor?— is saying, "Live from the DelMar." Sasha lifts her head.

The Channel Eight crew is in the room now, filling the space as the chief of detectives steps in to make a statement. Someone is brushing Sasha's face with powder and helping her to her feet. A reporter thrusts a Nerf-ball mike under her chin, asking the classic, "How does it feel?" as the power of speech returns and with it the first clear thought she's had on this terrible night: *television*. She will use this to flush him out.

"How does it feel?"

Now Sasha Egan is transformed. The change is complete. Where she was taut with rage, she is electrified. Passionate and articulate. She seizes the mike from the startled reporter and glares into the camera. She isn't speaking to the reporter or the personnel in the room. She speaks only to him. Wherever he is.

"You, who took my baby, you bastard. Thief. Monster. Hear me," she says with her voice vibrating with fury. "Hear me now."

32.

When he finally crashed into sleep in his dim motel in Myrtle
Beach, Starbird still thought of the transfer of property as a
win-win proposition. Good home for the baby, the girl will be relieved. Forget Galveston, do this soonest. Meet Zorn and the
wife in Washington, D.C., he needs to look into the woman's face,
make sure she's a good person, stable, fit to handle a kid. Do that
and the girl will thank him. Correction. Would thank him, if he
made the suicidal move of revealing himself. He'll tell Zorn to
bring the wife when he calls to give him the details: which hotel
and what time. Before he shut down for the night he opened his
laptop and scoped his route on the Web, down to the stop he would
make to phone Zorn. Surfing for the comfort surfing brings, he
found a hotel where he could simply walk in and get a room, pay in
cash and leave no tracks. By then it was beyond late and the product was awake and crying again. He fed and changed the baby and
patted it down in the pet carrier. Then he dropped like a stone into
what little was left of the night.

The first thing Starbird did when he woke up screaming was
turn on CNN. It wasn't a scream exactly, but it felt like sound—
something profound ripped right out of him. How long had he slept?
An hour? Two? Too much and not enough. It was the baby screaming, he realized. Still it left him raw and jangling, as though the
noise that roused him had been pulled out of him by the roots. The

parted curtains showed a wedge of pink sky. He lurched to his feet to slap on the TV before he realized that he was holding the remote. White sound worked on the baby when he first took it from the DelMar and he was looking for the adult equivalent— that predictable tickertape banner spelling disaster along the bottom of the screen, the talking head that can smile while all hell implodes in the background and the earth caves in, describing the scene in that same reassuring drone. With the TV running Tom took a bottle of premixed formula out of the cold pack and put it in the sink to warm while he pulled the baby out of the pet carrier— gently, because he's been doing this for so long that he is extremely good at it— and changed the kid and sat down to feed it while they zoned out on CNN. Where the baby ate and snoozed, Starbird sat with his mouth cracked wide, waiting. At some level, he understood what he was waiting for. What he didn't understand that night— will never know— is why.

He didn't wait long.

She sprang out at him. Pre-dawn press conference, direct from the scene in Savannah. The victim— when did you start thinking of her as a victim, Starbird, bad move— the girl was strikingly pretty and the local TV news people persistent. The police called the press conference to draw possible witnesses, to keep her off guard, prop her up and let her make a plea.

He recognized the sterile, tidy room at the DelMar.

The girl looked haggard and ashen, what did they do to her? Sweet woman, baby's fine, what does she need with the cops? The chief of detectives wiped his mouth and read from a piece of paper giving details, what little they had. The room was filled with bobbing cameras but the local news had shouldered into the front row. Sitting in Myrtle Beach Starbird watched the woman he couldn't dismiss and could not quite let go of shove aside the local reporter— whose makeup was perfect in spite of the hour. The girl batted at the globe of orange fuzz protecting the microphone with such force that two hundred miles away, Tom Starbird flinched as he heard the smack. He put the baby over his shoulder and got down on his knees to stare into the motel TV. Rocking the baby, he leaned close, opening his mouth wider, as though that would help him take it in. He studied the screen carefully. He was looking for something. He wanted to examine that face and know for certain that when he took her baby and left this girl behind at the DelMar he had made her, if not happy, then relieved.

Instead the girl he thought he was doing a favor was vibrating with rage. When the reporter asked, "How does it feel?" she seized the microphone and jerked it away, advancing on the camera. Now Sasha Egan's voice cut through time and space and into Tom Starbird, severing some part of him that he didn't know he had.

Two hundred miles away, he groaned. She was beautiful and she was articulate. What did he expect? This woman whose life he had disrupted was nothing like the hapless victims who parade their grief for the cameras, fresh from the beauty parlor and facing the lens with those shaky, inadvertent smiles. Unlike the usuals, who spoke from the safety of their sofas, this girl lunged into the frame with her eyes wide and her teeth bared. She didn't plead and she didn't talk at length, which most victims take as their inalienable right. The woman whose baby Tom Starbird had stolen, yes, stolen, advanced on the camera, glaring and intent. Before the local reporter could lick her lips to bring up the sheen and repeat, "How does it feel?" she started to talk. She wasn't interested in telling anybody how it felt. Instead she told them exactly what she thought. She could have been speaking directly to him.

If she'd only looked down, if she'd lost it and begun crying the way they usually do, Starbird would have been able to handle it. He could have turned off the television and moved on.

But this was no run-of-the-mill, bewildered victim and she was nothing like Daria Starbird, greedy for praise and anxious to put her burden down. Sasha Egan glared into the camera. She was looking right at him, and as she spoke, something ended. It ended and grief rolled into Starbird and reamed him out. Never mind what she said. Yes, mind it. He needs to play and replay the diatribe, he has to deconstruct and reconstruct it, he needs to study it and parse it. For the next thirty-six hours it will draw him back to the television here and in Washington, in a terrible, agonizing need to see it play out again and again.

He heard himself shouting, "I'm not like that!"

Sasha Egan finished as the sun came up.

"God." Staggered, he wanted to jump into the box and pull the woman out. He wanted to grab this girl Sasha Egan and shake her until she looked into the center of him and saw who he really was. He was hurt bad and shouting, "Oh, lady. Let me explain!"

But he had to take the baby to Washington. Contact Zorn and set this up for Friday night.

Stabbing at the air with the remote, he flipped her rage into oblivion. He had to research!

After what he had just heard, the still, predictable images on his laptop came as a relief. He didn't even know he had a plan until he started lining up equipment he never dreamed he would have to use. What is he going to do with it once he's . . . That will have to wait until he plays this out. Choosing equipment, he began by locating computer stores in the D.C. area. He needed the best, the one with all the necessary supplies. For the efficient organizer, need ran ahead of the details. She had to know the truth about him no matter what. He would do this, he had to do this, step by step. Spell out what you have to do the way you do everything, Starbird, with great care. You are nothing if not meticulous. Take it step by step and maybe you can figure out what comes next.

He's as good behind the wheel as he is at everything else he does and he paid top dollar for the car he drove out of Myrtle Beach Friday morning— a gray Volvo, steady at high speeds. He left on time and proceeded on schedule, everything carefully planned. Once he rolled onto the Interstate he rode the fast lane all the way up the coast. That put him in the D.C. area by late afternoon in spite of scheduled pit stops to feed and change disposable diapers on the product, with a little something extra in the formula so it would sleep. At the designated rest stop north of Raleigh, North Carolina, he made the call to Zorn. MapQuest put driving time at seven plus hours; he made it in closer to six. He waited out the D.C. rush hour in Computer Warehouse in Alexandria, Virginia, where he scored the necessaries. Big place. Latest technology. Everything he needed in stock. Excellent. That left him with an hour to find his hotel and check in, plus an hour alone with the baby. No. The product. Time enough to bath it, feed and change and— Starbird, what the fuck is this?— hold it a little, just a little, before Zorn and the wife came and he handed it off.

33.

If the baby Jake says his contact is arranging had come right away, said arrangement might be tolerable, but time drags and questions rush in to fill the space. Something's wrong; Maury knows the signs. A guy like Jake never just waits. He won't answer questions, either. Like a seasoned scam artist, he's too busy creating a diversion— in this case, his celebrated upcoming exposé.

Where she should be excited and happy, Maury is tense. She wants to talk about the baby. All Jake does is talk about the show. She doesn't know who his newest target is, exactly, but she knows that look: wily predator, grinding his jaws. Woman, is all he'll say, Nobody, really, but wait for the show. Writer you've never heard of. Look, I'm doing her a favor. When I'm done her books will sell like poppers at a rave. His verve makes Maury tremble. Whoever she is, Jake will hunt her down and nail her hide to the wall after he's flayed her alive on TV. At night he crouches over the display on his laptop. If she speaks he jumps like a cat surprised in the jungle, glaring over its half-eaten prey: don't bother me. Her laughing, ambitious man, who wants life to fit the patterns he draws, is grappling with problems beyond his control.

Use his name the way you do, like a weapon. "Jake, what's going on?"

He slams the laptop shut. "Don't! You made me lose my thread."

"At least tell me how much longer we have to wait."

Anger flares. "I told you, I don't know!"

Maury started out hopeful; she starts out hopeful every time, but every new day diminishes her. This is in the hands of a real professional, expert, tops in his field, Jake tells her. Lay back, you'll have your baby soon. She was happy and excited; it was like being stoned all the time, or out on one of the drugs they gave her the year she completely lost it and tried to off herself. With a baby so close her world expanded like a fresh, green field dotted with flowers. With a baby this close, she floated through perfumed air like a new mom in a commercial, happy and minty-fresh, unless she was freshly minted.

Hope. You can only travel so far on hope.

Time works like acid, eating it away.

If Jake's connection had made the match within that first week their mysterious arrangement would have flown, no problem. Who has time for questions with a new baby to love? But days went by. Weeks.

Maury hates being this person but she is too intelligent to take the story at face value. The questions she tried so hard to avoid pop up like hatching aliens in a science fiction movie, proliferating until they fill all available space. Who is this supplier Jake's found, and why can't she meet with him? Are they hiding something? Where's this baby coming from, who's the birth mother and why is everybody so close-mouthed? What are the legal ramifications, really. Are there legal ramifications?

Don't go there, Maury. If you want your baby, you can't even afford to look.

Instead she zeroes in on questions she can ask. About the timing. The secrecy. Why the man she knows and loves treats her like a stranger, fobbing her off with that grin. This is a business arrangement but so far Jake hasn't touched on the money, only that it will be a lot, don't ask, Maury. Just don't ask. So far in her childless life Maury Bayless has been through grief and disappointment and a string of medical indignities; she's been through humiliation and bloody horrors and come up smiling, but the secrecy is eating her alive.

She may get a baby. It may be here soon, barring the unforeseen. Jake won't tell her anything about the arrangement so she can't even guess what might go wrong. If she knew, she could plan. If he'd only tell her she could deal in terms of contingencies, devising Plans B and C, but the more this drags on, the less she knows. The less she knows, the harder it is. She may never have a baby and this is bad, but it's not what Maury fears most.

She's afraid she'll get her baby and somebody or some *thing,* some unforeseeable accident will rip it out of her arms.

Maury does what you do when you don't know what's coming. You prepare. This time she is beyond ready— oh, there have been so many times! The baby's room is freshly painted. Again. Bad karma, she thinks with a visceral twinge, but the baby could come any time, and the room has to be pitch perfect. With babies, stability is important because they can't tell you what they need. Whatever her baby needs, she has it! The crib is ready— blankets, mobile, God's plenty of stuffed toys washed or carefully vacuumed and inspected for choking hazards. The little changing table is loaded with wipes and diapers and cotton balls and Q-tips and Kleenex and talcum and ointment and baby oil; safety belt so her baby can't roll off while her back is turned. The dresser's filled with caps and bibs and onesies— everything the books say a baby needs— all freshly washed, which is a given. She has velvety towels and baby washcloths, tiny socks and nighties in graduated sizes because you know how fast they grow. On top of the dresser, of course, she has her shelf of how-to's for new mothers, and a little library of soft books, printed on cloth stuffed with cotton— no sharp edges anywhere. Everything's in place: self-warming baby bathtub, baby monitor, bottle warmer and music box, night light.

In the absence of a functional uterus Maury Bayless has all the right equipment. You don't have to carry a baby and give birth to know how to love and take care of one. Nature doesn't make you a mother. The baby does. She loves him so much! Jake says it's a boy.

Even though she works long days Maury comes home at night and cleans in an excess of energy that precludes thought. Her house is in order, bathrooms immaculate and the kitchen shining in spite of the fact that inside, she's wrecked. She is walking under water, dragging memories like chains— ghosts of babies past warning her not to hope too much. She is home less and less now as the wait drags on because at work, at least, she can pretend this is a world she can control. When everything else is at risk the law is stable, with its rule of precedents and provisions for every contingency. Even when clients are volatile the practice of law has its set parameters, precedents, inviolable rules; in an unstable world it offers a series of probable and possible outcomes. A range of events that can be prepared for because they are expected.

When they run into each other in the daylight, fully dressed and standing, Jake flashes that swift, vulpine grin that worries her because there's no telling what it hides. He hurries past to keep her from asking questions: *Don't slow me down.* Slow him down and he'll have to think. Jake always says a moving target is harder to hit. For the first time Maury knows exactly what he means. They don't talk but in bed at night they are voracious— sublimated hunger, she supposes, unless it's denial.

Days, she hides in her work. With her life in flux, the only safe place is the office.

Or it was.

She's in the middle of a settlement meeting when a tick on the plate glass distracts her. Looking up, she sees Jake hulking behind the Levelors outside the conference room. Sliver of Jake through the slats. Jake, don't you see I have clients sitting here? She jerks her head in the direction of her office. Wait. He taps again. This won't wait. Maury can't excuse herself, not at this stage in the negotiations. Her eyebrows shoot up. *Please.* Jake's brows draw their own line: that scowl. As the meeting proceeds she sees Jake's restless shadow stalking in tight circles, a blur of compressed anger crowding everything else out of her head.

When she excuses herself and goes out he pounces like a hawk on an owl. He is laughing. "Let's go. Let's go!"

"Jake, I'm due in court in ten minutes."

"Hell with that. I need you now."

His bark brings her head up so fast that her neck snaps. "Is something wrong?"

But her Jake is grinning, triumphant hunter-gatherer bringing home the biggest trophy yet. "Hurry. I've booked the shuttle."

"Shuttle!"

"We're going to D.C."

"Washington." Yes Maury is playing for time, repeating Jake in an attempt to understand. She can't decipher the subtext unless she makes time to absorb the details here.

"Maura, come on! Cab's waiting. We have to go."

"Jake, I can't go to Washington, I'm due in court."

"We're due in Washington tonight."

"You go ahead." She is calculating. Times. Possible flights. "I can be there by nine."

"I need you now." He grabs her arm. "You have to come."

Now he is giving her orders. Disturbed, she pulls away. "I don't have to do anything, Jake. Why all the pressure?"

All his breath comes out in a rasp of exaggerated patience. "Maur, our baby's in Washington. He's waiting. Are you coming or what?" When she does not move Jake says grudgingly, "He wants you to come."

Stalling, she repeats, "Our baby."

"I thought you would be more excited."

"I am, I'm just . . ."

"You don't sound very glad about it."

". . . scared." Fall down and land in a rose garden. Touch the petals and wonder why they are decaying. Use his name again the way you do, like a weapon. This is Maury today, unseated by suspicion. "What are you not telling me, Jake?"

"Not now, Maury. There isn't time. We have to go."

"What's the matter here?" *God why am I so careful.* "Why can't you be straight with me?"

Jake shakes his head. He is beyond answers. Seizing Maury's hand, he tugs her like a large child. "Are you coming or what?"

God why do I hate myself. The group in the conference room is waiting. They are due in court within the hour. She says, "I need you to explain." Pull away from him, Maury, even though you want this baby more than anything. Pull hard. Make him let go. Don't let him see you cry when you have this to do. "Let go."

"Honey, the baby's ready, you have to come!"

The possibility of joy is terrifying. Lawyers are trained to look for hidden flaws. Her voice is tight with pain. "Not until you tell me where this is coming from."

Jake lets go. In that second Maury looks deep into her mate and sees his soul stripped naked, bleak as an unfurnished room. *Do we even know each other?* Shuddering, she thinks, *Did we ever?* After a pause that is too long for what it does, Jake says grimly, "Believe me, you don't want to know where this is coming from."

"At least tell me why."

"Don't do this to us, Maury." Jake fixes her with a look so compelling that in that second they are connected. "Not now."

Shaken, she falls into the old courtroom stance, masquerading as a lawyer: question-question-question, spraying him with doubts. "You wouldn't let me meet him and now you're trying to make me meet him, what's going on? What is it, Jake?"

"It's our baby, Maury. That's all you need to know."

This stops her dead. Yes she's angry but there's more to it than that: the dread that runs in on the heels of joy. She is suspended over a fresh area of vulnerability, skating on risk. What if she sees the baby and they don't let her have it? What if somebody rips it out of her arms? Shivering, she says, "You started this without me, Jake. You finish it. You go bring the baby home."

The elevator comes up. The doors open. Jake tries to walk her inside but he can't budge her. It kills him to say what he says next. He squeezes out the truth. "I can't. Not without you."

"Why?"

Look at him. Jake Zorn, husband and provider. Hunter-gatherer, remember? Triumphant only a minute ago. So proud. The strong, weathered face falls apart. Up against the wall now, he makes a terrible admission. In the daily battlefield that is Jake Zorn's life this is a defeat and he knows it. "Because he won't do it without you there."

She falls back a step. *Oh.* "Won't do what, Jake?"

"Make the transfer!"

"Transfer?" Oh, this is bad. She won't ask: transfer of property? He hasn't said it for a reason. "Jake, are we into something hinky here?

He wheels. Tears fly. "Maury, do you want this baby or what?"

And so they have come right down to it. Under the skin Maury is just as hungry and guilty as Jake. Everything inside her goes soft. Helpless now, she flows into him in a stunning act of complicity. "Yes!"

"Are you sure?" Jake falters. This is hard for him too; it always has been. He grimaces. "You always want everything aboveboard. You always have."

"Aboveboard. I do, Jake. I did." They are stalled in the hall with the elevator doors rolling shut against Jake's big foot and then open, shut and open again. Why is it that when you find out you're just about to get what you want, it makes you feel bad, like happiness is a sin? Guilt, Maury supposes, without knowing why. She has no idea whether it's for her failure or for whatever crime they are about to commit. In a way, she is grateful to Jake for not telling her. In a case like this you are better off not knowing the details. Ignorance of the . . . Stop. Just stop.

He says bitterly, "You're always such a fucking stickler."

"I am." Maury Bayless grew up believing in sin and in guilt and she knows better than anybody that these can run along with joy even and especially in moments of the greatest arousal. This is what she feels right now: guilty arousal. Their baby's in Washington and they are flying down to get it, no questions asked, don't even try; they're going on the shuttle, Jake has booked it, and as she numbers these items, least to the greatest— their baby is in Washington!— she understands that whether or not Jake ever lets her know the truth of it, they are engaged in something wrong.

Helpless with desire, she flows toward him, but in the rhetoric of wrong and acceptance there is always the dubious pause. She finishes, "Just not this time."

They are at the ground floor. Jake takes her hands. Urgently, he put the last question. "So you want this baby, no matter what?"

This is what the hunger does to you.

In the crunch, intelligent, ethical Maury Bayless is no stronger than anybody else. Need outruns reason and she follows Jake out of the elevator, helplessly excited, guilty and breathless as a virgin on prom night. "No matter what."

34.

Tom Starbird ought to be in orbit by this time, smoothly lifted off the globe. Gone from this place. In mid-ocean on a Polish freighter, on a flight around the world or mysteriously vaporized, vanished from the knowable earth. Because he is the best at what he does, the baby merchant always disappears the second the job is done.

But here he is. Starbird is holed up in a small hotel in the Northeast section of downtown Washington, in a dim neighborhood where questions don't come up and outsiders know not to ask.

What's the matter with him?

He is hung up in front of a blank TV.

Even he can't tell you what's the matter with him. The transfer of property is complete. The pet carrier he used to transport the product is empty. The product and the supplies he bought to tide it over are gone. Without the baby here the room is peculiarly empty. It's as though a cold wind just blew in and cleaned him out.

Except for the sophisticated equipment he bought on his way into the Capitol— digicorder with a 150-gigabyte virtual drive, compatible blue laser DVD burner, blanks big enough to store three hours of video— the room is empty of Starbird, too. There is the Lands' End bag filled with cash that Zorn brought, but Starbird doesn't want the money. He'll leave it in a Dumpster when he goes. There is nothing he wants to take away from this. He wants to start clean.

He doesn't need much. When he divested, stripping his life down to the bare walls, the discovery liberated him. He doesn't need much at all. He is cleaned out now. There is nothing left of Tom Starbird but bare walls and a dawning grief that he can't quite source and can't shake off.

In a way, he'd hoped Zorn's wife would turn out to be— not all wrong, exactly, but not quite right, so he could pull the chain on this operation with a valid excuse: I'm sorry but your wife is unstable, Zorn. Not fit to take care of a child. He'd make other plans for the baby, not sure what, and if Zorn made good on his threat to lay Daria Starbird wide open via satellite news? *Look, lady, I did what I could. I tried.* Unfortunately, where her husband was sealed tight as an armored car, the wife's face lay open like the door to a lovely room. A little apprehensive but smiling. Kind. Good as Starbird is at what he does, there was a bad moment in which she reached out for the baby and he gripped it tight and fell back a step, surprising both of them. Foolish, Starbird. Getting attached. Her breath came out in an inadvertent, "Don't!" Shaken, he understood that he and Maury Bayless were weighing some of the same things. Unless they were afraid of the same things. As though she expected him to hurt her in some new and profound way.

He studied her, looking for the flaw that would justify defaulting. Instead he saw the intelligence in her face, the fear battling unquenchable hope, and he softened because with everything at risk in that moment, she still made a nice smile for him. Unlike some women with a new baby, he thought bitterly, this one is happy to see him, and he was not clear whether by *him*, he meant the product or himself. "It's OK," he murmured, "really. It's all right. It's going to be all right," and with a pang, put the baby in her arms. *Product, Starbird. Think product. Bye, kid.* She reached out and with beautiful certainty, clamped him to her heart. Starbird coughed. It was as if a pin had lodged in his throat. The woman glowed as the baby snuggled in. *Oh, don't turn that smile on me.* Her face was so bright that he had to look away. He kept his head bent over his PDA until they finished the transaction and took the baby away.

Right, he thought when Zorn slapped him on the shoulder before he could dodge. Right, he kept telling himself, struggling with what he had done. It was right. Look at her rocking him with that sweet, sad smile, so I did a good thing.

I think.

Still, he'd thought to turn on the glittering eye of his laptop to record the transfer of property. It's just something he knew he had to do. The transaction went smoothly enough: in exchange for Zorn's verbal reassurances, which he has recorded, he handed over the kid. Zorn and his wife have the baby, so the Conscience of Boston can shut up. The Daria Starbird exposé will never air. All parties can go their own ways in safety.

First, he has things to do.

After Zorn left with his trophy kid in the Baby Björn he'd bought for it, Starbird set up the equipment he bought in preparation— not for a confession, necessarily— but for something like it. He needed to explain! The together man who always had a plan found himself empty-handed and oddly disassembled. For the first time since Tom Starbird could remember, he didn't know what to do. Taking a deep breath, he stepped in front of the digital camera, talking as if he had the girl standing here in the room with him. What did he think, he'd give it to her later and make friends? He doesn't know. He's been talking for hours.

I am very good at what I do.

Sorting out the truth of this, talking for the camera, Starbird kept himself going by giving meticulous attention to process: from the detailed narrative he's building, step by step, to the physical business of recording to the mechanical procedure of getting his story out there, wherever he wants it to go. OK, he wants the world to know. More than anything, he wants the girl to know. She may never forgive him, but at least she'll understand.

Or he will.

It all depends on the logic of process. What Starbird does next, and when. If he can do this part right, maybe he can figure out what else he has to do.

When he bought the recording equipment, he thought he was doing it for insurance, but he understands now that he always had the girl in mind. Therefore he spent some portion of the night and much of today recording. The rest, he spent deleting his old files. It was a pleasure to watch them vanish one at a time. It's like unwriting chapters of his life. The night and most of the day have gone by. It is midafternoon. He has finished telling the digicorder everything he has to tell. When he began, he thought he was explaining it for the girl— not for now, for when they're older and she's had a chance to cool down. *You will thank me for it later,* he thought, winding it up. *Won't you?*

He's downloaded the video he made of the transfer of property, spent hours editing to his satisfaction and burned his DVD. Six copies. That should be enough, no matter what he decides to do. The same-day messenger service will pick up the Jiffy Bags and deliver today, guaranteed. All he has to do is make the call.

If he makes the call.

He's still figuring it out.

Working mechanically, the way he does when he needs to keep grounded, Tom has queued up the emails he can send the minute he decides. Unless he deletes them. He still doesn't know. There they are: mails to go to the major networks and Boston area affiliates, with his one-line pitch and a brief description of the low-res three-minute videos he plans to attach and send as ZIP files. Not top quality video, but the files are small enough to travel fast and make it past spam filters and firewalls alike. They're built for a quick download at the other end, which is the issue here. Getting attention and getting it fast.

There is a comfort to be found in this kind of work. Who doesn't love computers? The monotony of logic. The wonderful predictability of the analog mind. The magic of connectivity and the illusion that everything is happening right here, in this very room. Tom Starbird has spent his life connected, no problem; he can make a wireless connection anywhere, darting in and out of servers without leaving a trace. It's one of the talents that sets him apart. He understands now that he's always been a man apart and he has no idea whether this is a burden or a gift.

And now that he has these emails queued up?

All he has to do is hit SEND.

So what if he left a paper trail in that high end computer supplies store in Alexandria, Virginia? No problem. If a blind bull mastiff could find Starbird's footprints on the emails he has queued to send, that's cool. Everything he ever cared about is gone. He has nothing more to lose. Whether he decides to hit SEND today or deletes the files and walks away, it no longer matters that he can be traced.

Once you've agreed to shoot yourself in the foot, no matter what your motives you have shot yourself in the foot. The interesting part is discovering whether it hurts and what comes down after.

He only took this job to stop Zorn. He made a deal for his mother's, he supposes it's freedom; the deal was his mother's freedom in exchange for what he has done. The Conscience of Boston hit Tom here with things that he's spent his life trying to forget. The abandonment, which yawns inside him like an open wound. Examine Starbird's motives— and he does— and even that girl Sasha would have to understand that he got into the work because he wanted to make things right. Outsiders may look at what he's done and say it was wrong, but they don't know. How could they possibly know? Tom Starbird has spent his life trying to do the right thing, he has given his heart to it and he still doesn't know what, exactly, that is.

This as much as anything is what draws him back to the TV. Flicking it on, he drops to his knees. Empty now, unless he is reamed and bereft, he kneels there watching CNN. Not watching, really, just physically present like a whale watcher staring into the Atlantic. He is waiting for the Savannah press conference to surface again. In most cases, a TV moment like this one runs on the day the story breaks and then disappears, but this kidnapping—

Wait a minute. Kidnapping?

This *event* is being played up because even exhausted, raging and desperate, the girl is so pretty and so articulate that the mystery of the missing baby looks like a better story than it is. Yesterday's press conference is old news but the Egan sound byte still surfaces regularly. CNN surrounds it with new information to keep the story fresh but those first shots of the girl Starbird wishes he'd never met and knows he never should have spoken to are deeply embedded in all the second-day video on the case. If nobody starts a new war and no explosions preempt, the network will go on replaying it until new footage comes in.

Terrible and amazing to know that a woman who can't get 911 to come in time to stop a thief knows how to reach millions before Starbird can complete delivery of the property and walk free, that she knows how to cut into his guts and turn the knife, that she can do it from six hundred miles away and she can do it again and again.

Starbird's mind has been going around the block nonstop ever since he first turned on CNN in Myrtle Beach. He has played and replayed her diatribe in his heart and he knows in his heart that nothing he can do or say will change what Sasha Egan thinks of him.

He can't bear it. He can't shut it off.

"Whoever you are, wherever you are," she says with her eyes crackling and her hair wild, "do you know what you've done to me? Do you know what you are? Do you really know?" That pause that breaks her heart. Maybe this time she won't say it. Then she does. "You are a monster!"

Again and again, she advances on the camera with her teeth bared and her dark hair flying and she and Tom Starbird, whose fatal error turns out to be caring, are *connected,* like it or not. Whether or not he is watching, he will see her advancing on him for the rest of his life. Even with the television set on MUTE, he hears. From the far side of the moon he will know. He has it by heart. Judgment rolls down on him like the great stones into the pharaoh's tomb, sealing him in. Outraged and coming at him from a place he didn't know existed, the girl he told himself he was helping flows into the room in full cry.

"Do you have any idea what you've done?"

What's the matter here, Starbird, why do you need to keep seeing this? Why do you need to see it again and again?

Bizarre, getting hung up on this, considering what he's been through. Dangerous, being in stasis when he should be on the run, but necessary. He is deciding what to do.

In theory, he's free to go. He and Zorn are protected by a mutually assured destruction pact. If Zorn gives so much as ten seconds of air time to Daria Starbird, he risks having this transaction exposed, and given the nature of the supplier— the jaws tearing at the inside of Starbird's stomach tighten and start grinding whenever he thinks of her— Zorn could go to jail for kidnapping, slavery, whatever the courts dish up. Of course Starbird would go to jail if they caught up with him, but that's been a given from the first. Trial and conviction, death penalty implied. Secrecy is the glue keeping this arrangement in one piece. It's a matter of collaborative protection. The Zorns are safe and Tom Starbird is safe.

Unless, of course, he tries to take the baby back.

Everything is open to question now.

Interesting, how you can know you're doing something wrong and rationalize until you convince yourself that what you're doing is absolutely right. Starbird knew at the outset that this transaction was a mistake. If you're quitting the business, you don't take on a job. What happens next is preordained. It's bound to play out like a movie— the cop's partner says, *after this case it's, hello, Sun City, Florida,* and you see this stamped on his forehead: MARKED FOR DEATH. Tom should have whacked Zorn's smooth face with the flat of his hand and walked away. Letting the Conscience of Boston stampede him was the first mistake. Unless the central mistake was caring what happens to Daria Starbird, who could care less what happens to him. His encounters with the girl— correction, the mark— compounded the, OK, the felony. Then, shit. He interacted with the baby. Handing him off was like losing a friend. The baby he handed off to Zorn last night looked at him over the wife's shoulder as they left. It had her eyes.

What have I done?

Staring into the screen he sees the mark— no, the girl whose baby he took— come blazing into the room, and where he has run on through life unencumbered, they are connected. He needs to see her again. Again. He has to know!

He is torn. There was Maury's smile when he proffered the baby. That baby snapped into her arms like a key in a lock or a space shuttle docking, he could almost hear the click.

There was that, then. Now there is this. Tears flying as Sasha Egan whips them away with an angry hand. Again. For as long as he lives. The tirade on a perpetual loop. Stricken, he shouts, although she is nowhere near, "I'm not like that!"

OK! He will expose Zorn. Forget the wife, he wants to expose Zorn.

He wants the girl to understand.

He wants to leave the country with everybody happy, and this is where the plan destructs. Happy as Maury Bayless was to have that baby— happy as she was and happy as the baby seemed when she rocked it and whispered the new name she had chosen for it— it isn't hers. And the girl, the girl he thought he was doing a favor? She thinks he's a monster. She always will.

Unless, he thinks. *Unless I get her baby back.*

There is no way to do it without hurting somebody.

Defeated, he closes in on the TV. He's in so tight that he can see his breath condensing on the screen. Sasha Egan reduced to glittering pixels, condensed fury in HDTV. He needs to look deep into her because it's the only way he can see into himself.

All his life Tom Starbird has run ahead of consequences. He could do what he did as long as he worked fast and moved on, so he didn't have to see what happened next. He did what he had to and that was it; that was all. That would be all, for as long as he kept moving at tremendous speeds. Consequences are nothing he has time for. It's why he is so good at what he does.

Now look. No matter what he decides, somebody will get hurt. The girl. He doesn't mind hurting Zorn, but he feels sorry for the wife. There is his mother to think about.

The man who always has a plan is completely empty now—bone-dry. Has he eaten? He forgets. Staring into the dancing pixels, hypnotized, he falls into the truth of what he's been doing.

No. What he is.

"Oh!"

Staggered, he turns off the set and retreats to the desk. Picks up a pen.

Years' worth of consequences accrete and roll in, sealing the exits as they pin him in place. He can forget about flight. Motives aren't the issue, he realizes. Outcomes are. You go along in good faith; you go along telling yourself that you're doing the right thing but sooner or later what you were really thinking catches up and you discover that you have done something terribly wrong. There are ways out, there have to be. Right now he can only think of one.

A noise outside pulls him back into the room where his body is sitting. Surprised, he looks down. Without thinking it through, he has drawn a diagram. The street below: the sidewalk, the curb, the Dumpster. An X. A string of words. *I will land here.* At least it would be over. For him. End it and he'll never make up for it. Stand on the sill and aim for the X and everything you've done so far will damn you. Hit the X and nobody wins.

Scratch out the drawing. Crumple it up. You want to throw it into the street but you're afraid to open the window. No telling what else might drop into the street.

He has things to do.

It becomes important to let her know that the baby is safe.

For Starbird, this is not the most important thing. Before that, before anything, he wants her not to hate him. He wants to hear her voice when he tells her the baby is safe.

He waits to make the call. First, finish up with FedEx. He orders an express pickup. By the time he lets himself pick up the phone to call the girl the same-day delivery messenger has been. His DVDs are on their way. His laptop is connected, with the emails queued up, complete with the short video, high concept late breaking news. All he has to do is hit SEND.

The complete package he produced today is on its way to major markets in Washington, Boston and New York. The complete Zorn scandal, on high-res DVD. It will be in news directors' hands by tonight, but the three-minute preview he is emailing will hit its targets first. He wants the teaser to air on the early news in all three cities and, in Boston, on the local stations that Jake Zorn and his exposés have leached of viewers like a sprawling carnivorous plant. Because Zorn takes no prisoners, his enemies will probably preempt whatever they are showing, interrupting regular programming for the bulletin. You bet they'll go with it. In Boston, where he is much hated, his rivals will run for the barn.

Jake Zorn will be ruined before he can ever do the show. It won't matter what he tells people about Starbird, Daria, anyone. Nobody will believe him now. Whether or not his station fires him, whether or not cops close in as he leaves for the studio today, the network will drop him faster than a glob of steaming shit.

With everything in place, Tom phones the DelMar. He can hear the double click as mechanisms kick in, tracing the call. So, fine! In the background he hears muttering— police or Feds— the buzz of an argument. Then they call her to the phone.

His whole life rushes into his mouth. "It's me."

In the long silence Tom Starbird can hear her breathing. He hears a fusillade of clicks. The police audio guys will lock onto the source, no problem. *You want to come and get me? Come and get me.* In full knowledge of what he's doing to himself, he is calling from the hotel telephone. Land line, in seconds the cops will know what city, which hotel and which room. Still she doesn't speak. *I love you. Say something!* Holding his breath, he waits. He waits for a very long time.

When he's sure police trackers have locked on, he says, "Don't worry about the baby. Your baby."

He hears her draw a little breath.

"He's fine."

He thinks it doesn't matter what she says, as long as she says something to him. *Please.* She does not speak.

"I just wanted you to know."

Oh, please! Why should she respond after what he did? What he did to her? How can he explain that he wasn't doing it to her, he was doing it for her? What is Starbird waiting for her to say to him, thanks for calling? That she's glad to hear from him?

"Sasha." Saying her name makes his heart stumble. "Are you there?"

She won't answer.

"I know your name but you don't know mine."

He can't even hear her breathing.

Oh, Sasha. Say something. Anything.

"It's Tom Starbird."

The long silence is punctuated by clicks. He knows what they are doing; he knows. Finally he says:

"My name is Tom Starbird." It seems important for her to know him exactly. "You know, Tom, from the Food King?"

In the background somebody mutters, "Answer him." Somebody else says, "String it out. Keep him on the line."

Nothing. *Naturally she will give back nothing. Not after what you took from her.* Get off the phone, Starbird, you can still make it out of here.

He will do anything to break the silence. "Please?"

Just her breathing.

Idiot, stop. Clumsiness overcomes him and he blurts, "I did it for you."

So Sasha Egan's voice comes into the receiver at last, and it's nothing like he imagines. It is low and charged with loathing. She speaks and the air around him trembles. "Did you really imagine I would thank you?"

"Just listen," he cries.

She breaks the connection before he can get the words out.

"I'm sorry," he says anyway. Even though she's long gone Starbird says to the empty room, "You'll know where he is by six tonight."

He hits redial. There is the sound of steel jaws snapping as four people pick up on four phones.

"Tell her she'll know where he is by six tonight."

"Where are you?" They don't need to ask. By this time they know.

The only thing that remains is to go to his computer and hit SEND.

The files are so big that it takes them a minute to go. As soon as this part is done Starbird destroys the copies on his hard drive. No need to keep a backup. He knows what he said. The short version is burned into his heart.

My name is Tom Starbird. I am very good at what I do but I am done with it. For eight years I was a baby merchant. I stole children to order and sold them to high end buyers at a tremendous price.

Over the years I have stolen more than a hundred babies and put them into new homes, and I did this for profit, although I wanted them to be happy. I told myself I was doing it for their own good. I stole the Egan baby and delivered him to the television Conscience of Boston, Jake Zorn, a walking slime mold who tears up innocent people on national TV. Now, Zorn knew what he was doing and if I am guilty of a crime here, so is he.

I did what I did because . . . no. No explanations. What I did was monstrous. Sasha Egan, wherever you are when you see this, I was only trying to help, and this is the hell of it. You can use up your heart trying to do right and still have it come out all wrong.

35.

The Savannah police detective's voice is rough with exhaustion and loaded with apology. They've been together in here for entirely too long and she's having a hard time remembering his name. Dwight, she thinks. Dwight Larcen. Detective Larcen to you. The room Sasha fixed up for her new baby is littered with equipment and takeout cartons, the detritus of a long wait. Except for Larcen, the police and FBI people come and go in shifts. He sleeps in a chair. Sasha is on duty here full-time. She sleeps when she can. Not for the first time, the detective is trying to get her to the phone.

"No," she says. "I've said everything I had to say to him."

"Not the perp." Larcen shakes his head. "It's your grandmother again."

"I don't want to talk to her."

"She's at Savannah International."

"Here?"

"Yes Ma'am. She wants to talk to you."

When the animal who took her baby called, everything changed. Sasha has the power now. She hisses, "No."

"She wants to take you to a hotel."

"Tell her no."

"As soon as we know anything, you'll know, I promise." Sasha knows the look. He's afraid to refuse the old lady, everybody is.

"Yes Ma'am, I'll tell her, Ma'am." He says to Sasha, "Really. You'll be a lot more comfortable. We can patch incoming phone calls to your hotel."

She's too tired to repeat. She waves him off.

"You can relax, Ma'am. Your baby's safe."

"You don't know that." Interesting. Through all the hours of interrogation, Jimmy wasn't "your baby," he was "the baby." He was "the baby" until the kidnapper called and their positions slid into flux. He's "your baby" now. She wants to be happy but she can't. She won't be happy until she can hold her child. She won't relax until her arms close around him, strong and tight enough to keep him safe for as long as she lives. Understand what is happening here. Sasha is not so much planning as admitting a bond that will outlast her; she is opening the door to a huge and powerful force that rushes in to fill up the rest of her life. There is no physical change in her, not really. There is only a ripple of— what, excitement? Joy or fright? None of the above or all of the above, because Sasha Egan is no longer autonomous. With grace she may grow up to be an artist, but she's Jimmy's mother first. What happens next will, miraculously, happen to both of them.

The detective is saying, "It's all we know." Larcen sees she has slipped into another zone and touches her arm to bring her back. "It's OK to leave here, now that your baby is within reach."

"You mean, now that I'm no longer a suspect."

Embarrassment creeps up the man's face until the skin under the combover goes red. "I mean, you look like you could use the sleep. Your grandmother . . ."

"No."

How powerful he was, when they first began this. How anxious he seems. All his teeth show. He can't seem to get her to take the phone. "She says put you on or she'll sue the city."

Sasha's sudden laugh is more like a sob. "That's not my problem."

The detective's sweaty face is filmed over with desperation. In his hand the phone weaves like a rattler's head. "Ma'am, please."

All these hours, she thinks. The questions that were really accusations. The clumsy search. The false apologies when the man who stole her baby telephoned. Did he really say, *I'm not like that?* So her baby is safe, but where? All these hours. Larcen slides the handset across the table and Sasha shoves it back. Her voice hardens. "When did you start calling me Ma'am?

"Just talk to her, OK? Then we can get out of here."

"You'll take me to my baby?"

"We can't, not until the D.C. cops find out where."

Her teeth close on this like a bear trap. "Then take me to D.C." The grim, murderous rasp surprises her. "I'll get it out of him."

"Yes Ma'am." Bastard, he temporizes. "After the D.C. police bring him in."

"Not good enough . . ." Sasha is as anxious as anybody to get out of this terrible, crowded room. The knotty pine-paneled walls, the dingy pink bedspread, the welter of equipment and people cluttering the space are all she knows. They've been together in here for so long that her room at the DelMar is its own snow globe, filled with particles and hermetically sealed. Within this reality, their positions have reversed. She adds a condescending period. "Dwight."

Like a flight of hornets, her grandmother's voice comes boiling out of the handset halfway across the room. The detective is no longer in a position to give orders; he is pleading. "All she wants to do is talk to you."

"It's never that simple."

"It isn't just the lawsuit," Larcen says. "She'll crucify us in the press."

"Will she." It isn't a question and he knows it. Sasha stands, resting her fists on the table between them. "I have to go."

"I'll do what I can."

"You'll do what I want." She leans in with her jaw drawn taut. Their faces are so close that he can't look away. "You might as well know, I've had offers for my story too." She has.

"I'll try, but I can't promise anything."

"How do you want to look to the audience, Dwight? How do you want to look to the world?"

Defeated, he groans. "I'll get on it."

"I talk her off the phone and then we move out. You get me to the airport. Fast."

Exhaustion has left him shaky and dubious. "I'll see what I can do."

"No. You'll do it. Now give me the phone. Hello," she says. "Hello, Grand."

At the other end of the line Maeve Donovan is talking but none of her threats and none of her extravagant offers can touch Sasha now. Ugly custody suit, trip to Europe, ancestral diamonds, nothing Grand says will make any difference. Sasha doesn't assent and she doesn't protest; after the first hello, she doesn't say anything. She just holds the phone at a slight distance until noise stops coming out of it. Across the room, the detective, her nemesis, her designated driver, is taking a call. His eyebrows lift at the news. He gestures.

"No need to go to D.C."

What, Sasha mouths. *What?*

"Baby's in Boston."

Her voice goes up like a rocket. "Yes!"

Grandmother talks on as though none of this has happened. Trust fund. Bearer bonds. Volvo wagon to keep our baby safe. *It's not your baby, Grand.* You don't have to live with us, I'll buy you a house of your own. "Thanks for calling," Sasha says right before she hangs up on the old lady forever. "I'll keep that in mind."

The detective is flushed with relief. "So it's only a matter of time."

She wheels on him. "Time!"

"They said Child Services will fly him to Savannah as soon as they pick him up." What's the man grinning about? Oh, right. He wants her to hug him but she isn't giving anything away.

"Not Child Services, Mr. Larcen. I'm picking him up. Me."

"I don't know if that's . . ." He is backpedaling. "OK, we'll go in the cruiser."

"Police helicopter, please." Sasha is trying to sound stern but her voice lifts, bubbling in spite of her. Her heart is inflated and jumping like a Mylar Happy Birthday balloon. She taps a business card on the table: never mind which one. "It's the least you can do."

"OK." Anything to get her off his back. After all these hours of grilling and cruelty and refusal to listen, what else can the man do? What else can he say to her? "We'll get you to the airport soonest. We'll get you out on the first thing Delta has."

"No."

"Ma'am?"

"I don't wait." Like Starbird, Sasha has seen the CNN press conference a dozen times. She is surprised by what the crisis has made of her. In this tight enclave, the baggy, awkward detective was in charge. Now she is the one dealing from strength. She summons the cold, furious tone that comes up again and again on CNN, the glare that brought the baby thief to his knees. "I need a private plane."

"That's a lot to ask."

She has backed him up against the crib. Now they are standing nose to nose. "After everything, you can damn well front for it."

"We found your baby, he'll keep until you get there."

Sasha Egan, who has never in her life hit another person, slams the heel of her hand into the detective's chest. "You didn't find him." Again. "I did."

"Ma'am!"

Harder. "My grandmother isn't the only one with grounds for a suit."

He goes white.

"Clear?"

"Clear." The detective backs off with a tight, gray look. He gestures to his partner. "Get on it. A.S.A.P."

Weeks from now, when she and Jimmy are settled into the place she will find for them in Santa Barbara, when she's banked the modest down payment on her story and given the first in a series of taped interviews, she may take one of her grandmother's calls. The money isn't huge, but it will keep her afloat until she finds somebody she can trust to take care of Jimmy at night while she goes out to the local art center to teach. In exchange for X hours of teaching, her tuition will be free. When she does talk to the old lady, which won't be until she's damn good and ready, the conversation will be short. "Teaching art classes, thanks. MassArt is transferring my credits so I can finish up out here. He's fine. I'm fine, thanks for asking. No, thanks. Thanks, really. We don't need anything. Yes I know what I'm doing, thank you. Oh, if we ever go east again . . ." The *we* comes out in a little zig-zag of delight, ". . . If we ever do, we'll certainly keep that in mind."

36.

Maury is settling the baby in his pretty new bed when Jake steps into the archway leading into the living room, where she's keeping the bassinet. His face is such a confusion of joy and avarice that she has no idea what he's about to say. Then the rocky facade softens and he smiles. "Are you happy now?"

"Yes." Her heart jumps. She can't help adding, "I think so." There is always the chance that they will be caught. Caught is the way she thinks of it now, the way she's been thinking of it ever since they got back on the shuttle at National Airport and she peeled off the little hat and saw that the baby hadn't been chipped. She sat with Jake tapping on his laptop and the new baby sleeping in her arms, fixed in a silence so complete that she had too much time to think. She's not sure how Jake brought off this transaction or where the baby Maury is stroking came from or whether there's anybody looking for him but she is nursing an odd, visceral ache that lets her know that whatever they've done, whoever may be the victim, she and Jake are engaged in something deeply, terribly wrong.

Her man, whom she loves but doesn't really know, squints like a cryptographer trying to decode her face. "You sure?"

"I am," she says. "I am happy, but . . ." It's the look, she thinks. The last look Jake's paid go-between threw at her followed her out the door as surely as a Ninja throwing-blade, hit its mark and stuck. Like the microchip that all babies have— well, all babies except this one— it is lodged deep in her hide.

Relieved, Jake says, "Good. He's a great baby, isn't he?"

"He is."

He relaxes into that wonderful Jake Zorn grin. "Great, I knew you'd like him. I know a guy who can get him registered with the government, no questions asked. Tomorrow we'll do the paperwork so we can get him chipped." Before she can respond he flips the remote toward the TV and the portrait-sized plasma screen comes to life.

"Don't, he's sleeping."

"Gotta see this." He puts it on MUTE.

Can't he leave TV alone for a minute? Going to and from D.C., Jake was too preoccupied with the mission to check on the competition. He stayed focused on the canvas bag at his feet and it came as a welcome relief. At the airport hotel he was tired and distracted by the child. Coming home this morning, Maury hoped having a baby had changed him, but she sees now that it was the briefest of vacations. A temporary respite is no respite.

Her mind runs ahead to newscasts. What if there's been a . . . She can't let herself complete the thought. "I wish you wouldn't, Jake."

"They're running a sixty-second promo— preview of my Nebraska baby ranch exposé. Engineered multiple births, infants caged like so many cocker spaniels. It goes on at six."

"Oh, Jake."

"It'll only take a minute."

The new baby begins to whimper. With a shudder, Maury turns to the bassinet. She says, "Please. It's so sordid," but that isn't what she means. That just may be the problem here.

"Shh, honey. Be quiet." He hits the MUTE button again. Sound bleeds into the room. "I think it's the next thing up."

Thus they are both listening when the voiceover cuts in. "We interrupt this broadcast for breaking news." There is the inevitable background thunder of a helicopter as the airborne unit approaches the scene as in the studio the squirt from Jake's office says gravely, "Now, live from suburban Auburndale, where . . ." Therefore the Zorns are both watching the screen as the airborne camera picks up the TV ground crew's van and a flying wedge of police cars converging on a quiet, leafy street. As it becomes clear that the helicopter is directly above them, Maury will see— both on the screen and out their front window— police and child services workers and FBI and the Channel Five news team— Jake's rivals!— spilling out of their vehicles and trotting up the front walk to the beautifully kept Boston Victorian Zorn-Bayless house. "And now, from Washington, D.C., an astonishing confession . . ."

Seizing the baby, Maury buries her face in him.

She hears a new voice say, "My name is Tom Starbird. I am . . ."

"It's OK," Jake says vainly. He grabs her, pointing her toward the screen. "It's OK, Maury. Look!"

As the doorbell rings she nods and looks at the screen just in time to see her husband and the baby merchant exchanging handshakes for a camera she hadn't guessed was in the room. She sees the bag full of money, noting that Jake is front and center for this exchange. In the background she sees the pet carrier their contact used to carry the baby; although she knows that by the time he had handed the child to her . . .

The doorbell rings again and she groans aloud.

. . . although by the time they shook hands she was holding the baby, the little grate on the pet carrier is shut and her sobbed thank you has been swept from the recording. She is nowhere visible on the screen. As though the baby merchant wanted to protect her which, as a lawyer, she knows is impossible.

". . . so-called Conscience of Boston," Starbird is saying and now the video is superseded by a picture of Jake Zorn, full-frame, "a walking slime mold who tears up innocent people on national TV . . ."

A blue band runs across the bottom of the screen with block letters flashing again and again, on a perpetual loop:

CONSCIENCE CORRUPTED. DETAILS AT SEVEN.

The knocking begins. Jake turns to her and with a stupendously mixed expression of love and guilt and resentment, flicks the rest into oblivion. "I only did it because I love you," he says and, moving faster than he has since they were eighteen, he picks up the baby and trots to the front door. "Coming. I'm coming," he shouts. "With the baby. Don't shoot. I'm giving myself up."

A weaker woman would have thrown herself at him, begging him to give her baby back. *This is right,* she thinks, dying. And lets him go.

Although the fates are not famous for being open-handed, Maury will be all right. She'll survive Jake's trial and of course she'll promise to wait for him and settle in to do exactly that, although there is some question as to whether when he comes out, anything will be the same. Still, rough-hewn as he is, self-centered and tough-minded, he loved her enough to convince the law that she had nothing to do with the illegal aspects of the transaction, and to make it stick. Remember, they've been together since they were kids. She loved him then and she loves him well enough now to wait, and to pick up whatever pieces are left of his ego after he gets out of prison. There was the possibility that she'd be charged as an accessory but the last thing the firm did before they let her go was see to it that all charges against Maury Bayless, who was in fact an accessory, were dropped.

There were no charges but there will always be gossip. Maury will never work in the private sector again. At least she wasn't disbarred. Instead of working with rich, intelligent clients, she'll spend the rest of her working life in the State Attorney's office, chasing deadbeat dads for unpaid child support.

There is no apology she can make to Sasha Egan. She won't even try, but for the rest of her life, in odd hours Maury will scour the Web, looking for images of Sasha and her little son.

She will, in time, be engaged in a custody matter— murder-suicide, no surviving adults— and become legal guardian of the orphaned child because she'll fight all the way to the State Supreme Court to keep her from becoming a ward of the state. After seven years during which no other claimants come forward, the court will allow her to adopt.

37.

Tom Starbird spent his life trying to do the right thing and until today, he's never known exactly what that is. He still doesn't know, but this, at least, feels right. Everything he had to do today has been accomplished. Zorn's ruined. Sasha will get her baby back. The girl won't thank him, but that isn't the issue. It's that he's done it. Try not to think about Maury Bayless with her sweet face and that sad mouth trembling, the glow when he settled the baby in her arms. Think about tough, fiery Sasha Egan, getting back what she fought so hard to keep. At least he has done one thing right.

Keep going on this and try to forget her accusation, the cold, hard blade of hate.

Try to be cool, try to understand, try to be what you must become, Tom Starbird, even though you have no idea what that is. Maybe this is all he is and all he'll ever be, the sum total of his efforts.

Maybe this is who he's been all his life, the person he was trying so hard to find, or to get back to and get to the heart of, his deepest needs distilled and driving him forward, in pursuit of something he can't see and may never understand.

It isn't the act that matters, he tells himself, it's the compulsion. *I want*, he thinks, a fact that he always refused to recognize. *It hurts*. This is the only sign he has that there really is something out there, the concept or the entity that he's been trying so hard all his life to find and has so badly failed to reach. Whatever it is, he'll have plenty of time to think about it wherever they put him, unless he gets bushwhacked and murdered on his way to Death Row. Would that be the hand of justice? Fitting retribution? He doesn't know.

In a funny way, the failure to comprehend is his answer. Unless the question is. That there is a question he can't begin to ask. It exists, whoever or whatever It is, and the proof? The merciless, inexorable *want.*

It's time to turn it all off. Computer, television. Everything.

He sits and waits for them to come.